DRAGON'S HOPE

Leah E. Welker

LIGHTBOUND MEDIA

Library of Congress Control Number: 2024947925

Print ISBN: 978-1-964174-13-6

Ebook ISBN: 978-1-964174-12-9

First Edition

CONTENTS

To Tia, cherished sister and friend, who has done so much to support me—and who asked me for months whether Sarah and Ben were married yet.

Always we are following a light,
Always the light recedes; with groping hands
We stretch toward this glory, while the lands
We journey through are hidden from our sight
Dim and mysterious, folded deep in night,
We care not, all our utmost need demands
Is but the light, the light! So still it stands
Surely our own if we exert our might.
Fool! Never can'st thou grasp this fleeting gleam,
Its glowing flame would die if it were caught,
Its value is that it doth always seem
But just a little farther on. Distraught,
But lighted ever onward, we are brought
Upon our way unknowing, in a dream.

Amy Lowell

KEY TERMS & TRANSLATIONS

Races

draká ("druh-KAH"): the original "dragons."

amá ("ah-MAH"): human(s); the sentient inhabitants of Earth.

dramá ("druh-MAH"): the race that emerged from the combination of draká and humans.

Blood Manifestations

drakón ("drah-KOHN"): dramá chosen to have far greater magic and gain a drakáform.

amón ("ah-MOHN"): dramá who are not chosen, yet still have the Blood of the Covenants and cannot accurately be called "human."

Distances

Rough equivalents

ild: inch.

foot: literal translation.

erd: yard (only a couple dramá feet).

ald: 100 dramá feet.

eld: half an English Imperial mile.

elden: an English Imperial mile.

Time

dek: Roughly 1 minute, made of 56 moments.

deken: Roughly 1 hour, made of 56 dek.

day: 28 deken.

THE SIX REALMS

Sun	Planet	Capital	Clan	Color	Specialty
Kaldrir	Ythra	Crownhold	Sunfilled	Gold	Central governance, priesthood, guarding Tree, maintaining sungates
Kyalid	Ekrel	Krevenyir	Battleblood	Violet	Battle, smithing, exploring, peacekeeping
Ashga	Oshal	Rosin	Starkissed	Sapphire	Magic, scholarship, diplomacy, artistry
Olmen	Romskal	Palla	Strongshield	Scarlet	Civil service, law, administration
Winalken	Yonvey	Remik	Brightflare	Orange	Tinkering, financing, mining, farming
Yedrik	Ykran	Danyeth	Peacegrowth	Emerald	Healing, farming, conserving

PROLOGUE

SOLIM

THE TREE OF ICE—IMMORTAL of the First Creation, one of the oldest and most powerful of all Trees, guardian of Earth and spiritual Mother of humanity—was dying.

The latest evidence of that was in Solim's presence here, on Her very shores.

Technically, he had been here before. He idly kicked some of the broken boards and metal scraps that were all that remained of the hut that had briefly sheltered the Heirs of Ice and Flame as they fled from him, before he obliterated it in his pursuit. The torched cowards had fled somehow, denying him his rightful prey and delaying for a small eternity his promised reward for their Blood.

On that day, Solim had had to emerge far offshore and fly after them in his draconic lish form. Yet just a few moments ago, his master had created a darkrift on this very spot, and all Solim had to do was walk through in his amáform and into the dark night onto Her very soil.

True, he was standing somewhere in the southwestern corner of the land these insipid Earthren called "Green," and the Tree of Ice was somewhere beneath the ice to the northeast. He could feel a great Power in that direction, pulsing, and a great Awareness of him so intense that Solim spit in Her direction, so great was the loathing—and, though he did not admit it to himself, the fear—it stirred in his darkheart.

Black triumph also stirred in him, for his proximity now was the surest sign yet of the Tree of Ice's weakening.

Once, not even the Tree of Flame, one of the Devourer's most formidable opponents, had had such tight and thick protections against the Devourer's intrusions as the Tree of Ice had. The Devourer had to chip away at Her shield for thousands of years to even make one darkrift—a small, temporary tear in that shield—on Earth to send its slaves through, and even to this day, those darkrifts were difficult and rare.

Thus the weak and foolish humans of Earth had not yet had to face one of the Devourer's full invasions, despite their severe neglect and almost complete *ignorance* of their Tree. When Solim had first come to Earth, he could not comprehend how oblivious these bleating sheep were of their Shepherd—and how blind they were to the black wolf that hungrily prowled at the edges of their fold. How willfully they resisted Her whispered warnings, how eagerly they tried to push through the fence, undermining the very Being that preserved their existence.

That was not by chance, however. Though the Devourer could not attack and consume Earth *directly*...it had long since learned how to send out its own whispers—ones that these short-lived and even shorter-sighted humans were all too eager to heed.

First came rebellion against the strictures of the Tree, then greed, then bloodshed to satisfy it, then secret agreements to keep their atrocities in the dark. Then came famine and war. Tyranny and disease. So soon, so incredibly soon after the Tree of Ice was given humanity as Her children, the Devourer persuaded them to turn away from, abandon, and forget their Mother entirely. For what was the purpose of heeding such a tiresome Being, if no monster waited in the shadows?

Or so the Devourer led them to believe. So thorough was its deceit that the only records left of either the Tree or the Devourer were the scantest traces in myth or fable. All other records, the Devourer had its most devoted listeners methodically hunt down and destroy long ago, while it twisted other myths about humanity's once and future allies, the draká—or "dragons"—in its favor.

Then, in the last few centuries, the Devourer's seeds had truly born fruit, as humanity created ever more effective ways to slaughter and subject each other. Even the most brilliant and well-meaning of them made machines that devoured after their own fashion, until they had unintentionally begun to weaken Her with the Earth's rising heat and polluted surface. That was the most hilarious part to Solim: led by the noose, the children of Ice were willingly destroying their very foundation, their very birthright. The sheep were beating their heads against the fence to let the wolf in.

And now they knew it.

At least in part. Yet even the warnings from their brightest minds and purest hearts could not sway the whole of the herd, who would rather plod or even run headlong to their deaths than change their ways now.

It was all uproariously tragic, and one of Solim's favorite pastimes now was to slip away to Earth when he could to watch the disaster unfold.

Of course, Solim had another motive for slipping away....

Pain—agony—lanced through his whole body. He raised his trembling hand to glance balefully at the veins there, at the blackened blood becoming ever more visible beneath his paling skin.

Pain the likes of which he could never have comprehended before was his never-ending companion now, and a small, largely ignored part of himself suspected it was slowly driving him mad. Loathing boiled up like black tar in his chest and into his throat as he thought of the one who had done this to him.

The newly crowned "Queen" of Ice. Who, for all her lofty title, had seemingly abandoned Earth to its fate.

If he had his way, she would pay in agony tenfold for this poison that had taken hold of him. One of his greatest comforts was in imagining ways to make her suffer. Yet one of the greatest edges to his pain was that he probably would never get the chance.

Do not lose sight of her usefulness to us, a cold, unfeeling voice reverberated in Solim's mind, and he flinched as an even greater darkness formed itself from the shadows around him into the shape of a hooded man.

Here was the real reason Solim came to Earth so often these days. He told himself he was not hiding—he was merely regaining his strength, and one of the primary ways he did so was by trying to stay out of his master's way. The Devourer had no patience for its greatest, most powerful servant's condition—and absolutely no remorse for its part in that condition, for it was the Devourer's own plague that now tainted him. The Queen of Ice had only done the unleashing.

Solim gritted his teeth.

Soon, he told himself to hold yet another surge of spite in check. *Soon it will give you everything, this agony will end, and you will have your revenge on her, on Korinth—on all of them. Soon.*

To the Devourer, however, Solim tried to appear at ease and indifferent. His master punished displays of weakness almost as readily as insubordination. *Weakness* meant a lack of *usefulness.*

The only reason the ever-hungry Devourer kept anyone alive was because they were useful.

Hence its chiding words just now about the Queen, who would have been rightfully dead by now if that had been the Devourer's only objective concerning her.

Solim snorted. "Lot of good the Queen's Blood will do us if she gives it to *that* instead."

He knew better than to mention a Tree by name in front of the Devourer, so he instead merely gestured to the northeast.

"Yes," the Devourer said, its tone frosted, emotionless. "And yet She does not call on the Queen to do so, even as She weakens to an unprecedented degree. Why?"

"Sentiment. It's always Their greatest weakness when it comes to Their favorites. That, and adherence to Their 'laws.'"

"Do not presume a knowledge of Their ways, *boy*," the Devourer said, a hard edge entering its detached voice, and Solim felt another increased spasm of pain that he knew wasn't coincidental. He had to lock all his muscles in place to prevent himself from buckling or gasping.

Yes, he avoided the Devourer now for very good reasons.

The dark, hooded head turned back to the northeast, and its voice lowered. "I have fought against Them for eons your mortal mind cannot even comprehend. They are planning something...and all of it seems to center on that new queenling of Hers. But how? And why...her?"

Solim knew by now it would probably be better for him to remain quiet, but even after six years in the Devourer's service, climbing his way tooth and claw to emerge as the most powerful of all his slaves, Solim still could not accustom himself to the fact that the Devourer never wanted his opinion. Solim wasn't just the first lish in nearly a century, nor the most powerful to have ever been. He also had the most brilliant mind of his time, and a breadth of knowledge that his pathetic "brother" could never imagine. How could he remain *silent*?

If the Devourer did not listen, it was a fool.

"Tolsyon's prophecy, then," he said flatly.

He was paid for his trouble with another flash of agony.

"The 'prophecy' you refer to," the Devourer said derisively as Solim silently suffered, "is a scheme of Theirs that I have been anticipating for much of those eons, as you should know by now."

Solim felt a separate sting, this one of memory. He had been so certain when he had come to the Devourer that one of the greatest evidences he had of his usefulness was in revealing to the Devourer the Trees' plot for its downfall—only to discover that the Devourer was not only utterly unimpressed, it had an even greater knowledge of that plot than he did.

The Devourer's voice grew impassive again. "Some of the signs of it are there, but they are...confusing. It should not be a Queen of *Ice* to begin it all. Let alone one so...unremarkable."

"I never said there was anything *special* about her," Solim said through clenched teeth. "There's nothing special about any of them."

Korinth, most especially, he thought savagely. Of all his many hatreds, his loathing toward his former blood and the current Tolsyon heir lay underneath them all, simmering until the slightest prompting brought it gushing forth.

Korinth was the reason for everything Solim had unjustly suffered. Always. And *still* the wretched younger man had the audacity to live, to breathe, to smirk and charm them all.

Solim had no words for the loathing he bore for Korinth, for how much he longed to shatter everything around his former brother until he was left alone and tortured by his failures, and then, *then*, at long last, make him suffer for days, months, years even before Solim finally claimed his life.

He thought it a pity that the Queen of Ice had clearly rejected Korinth's offered heart. Surely Korinth had hardened enough by now that her death wouldn't cause him nearly the same amount of suffering. Ah, well. Solim would find other ways to emotionally cripple him.

Soon, he chanted to himself, and this time, the pain in his blood felt like pleasure, because it was a sign that the day of his greatest desire was coming.

He yanked his attention back to the present, because it seemed the Devourer always had to disagree with him. "Not so. This new King of Flame shows...an unusual amount of power and skill, particularly for his age. Already, he nearly surpasses his formidable sire. He, of all the pieces, fits in place the best. With the Queen of Ice to give him even more power, he is a nuisance I will not tolerate for much longer, lest he grow to become a threat."

Solim gritted his teeth. *And what are you going to do about him?* he snarled in his thoughts. *We've already failed to take his Realms and Tree. Twice.*

And with each attempt, not only did their consumed army shrink to a dangerous degree, the Tree of Flame grew even *stronger*, better able to protect Her children and thwart the Devourer's attempts to enter Her Realms.

During the second battle, the one that had occurred just yesterday, Solim had still been too weak from his poisoning to fight in. If forced, he probably would have been killed. Solim had half expected the Devourer to order him to anyway, it was so furious with Solim's impotence and the Monarchs of Ice and Flame. Yet it did not. Nor did the Devourer kill him after that failed battle, as Solim feared for a moment it would.

It came close. In the Devourer's wrath, it caused Solim agony the likes of which he still was recovering from, pain that almost sent a tremor through him just from the memory. Yet the Devourer did not end him, and in fact, it calmed itself and spared Solim before permanent damage could be done. Solim still didn't know for certain why, and that made him more afraid than he ever admitted to himself.

It wasn't for his wisdom.

The problem with being the Devourer's consumed slave was that it could know even his thoughts. It just generally did not care about them, almost always tuning them out as the most trivial of noises.

Yet, in a rare moment of the driest amusement, the Devourer answered his unspoken question. "True. Then I think it is time to strike at his weakness."

Solim blinked. "At the *girl*? But she's even more protected than he is!"

And that's while she's in his Realms! Solim thought with frustration. *We still don't even know where in the hellfrosted universe the Tree has hidden her* family.

Searching for the newly restored, incipient Moontouched "clan" had been one of Solim's main tasks (and thus failures) during his recovery. His strict orders to comb the universe so diligently had made Solim suspect the Devourer was more concerned about the Queen of Ice than it let on—or, at least, about her clan. The spectacularly failed siege of Rosin, thanks in no small part to the Moontouched, seemed to confirm the cause for such a worry.

Solim's hopes that the Devourer had once again tuned out of his thoughts were fruitless, because Solim felt another lance of intensified agony. Whether for his insolence or at the reminder of that failure, he didn't know, and it probably didn't even matter which anymore. Solim had failed the Devourer so often now that it seemed to think of him as little more than a cur to keep at its side and beat at its slightest whim.

Once, the Devourer had been different toward him. When it first began whispering in his heart, it had been cordial—*flattering*, even. When Solim was betrayed by his own brother and sentenced to death by his own people, he had come to the Devourer, confident in its promises that he would at last be welcomed and valued as he deserved and immediately given the power to enact his revenge.

Yet the Devourer had been cold with displeasure at Solim's failure to kill the then weak, adolescent Heir of Flame (now the matured King the Devourer watched so guardedly) and dismissive of Solim's consequent treatment at his people's hands. Though Solim now had all the sniveling adoration and fear he could have asked for from the rest of the Devourer's slaves, he'd had to *earn* it; the Devourer had granted him no special status from the beginning, and Solim had spent years of scrambling for power and outmaneuvering his fellow slaves before he had felt secure in even his own life. Despite his rise, the Devourer had only grown colder and more displeased with him the more time went on.

He knew, now, that the Devourer's flattery in the beginning had only been to sway him to the point of no return. Yet Solim only despised himself for not expecting as much. He had grown wiser and more cunning now—he knew that was simply the way true power worked.

So he now played a very dangerous game with the Devourer in turn, keeping his plan too deep within his heart for his "master" to care to discover, never daring even think it—only feel it in shoots of resentment or bouts of lust for more power. Those were all emotions the Devourer understood and could pin to other causes, ones entirely in alignment with its will.

Solim had nowhere else to go now, no place to be safe from a Tree's condemnation and the burning that awaited him for the breaking of his blood oaths except by the Devourer's side. The Devourer knew it, and it took Solim's keen awareness of that for granted, thinking that dependence was all the Devourer needed to keep him in line.

But when one had nowhere else to go but up...that was where one went.

Soon. That was the only word Solim let himself think. He let the rest boil underneath.

"Yet," the Devourer said coolly, "there is one sure way to draw the Queen out."

Its hooded head looked again to the northeast.

Solim stared, darkheart thumping. "You're...going to go after *another* Tree?"

Hadn't they lost enough by now? Their slave army was reaching dangerously low levels, considering how many of them the Devourer had to consume to retain its power. Their strategies weren't working, and with every day, the peoples of Ice and Flame and the Tree of Flame seemed to grow in power and unity. Only the Tree of Ice seemed to wane, but even She was still strong enough to prevent any consumed from touching Her, even as un-guarded as She was.

They should be retreating to their strongholds, conserving their strength, and waiting for another few years, another few world conquests *at least*, before taking Her and, inevitably, the peoples of Ice and Flame on. As much as that delay would grate on Solim like nails being dragged across his skin, he knew that was the path of wisdom, of preservation. He hadn't come so far to throw his life away now.

Solim only realized he'd said the forbidden word when it was too late, and the pain that shot through him was like his flesh was being simultane-ously burned and frosted and consumed from the inside out. He couldn't help but stumble to his knees, falling amid the rubble of the destroyed hut. He didn't even notice the discomfort of his knees and hands hitting metal, splintered wood, and concrete. Ironically, his poisoned yet empowered blood healed those minor cuts and bruises faster than ever. It was the Devourer's inflicted pain—and humiliation—that lingered.

In contrast with the fury with which the Devourer had lashed out, its voice was emotionless as it turned its attention back to the northeast. "It is a risk, but a necessary one. It is time to draw Her out. Time to see what game She is playing this time...before She turns that game against me."

Only then did Solim realize that the "her" this time was not the Queen of Ice but her Tree. Solim resentfully struggled once again against a feeling of nothingness, of being only yet another pawn on the Devourer's board as it played the game of eternity against the Trees of Life.

Sometimes, terrifyingly, his master seemed certain to lose. Even so, Solim wasn't one to stop it from trying to win. If there was anything Solim hated more, wanted to see burned to ash more than Korinth...it was, perhaps, his Tree—his fickle Tree, who had so easily turned Her back on him and cast him aside for Her new *favorite*.

One day, She *would* burn. But because Solim cared about his continued existence too much to tackle Her first, he focused all his hate on the one that would soon be within his power to destroy. He told himself that Korinth encapsulated in one mortal body all that he hated in his Tree, that to crush him was to deal a blow to Her that he could inflict in no other way. For now.

Soon.

"Yes, Solim," the Devourer said, the slightest derision entering its implacable voice. "Soon. Serve me well for just a bit longer, and I will fulfill all my promises to you. In fact...yes, I will even go so far as to say that if you bring me the girl during that battle, I will use her Blood to finally grant your wish, rather than to claim her world."

Solim couldn't help a flutter of dark excitement. "You will?" he asked, rising.

Set aside the satisfaction of finally having his revenge on her in such a poetic way, for her poisoning of his blood to be transcended with her own. The truly *exquisite* part would be the utter *anguish* it would cause the King of Flame and Korinth when he told them of her fate.

Surely enough of Korinth's affections for her still lingered to make such a cruel end to her life deal him a powerful blow.

"Indeed," the Devourer said. For the first time, its voice grew softer, approaching something close to its flattering whispers of long ago. "Of course...there is one way I could grant your wish even sooner."

Solim reflexively placed a protective hand over his heart.

That was, perhaps, the one reason the Devourer had kept him alive until now. Death was, indeed, the other way for Solim to transcend mortality as he wished. But if the Devourer killed Solim against his will...the magic could not work. He had to be willing in even his death.

Even the Devourer was not above the laws of the Creators. Yet.

"No," Solim snarled. "I will take the *gashren's* Blood, thank you."

The foul word he'd used for the girl reflected woefully little of his hate.

"Very well," the Devourer said, voice turning cool. "Then here are my *generous* terms: during the battle for Earth, bring the girl to me...or die trying. Either way, I will fulfill my promise."

Solim smiled, black lips pulling against blackened teeth.

Soon.

Chapter One

Authenticity

Koriben

After the mourning feast and dancing to honor those who had fallen in the defense of Rosin, Sarah and I returned to our suite in the King's Wing, and Sarah, her father, and her brother got ready to leave.

We had decided they would sleep in their own hold and Realm tonight. That way, our entourage could pack up first thing tomorrow and leave Rosin for the Battleblood Realm of Ekrel, the final formal stop on the grand tour, and Sarah could visit her family and consult with her Tree before rejoining us in the early evening.

I had mixed feelings about this plan. I wasn't thrilled about being separated from Sarah, especially so soon after the siege, but if the Devourer still had not discovered where her Realm was, it was the safest place for my betrothed to be. Hadn't I been thinking of ways to persuade her to go back there all along?

And Sarah *needed* to consult her Tree—there was no question about that. Even if she believed what the Tree of Flame had told me we had to do, she shouldn't decide something so important on my word regarding my Tree's will. She needed to hear it for herself from her own.

If Her Tree said something else, well...we would figure that out if it came to that.

I had no reason to think that would happen, though. In everything else up to this point, over the entire history between our two peoples, the Trees of Ice and Flame had never contradicted each other. I was more likely to be mistaken than for the Trees to disagree.

But...I couldn't be. As hard as it sometimes still was for me to have faith in myself, I knew what I had seen and felt in that dream. I simply...knew.

While I waited for the Linds to pack, I tried to catch up on some reading, so I was sitting in our suite's reception area with my archival-stone tablet and a steaming mug of tsha when an attendant opened the door and ushered Sarah's brother in.

"Here you are, rightwing," he said to Michael. "King's suite. And there would be the King."

"Ah, thank you, Tobi," I said, blinking as I looked up from taking a sip. I set my mug down on the side table, feeling sheepish. I hadn't thought about the fact that Sarah's father and brother might not know where to find Sarah and me in the vastness of the King's Wing of Rosin, even though Kor had graciously given up a small spare bedroom in his suite meant for an assistant of his own, meaning they were just down the hall.

Michael shuffled into the room. His awkwardness was partly because of the large bag he once again carried—but only partly.

"We can bring that with us when we move to the next hold, if you like," I offered, though I had little expectation he would accept.

Sure enough, Sarah's brother gripped the bag more tightly and stiffened. "No thanks."

I gestured to one of the couches in the sitting area. "Well, have a seat. Sarah's not quite ready yet, but I'm sure she will be soon."

"I figured," he said. Yet he still stood there.

I sighed but figured there wasn't much more I could do to make him comfortable—and perhaps nothing I could do to make him like me. So, I philosophically returned to my reading.

Or tried to. To my surprise, I saw movement out of the corner of my eye, and when I looked up, Michael was setting his bag down and sitting on the couch perpendicular to mine.

I tried not to blink in surprise. There were plenty of seats in the room, and he had chosen the one closest to me without being on the same couch. His spine was rigid, and he perched on the edge, but he was there.

It was a good thing I'd already set my expression to neutral, because abruptly, Michael said, "How are you feeling?"

My mind blanked. Not even the most basic of civil trivialities would come to my head. "What?"

Michael's face was heating. "Health-wise, I mean. I mean, you look OK. Physically. But everyone said...Sarah said...well, last night I saw.... Yet, you know, magic. Fast healing. And stuff. So...are you good now?"

Ah, he was talking about my injuries from the lightcannon blast during the battle for Rosin. I stalled for time to compose my answer by lifting my mug, taking a sip, and setting it down again.

"Thank you for your concern," I said slowly. "But you're right. I'm fully recovered."

I smiled, not sure how long his new goodwill would last. "It probably seems surprising, considering the state I was in. But we have a saying: 'To kill a drakón, one must do it in one beat of the flameheart.'"

"So that's what I nearly did, didn't I?" Michael said quietly, looking down.

I stilled as I realized what this was about. I had forgotten that he had been the one behind that lightcannon blast—that's how meaningless his culpability was to me. Yet not, apparently, to him.

"Michael...."

He straightened, setting his jaw as he met my eyes. "No, let me do this. I don't like having things hanging over me, so...let's just have out with it. Ben...I owe you an apology. Because last night...I nearly killed you."

I set my tablet down next to the mug. "Michael, what you *did* was save my life."

He had been aiming for the shadow of the Devourer that had launched itself out of the water at me and Sarah. Except the Devourer had been too close to me, and I caught some of the shrapnel from the blast of light and ice that repelled it. I shuddered and thanked the Tree once again that Sarah, who had been riding on my drakáback, was unscathed. I hadn't been able to turn quickly enough in the air to torch the Devourer's shadow with my drakáflame, but perhaps I had turned just enough to shield her from the lightcannon blast with my body.

I had only a few vague impressions of light and agony from that moment before everything went black, then an even hazier one of coughing up saltwater after Sarah had pulled me out of the sea through a series of miracles I was still wrapping my head around. Michael had good cause to be surprised. Despite my casual attitude to set him at ease, by all rights, I shouldn't have been sitting there. Most of that had to do with the will of the Trees, who, for some reason I couldn't comprehend, had decided I was to live.

But a large part had to do with Michael, and I was surprised he couldn't understand that.

"No," he said, jutting his chin. "I was saving Sarah's. Except I panicked, and shot too quickly, and I—"

"Saved my life," I repeated. "Sarah *is* my life, Michael. You saved her when I couldn't."

Michael snorted, some of his stiff demeanor disappearing with the rise in his derision. "Please. I've heard this from you before, so spare me. Just because I owe you one doesn't mean I believe you."

"Fine," I said. "You want impartial facts? You think the Devourer would have stopped at killing Sarah?"

Michael paused.

I sat back. As objectively as I could, I said, "Of the two of us, I have more experience dealing with it, so maybe you'll finally believe me when I say the answer is no. It most definitely would have killed me if it could have. The only reason it wouldn't was if it thought that the only way for it to take Sarah would be to do so immediately, leaving me alive. For the moment. But if the Devourer had Sarah...."

I closed my eyes and forced myself to breathe and to speak. "Then we *all* would have died not long after. Within days...perhaps even deken. Maybe even that very night."

Michael was quiet for a moment. I opened my eyes and saw him thinking.

"Oh, right," he said. "That...blood thing."

With a Monarch's Blood, filled with their Tree's Power, the Devourer in its entirety could enter and consume a world—Tree's protections or no.

I smiled thinly. "Yes. 'That blood thing.' Which is why all Oshal, if not all the Six Realms, now owe their lives to you. Including me. You don't owe me anything, Michael."

"Why risk her at all, then?" he demanded.

I controlled my irritation with a few more deep breaths. I had been trained in how to negotiate with resistant people, and one key was asking thoughtful questions that got one's counterpart thinking deeply.

"How do you think that battle would have gone without her? You must have been watching it closely. Imagine what it would have been like if none of us could use our drakáforms, and we only had a fraction of our power available."

I took advantage of Michael's thinking time to take another sip of tsha. It was getting cool. Not that I minded compared to the importance of this discussion, but it also seemed like a benign, normalizing gesture.

From his body language, I was getting a feel for one source of his dislike, and my miraculous recovery wasn't helping: he saw me as different from him, other. No, not just other, but dangerous, unpredictable. The more mortal—no, the more *human*—I could appear, the more I could show human needs, motivations, and habits, the safer he might feel.

It wasn't right, but it was a part of life—especially *my* life. I was all too familiar with trying to make people not afraid of me, and those were *my* people, who knew me and knew my powers, my limits, and all the rules I abided by. Even then, I used to bend over backward to convince people I wasn't a monster. Sarah showed me that not only was that attempt unhealthy, but it also wasn't possible—especially not when I believed I was a monster too.

I still slipped into old thought patterns sometimes, but I had noticed a gradual change in me ever since that first conversation with Sarah about my inner darkness. The more I accepted my worth despite my mistakes, the more I trusted myself to be in control and do the right thing...the more I was, and the more others trusted me in return. My footing was still shaky, but I was finding that balance.

I reminded myself of that as I drank my tsha. Normalizing gestures were well and good, but going out of my way to reassure Michael would be unhealthy, and self-defeating besides. Balanced confidence, that was the key. Trusting in myself, believing I wasn't a monster, yet still practicing gentleness and restraint. Like Avva.

Hopefully that subliminal communication, combined with time and patience, would finally set Michael at ease.

If it didn't...well, I would just have to accept that. It would hurt to be rejected by a member of Sarah's family, and it would make my life harder as King of Flame, but I couldn't afford to let someone else's opinion of me darken my soul. Not any longer. Otherwise, I would become the monster Michael feared.

"It...wouldn't have gone well," Michael admitted at last. "From what Mathya told me, there were some creatures out there big or nasty enough to have done some damage to the mountain, right? We couldn't have just holed up the whole night. They could have caused cave-ins or even broken in."

"Right," I agreed, surprised and a little impressed at his grasp of the situation—and relieved. Sarah needed a rightwing who knew his business—or could learn what he didn't know. Quickly.

"Do you know what would happen if consumed got in?" I asked, continuing the tack of asking questions, since it seemed to be working. "Especially while we were still limited to amáform?"

Michael grimaced. "A lot more people would have died."

"And what about if they got to the Tree?"

"That's right. There's one of those here. One of Mathya's worst contingencies was falling back to defend it."

I sent a quick prayer of gratitude for Mathya's thorough work in preparing Michael, even with how precious her time would have been that day. Though, considering how Michael had saved us all, that was time well spent; I was impressed enough with the Starkissed rightwing to suspect she had been wise enough to anticipate as much.

"Her," I said mildly, risking one correction after taking a sip.

He blinked. "Excuse me?"

"Falling back to defend Her. The Tree. She is female and prefers us to use feminine pronouns."

"But...it's a tree."

I reminded myself that he had grown up with no knowledge of Trees, and he had only had a short time and not much training to adjust. "Trees can have gender. Even normal ones. And She is no ordinary tree."

Still, I hadn't meant to sidetrack us. "Did Mathya say what would happen if harm came to the Oshal Tree?"

"No," Michael said with a frown.

Unsurprising. Even Mathya would have assumed the horror of such a thing would be self-evident to him by now.

Michael continued, "But...that's bad, right? From what Sarah's said, Trees protect your worlds from this Devourer...thing."

"They protect yours, too."

Referring to Earth, the world they had come from. Though tragic circumstances had since separated them from their former home, I knew the Linds still felt a deep emotional connection to it.

He raised an eyebrow. "Not the one we're currently on."

"Yes, I've thought about that," I said with a frown. "I'm not sure why the Tree of Ice hasn't given Sarah a Branch to plant in the Seventh Realm yet. That means that right now, the only thing protecting your Realm from the Devourer is its anonymity—the Devourer doesn't know where in the vast universe to find you."

"Perhaps that's the reason," Michael suggested. Then he scowled and looked away, as if I had baited him into being engaged, and he resented me for it.

I played dumb. "What do you mean?"

He wrinkled his nose and waved a hand. "How should I know, when it comes to this gods and magic crap?"

"But you had a thought," I said, leaning back as I nursed my mug. "And that's all any of us have at this point. I'd like to hear it then, if you don't mind."

He gave me another scowl, but when he looked away, his face smoothed somewhat. "I dunno. I just thought…. Is there something about a planet *having* a Tree that makes it more noticeable to the Devourer? Maybe we hide better without one."

That thought had occurred to me, and a long time ago, but I made myself thoughtful. I didn't believe I was being disingenuous. I was truly impressed, and I wanted to encourage him.

"That's a good theory. Might be the best one we have right now."

Michael preened a bit, and I felt a flicker of amusement. That was the very basics of flattery, the kind even I was capable of—because it was genuine and well-meant. The Moontouched rightwing was going to have to get more accustomed to politics someday, and soon, before someone took advantage of him. For now, I was just glad he had allowed me to boost his confidence.

Now, I would just have to keep him from bringing his theory up in front of Kor. There was no one better at *squashing* one's theories than my genius leftwing.

I thought for a moment to remember where we were. "So yes, if the Devourer's minions hurt or especially killed the Tree, the Devourer could enter the world. And that would be the beginning of the end."

I thought about going into the ramifications of the loss of Oshal and the Starkissed, at least as an independent clan, but I decided to hold back. That would probably be too much, too quickly.

I was glad I did when Michael frowned thoughtfully. He was engaging again, despite himself. If only this time, I could keep him from noticing….

"But then, how did the Devourer appear last night?"

"That was just a small piece of it, what we're calling a shadow, for lack of a better term," I said with a shrug. "Trust me, if that was *the* Devourer, in its entirety, one blast of a lightcannon wouldn't have dealt with it."

Now that I thought about it, I was surprised that the lightcannon blast had done the trick. We hadn't had time to test many methods of hurting Devourer shadows, since we'd only just discovered both their existence and the fact that we could hurt them at all. But since Sarah's ice had only contained it before, we'd begun to think that only drakáfire could destroy it. And yet, if any remnant of the shadow from last night had remained, surely it would have continued to go for Sarah or me....

Especially since I was gushing blood.

I felt a chill go through me, which hopefully wasn't visible. Either I'd controlled myself or Michael wasn't paying attention, because he just continued to think, his eyes troubled.

Whatever it got *of my blood,* I told myself through clenched teeth, *it wouldn't have been all of it. Not enough for it to enter in its entirety.*

But perhaps I had discovered how its shadows had entered, because that was not the only time I had bled profusely, out in the open, in the past few months. The other time I could think of was back when I had been Heir...but perhaps that was still enough.

Michael drummed his fingers on his legs, and his mouth pursed, as if he were tasting something sour. "So let me get this straight: in an attack, you can either protect Sarah and her blood from the Devourer, and maybe lose the world...."

"And all life on it," I added quietly.

Michael's pursed lips turned into a full scowl. "...or...you put Sarah at risk, and maybe win the battle."

My agony as King, in an agshell.

But to Michael, I just said, "Yes. Then add to that the fact that if Sarah *chooses* to help, I have no right to stop her. I never did. But now, thanks to my blood oath to her, I can't."

"Svyer said it's a burning in your blood," he said, looking at my right hand. The covenant hand. "The blood oath thing. Once you've made an oath not to do something, if you so much as think about doing it...the fire that went into your blood when you made it burns you, from the inside."

"Right," I said. "Technically, you can still do that thing—or you can try to, anyway. But if you truly *try*, ignoring all warnings, all pain...the fire can generally finish you off before you can manage it."

His eyes flicked up to mine in surprise. Apparently Svyer—my cousin, who had joined Sarah's clan and now lived with her family in the Seventh

Realm—hadn't gone this far in her explanation. "Finish.... You mean it *kills* you?"

I cocked my head. "What did you expect?"

"I just...everyone made it seem like...." He put his hand on his neck and looked away. "Like it just *stopped* you. That was it."

"It's fire," I said quietly, looking into my mug. "When you misuse its power...it tends to be merciless."

Michael bent over, resting his elbows on his thighs, and stared at the floor for a long moment. "So, when you promised not to shut us out again...when you did it, you knew that if you ever tried to again, you would die?"

"Yes," I said.

Then I drained the last of my tsha and set the mug down to pour another from the pot there. Michael started a bit at the click of porcelain on wood. He glanced at the mug and smirked.

"Sarah implied you had a bit of a thing for tea."

"Implied?"

He looked away, face hardening. "She didn't talk about you much. During that time you shut us out. We mostly had to guess about you, from things that she *wouldn't* talk about...or avoided."

"Ah," I said softly, flameheart constricting.

He looked back and scrutinized me for a moment. I didn't know what he saw in my expression, but I didn't conceal any of the pain or regret I felt for my greatest mistake. He looked away.

Silence fell between us for long enough that I wondered if I should go back to my reading. On the other hand, it occurred to me that Sarah was taking an awfully long time to get ready. She wasn't one of those fussy girls who had to pack practically everything they owned every time they went somewhere, and she told me she was just going to change and grab a few things....

Then I realized that her star in my mind's eye was still and had been for a long time. That wouldn't match the bustle of packing....

I felt a jolt of worry, wondering if something was wrong, but when I glanced to the side at our bedroom door, I realized it was just the slightest bit ajar. Sarah's star in my mind placed her just behind it, close enough to be touching it...or holding it open.

Ah. That would be why. My mouth lifted at the corner the slightest bit.

"Why does it have to be her?" Michael said, breaking the silence. "I'm not an asshole. I don't think you all should die. But...if someone has to risk their life to help you people, why my little sister?"

I straightened my expression. Now that I was mindful of our eavesdropper, I was tempted to edit my responses, but that would risk Michael sensing a change in me and becoming suspicious. Now was not the time to stop being genuine—or human, like him.

So, I tried to forget that we had a listener at all.

I sighed. "I ask myself that question every day. Well...except for the sister part."

I colored a bit at that, and Michael became amused when he glanced at me. "Right."

I considered that progress, so I put myself out there even more. "Believe it or not, I *tried* to think of Sarah as a sister, once."

Michael smirked. For all his doubt that I cared about Sarah's wellbeing, he seemed to have no trouble believing I was attracted to her. I was a bit insulted that he thought I had so little honor, but I let it go for now. Flame knew I'd given him reasons to doubt me, and only time would prove my sincerity to him.

Besides, I *was* the one who brought it up.

"How did that go for you?"

"Terribly," I said with a grimace, then took another sip from my mug. "I don't think I lasted a day."

Michael let out a low laugh, and I considered that worth the price.

"My friendship strategy worked longer," I mused. "At least a couple of days more, I think."

"Well, isn't friendship supposed to be the basis of a lasting relationship?" Michael asked in amusement. Then his smile died, and he looked away again. "I mean, not that I care about.... Well, I want Sarah to be happy, obviously. And I guess you guys are engaged now. Not much I can do about that. So...."

"Michael," I said, softening my words with a smile. "If this is the part where you tell me that if I hurt your sister again, you'll kill me, then let me save you the trouble by telling you that you're going to have to get in line. Rachel already made that threat, and though Svyer hasn't, I'm certain she would be faster than you."

Michael's lips twitched. "Svyer?"

"You clearly haven't seen my cousin when she's mad," I said dryly. "But surely by now you have some idea of how much she loves Sarah."

He smiled wryly. "Guess so."

I paused to think. "Actually, there's quite a lot of people who would be ahead of you in line, some of whom you haven't even met yet or scarcely know. At least two of them, you will never meet, since they're beyond the Flame. So, I am *well* aware of what I'm in for if I should ever be that idiotic again, thank you."

"Well, good," Michael said, losing the battle with his lips and smiling. "Because if you *did* pass her up again, you *would* be an idiot."

I raised my mug to that. "I couldn't agree more."

"Speaking of Sarah, though," Michael said, frowning as he settled back. "Where is she, anyway? It normally doesn't take her this long to get ready. She's not *Rachel*."

He rolled his eyes, which made me smile.

I took another sip and said, "Oh, I'm sure Vadya pulled her into something."

Like eavesdropping. This had that Starkissed's mischief written all over it.

Isn't that right, Sarah? I sent to her silently, a smirk in my inner voice.

Sending one's inner voice was a bit like shooting an arrow of energy that could go through walls. Line of sight wasn't an absolute requirement, but the more precise an idea you had of your intended recipient's location, the more precisely you could send your voice with no one else being the wiser.

A lack of precise knowledge meant sending out a volley instead of a single arrow to get your message out. Because I had the power of a King, if I *had* to, I could perhaps project my inner voice across the King's Wing, but it would be in an indiscriminate "shout" that *everyone* within a certain spread would hear. (Once, charged with Sarah's power, I had apparently roared my inner voice across elden, but, given I was in a crazed, berserk rage at the time, I had only vague memories of this.)

Because I could visualize through my sight and Sarah's star in my mind *exactly* where she was right now, I could confidently send that statement just to her, even though I couldn't see *her*.

I knew at once that my shot had hit dead center. Michael's back was to our bedroom door, so he didn't see it abruptly swing shut.

Sloppy. She should have left it open; closing it in that moment was as good as admitting to guilt. These Linds were so bad at intrigue, it was adorable. Then again, that was one reason I'd fallen in love with one of them.

I wasn't much better, just from sheer ineptitude, but at least I had *some* exposure. I knew what I was *supposed* to do...even if I couldn't do it most of the time.

On second thought, that probably meant I was more hopeless than they were.

"Vadya?" Michael said, his face scrunching.

"Sarah's chief of staff," I explained, taking another sip. Now that the door was closed, I could offer a sincere compliment. "A highly capable, intelligent young woman, and a good asset to Sarah."

And, apparently, a corrupting influence. Then again, I wouldn't have expected anything less from one of Kor's *tol'lon* cousins.

Michael shook his head in wonder. "She has a *staff*?"

I raised an eyebrow. "She's a Queen."

"Well, yeah...but of what? Besides us?" He gestured to himself to indicate their family.

"Well, technically, no one else right now. But all of this—" I gestured around us. "—the grand tour and everything—is precisely because that's about to change. Hopefully in less than a sevenday."

Even if we secretly married sooner, no one else would know that until the public heartbinding.

Michael just stared at me. Had this not occurred to him yet? Jake knew; he'd said so himself.

"Michael, when Sarah marries me, she'll be Queen of my Realms as well as hers."

And I would be King of hers, though I didn't mention that bit. Besides, Kor and our lawyers were still working out what that even meant—if anything, beyond being each other's consorts. But I doubted the Trees intended it to be as simple as that, and Kor seemed to agree with me. The problem was getting a straight answer from either Tree. Not that...I'd been actively asking mine. Despite repeated, increasingly pointed inquiries from said lawyers.

I sighed. Yet another reason I should have talked to my Tree before now.

Before Michael could ask one of the dozens of questions I could see building in his eyes, Sarah opened the door, carrying a bag.

She had changed from her feast finery into the simple, practical clothes she preferred: a soft white shirt and form-fitting, yet comfortable black trousers and black slippers. Vadya had no doubt helped clean her light brown skin of makeup and body paint, and unpinned and brushed out her long white hair so that it was now tied in a simple tail over one shoulder.

Her wide silver eyes were trying—and delightfully failing—to look innocent. At least she'd had the presence of mind to wait just a bit before emerging. Maybe that was at Vadya's advisement; the young Starkissed woman slipped out a moment later, doing a much better job at acting blasé.

"Oh, hi, Michael," Sarah said cheerfully. "Sorry for keeping you waiting. Vadya had...something to discuss with me."

Should have come up with a different excuse, I sent to her. Now it sounded like we were colluding.

Her eyes darted to mine, and I just held my mug with both hands and grinned at her over the rim.

Michael frowned, then looked back at me, but I thought I schooled my expression in time. Once again, though, before Michael had time to question, the door to our suite opened, and their father, Jake, walked through, holding his own bag.

"Oh, good," he said placidly. "Looks like we're all ready. Shall we go?"

The timing was just a tad too perfect. So, though I nodded, downed the last of my tsha, and stood, I cast a glance and a raised eyebrow at Sarah.

You were doing so well with him, she sent with a flicker of sheepishness crossing her face. *I didn't want anyone to interrupt.*

Ah. Sarah had probably had Vadya pass on a message via call scale to Kor to ask Jake to delay, and then to tell Jake to come when Sarah knew she'd been discovered. She could have even prevented anyone else from coming into the room.

Perhaps she was better at this than I'd given her credit for. I didn't know whether to be proud of my betrothed or worried for myself. I settled on the hope that her words gave me.

I did well, did I? I said as she came up to take my hand.

Of course you did, silly, she said, giving my hand a clench. *You were you.*

Huh. Maybe that meant I didn't have to be good at intrigue after all. At least, not when it came to dealing with the Linds.

CHAPTER TWO

SEED

SARAH

WE HADN'T PLANNED FOR Ben to come through the crowngate with us into my family's hold. But when it came time to say goodbye, neither of us seemed to want to part, especially since we hadn't gotten our quiet evening time together, so I invited him in. Since he was going to spend the night in his rooms in Crownhold anyway (not being able to go back to Rosin with its sungate banked for the night), I suggested he come through and say hi to my family, and once things had settled down, we could slip away.

To my surprise, Ben took me up on my offer, even though that meant getting through my family first. Maybe his conversation with Michael had given him confidence. Whatever the reason, I was relieved. I'd always known the key to getting my family to accept Ben was putting them together long enough for them to get to know him and for him to feel comfortable enough to act like himself. Because once they really knew *him*, how could they not like him?

Fortunately, that meeting went well, even being unplanned. Perhaps that spontaneity worked in our favor, since no one had time to work up a sour mood, and Svyer was right there to greet him and smooth the way with the playfulness she brought out in Ben, even if it was by mercilessly teasing him about not calling or visiting her.

I could tell that their interactions were good for humanizing Ben in front of them; he could hardly act the formal Golden Royal they'd always seen before with Svyer poking him into the wall and him valiantly trying to defend himself with dodges and excuses. Even Ben's seven-and-a-half feet of intimidating muscle meant little in the face of his tall, green-haired cousin's playful pestering.

It only took a few moments for Mom's apprehension to fade into watching the two of them with the fond amusement of a mother. Even Laura, my prickly sister-in-law, had a hard time keeping her lips from twitching, but she solved that problem by stiffly walking away with Michael and their toddler, Tommie, as soon as they were done with their own family greetings.

Before that could sadden me too much, Michael cast a glance back at Ben over his shoulder. The look in his eyes wasn't soft, but it wasn't hard, either. It was...evaluating. Perhaps a begrudging acceptance that there was more to Ben than he'd thought.

I thought it would be easy for Ben and me to slip away, since I expected Mom to be the clingiest person to me now that I'd finally come home, and she was *still* an early bird that should have been longing for bed by then.

But, surprisingly, Abby was the biggest holdup. As soon as Svyer was done with Ben, Abby closed in, demanding that Ben pick her up, and once he did, she began chattering away at him as if they were old friends. Even though I could tell that he was baffled about what to say or do, Ben put on a show of interest that more than satisfied my five-year-old sister.

Unfortunately, his pretended enthusiasm—combined with the fact that he was the only person who had lately indulged (or even *could* indulge) the growing girl's lingering preference to be held—meant that Abby refused to be parted with him. Every time Ben tried to put her down so that Mom could take her to bed, she put up a fuss that had Ben promptly stopping in alarm, as if he were afraid he would genuinely hurt her.

I didn't like the feeling that I was setting a precedent, but I didn't want Ben's first primarily positive interaction with my family to end in one of Abby's rare tantrums, so I negotiated a compromise: Ben would carry her to bed, and I would tuck her in, just like old times. Abby pondered this and then said if Ben also told her a story, she would accept; with no more access to picture books,

Abby was always looking for fresh bedtime content. Ben, relieved, said yes before I could counter.

I had to roll my eyes. Much more of this, and Abby would have tender-hearted Ben wrapped around her little finger. What was worse, Abby seemed to sense that.

Though *my* heart was the one to melt to a dangerous degree after we finally got Abby into the bottom bunk bed in the room she and Lizzy shared, and Ben sat on the ground and sang her a couple of lullabies in lieu of a story. Abby didn't protest the swap, perhaps because they were still new, or because there were story elements in each song; or perhaps it was because she immediately discovered, as I had, that Ben had a rich baritone that you could listen to for hours.

Sadly, only a few other times had I coaxed Ben into singing around me. To sing now, Ben must have been desperate for something he knew that resembled a bedtime story, but I think there was also something about Abby's childlike eyes that set him at ease and let him ignore his small audience of Mom and me behind him.

By the middle of the first lullaby, Mom put her arm around my waist and rested her head on my shoulder. I knew her well enough to know what she was thinking: Ben was good. Truly *good*. That filled her with relief.

Of course he's good, I told her silently, throat closing up—from the sight in front of us, and not from her lack of trust. Still, I couldn't help adding gently, *Did you really expect me to love someone who wasn't?*

"Sorry," she whispered out loud. If she could use an inner voice, she had never tried hard enough to discover it. "I should have had more faith in you. But I worried."

You're my mother, I said, putting my arm around her waist and holding her against me in turn.

I was only getting the slightest inkling of what it meant to be a mother. I thought I'd known something of it before. I had half-raised the littles in our family, after all. Abby especially held a tender place in my heart, and she looked to me like a second mother.

But never before that moment had I had this...craving. This seed being planted in my iceheart that could crack it open and change it into something entirely new. Something expanded, something vaster and more powerful than I could have imagined.

Something inextricably connected to the good man sitting in front of me, crooning my baby sister to sleep.

"So, you tried to think of me as a sister, huh?" I teased.

Ben and I were sitting together in the most vacant part of my hold we could find: ironically, the assembly room. But when we weren't having a formal family meeting, we had little use for it, and especially at this time of night, it was empty.

It was a good place for us to sit, especially since Ben produced cushions for us to soften the hard surface of the solid stone "bleachers," and I thought it was a nice change for me to sit on the level above Ben, so that my head was above his for once. Ben didn't seem to mind; he just turned to the side to face me and rested his elbow on the level I was sitting on. It made for a different, but still comfortable dynamic.

I'd expected Ben to blush—his pale skin could turn an adorable red, even with his short gold beard—but he only laughed. "Like I told Michael—that didn't last a day."

"But why?" I asked, as I'd burned to do ever since I'd overheard him mention it. I had some ideas, but I wanted to hear the answer from him.

His smile faded. "It was Avva's idea, ironically."

I blinked. That, I had not expected. "What?"

He shook his head ruefully. "He made it clear to me after your conversation with him that you were going to be a part of our lives, one way or another. When I seemed a bit...uneasy, wondering what he was implying, he said I could think of you as a sister, if I liked. He was teasing me—he didn't mean me to take him up on it."

"Then why did you?"

He smiled, but the flicker of amusement faded before he answered. "Lots of reasons. Mostly, I was scared. Of how I was already feeling about you, and what you might think if you found out. Aside from the usual embarrassment that might have brought, I was desperate to keep you as a friend, and I was terrified that if I alienated you, you wouldn't help me anymore."

He sighed and looked away. His voice dropped to a murmur. "And there would go my last hope of saving Avva."

My throat closed, and my eyes stung. "Ben...."

He looked back at me, and he took my hand and clenched it three times—our code for *I love you*, since saying the words out loud was difficult for him right now.

"No apologies, Sarah. We've been over this. You *did* save him. Just long enough."

I sighed, but I let Ben look away and get lost in his thoughts for a moment. I tried not to sink too deeply into my own as I thought about my own memories from that time.

When he spoke again, his voice had dropped back down to a murmur. "Fear motivated so much of what I did back then. Almost everything, actually. Fear of losing Avva, fear of losing you.... But most of all, fear of myself—of the bad that I thought I was capable of, and the good that I thought I wasn't. I was *terrified* of becoming King. I thought I would bring the Six Realms to ruin within the first few days."

I smiled softly and clenched his hand. "Yet here they still are, standing. You're stronger than you knew."

Ben laughed faintly and clenched my hand back. "Well, thank Flame that I also figured out that not everything depended solely on me."

"That's true, too. You have a lot of good people to help you, Ben."

More than I'd ever realized before going on this tour with him. I thanked both Ice and Flame for that.

"To help *us*, you mean," he said, smiling slightly as he looked up at me. "You're sharing this crown with me, Sarah. Flame only knows why you think

I'm worth the burden...but I'm not stupid enough to bear it without you anymore."

My eyes finally spilled over.

Ben cleared his throat. "Ah, Sarah. I really didn't mean to...."

I know, I said silently, my throat too tight to speak—and my lips too busy moving against his.

I had no words to explain to him how much that single sentiment meant everything to me—that now, he was letting me not just love but also *help* him.

When we parted, I tried to lighten the mood. Otherwise, with the seed growing in my iceheart, I might end up pushing us further than we should go tonight.

"Would you like to hear that I felt much the same way about you at that time?"

"Really?" Ben asked, his gold eyes brightening—and they were already glowing faintly from the kiss.

"Mm-hmm. But I was scared, too. Aside from the usual, I thought a guy like you would never be interested in a girl like me."

Ben leaned back, stunned. "Wait, *what*?"

I could smile about it—now. "Ben, aside from being simply incredible, you were the *Heir*."

"So were you! Of Ice, that is."

"Well, you remember how hard a time I had believing *that*."

"I...guess," he admitted grudgingly. "But who else could it have been?"

I shook my head. "See, that was exactly the thing. I was terrified that as soon as you met the rest of my family, you would decide that one of them would make a much better Monarch than I would."

Ben seemed to be almost mad at me. "Even *if* that could have possibly been true, that wasn't up to me."

I shrugged and spread my hands peaceably. "I didn't understand that, Ben. Not really, and especially not those first couple of days."

"I.... You're right," he said, looking away. "I remember."

"Besides," I said thoughtfully as something occurred to me. Fortunately, long after the uncertainty had passed. "Wasn't it up to you, kind of?"

Ben looked back at me, eyes narrowed. "What do you mean?"

"I didn't know it then, but you had to marry the Queen of Ice, right? Maybe I understood that would be on the table, instinctively."

Ben blinked, then frowned. That thought clearly hadn't occurred to him either—that somehow his preference might have played a part in the Tree choosing me.

Now, with our decisions made, my confidence grown, and with my white betrothal earring glowing in his left ear, I could finally admit, "I was particularly worried about you meeting Rachel. I thought that as soon as you saw her, that would be it."

To my shock, Ben gagged. "*Rachel*? You honestly thought I would choose *her* over *you*?"

His vehemence took me aback. "Every other guy I've ever been interested in has."

That brought Ben up short. He leaned back to get a better look at me, anger fading as abruptly as it had come to turn into something much softer. "What?"

I shrugged, trying to make it look like it didn't matter—and to my surprise, it didn't. Not anymore. "If they met her first, they would never even look my way. If they met her second, they soon forgot about me. I got used to being invisible."

Ben's eyes tightened, and he clenched my hand. "You were never invisible to me."

Again, because it was in the past, I could smile and tease, "Because Rachel wasn't around."

An echo of his former anger came back, this time cooled to brief irritation. "No, because you were *you*. Even if for some torched reason, your places were swapped and Rachel came to the Six Realms instead of you, I'd never have fallen for her, Sarah. Not like I fell for you."

My iceheart pulsed. I tried to tell myself he was biased now, but his words still mattered more than they should have. I couldn't help but ask, "Why?"

Ben groaned. "I can't believe you're asking me this. Do you really doubt me that much?"

"No," I said hastily, clenching his hand. "No, it's not that. It's just...I'm sorry, Ben, I know this is stupid, but I just have to know."

He looked away, frowning. But the frown faded only a moment later. "How many times do I have to tell you that your feelings aren't stupid?"

He sighed and ran his free hand through his hair. "And I suppose, if that thing with Rachel happened every other time to you...then I can see why you would need to know."

"Yes," I said with relief.

Ben was silent for a moment. Then, still not looking at me, he asked quietly, "Why did you choose me and not Kor?"

I was taken aback, both by the suddenness of the turn and because...we had never talked about this. Not directly. I hadn't thought he wanted to. I was hoping for my own reassurance, and then he threw *this* at me?

But...that was fair, I supposed. It was essentially the same question I was asking him, and he had more cause than I did to ask it.

I thought about my answer, but I didn't want to take too long. There was a careful balance here between showing him I was taking his question seriously and making him wonder if I had regrets.

"Well, at first, because he drove me crazy."

I hoped that would bring a smile to Ben's lips, but it didn't.

"Then?" he asked, voice carefully neutral. "When he actually tried?"

My voice softened. "What you saw wasn't him trying, Ben."

It was a risky move, since it then begged the question of what Kor *had* done to try, and that was definitely territory we hadn't approached yet. But now I felt like Ben had a right to know, especially if he was feeling even more of the old uncertainty rise than I was.

Ben smiled thinly. "I know that. Now. That was for my benefit, wasn't it? He was trying to make me jealous."

"Yes," I said, face growing warm. "That's why I let him, you know. He convinced me it was...necessary. To give you a final push. I doubted him then, and I definitely do now, but...at the time, I agreed to let him try. I'm sorry."

Ben sighed and clenched my hand. "I...can understand. I still don't like it, but I...know I wasn't exactly being...."

He trailed off, sighing again. "Like I said, a lot of what I did back then was motivated by fear. And that didn't stop after I knew you wanted me."

I knew he was referring to the first time he'd pushed me away.

"Solim's attack didn't help," I said quietly.

"No. But I was...already panicking even before then. That was one reason I let Svyer lure me away. I was running from you, basically. It all hit me suddenly, and I just didn't know...what to do."

He shook his head. "So, anyway, what I'm saying is...like usual, I hate Kor's methods, but I don't have a current to carry me here. I certainly don't blame you for giving in to Kor's plan, especially at the time, when I hadn't given you anything to hope for. And I know how persuasive Kor can be. Which...is also why I have to ask...."

"About when he actually tried?" I said quietly.

Ben swallowed and nodded, still not looking at me.

"He didn't do much," I said gently. "Probably not nearly as much as you're thinking. He just kissed me and said that if I needed another option for a consort, he was 'amenable.'"

Ben stiffened. At first, I feared that meant it was *worse* than what he expected, but then Ben spluttered, "Wait, *what*? That's *it*?"

"Yup, that's it," I said in surprise.

I didn't count Kor's first kiss as him trying anything. For that one, Kor had thought he was about to die, to have to sacrifice himself to save me from his brother and get me to the moongate. For once, I think that action was wholly spontaneous and free of ulterior motives. Just Kor, charged on adrenaline, going out with a bang.

"'Amenable'?" Ben said incredulously, finally looking at me.

"Yes. I'm pretty sure that was his exact word."

"And...he kissed you just *once*?"

I winced. This was pushing into dangerous territory, since Ben still thought Kor and I hadn't encountered anything dangerous while looking for the Ekrel moongate. I probably should come clean to him now that he was in a healthier state of mind, but if I did that right at that moment, it would entirely derail our conversation. I needed to address his primary concern about Kor first, and he needed to finally answer my question about Rachel, and that wasn't going to happen if Ben found out that Solim had gotten that close to me.

"Technically, twice," I said carefully. "But the first time was more of an accident."

Ben raised an eyebrow at me.

"Really, I swear. I *don't* think he was trying anything with that one."

"Alright, fine. I trust that was what it felt like to you, at least. But...." Ben clenched his jaw for a moment. "He honestly didn't say anything about...."

"About what?"

Ben answered from between clenched teeth. "Feelings?"

I laughed. "Ben, this is *Kor*. Personal feelings had nothing to do with it. He was making me an offer out of duty. To give me an option, for the good of the Realms. So I wouldn't feel like I had to either marry you or reject my birthright. He said so."

Ben swore, looking away. His free hand clenched and unclenched where it rested on his thigh. "That torched...."

Ben closed his mouth, looking like he was trying very hard not to say the expletive that was in his head.

I stared at him. I was struck by the parallelism of this moment and when I'd told Kor about the first time Ben had told me he loved me. And just like last time, I had no idea where the emotion was coming from.

"Ben, I'm...sorry. I really am—"

"Sarah, you have nothing to apologize to me for," Ben said, running a hand through his shoulder-length golden hair impatiently. "If I'm guessing right, this all was just after I pushed you away the first time, right? While I was unconscious on Ekrel?"

"Yes."

"You didn't owe me anything at that point. Hellwinds, you didn't have to tell me now, but you did, because I was rude enough to ask. I'm not mad at you, Sarah. None of that was your fault. Or even your *doing*. Sounds to me like you were far more loyal to me than I deserved."

"Then why are you mad at Kor? For what seems like *less* than you were expecting?"

Ben didn't answer—just stewed while glaring at the far wall. Then it hit me, and I groaned. "Kor made you *think* there was more to it, didn't he?"

He still didn't answer.

"Look, Ben, I'm sure that was all part of the jealousy ploy. I'm sorry he did that, and that I didn't know he did that; otherwise, I would have dispelled that illusion for you. I'd already told him back in *Olsdak*, right after the feast, that I was done with his games. And when he made his 'offer,' I told him thanks, but no thanks."

"But why?" he said quietly. "You still haven't said."

"Isn't it obvious?" I murmured. "Because I didn't love him. I loved you."

He sighed and leaned back. "But if things had been different...if Kor had been the Heir...."

I snorted.

"What?" Ben asked heavily, looking at me. "It's the same question you asked me."

I sobered. "You're right. Sorry. It is. It's just, the thought that I would choose Kor over *you*, no matter the circumstances...."

Ben smiled thinly. "Do you see why that question bothered me so much?"

"Yes," I said ruefully.

He looked away. "And do you understand why, now that you've brought it up, I need to know the answer?"

He paused only long enough to take my silence as confirmation. "If Kor had been the Heir, then the King, would you have married him?"

I hesitated. I knew Ben needed full honesty from me now, but it wasn't a simple question to answer—to find the answer inside me or to say it. "Are you in this scenario or not?"

"Does that change your answer?" Ben asked quietly.

"It might."

"How so?"

I took a deep breath. "Because...because you taught me to reach for happiness, Ben. If I never knew you...then yes, I might have married Kor, if that was what I thought I had to do. Because, even as much as the thought terrified me, I wouldn't have known I could have better."

He shifted in surprise and looked back at me. "Terrified?"

"Yes," I said, rubbing my arms nervously. "I'm getting goosebumps just remembering Kor's offer. He scared the living daylights out of me."

Ben hardened, getting a dangerous look in his eyes, but I realized my mistake and threw up my arms almost immediately to forestall him.

"Kor didn't do anything wrong! Nothing! It was all me."

Well, and a bit of Solim's lingering influence of lies over me, but those only gave my fear an extra edge—they weren't the source.

"It's just...." I struggled to find the words to explain. "I trust Kor, and I like him as a friend. But there's something about the thought of *marrying* him that just...terrifies me. Especially in contrast with you. It's like...you're a warm, comfortable campfire. You invite me in simply by being you, but you never push."

Technically, he *pulled*, but that seemed to be unconscious on his part, and that mysterious connection between us only began after I'd fallen for him anyway. I hadn't yet admitted to myself that I loved him, but I'd been willing to die for him that night—and what was love but that?

I continued. "You just sit there, warm and accepting, willing to take whatever I give you, and giving me twice as much in warmth and light in return. You're bright. You have your shadows, but you don't hide them from me. You encircle me but don't make me feel trapped. Just protected. Loved. You are...safe."

Ben smiled softly as he tilted his head at me. "Safe," he repeated, almost in wonder.

I shrugged. "And many other things besides. But that's just the best word I can come up with to describe the difference between what I feel with you, and what I feel with Kor. You're safe. In all the best senses of the word."

Ben laughed quietly and squeezed my hand. "I believe you. It's just...only you could have ever called me 'safe,' Sarah."

"That's not true—"

"Sarah, you're perhaps the only person who has seen all my shadows," he said, shaking his head. "You have more right to be frightened of me than perhaps anyone. And yet, you think I'm safe."

He wasn't questioning me. His eyes were full of wonder...and love. I couldn't help but touch his face, derailed for a moment. Those were the eyes of my sun.

Had I even explained a hundredth part of what he meant to me? How the thought of going through life never having known him frightened me?

That explained some of my terror of Kor, but still not all.

As if reading my thoughts, Ben prompted, "And Kor?"

I took a moment to bring myself back. "Kor is different. First off, he doesn't love me—"

"Pretend he does," Ben said abruptly. "Or, er, did. In this scenario."

"What?" I said blankly.

Ben grimaced. "Just...indulge me. Say, for the sake of argument, that, when Kor made that offer to you, he didn't do it out of duty, but because he...loved you."

My iceheart pulsed, especially when Ben just continued to look at me.

I looked away, swallowing. "Well...that would have...terrified me even more."

"Why?" Ben asked intently, leaning in.

"Because I trust him with my life, but that's a very different thing than trusting him with my *heart*."

Or with my body, which would have been a factor in even the dutiful marriage scenario. But Ben was too keyed up for me to imply that I felt any danger from Kor in that regard. Which I didn't, not in the way Ben would assume. I didn't know how to explain all that adequately to Ben, though.

Ben scrunched his face in confusion. "You think he'd be unfaithful to you? If he gave you his word?"

"Goodness, no—not if he gave me his word." Kor was almost as much of a stickler as Ben in that regard. They both had "oath" in their name, and I'd found out that was for good reason.

"Then...?"

"Give me a moment. I'm thinking. I haven't had to put this into words before."

"Take your time," Ben said, settling back. "I know I'm...demanding a lot."

"No, these are good things for us to talk about, and think about," I said firmly. "I see that now. They were questions we still had for each other that we've been covering up in the rush of other things, and now that we have the chance—" And the courage. "—we should have out with them. It's all part of being sure."

I *needed* to be sure, because I wasn't certain how much longer I could hold back from Ben. Or from...a possibility that was growing inside me into something frighteningly close to a desire.

"Right," Ben said heavily. There seemed to be a deeper meaning there, but when I looked at him, he just looked away. So, I refocused on articulating my feelings about Kor.

"Kor is...not like you," I said slowly. "He doesn't wait. What he wants, he pursues. Relentlessly. What he thinks he *has* to do, he does with a single-minded drive and brilliance that's frightening. There's just...no saying no to him in that scenario. You know he'll find a way eventually, so what's the point in resisting? He respects choice...to an extent. But if he were convinced that he was the right choice for me...he wouldn't rest until he convinced me of that, too."

"Ah," Ben said quietly.

"Are you beginning to see what I find scary about him, in that sense? He's not *restful* like you are, Ben. He's not a warm campfire. He's all cold shadows and mystery, all secrets and plans. He's too...everything. He's not safe. Not in that way, for me. As an ally, and even as a friend, yes. But if he were to try to become something more, to go deeper inside my heart...."

I shuddered. "I would never have chosen him, Ben. Not knowing both of you. Not even if he had been Heir and you had been his rightwing or something. As soon as Eskala told me that if I became the Queen of Ice, I would have to marry Kor, the Heir of Flame, I would have been out. I would have told the Tree to pick someone else...and I would have stayed with you."

Ben seemed to be trying hard to suppress a wild joy I rarely saw in him...and he was failing. His eyes were soulflaring from the force of it.

He didn't speak for a long moment as he searched my eyes, and I, captivated by the glow of his own, couldn't look away. Eventually, he looked down at our joined hands, and I took in a rasping breath, realizing I had forgotten to breathe.

His voice was hoarse. "Even if you knew you were your best chance to save your family?"

I was now prepared for that question. "I don't think, in that scenario, I would have been."

"What?" Ben asked, looking back up at me.

I shook my head slowly. "The things we've done together, Ben...they required complete trust, even before love. The kind of trust I would never have been able to give Kor, at least not for much, much longer. Time that my family and the Seven Realms didn't have. I think Kor and I would have proved to each other long before we got to the Tree of Ice that a closer partnership between us wouldn't work. Regardless of how he *felt* about me, I think Kor would have been relieved for all our sakes if I stepped down."

And gave the crown to someone who *could* work with him to save the worlds. Someone like....

I shook my head to dispel that thought before it could fully form.

"The only scenario I can think of in which I would marry Kor was if I thought I had no choice. If I never met you, and I never felt the kind of love you give me, and I thought I had nothing waiting for me in this life but duty—and, in your scenario, the kind of crushing, frightening love Kor could offer. And thinking I had no choice...that's hardly choosing him then, is it?"

Ben smiled faintly. "No, I suppose it's not. But is that choosing me?"

"Yes, it is," I said with a much stronger smile. I cupped his face in my hands and leaned in. "Because with both of you, standing side by side, Kor showed me more clearly than any other way possible just what I'd found in you."

Ironically, Kor had made my own choice clear. That was when I finally found the courage to choose Ben, once and for all. Even when he wasn't giving me much hope. The happiness I'd just begun to taste with him was worth hoping for.

Ben reached up with his free hand, grasped me gently behind the neck, and pulled me down for a kiss, a burning one that echoed the wild joy I'd glimpsed before.

There it was—the taste of happiness. Every time he gave it to me, it was worth every moment I'd waited.

But I thought I'd waited long enough for one particular answer.

I pulled away after a few moments and smiled at him. "Your turn."

"My turn for what?" Ben said, blinking dazedly. He looked like he was having a hard time remembering even his name right now.

I laughed. "Your turn to explain why you would never have chosen Rachel."

"Oh," Ben said, clearing his throat. "Erm. Right. Well...that answer is straightforward, because, funnily enough...it's exactly the same."

I frowned. "What?"

Ben colored a bit and rubbed his neck. "Now, try not to take this the wrong way.... I know Rachel is your sister and everything, and I'm sure she has...redeemable qualities...."

"Redeemable?" I said with a startled laugh.

"Ah, torch it. I'm just going to say it, alright? Be mad at me if you will, but the truth is this: Rachel terrifies me. In much the same way Kor terrifies you."

I stared at him in incredulous bemusement. "*Rachel*? Rachel Lind, my sister, scares *you*? You hardly even *know* her."

"Well, then," Ben grumbled, "I should probably say that, more accurately, Rachel's *type* terrifies me—and trust me, I know her type. They've tried to foist themselves on me for years. I've had *nightmares* about girls like her."

It finally clicked in my head: The characteristics that made me different from Rachel, that I'd grown up thinking of as flaws. Everything that Ben seemed to find inexplicably appealing about me. All Kor's hints about my unintentional seductiveness....

And then I burst into laughter so long and loud that Ben went completely red.

"I'm sorry, I'm sorry," I finally wheezed, wiping my eyes and clutching my side. "But, to finally realize that all the qualities that have made Rachel irresistible to every other guy before...are the very ones that *repel* you...."

Another giggle escaped me. "Sorry, it was too much. I can almost picture Rachel's face if she found out. And now I almost want to tell her myself...."

"Don't you dare," Ben said in genuine alarm, his eyes going wide. "She has enough ammunition to use against me as it is. Don't give her more!"

"Oh, don't worry, I won't," I said smugly. "As satisfying as it would be to gloat, I'm perfectly happy with the two of you keeping a...friendly distance."

Ben rolled his eyes. "Oh, trust me, that won't be difficult. I wouldn't touch her with the tip of my longest blade."

Which I assumed was less threatening than it sounded if it was merely the dramá idiom equivalent of a ten-foot pole. Either way, I tried not to wiggle with satisfaction at hearing him express such a complete lack of interest.

Ben slowly smiled. "I suppose my request of you means *I'm* not allowed to tell *Kor* just exactly why you find him so unappealing?"

"Oh, I think from my reaction when he offered, he already knows," I said dryly. "Besides, he'd probably just laugh if you tried, since he's perfectly happy with the way things are now. He doesn't actually love me, remember?"

"Oh, right," Ben said with a straight face.

I didn't let myself read too much into that, convinced Ben's needless jealousy was making him assume things he could have no real authority on. After all, Kor would hardly have *told* Ben, even if he felt anything for me.

And even if he did...well, that wouldn't change my choice.

Chapter Three

SPROUT

Sarah

The next "morning" (more like afternoon, given my new sleep schedule) I did my rounds around my family's small hold for old time's sake. Or that's what I told myself at first, but each stop proved to me something unexpected, even though it shouldn't have been: over the course of my time away to tour the Realms with Ben, my family had come to no longer need me.

Oh, they were happy to have me; there was a kind of campfire warmth from each of them like the one I got from Ben, even from Laura—though her fire was the kind that warned you it would burn you if you got too close. I thought Laura still loved me like family, after her own fashion; otherwise, she wouldn't even bother disapproving of my relationship with Ben.

Yet in every place I stopped, I saw I was no longer needed or even expected to step in.

Laura pushed me away as soon as she could so she could refocus the littles on their lessons—which I saw she had supplemented with dramá materials.

"Might as well teach them to read both," Laura said grudgingly when she caught me looking at a poster with the Drona consonant letters and vowel notations. I thought that was yet another reason she wanted me gone.

David was down helping Mom in the garden, and though Mom enthusiastically showed me the progress she'd made and gave me a tour of the new underground "fields," she no longer asked me questions in the faint hope I might have answers. Instead, she confidently reported all she'd learned from Svyer. Her plans for who would help her with what didn't have any mention of me.

Michael was training with Rachel again, except this time the two of them were sparring with ice. They looked like they were having a blast trying to kill each other, but I took one look inside the frozen, jagged wasteland of the training room and decided I didn't want to risk interrupting. Still feeling a bit of residual possessiveness over my hold, I grumbled to myself as I left that they'd better know how to clean all that up when they were done.

Finally, Svyer was with Dad in the library, working on some more translations—this time of some schematics and accompanying literature for a complex Moontouched technology that even Svyer didn't recognize or guess the purpose of.

"You know what would be really helpful, Sarah?" Svyer said with a frown as she scrolled through the text on the large black archival stone—the dramá equivalent of a hard drive and display in one. Their "tablets" (in the old, "stone block" sense of the word) were just miniature versions.

"What?" I asked curiously.

"Getting an artificer in here. I'm a healer, with an herbalism specialization at that. My only contribution here is that I'm dramá. I don't know a third of these words, and when we look them up, I *still* can't explain to Jake what they mean."

"Agreed," Dad said. "But it would have to be someone we trust. Not just to live with us, or join our clan if that's what they like, but to safeguard these secrets. I won't be partisan to weapons proliferation. Or the spreading of *any* new technology without a careful consideration of its effects first."

One of the few reasons Dad agreed to help with the creation of the lightcannons was the fact that he could guarantee that only a Moontouched—meaning a member of his family—could supply the power. Even then, he'd obtained promises on how the Warflight would secure the lightcannons from then on.

"I think I might know an artificer like that," I said, thinking of Alya. "I'll get in touch with her. Kor should know how."

"Is this the one who made your watch?" Dad asked, becoming thoughtful as he looked at the device on my wrist.

"Yup," I said, holding it up. "She's brilliant, and she's Strongshield to the core."

"Good," Svyer said with a nod.

For Dad's benefit, I said, "That means she's dutiful to a fault and as hard to read as you are." I chuckled. "You two should get along great."

Dad smiled thinly.

"Do you think she'd be interested?" Svyer asked curiously.

"I think so," I said slowly. "But she's a member of the First Flight of Goldek Gate on Romskal...."

Svyer nodded. "Ah, so if she *is* interested, you would need to get her excused from her duties, perhaps released from the Warflight altogether."

She winked at me. "Fortunately, you happen to know the head of the Warflight."

I raised an eyebrow. "I doubt Yvera is about to do me any favors."

Ben's lethal, prickly rightwing, primary bodyguard, and lifelong friend might not think I was a threat to Ben anymore, and therefore she no longer wanted to kill me on sight, but I thought she was still getting over her jealousy and dislike of me.

Svyer smiled knowingly. "You might be surprised. But if all else fails, Yvera will do it for Ben, and Ben will do it for you, and that amounts to the same thing."

Dad frowned marginally at Svyer and looked at me. "Even so, it is better to ask Yvera first. That's the path of least resentment."

"Makes sense," I said, nodding.

"If Yvera agrees, I would appreciate an introduction to this artificer. I'll interview her and give you my thoughts. Technically, her admittance is your decision, but I would prefer you follow my lead in this."

"Fair," I said. "You're my leftwing, after all, and you're the one who's going to be living and dealing with her on a regular basis."

I looked away and tried to seem casual, even as my eyes stung. "Seems like I won't be needed much here in the future."

"Ah, Sarah." Svyer sighed and gave me a side hug. She was tall enough that she could lay her head on top of mine. "I was worried about this."

Dang it, the stinging in my eyes had progressed to dangerous levels of moisture. I had *not* intended to cry about this, much less in front of anyone. "About what?"

Svyer glanced at Dad, and he nodded. Without a word, he smiled kindly at me and walked past us and out of the library, leaving us alone in the cool dimness.

"I was worried that when you came back, you would feel like I had replaced you," Svyer said softly. "I didn't, you know. I couldn't."

"I know. That's not what I feel...exactly," I said thickly, still valiantly fighting off tears.

"Then what is it?"

"I guess...I knew things would have to change. But I wasn't ready for this place to no longer feel like...."

"Home?"

"Sort of. Except not to that extent. It still feels like *a* home, because my family is here. But...it doesn't feel like I need to stay. Or that I'm meant to. And that makes me feel...."

The tears spilled over. I tried laughing through them, wiping at them with the hand that wasn't hugging Svyer back. Her warmth in this moment meant more to me than I could tell her. Even if the thaw had finally made me cry.

"Lots of things," I finished thickly. "Sad. Relieved. Guilty. But mostly...lost. Adrift. They're all I've ever known, Svyer. At least before I came to your worlds. To start letting them go...*really* go...."

"That's all perfectly understandable," Svyer said, clutching me gently. "Let yourself feel those things, Sarah. Don't fight them. Now that you've named them, just give them a moment to speak to you, and listen to what they have to say."

She fell silent, so we just stood there, holding each other, while I let myself feel. That was hard at first. I struggled with guilt, trying to push them all away.

Thoughts of, *I should be happy,* or *I should have expected this* arose until I finally silenced them. They didn't have a place in the circle of warmth Svyer had created around me.

And then, as she had asked, I just let myself...be.

Surprisingly, the feelings then settled down, as if they were turning from squabbling children to patient adults now that they knew I would hear them. One by one, I let myself feel them, be in them, and listen to them. Then they left. As they did, each gave me a subliminal piece of a mosaic of truth that was as beautiful as it was simple.

"I am no longer a child," I whispered. "I've outgrown what I was. It will always be a part of me—*they* will always be a part of me—but now it is time for something else. And I'm strong enough to face it. I *want* to face it. I want...to create another home."

And not just another home. Another....

Family.

Again, the guilt tried rearing its head—*Isn't one good home, one good family enough for you?*—but again, I silenced it. Why should there be only one of each in the universe? What was so wrong about creating *more* good things?

Nothing, that was what. In fact, doing the opposite would be the evil thing.

I wasn't cutting my old ties; I wasn't adrift. I was growing. I was...branching.

As if echoing my thoughts, Svyer said, "That is a *good* thing. A natural thing. We're all a bit like trees, Sarah. We're all part of the forest; we're all connected at our roots. But we're not meant to stay as roots. We're meant to grow up side by side, tall and strong. You can always come back to your roots for strength, but don't let them keep you from reaching for the stars."

"How'd you get to be so smart, Svyer?" I mumbled, sniffling.

She laughed and handed me a handkerchief, and I released her to use both hands to blow.

"I can't take credit for that one, I'm afraid. That gem comes from Aunt Nyethra."

"Ben's mother?"

Since she had died long before I ever came to the Six Realms, and Ben still loved and mourned her deeply, I was always eager for any scrap of information about her.

"Yep." There was a smile in Svyer's voice as she held me tighter for a moment. "Now *there* was a wise woman. I can only dream of being like her someday."

"Well, you have a few years to manage it," I said with a weak smile.

Svyer rested her cheek on my head again. "We both do."

Not long after, I was climbing the frost-covered steps up to my Tree, in the great cavern She rested in beneath the icepack of Greenland. Her underground Temple was the only accessible place on Earth left to us Linds, now that our home in Pennsylvania was destroyed and the nearby moongate rerouted to this location.

Here's another home, I thought.

It had been a while, but with each step, those familiar feelings of peace and power settled into me like snowflakes until I was covered in them.

Except something was different here, too. Perhaps if I hadn't been gone for so many days, I might not have noticed, but I had. The air felt...heavier. Sleepier. I didn't know what it meant, but it troubled me. Was it just me, or were the lights inside Her ice leaves, the principal source of illumination in this cavern, just a tad dimmer than before?

I reached the circular terrace at the base of Her mighty trunk and crossed the distance to the well at the terrace's center. I set my feet, clasped my hands behind my back, lifted my face to Her frost-covered branches a hundred or more feet above me, closed my eyes, and breathed deeply. The air here was still the purest I'd ever inhaled anywhere; at least that much hadn't changed.

Minute after minute passed. I used the time to gather my thoughts, thinking about which questions to ask and how. After about five, and just when my thoughts were settled, the Tree spoke, Her voice like the whisper of a winter wind.

It is well you have come, child.

I opened my eyes and looked around. But like last time, She did not appear. Only Her voice came to me.

You have been faithful in doing as I ask, and for that, I commend you. Now there are things we must discuss, you and I.

Would you like to begin, my Lady? I asked, iceheart pulsing.

No. You may first ask your questions you have brought to Me.

I took a deep breath. *My first is regarding the dream Your Sister sent to the King of Flame.*

Her voice was mild, merely prompting me to continue. *What of it?*

My inner voice lowered to nearly a whisper. *In it, he was warned that the Devourer would come for me.*

That much is true, and it was all the King of Flame was told, for that was all that was his burden to know. Although to you, My daughter, I say that first, it will come for Me.

"What?" I choked, feeling a surprisingly sharp lance of fear.

Why, when Ben had told me I was the target, had I been calm, but now I felt threatened in the most primal of senses?

Perhaps because the Tree was the collective heart of my family. Of my *worlds*. The world that had birthed us, and the one that now sheltered us.

To threaten Her was to threaten us all.

The Devourer searches for you, but particularly for your family, and your sanctuary, the Tree whispered through Her winter winds. *It rages across the cosmos, but still it has not found you. Yet it knows where to find Me. It has not thus far focused its full might on claiming the world you call Earth, for its own dark purposes, but now at last it is turning its power to reach Me. And when My last defenses finally fall, it will strike, knowing you will be there to defend Me.*

I would. I could already feel myself tensing, my fists clenching, my iceheart pulsing with power. I finally and fully understood Ben's horror when we saw the vision of darkness claiming his Tree. After the Tree of Ice had given me a new heart, a new life, a new purpose, and more peace, power, and happiness than I could have dreamed of, the desire—no, the *need*—to protect Her was in my very blood, ingrained into my soul.

She was my life, and the life of all I held dear outside the protection of Flame. I could feel in that moment our interconnected web of life; I could feel the billions upon billions of precious lights that would be snuffed out should She fall. That degree of horror was unthinkable.

I saw then, the inevitability of it. How Ben could not save me—could not even prevent me. No more than I could have prevented him and his father from defending their Tree at the Battle of the Solstice. I *would* be there on that dark day, and I *would* defend Her...or I would be the first to die trying. I had no other choice.

Neither did any of my family. All of us old enough to fight, to make a difference, would be here to try. It was either that or die later, when the source of our life went out.

"Why?" I said out loud, an edge in my voice close to a wail. Tears stung my eyes, and the cold bit bitterly through that moisture. "Why us? Why now?"

Because the Devourer fears you and the other children of Ice. Now, more than ever.

That answer brought me up short. It was not the one I had expected, if I thought there would be any. I wasn't seriously questioning the motives of a voracious force that had seemed so vast, invulnerable, and unknowable. I didn't expect to understand it.

Yet fear...fear, I understood.

And fear was not the emotion of an invulnerable being.

Yes, child, the Tree whispered. *There is hope. The Devourer* can *be defeated. My Sisters and I have done so many times, and Flame and I have planned this defeat for eons. The Devourer does not know Our plans, but it can recognize they are coming to fruition. It knows you are the final piece—which means it will stop at nothing to destroy you, and all who could take your place.*

"Rachel," I whispered, staring at nothing. "Dad, Michael, David, Laura...."

It will not stop with them. It seeks the death of all My children, down to the last.

An image flashed into my mind of Abby, huddled in a corner holding her favorite stuffed purple dragon, with hungry shadows reaching toward her.

My teeth snapped shut and my fists clenched. My body glowed with swirls of white power under the surface of my skin, and I could feel my eyes blazing silver.

"*No,*" I snarled.

They were mine first, before they were yours, the Tree said, Her voice heavy. *I have done and will do all that I can to protect them. All that I do is to save My children. For one more generation, one more century. For as long as I can....*

Her voice dropped to the faintest whisper. *For as long as they will let Me.*

That led me to another question I had, and I was happy to delay the most difficult for a bit by asking. *My Lady, how long has it been since the children of Earth heeded you?*

The dramá had shown me what a sentient race's relationship with their Tree was *supposed* to be like, and the humans of Earth were so far off the mark, I could scarcely believe our world still stood. Now I could understand Ben's initial shock at how little I had been taught. How could humanity have even survived without knowing their Tree?

Millennia, the Tree said, every whisper laced with sorrow. *They turned from Me so quickly, then forgot Me entirely. The Devourer, discovering their neglect and their cleverness, planted its own seeds in their hearts long ago.*

I felt a chill. But then, this truth had been forming in my mind for some time. *It has a hold on Earth, then?*

Even with their neglect toward Me, the Devourer cannot yet break through My protections to consume My world, or even to send its minions in force, for I am one of the oldest and most powerful of My Sisters. That is why the Creators entrusted Me with this, one of the brightest and yet most troublesome races of all Creation. I guide them as best I can, but I must do so more subtly than My Sister of Flame. Yet so must the Devourer.

As you have begun to see, the more a heart inclines itself toward Me, the more I can protect it and nurture it in the ways of life. The more a heart turns from Me, the more it leaves itself vulnerable to another influence, and there the Devourer has found its only true entrance. Thus, the Devourer and I have struggled over the hearts of My children through the ages. What I build up, the Devourer attempts to destroy in petty revenge for being able to do no more.

Yet of late, it has become more cunning. Discovering the horrors humanity's cleverness has allowed them to create, the Devourer has encouraged a kind of building of its own—yet it is the kind that it hopes will ultimately lead to humanity's ruin.

I didn't need to ask what kind of horrors those were. It could have been anything: from overt development of nuclear, chemical, or biological warfare, to more covert campaigns of hate, greed, and ambition. The latter weren't as flashy, yet they were the destructive elements that had brought eventual ruin to every Earthren civilization in recorded history.

The only reason the dramá had not gone the same way was their collective devotion to their Tree. Not every heart would be perfectly inclined toward Her, but so far in the thousand years since the First Invasion, they seemed to have built up a kind of herd immunity to the Devourer's influence that left its primary recourse to be its sending in its slaves from other worlds and creating the occasional one from the dramá when it could lure them in through overt promises of power and revenge.

Unlike on Earth. How strangely tragic for both dramá and humans to have the Devourer threaten their very existence, and yet in such opposite ways. Still, I knew which one I had less hope for.

I swallowed. "Will it succeed?"

The affairs of humanity are not your concern, my daughter, the Tree said gently. *They are the people of your birth, and one day in the years to come, you will have a part to play in their salvation—if they will allow themselves to be saved. Thus far, I have answered the questions you have long pondered, but here I make an end of speaking of them.*

She paused a moment, and when She began again, Her voice was both harder and softer, quieter and louder, resounding throughout my core.

If I am to survive long enough to save them, I will need you—and the life that the King of Flame can create with you.

I froze, existential concern for humanity dying at that sudden turn. I swallowed. "So...it's true?"

Yes, She murmured. In Her voice, I felt the weariness of ages untold. *I know your heart, daughter. I know how Our command that you have a child troubles you. I would not ask it if it were not necessary. I never ask unless it is necessary. You will not survive what must be done as you are now.*

"How? Why?" I asked, swallowing.

That, I cannot tell you.

Can't or won't? I thought to myself.

I should have known that was as good as asking it out loud. A Tree knew all the thoughts of Her children.

I cannot, the Tree said, with a dry winter wind. *It is not something you would currently understand if I were to try. You must trust Me in this.*

I took deep breaths to gather my thoughts, looking at a fixed point on the Tree's frosted trunk.

What troubles you, My daughter? the Tree whispered, Her voice softened.

"A child is not a tool, my Lady. Even if both the King and I were willing and ready, what of them? What of their choice?"

Ah, that *is the question you should have asked Me, dear one, for it is the most important one—and the one that I may answer.*

I blinked in surprise, and my iceheart pounded.

The Tree's voice was as soft as snowflakes melting against my face. *Worry not about their willingness: they have made their choice already. Just as you and the King each made yours before* you *were born.*

I inhaled sharply and gazed upward at Her branches. "*What?*"

I felt a tender wind stroke my face, as full of goodwill and promise as the first breath of spring.

Did you think your existence began at your mortal birth, dear one? That the Creators made your soul from nothing before giving it to My care? You are made of something more precious and eternal than the stars. Something that had thought and choice long before you first drew breath, long before you first formed in your mortal mother's womb. What you were and are will go on after you draw your last breath, and after your mortal body returns to the dust from which it was made.

I was staggered, unable to think or feel.

The Tree wasn't finished. *Long before you were born, I chose you to be My Queen. I came to you and showed you all that would be required of you for the sake of Creation, and you chose to accept. As did the King of Flame, when My Sister came to him.*

I stared at nothing. "I...don't remember this."

And yet, as soon as I said that, I realized that wasn't entirely true. Something *deeper* than memory struck chords in my body—in my soul. Playing a melody I once knew but had long since...forgotten.

A melody I had heard the first soul-trembling notes of when Ben and I had once discussed the meanings of our names in our respective worlds, both of us troubled by what we discovered.

Princess. Valiant.

Oathbinder. Son of the Right Hand.

By the Creators' decree, no mortal may have knowledge of their existence before or what awaits them thereafter, for that knowledge would interfere with the purposes of that mortal life.

"But how was I expected to do what I'd agreed to if I didn't remember agreeing?!"

For that reason, you had to learn and choose again. It was a risk My Sister and I had to take. We had other plans, should you or the King refuse in this life, as was your right. But those plans would have saved fewer lives and brought all—yes, even you—less joy. Thus far, you have done well, daughter—all that I once asked of you. What remains is still yours to decide.

My head was spinning. I didn't care if it was disrespectful—I sat down where I was, in front of the well. I figured it would be worse if I just fell over.

I swallowed with difficulty, then whispered, "Did I agree to do *this*?"

Yes. As did the King. As did your seed. They stand here with you now.

My head shot up again. "*Now*?"

And yet, just as when Ben and I had come through the crowngate after he first let me back in, I felt...something else there. Something full of love and light and intelligence.

Something...just behind me.

Even though I wasn't afraid, the hairs on the back of my neck stood up in prickling awareness. But again, I didn't dare turn. Yet again, I felt something: bodiless hands settling on my shoulders, as if whoever it was stood just behind me, lending me a surge of strength and reassurance.

They made their choice long ago, the Tree whispered. *They have waited ever since for this moment. They are ready.*

Tears were spilling down my cheeks before I even comprehended why. After feeling them *there, with* me, feeling their love for me...I couldn't help but love them in return.

The seed that had been planted inside of my iceheart burst into life, cracking it wide open, as I'd known it would. Yet this new desire was far more explosive than I could have imagined, sending up shoots and putting down roots with unbelievable force and speed. After that moment, I knew I would never be the same.

I *wanted* that child.

Not just any child—*mine.* Mine and Ben's.

The one that had waited patiently for us to come to this point for so long. I wanted to hold them in my arms, while Ben wrapped his around us both. I wanted to rock the child as Ben sang them to sleep. I wanted to hold their little hand as they took their first steps, with Ben holding the other. I wanted to sit with them in my lap, laughing as they squirmed while someone tried to sketch the three of us, as Avva had done to Ben and his mother. I wanted to hear their childlike yelps of joy as they discovered the world they had chosen to enter. I wanted to wipe away their tears and soothe all their fears. I wanted to guide them and help them, as much as they would let me. I wanted to see them grow up and grow old, and know that our life and love and happiness would go on, as pieces of us inside of them, long after Ben and I were gone.

I wanted that child more than I had ever wanted anything.

CHAPTER FOUR

FLAW

KORIBEN

I SURGED TO THE Temple of Flame a couple deken after dawn. I'd intended to go *before* daybreak, so no one would be the wiser, but I also hadn't intended to stay up so late with Sarah, and I overslept. A promising beginning to such a crucial and well-overdue communion with my Tree, I was sure.

I sighed as I stood on the dais next to the sacred flame, while the high priestess sent out the signal that would ask everyone else to leave so that I could have a private audience. If I had come even a deken before dawn, the seven gates around the Temple Heart's perimeter would have been full of fire, blocking anyone from entering; the giant sandstone chamber would have been empty, and I could have surged straight to one of those gates as if they were the normal kind.

But no. I had to sleep in and arrive long *after* the Heart was opened to the public. Now, the entire Six Realms would know within the deken that I had openly gone to speak with the Tree for the first time in my Kingship, and speculation would run wild as to why. Some rumors would be fear-based, wondering if there was an imminent disaster. Others would be critical, questioning my faithfulness for not having come sooner. Very little of that gossip would paint me in a positive light, especially with the timing being just before the last stop of the grand tour, which would make little sense to anyone.

Kor is going to give me an earful for this, I thought morosely as I counted all the questioning looks I got as the worshipers filtered out through the empty sandstone gates.

"Well, there you go, my boy," High Priestess Tivien said cheerfully as she turned back to me, her humble golden robes swishing over the dais flagstones.

"Thank you, Mother," I said, nodding deeply.

She had earned that most prestigious of titles by virtue of her position as High Priestess and her status as the oldest member of my clan, at two hundred and two summers. A drakón's hair never turned gray as an amón's did, but their skin did eventually wrinkle after about a century and a half, and she had plenty of lines by now to prove her illustrious age.

The cane was new since last I'd seen her, and that troubled me; weakness was one of the last signs before the fading truly began. Still, her golden eyes were as sharp as ever. She had been the High Priestess since before I was born and knew me well.

Sometimes a bit too well.

"You took your time in coming, Koriben," she said, softening her words with a wink.

"I know," I said with a sigh. "I'm sorry."

"Not me you need to apologize to. If indeed an apology is still needed."

I glanced at her in surprise, and she shook her head fondly at me. "You've always been so quick to believe yourself unworthy."

"But I am," I protested quietly, hoping my expression gave little away to the worshippers who were walking out as slowly as possible, watching out of the corner of their eyes.

Mother Tivien snorted inelegantly. "Have you asked *Her* that question? Seems to me like She's the judge of that."

"Well...no," I said. I felt like I was getting a scolding, even though technically it was the opposite. "But She was pretty mad at me last time we talked."

"Mad or stern, boy? To a mother, there is a great difference. Granted, I agree you needed a bit of a slap to wake up. I nearly went and gave it to you, but She told me to be patient."

I stared at her.

She laughed. "What, does that surprise you? That the Flamemother could have some compassion for your grief?"

"She didn't seem very compassionate at the time," I mumbled.

"Well, She didn't revoke you, otherwise She would have told me, so take that as a good sign. After all, it meant She thought you were still worth bothering with. 'For those who love Her and do Her will, Her fire imparts correction as well as warmth, else Her children lead themselves into darkness. But those who will not heed Her, She abandons to the frost.'"

She was quoting the Liturgy of Flame, of course.

My lips twitched. "Going to give me a sermon, Mother?"

"If necessary," she said, her eyes dancing.

"You have to admit that She's probably at least a *little* mad that it's taken me this long to come."

Tivien shrugged. "Lip service means nothing to the Tree. So do visits, if that's all they are. The most hypocritical of Monarchs could visit Her every day in a show of devotion, and She would never so much as speak to them."

She shook her finger at me. "You're no hypocrite, boy. You came when you were good and ready, as I knew you would, and so must She. And meanwhile, you've done everything She's asked since the day you woke up from your grief. Haven't you?"

"More or less willingly," I muttered.

She barked another laugh. "Son, if all of us were always happy to do Her will, we'd be a bunch of mindless puppets, and She's not interested in those."

I sighed, glancing at the ritual fire burning in the shallow pit beside us. "But Avva...."

She smiled thinly as she shook her head at me. "If you think your father was always cheerful about what She asked him to do, then you know very little about him."

She looked into the flames, and her voice lowered to an unusual degree. "It broke his heart to leave you."

I inhaled sharply and looked at her. She was smiling sadly. "He put it off for as long as he could, and at the end, when he asked us to leave him, he was weeping. For you, Koriben. 'Take care of my son,' he asked me."

Moisture clouded my eyes and clogged my throat, and I needed a few moments of looking at nothing before I could rasp, "And what did you say?"

"I told him I would do my best, but that I had a feeling you would be stubborn about it. He laughed through his tears and said that I would just have to have some patience in my old age to raise another young King as difficult as he had been."

"What?" I glanced at her in disbelief.

She was still smiling sadly. "I wish you could have seen Kavarian when he was your age, Koriben. You are your father's son—far more than you know."

Then, without another word, she left me, cane clacking against the flag-stones as she crossed the dais and gradually lowered herself down each step to the priestess waiting for her below. I just stood there uselessly, frozen, unable to move.

I wish I could just dismiss her words, but Mother Tivien didn't speak frivolously. What she said, she meant. Every word.

I...my father's son? Already so much like *him*? How could that be? I was....

My own voice came back to me, an accusation I'd hurled at him on this very spot. *You don't see yourself for what you are. You never have.*

It was, as far as I was concerned, Avva's only flaw.

Could it be that I...had the same one?

When Tivien and her assistant reached the gate, she turned and raised her hand to me. Numbly, hardly thinking about what I was doing, I raised my hand in reply. Immediately, fire filled all seven gates around me, leaving me alone in that vast sandstone cavern with the enormous Tree of Flame behind me.

With no small amount of trepidation, I turned back to face Her trunk, expecting to wait for ages before She would deign to speak with me.

Yet my flameheart got a jolt when I saw Her avatar standing there, on the other side of the pit of fire, flames licking Her charcoal body, Her ash hair swirling around Her face in an unfelt wind. Her eyes of flame were as soft as I had ever seen them.

For the first time I could remember...

...my Tree was smiling at me.

"Hey," Sarah said with a grin as she walked through the crowngate and hugged me.

"Hey," I said back, in English, smiling just as widely. Though I returned the hug gingerly, with her father and brother stepping through only a moment later.

She stepped back and looked me in the eye, and I looked at her in turn. There was something new in her eyes, an added light there.

"Have a good visit?" I said tactfully, knowing now wasn't the time to go into details.

"Yes," she said peaceably. "And you?"

I knew she wasn't referring to the fact that I got to sleep in my own bed last night. She, like me, clearly saw something different in my eyes.

"Surprisingly, yes," I said with a slight smile, remembering.

Her smile widened. "Told you so."

"Yes, yes, you were right, I was wrong. But who is surprised about that?"

"Not me," Michael quipped.

I looked over Sarah at him. "*Thanks,* Michael."

But I grinned to show him I took no offense. Actually, his jab gave me more hope than I'd ever felt that one day, we might find some equilibrium. Maybe we'd never be great friends, but I'd settle for good-natured sparring.

"Hey, she's my sister. I have no idea what you guys are talking about, but I have to side with her by default. Besides, she *is* probably the smartest person I know, apart from this guy."

He elbowed his father, who just lifted his eyes for patience.

"Perhaps we should be going?" Jake suggested. "I believe there is an escort party waiting for us."

I looked at Sarah. "You told them what to expect? With sungates and everything?"

"Of course I did," she replied with a twinkle in her eye. "I learned from the best."

And by that, you mean my mistakes, I said dryly.

Oh, hush, you, she said, taking my hand. *You did better than anyone else could have, and more than good enough for me.*

"Gather round," she told the other two, gesturing for them to come closer. "Ben is going to surge us up to the closest gate to the takeoff point."

While they did so, I couldn't help but add, *I seem to recall that you said I deserved a slap for not explaining sungates to you before taking you through one.*

And you nearly had a panic attack when I didn't explain airplane cruising altitudes to you before we were taking off, so I'm not perfect either. No one is, Ben. You're just the unlucky one who got to make all the mistakes first.

Before I could say anything about that, she said out loud, "OK, Michael, why don't you try lashing us this time? You've seen me do it twice now, so...."

Michael scowled. "I tried, earlier—with Dad and David. Still couldn't do it. Not enough to make it hold when one of us surged."

"Really?" Sarah said curiously. "Dad?"

Jake shook his head. "Same."

"Well, try now," Sarah said, looking at her brother. "Maybe I can see...or, er, feel what's wrong."

Michael cast me a glare that said what he'd do to me if I laughed, then closed his eyes with a huff.

I didn't feel much when Sarah lashed me to her, but I usually felt *something*: a pull from inside me—which I assumed was part of the attachment process, like sinking a hook into my essence—then a wrap of her energy around me.

Though I could feel Michael bringing power to the surface, I felt no pull, and the power he threw around us felt as flimsy as straw; it faded a moment later when Michael presumably gave up.

"That's...interesting," Sarah said slowly.

"See?" Michael huffed. "It's nothing more than what you did for us until *this* guy showed up again."

He waved at me, and I blinked in surprise. Sarah's lashes had been *that* weak at some point? But they never had been while she was with us. They'd always felt flexible yet unbreakable to me—like scarves woven from steel fibers.

"You're right...." Sarah said, looking at me with wide eyes.

"What?" I asked self-consciously.

"So, what's your secret, huh?" Michael demanded. "What haven't you taught us?"

"Michael, I think you answered your own question," Jake said thoughtfully, folding his arms as he looked between Sarah and me.

"What?" he said, taken aback.

"It's Ben, isn't it?" Sarah said, looking back at her father. "He's the difference."

"Huh?" I said.

"How is freakin' *Ben* the difference?" Michael said in exasperation, waving at me again. "You said he can't lash. This isn't his magic. This is ours."

Jake's reply was measured. "Except Ben is the only one she has successfully done this with. Isn't that right, Sarah?"

Sarah's cheeks heated. "Well, with...only one tiny exception. There were...extenuating circumstances."

"Like what?" Michael said intently. I could imagine how little he liked the thought of depending on me for yet another thing, and how eager he would be to disprove this latest theory.

Sarah seemed to realize that she wasn't going to satisfy him with vague details. "Er...at one point, to save Kor's life...I had to switch the connection I have with Ben...to Kor. Then later that same night, I surged with Kor."

I stilled as I realized what she was getting at. I tried hard to think about the common factor and not about the other details of the second scenario.

Unfortunately, Sarah's brother made that difficult.

"Wait, hold up," Michael said, slowly grinning. "You're saying that this mystical connection you have with Ben...you had with *Kor*?"

"For one night," I said tightly.

"To save Kor's life," Sarah repeated emphatically. "It returned to Ben as soon as we got back together again."

"Wait, by 'got back together,' do you mean literally or—"

The linguistic nuances were going over my head, but Sarah narrowed her eyes at her brother and snapped, "Literally, Michael. We were separated in a blizzard, OK? Kor got hurt in a fall while saving *my* life, then he didn't have enough energy to heal himself, so I had to switch to him *temporarily* to share enough energy with him to save his life. Just like performing CPR. OK? That's it. I didn't even consciously know that was what I was doing. Or I might have had second thoughts."

"CPR, huh?" Michael said, still grinning. "So, like, mouth-to-mouth—"

"The point being," Jake said, looking at the ceiling again, "it is the connection. Just as their connection allows Ben to unconsciously impart his healing ability with Sarah and Sarah to share energy with him without entering light-form. There is something about this symbiotic connection between a child of Flame and a child of Ice that strengthens the lashing we can do to the point that it can survive a surging. It makes sense, in a way. Lashing is about building connections."

"But we're *family*," Michael said. "Isn't that being connected enough?"

Jake raised an eyebrow. "I'm not minimizing the importance of family connections. Or even marital ones. But can you do an effective lashing with Laura?"

Michael's sullen silence was his answer.

"It's the magical symbiosis, the synergy," Jake said pointedly. "The joining of two different powers that together form something greater than the sum of their parts. It's why we're working together in the first place."

"Well, I'm sure as hell not bonding with one of *them* just to lash properly."

"No one is expecting you to, Michael," Sarah said hastily. "It's not that important. Besides, as Dad pointed out, you're, er, already married."

That made Jake curious. "You think this connection is always going to be an intimate kind, between couples? If it ever repeats, that is?"

Sarah and I glanced at each other, then back at him.

Sarah's cheeks looked as warm as mine felt as she replied. "I'm just going to keep things simple and say that's a definite yes."

ABOUT HALF A DEKEN later, we emerged from the Krevenyir sungate and soared out over the lush fields of its tropical valley. Technically, the sungate wasn't on Mount Krevenyir itself, but on another mountain just south of it. Because Krevenyir, the mountain and hold we were now flying north toward....

Is that...a volcano? Sarah asked faintly.

Yep, I said.

Tell me the hold isn't inside that.

Well...sorry, it is.

Krevenyir rose abruptly out of its verdant valley like a steep anthill whose top had been chopped clean off by a giant's blade and then dug out with an equally enormous spade. Greenery crept up its smooth slopes daringly high before fading to crumbled black stone near the tip. The vast, tiered crater let out minor plumes of pure white steam—a low-activity day with strong winds, which meant that Sarah got a good view of the red and black lava lake at its bottom as we circled the mountain to approach the main landing.

But...why? Sarah asked, inner voice still strained.

This is the Battleblood clan. A better question would probably be why not?

Right. Forget I asked.

Don't worry. It's always monitored for signs of eruption, and it's in a low-activity phase right now. Chances of an eruption while we're here are minimal, or I wouldn't have brought you.

I trust you, Sarah said quickly. *It's just...wow. I'm going to be sleeping inside a volcano tonight.*

You've slept in them before, I said in amusement.

What? she asked flatly.

Alright, they were inactive. But Olsdak, Rosin...I think even Palla is an extinct volcano. We gravitate toward warm spaces inside mountains. We've found all sorts of ways to use the heat from the magma: hot water, steam rooms, heat vents....

Alright, I get the picture, Sarah said, a laugh in her voice.

Krevenyir is also known for its smithing and mining, and this is one reason why.

Vadya said that when she was briefing me. She just failed to mention it was because it was inside a freakin' volcano.

Then it was time to come in for the landing, so Sarah quieted as I dove in and touched down, and Yvera and Kor followed suit on either side of me. The half dozen elites who had accompanied us remained circling overhead, since the landing was taken up by the hold's honor guard, standing at attention in drakáform. The closest two roared in welcome as I landed.

Then all of them had to wait for not just Sarah but also Jake and Michael to descend my, Kor's, and Yvera's backs, respectively. I could have carried all three Linds easily, and I even offered, but Kor thought the best symbolic arrangement for the first formal arrival of the White Crown was for all of us to be paired with our counterparts. Though Yvera had needed a direct order from me to accept Michael as a passenger, and Michael hadn't acted too pleased either when he'd been led away from Sarah to the ladder at her flank.

Sarah reminded me as they mounted that this was only the second time Michael had ever flown drakáback before, and the first time for Jake. Jake, however, took it with the equanimity he took everything, and he'd looked like a natural when he finally was settled astride Kor.

He dismounted just as naturally now, his feet stepping off the ladder and onto the flagstones not long after Sarah and long before his son. The rest of us were gathered and standing in formation by the time Michael joined us, and Yvera hurriedly changed into amáform and strode to follow.

"A volcano?" he muttered—thankfully, quietly enough that no one from the welcoming party would hear. "Really? You people are nuts."

Be polite, Michael, Sarah said. *Especially right* now. *It's showtime, remember? You don't have to fake a smile, but at least don't look like a thundercloud.*

Yes, ma'am, Michael said dryly, but he wrestled his face into a more neutral expression. He also straightened his shoulders, brusquely resetting the jacket of his uniform and giving his father's matching set a quick once-over out of the corner of his eye.

The uniforms were Kor's doing, of course: white militaristic jackets with high, black-lined collars and black borders; black trousers with white trim around the hems and outer seam; and black boots with silver accents. A white leather holster at their hips held their now infamous silver guns. The uniforms were identical except for the diagonal line of silver buttons across the chest, which were symmetrical to each other: Michael's went from right shoulder to left hip, and Jake's from left shoulder to right hip. I belatedly realized that while they stood in position behind Sarah like this, the silver lines together formed a V like a pair of raised wings, especially in the continuation of the silver V on Sarah's white dress that began at her navel and ended at her shoulders.

I decided my leftwing was officially having too much fun.

Because of course he didn't stop with the Moontouched. I too had a V on my black jacket, formed by two diagonal rows of gold buttons that, functionally, made no sense whatsoever, and I'd have been lost if an attendant hadn't shown me how to put it on. (Good thing it was so easy to default to the last clothes I'd been wearing in amáform when I changed back.) Aside from the colors and weapons (mine was a sword in a black and gold scabbard), my uniform was similar in shape and style to Jake's and Michael's, except I had a full-length black cape with gold silk lining, attached at the tips of the V. That cape matched Sarah's own, which was also black, though her lining was silver.

There, Kor's reign of fashion finally reached its limits. He knew without being told that there was no getting Yvera into something besides her customary violet scale armor, especially not when her scale normally did just fine for a rightwing's uniform on pretty much any occasion. To top it off, this was her clan homecoming, where every other drakón in amáform would be in *scale*. Not flimsy, vulnerable cloth.

So, Kor had picked his battle carefully and instead cajoled Yvera into wearing a simple gold sash tied across her chest. He'd argued that it showed her status as the King's rightwing and not just any Battleblood, or even any Battleblood elite, and that appeal to her pride finally did it. What he didn't mention was that his and Yvera's sashes paralleled Jake's and Michael's rows of buttons, though it looked to me like she still hadn't realized that.

Kor wore a very neutral expression, but I knew that meant he was suffering inside from the fact that he had to be in his blue scale set right now to match Yvera. I couldn't even imagine what his uniform would have been otherwise.

I had expected Michael to protest the uniforms like he had most everything else, but I'd guessed wrong. He had accepted his with poorly concealed enthusiasm, and I'd overheard him asking Sarah in a whisper if she thought he was meant to keep it. That's when I remembered he had been a lawkeeper on Earth; perhaps wearing *any* style of uniform felt right to him, no matter how dissimilar it was from the one he had been wearing when I had first met him. There was definitely a different air about him right now, especially after Sarah's reminder that we were on display: a much more professional, even settled look to him. In fact...he looked more like his father in that moment than I had ever seen.

Ready? I asked them as soon as Yvera fell in behind me on my right. All together now, with Sarah standing on my left and her wings behind her, we would probably form two inverted triangles from above.

Looks like it, Sarah said, giving my hand a clench.

I clenched hers in return and looked ahead. *Then let's go.*

Together, we walked between the rows of violet draká. I set a measured pace, even slower than I usually did to accommodate Sarah's shorter legs, just in case Jake and Michael found it strange walking in this formation. Even Kor and Yvera weren't used to having another set of wings walk beside them; before, when we had arrived in state with Avva and his wings, we three had always walked behind—one triangle following the other.

Considering we had only briefly discussed this and hadn't had time to practice, I thought we did rather well. At least as far as I could tell from hearing the measured steps behind me.

I couldn't glance back. Sarah was right—smiles were not only unnecessary, they would be nearly as garish to the Battleblood as they would have been to the Strongshield, but for different reasons. Emotional displays were rude, almost childish to the Strongshield. To the Battleblood, anything aside from stoicism could be taken as a sign of weakness. Along the same lines, they would expect me to keep my face serious and my gaze fixed firmly and confidently ahead. Glancing to the side would indicate I was nervous, looking for danger—and, most of all, distrustful of their hospitality.

Sarah, having been forewarned by her chief of staff, did the same. Of all the things around me, she was the hardest for me not to glance at. Even if the confidence I could feel her radiating was a show, I doubted anyone who didn't know her could tell. Yet I also doubted it was entirely put on. She was changing so quickly from the girl I'd found in that jungle on Ykran into the woman walking at my side, it was dizzying. I was certain she looked magnificent, and I thought it a crime that I couldn't be one of the witnesses.

Instead, we both looked ahead, to the Battleblood Lady that awaited us.

Lady Yalda was a formidable woman. Only a handful of ild shorter than me, she towered over almost everyone, male or female, around her. At one hundred and fifty-six summers, she was now the oldest clan leader after Lady Maya's passing, but, despite the scars slashing across her face, she didn't look a day over a century. Her violet hair was wrapped into a severe bun at the back of her head, and she was dressed in her scale (of course) with an even bigger claymore than Yvera's at her back. She watched our approach with a severe eye; I doubted deken of practice in our formation could have satisfied her. For as long as I had known her, she had never been satisfied with anything.

And that included her granddaughter, who walked just behind me, having achieved the highest position a Battleblood could hope for as the Monarch's rightwing.

Alyish was Yvera's great-grandfather on her father's side—a much different strain of Battleblood hailing from a local hold, whereas Yalda was the relative newcomer, hailing from the far north, as her pale skin attested. Yalda's daughter, Yvera's mother, died defending my own mother when Yv and I were just hatchlings, and Avvi then took Yvera and her brother under her wing in recompense.

Yvera and I, being the same age, had already been thrust together on occasion as playmates, but she hadn't been the friendliest one—in fact, she'd been something of a bully—so I was nervous when she came to stay with us. Still, I could see she was shellshocked and hurting. Even though I couldn't fully comprehend her grief, at Avvi's prompting, I tried to help as best as I knew how.

She, in turn, decided I wasn't so bad after all. In typical Yvera fashion, she did a complete one-eighty and turned from being one of my greatest antagonists to my staunchest defender—a shield that I, being as shy and uncertain as I was back then, already desperately needed. No bully dared come near me after that, not with her at my side. Almost overnight, we became inseparable and had been ever since.

Did Yalda blame your mother for her daughter's death? Sarah asked me softly, echoing my thoughts.

If only, I said, gaze resting on the Lady.

What? Sarah asked, baffled.

I think Yalda blamed her daughter for dying.

To a Battleblood, danger wasn't a thing to avoid—it was not only a fact of life, it was an opportunity for glory. Being a member of a Monarch consort's elite guard was an honor, one a softer Yalda might once have been proud of, despite or perhaps even because of the risks. But death was defeat, and Yalda never accepted defeat.

I think she did resent Avvi for taking in Yvera, though, I said grimly. *Not because she's fond of Yvera but because...Yalda thinks she could have made Yvera into a better warrior.*

Yvera? Sarah said incredulously. *A better warrior?*

Don't ask me to explain how Yalda's mind works. Only the Flame knows that.

I didn't mention that I shuddered to think how my foster sister would have turned out being raised by Yalda. Avvi claimed a mother's guilt and sympathies when she took in Yvera and Aldrek, and that could well have been true; but I'd often suspected another, more farsighted motive. Avvi knew she couldn't save everyone, but she seemed to have a sixth sense for those who needed her the most.

Now, I wondered for the first time if she'd had a third motive. Had she known, somehow, how much I would need Yvera? How I'd probably be dead a hundred times over by now if it wasn't for her? Had she seen *that* much?

We stopped the proper distance from Yalda and her entourage.

She gave the traditional greeting, her contralto voice cold. "Welcome, King Koriben, to Krevenyir of Ekrel."

"I thank you for your welcome, Lady Yalda," I said coolly. I wasn't being impolite—any more warmth and I would have been seen as being too forward. Or simply foolish.

Still, Yalda's voice could have been a *tad* less icy when she said, "What brings my King to my Realm on this day?"

"I come to present my betrothed and your future Queen: Queen Sarah Moontouched of the Seventh Realm and Crown of Ice. I also present her wings, Jacob and Michael Moontouched."

Yalda's sharp violet eyes fell on each person as I named them, but she only nodded to the bare minimum depth required for Sarah, and her eyes soulflared as she did so. That irritated me more than anything, but it wasn't worth breaking decorum to fuss over, and it was no less than what we had expected from her.

If Yalda, one of the most traditional of the Traditionalist faction, had greeted *Sarah* warmly, I would have unsheathed my sword, thinking she'd finally lost her mind and was concealing an attack. Or that the Devourer had somehow put one of its agents in her place—though that agent would have been a poor one indeed to give itself away like that.

Her coldness, though expected, *was* confirmation of what Kor had warned me of again that very day. I would have my work cut out for me on this visit to convince Yalda—and more importantly, the radical elements of the Traditionalists who saw her as a figurehead—that my betrothed was not to be trifled with.

Or they would have to answer to me.

Chapter Five

AGREEMENT

Sarah

It felt like forever until Ben and I could finally shut ourselves away, but it was only a couple hours—and that counted the brief, uncomfortable ceremony with Lady Yalda, getting to the King's Wing of Krevenyir Hold, and having our customary dinner with all the people from our entourage that we could fit into our dining room, including Dad and Michael for the first time.

Really not much time at all, and it was probably only possible because we had arrived in the evening, after our entourage had already settled in and it was too late for anyone to ambush us with real business.

I collapsed on the couch in our bedroom with a sigh, and Ben didn't look much more energetic as he settled down next to me. I cuddled against him, and he put his arm around me.

"So, Michael seemed...comfortable at dinner," Ben said.

I'd noticed. My brother had tried acting all stiff and formal at first—perhaps one reason he didn't change out of uniform—but then one of the male elites sitting next to him got him talking. From how they were enthusiastically showing their respective weapons to each other and making animated motions, I could guess the topic. The two of them disappeared before the main tranche started leaving, and I guessed they were heading to the training room.

From Kor's smirk as he watched them go, I had a hunch that the seating arrangements hadn't been an accident—at least around Michael. I didn't think

Kor's interference was overly manipulative. The elite's friendliness seemed genuine to me, and any good host tried to make sure their guests had someone to
talk to. Kor just happened to be a particularly good host...among other things.

I chuckled. "Michael is not that hard of a nut to crack. The only reason he's
been able to build up such a resentment against dramá this whole time is because
he hasn't had a chance to get to know any of you. Svyer changed that a bit, but he
could have told himself she was an exception to the rule. Now he's confronted
with you guys twenty-four-seven, and it's a lot harder for him to keep deluding
himself. Really, this is the best possible thing we could have done to finally soften
him up."

"Hmm. Perhaps I should be glad that your father seems already inclined to
give us a chance, then."

"Yeah. Like I told you in the beginning...Dad and Michael were going to be
the two hardest ones to bring around. Michael may bluster at first, but he's
a simplistic softie inside. Dad, though...there's nothing you can do to fool or
coerce Dad. If you're not legit—heck, if you're not one-hundred-percent worth
his time—he'll see it, and he'll let you know."

Ben sighed.

"Hey," I said gently, looking up at him. "The good thing about that is you
are legit, and you *are* worth his time. He sees that. That's why he's giving you a
chance."

Ben grimaced. "Despite all the reasons he has not to."

I huffed. "Believe it or not, Ben, I think he actually likes you."

Ben gave me a look that told me he did *not* believe it, and I insisted, "Really.
Why are you so determined to think that people don't like you? It's stupid, Ben,
and you're not stupid. You're not letting yourself see things clearly."

He opened his mouth, then paused. Then closed it thoughtfully.

"For that matter," I pressed. "Why do you let it bother you if they don't?"

"I don't, generally. I can't afford to, I know that. For example, Michael's
dislike doesn't bother me nearly as much. But for some reason, I want Jake's
good opinion. Badly." Ben sighed. "Maybe *because* I know it's worth so much.
Because if *he* looks at me and finds me lacking...then maybe I really am."

I cringed. I wasn't one to say much about that. I'd grown up with that very insecurity, after all. Needlessly, I'd learned by now—just like I was almost certain it was in Ben's case, but that was the problem with having a father who expressed so little emotion, in word or expression. You just could never...tell.

"Yeah," I said finally in a quieter voice. "I can see that."

Ben glanced at me. "Your father loves you, Sarah, *and* he's proud of you."

I smiled thinly. "How is it that you can tell that about me, but not about you?"

He hesitated. "That...is a fair point."

"Look, I'll just ask him how he feels about you. That's usually best—just to be upfront with him. He really can't tell that we can't tell these things."

"In that case, I should be the one to talk to him, not you. Unless you're just going to talk to him about yourself, in which case, by all means, do."

"We've had that talk," I said, regaining my confidence at the recent memories. "He's made that clear lately."

"Then let me talk to him about me."

I shrugged. "Sounds good to me."

He was right—that was best.

After a moment, Ben glanced at me and shifted. I could sense a change of topic coming. "So...how did your visit with your Tree go?"

I paused. "It was...informative."

That was scarcely adequate. It had been many things, full of paradigm-shattering revelations and every type of emotion—fear high among them, and desire, especially toward the end. But now, far removed from the moment, I felt doubt creep back in.

Was I ready? *Truly* ready?

Did I have any other choice?

"Meaning?" Ben asked hesitantly.

He, of all people, knew how much "informative" could mean when a Tree was concerned.

"I...can't tell you all of it," I said carefully. "I'm sorry, but the Tree said I couldn't."

Particularly the part about what we both had agreed to before we were even born—and what our *child* had agreed to. The Tree said that was knowledge Ben had to find out for himself, when he was ready...if he ever chose to be.

Ben shrugged. "That makes sense. I don't hold it against you. But what *can* you tell me?"

I sighed heavily and looked away. Softly, I said, "You were right. The Devourer is coming. Again. Except this time...it will strike at *my* Tree."

Ben inhaled sharply and held me closer to him. "*What*?"

"It's the surest way it knows how to lure me and my family out of hiding. Because we'll have to protect Her."

Or die trying.

Ben knew that part as well—knew everything I knew and more, as I had known he would. This was the role he had been born into: protecting his people and his Tree from the Devourer.

He was silent for a few long moments as he held me tightly. I curled in closer to him, resting my head on his chest and my hand over his heart. It was beating so quickly, rapid warm pulses sending out power at a heedless rate beneath my fingers. I thought of giving him power, then decided that he wouldn't like it. Not now. Right now, I had to let him feel the full horror of the situation sink in and simply let him hold me.

Finally, he sank back, slumping down so that his head rested against the back of the couch. He let out one choice curse as he put his free hand over his face. When he dropped that hand, he let out a heavy breath and turned his head to me.

"You won't be alone," Ben said flatly, his eyes soulflaring. "I'll be there, and I'll bring as many as I can with me."

I smiled slightly. "I know you will."

The *but* still hung in the air, unspoken.

It might not be enough.

The glow faded from his eyes under the weight of that despair.

"That's why, isn't it?" he said quietly. "Why you won't be strong enough to drive it off, unless...."

"She still didn't explain exactly why, but essentially...yes."

Ben crushed me into him, pulling me into his lap and on top of him. He was trembling slightly. He buried his face in my hair. I could feel his warm breath against my neck.

"I can't lose you, Sarah," he rasped, still trembling. "I can't. I *can't*. Not like...."

Not like he had lost his father. Because if the Tree had not offered another way, that would be my fate—sacrificing myself to save my Tree and my people. There would be no other way.

"You won't."

He clenched me even more tightly for a moment...before gradually loosening his hold. He leaned his head back again. After a few moments, the worst of his tremors passed.

"Does that mean you've decided?" he whispered.

I took a deep breath, then let it out.

"I have," I said with quiet conviction. "Not just because it's the right thing for me, or for you.... Because it's the right thing. For everyone."

Even the child. After all, if I sacrificed myself...their courageous choice, their waiting, and their love for me...would be for nothing. Maybe they could still be born to some other mother and father, but they would never become what they had been meant to be.

And I so badly wanted to see what that was.

I craned my head to look up at him. "Have you?"

Ben laughed shakily; the movement felt strange with him beneath me; it made me feel hot and flustered. Especially given the topic.

"Sarah, I made my choice, such as it was, the moment the Tree told me it was my only chance to save you."

His arms tightened around me again, and his voice thickened. "I just...can't.... Not again."

"I understand."

So, I let him hold me, not saying anything else.

A few minutes later, after his heart pulses had slowed to a steadier rhythm, I broke the silence, trying to lighten the mood with a teasing tone.

"So...now that we're both decided...when are we getting started?"

Ben chuckled. Again, the vibration twisted my insides in the best and worst ways. "About that...."

"Hmm?"

"Well, as you know, I talked to *my* Tree."

"And how did *that* go?" I said, trying to hide a flicker of unease.

"It was also...informative, but less heavily than yours. Mostly, I found out that, shockingly, She was generally pleased with me."

The unease turned to relief. "Told you so."

"Yes, yes, I already *said* you were right. But we did talk about one thing, and that was the heartbinding. Oh, we have Her formal permission for us to marry, by the way."

"Oh, good," I said with dry humor. "So glad to cross *that* nonconcern off my list."

Ben chuckled again. "I did have to *ask*. This is about my consort, after all. And you're still young enough that you need permission anyway."

I hurriedly did some math. "Just barely."

"What?"

"Well, if I've kept track of the days properly, then my nineteenth birthday is in..." I mentally double checked. "...ten days."

"Really?" Ben asked with interest.

"Funny," I said, scrunching my face. "We haven't talked about birthdays, have we?"

I was marrying this man, whom I felt like I knew better than myself, in hopefully less than a week, and yet I had no idea what day he was born.

But then it occurred to me why. "Not that...I guess, with our different calendars...and solar systems...it means a whole lot."

"Not really, I suppose," Ben said in amusement. "We celebrate the day marking someone's birth, sure, so it's good to know yours is coming. But traditionally and legally, it's the summers you've reached that matter the most. You've only seen eighteen, right?"

"Wait...." I did the calculation. "Actually...what's the threshold? When does it count? If you reach the summer solstice or the fall equinox?"

"The solstice," Ben said curiously. "Why?"

"Oh," I said in surprise. "Then I guess, since I was born at the beginning of October, I've seen *nineteen* summer solstices. Even though I haven't seen a full nineteen Earth years."

"Oh," Ben said, an odd note in his voice. That meant something to him. I didn't think it meant anything good or bad—he just had to make a mental adjustment about me.

I felt a trivial bit of satisfaction from that. It was just like thinking I'd gained an inch closer to Ben's height. Suddenly, in his mind, I was a year closer to his age.

Within my full legal rights to marry him, among other things....

I had a flash of insight. "Ben, my age didn't factor into your decision to not sleep with me yet, did it?"

"Er...."

When I looked up at him again, his neck and cheeks were flushed.

"Not consciously, no," he said. "But now that you point it out...I can't say it wasn't...a subconscious influence."

Figures.

I only laughed. "You're adorable."

"If you say so."

"Anyway, you were talking about the heartbinding?"

"Ah, yes," Ben said, but his flush only increased. "Since we were on the topic, I asked Her...if it would be better to...move it up."

I'd expected that. In fact, I had planned on asking my own Tree the same question but forgot in all the inner turmoil. I was glad Ben remembered, at least.

"And? What did She say?"

Ben grimaced. "She said, and I quote, 'It matters not.'"

I blinked. "Excuse me? *They're* the ones making this huge fuss over whether we have children. And the timing of it doesn't matter to Them?"

"Oh, I agree. I had the same reaction. But She just said that this is in Their hands either way, so They are leaving the timing of the heartbinding and any other related...activities...to us."

I raised an eyebrow. "So...They don't even care whether we start before or after?"

"I wouldn't go that far," Ben said slowly. "She seemed to...approve of my decision. To wait. Since She wouldn't tell me anything directly, I don't know if it was because it was *the* right thing to do or because *I* thought it was the right thing to do. But...."

He took a deep breath. "Torch it, Sarah, I can't believe I'm still saying this with your life on the line, but...I *still* think it's the right thing to do. Even now that you know, and you've decided. Waiting until we were heartbonded was always supposed to be a sign to you that I would put you before me, and I think that still holds true—perhaps now more than ever, now that I'm more terrified of losing you than ever. I won't...I won't let my choices about you be ruled by my fears anymore. If this is going to work, if I am going to be the husband and father you deserve...then I need to have more faith."

He paused a moment for another breath. "In the Trees...in you...and in me."

"In that case," I said quietly, "I agree."

"What?" Ben said, blinking at me.

"I agree. With all of that. You're right. You were always right. It is a sign. And it's not just one between us. It's also a sign to the child. That we're not just doing this for ourselves. We're doing it for...them. For our family."

That gave Ben pause. He clearly hadn't thought of it that way yet, which made sense. Our child still wasn't real to him—not in the way he or she was now to me.

I had *felt* him or her. They had *touched* me, giving me strength and love in a moment I had needed it desperately. They weren't some hypothetical, some unformed potential. They were there.

I had never been the type of girl to dream about kids, let alone pick out baby names years in advance. Yet I now wanted to *name* them. It seemed so wrong for them to be so real and yet nameless. And yet, what gender would they be? I couldn't call them something without knowing. I could pick a gender-neutral name, I guessed; surely there were those in Drona, too. But what if the name didn't suit them? What if they didn't like it?

How stressful a thing it was to not just create something but also *name* it!

These were the kinds of thoughts I would never have thought I would be having a week ago, and yet, now they were so pressing they distracted me from even a conversation as important as this. Fortunately, Ben used that time to think, and when he spoke again, I managed to notice and drag my attention back to him just in time.

"Then we're agreed? We wait until a heartbinding?"

"Yes, agreed."

He took a deep breath. "Then, I guess the only remaining question is...do we have a secret one now or not?"

As *sorely* tempting as it was to do it now—with my sudden baby hunger making it harder than ever to wait—I made myself stop, breathe, and think. That made the answer clear.

I sighed. "This is about faith, right?"

"Right," Ben said, sighing as well. I had a hunch we had both come to the same conclusion.

"If the Trees say it's in Their hands either way...then I say we wait. It's faith. Faith and a sign. To *everyone*."

Ben sighed again, even more heavily. "I...agree."

What that last rise and fall of his chest did to me was painful, given our decision.

"Well, then...." I said. "I guess I'd better get off you. Shouldn't I?"

Ben stiffened. "Er...yes, that would be best."

I laughed, but I slid off him. Still, I snuggled up to his side again, and he put his arm around me again. I took a deep breath and smiled.

As I'd told him before...for now, this was enough.

CHAPTER SIX

SPEECH

SARAH

"I HOPE YOU KNOW I love you," I said groggily, standing with Ben inside the shadows of an arch just before dawn. Beyond that arch was a balcony overlooking a giant stadium filled to capacity with what seemed to me like half the population of the Six Realms.

Ben squeezed my hand three times. "Oh, I know you do. I know this is an act of pure devotion. Trust me, I do."

According to Vadya and Ben, once a year, the Battleblood clan hosted what they succinctly called "the Tournament." Which, to me, sounded like a cross between a medieval tourney and the Olympics. With dragons.

Usually, it was held as part of the winter solstice celebrations, but that didn't happen last time because of the Battle of the Solstice. Now the postponed Tournament was the main event on the Ekrel leg of our grand tour. Combining the two was their main ask of the Golden Crown. Considering this was the clan of hardened warriors who occupied one of the most dangerous planets in the Six Realms, I didn't know whether I should feel like we had gotten off lightly or not.

On the one hand, Ben could have been stuck hunting rock wyrms or something somewhere, but on the other...the more I heard about this Tournament, the more I realized how big of a deal it was to not just the Battleblood but *all* the Realms. Even Ben seemed to regard it with the kind of appreciative fatalism he normally reserved for his Tree. Perhaps comparing the Tournament to the Olympics wasn't good enough—unless you thought of the ancient Grecian kind which were in honor of a god and seen as a form of worship.

The old King might have been partially to blame for the grand tour–Tournament combination. According to Kor, Kavarian had *discreetly* suggested it to Lady Yalda during an apology call as part of his preparations leading up to the Battle of the Solstice. I could only imagine how that conversation must have gone.

So sorry that we all must focus on the defense of our Realms instead of your pseudo-sacred Tournament, but if, hypothetically speaking, my son were to marry sometime in the next few months, you might think about doing it during his grand tour.

Not really, of course. If Kor said the old King was discreet, then I'm sure he was, even if my imagination ran dry on how. Yet ever since that conversation, that was that in Lady Yalda's mind. Not for the first time, I had to roll my eyes and wonder what everyone would have done if Ben and I *hadn't* decided to marry.

So here I was, standing with Ben, dressed in my Moontouched armor in full parade mode (meaning an added white, open-facing skirt), waiting for dawn so that we could step out and make an appearance at the opening ceremony.

This felt far too much like the start of the Battle of the Solstice for my comfort, but Ben assured me repeatedly that I would not be expected to give a speech this time.

He had also fought hard for me to be exempted from the opening ceremony altogether, but my semi-nocturnal Moontouched sleep schedule wasn't a good enough excuse for Yalda, and the sky would fall before she consented to start the Tournament at a different time of day. Not only had Ben given her only three days ("I couldn't give her *less* than I gave the Starkissed," Ben said with a sigh), so that every second of our stay counted, but also....

"She's a Traditionalist," Kor had said diplomatically.

"To the *core*," Ben added dryly.

If I had been more awake and charitable, if this hadn't been yet another day to throw my sleep out of whack, I would have felt sorrier for Ben. After all, he was the one who *did* have to give a speech this time. Even in my sleep-deprived state, I could tell that he was about fit to burst from nerves. He could hardly stand still beside me, which made *me* even more nervous. I trusted Ben with my all, but my weary primal brain still saw a twitchy, over-seven-foot muscular giant in golden armor and wearing an enormous sword, and it kept throwing up threat errors.

Then he pulled away from me and started pacing.

Do something, Kor urged me silently.

He and Yvera were waiting behind us, as were Michael and Dad. Though I didn't look back at Michael to check, I could imagine how he might have been eyeing Ben, not to mention all the other people in this antechamber with us. Only a handful of elites and a couple of event organizers, but still too many to see Ben in a state like this.

Do what? I asked.

I didn't disagree that action was needed, but my foggy brain was coming up empty. Why was I always Ben's comfort human anyway? On any other day, I would have been happy about that, not cross, but I wasn't in the best of moods.

Something, Kor insisted.

I caught Ben by the hand again to hold him still. *Ben, stop, please.*

Sorry, he said, trying to stand in one place again—and began fidgeting with his sword.

This wasn't going to work.

So, I started sending him a trickle of energy through our joined hands. Not much—just a dribble, but it was enough to get his attention. He stilled and glanced at me, scowling.

Sarah, cut that out. It's almost dawn, and you're exhausted.

I'll cut it out when you *can hold still,* I said.

I'm trying, he bit back.

For some reason, his irritation soothed mine. My next words were in a much more reasonable tone. *Show me you can do it, and I'll stop.*

He tried closing his eyes and taking deep breaths, but it still didn't look like it was working. His breath kept going fast and shallow. He needed a different focus, one outside himself. But what....

Then I had an idea. *Ben, can you feel my pulse? In the power I'm giving you?*

He stilled again, focusing. His next words had a tinge of awe. *Yes. It's carried in the current—as long as the current is steady.*

I upped the flow just a tad to ensure the current would remain unbroken. *Focus on* that. *Feel my heartbeat, Ben. Block out everything else.*

So, he closed his eyes and did, becoming more settled and relaxed by the moment. I focused on my own breathing to slow that heartbeat even more, and, surprisingly, Ben began to match my rhythm. My deep breaths were more like regular ones to lungs his size, but even regular breaths for him were an improvement.

I watched his chest move in sync with mine out of the corner of my eye, somewhat in awe—partly from how his miraculous plate armor moved to allow it, and the fascinating rhythmic motion those plates created as they shifted in and out, almost as if they were truly a part of him. But mostly I was awed that he was matching me at all, since that hadn't been the original intention. I even watched the center of his breath gradually shift from his upper chest to his diaphragm, where I was centering my own breath. I wanted to ask if he was doing it consciously, but I didn't want to disturb the zone he was entering, especially if he wasn't.

I don't know what you're doing, Kor said in relief, *but keep doing it—so long as it's short of knocking him out.*

I won't, I said, although I eyed Ben's expression. Now that Kor mentioned it, his face was nearly as relaxed as it became only in sleep. Was I putting him under? I hadn't expected this strategy to be quite this effective....

Then...I felt the slightest shift. Ben didn't move, but it was like his energy, his invisible essence, was pulling toward me. As if he were about to....

My eyes widened, and my iceheart jumped. *Uh-oh.*

Now was *not* the time for him to surge into me.

Either that spike in my heart rate or the draká roar outside finally made Ben snap out of it. He blinked his eyes open and shook his head as if he really had been asleep.

"Wait, what?" he muttered out loud.

An event organizer was waving us forward meaningfully. I wrapped my arm around Ben's. *I think that's our cue.*

Right, right, Ben said, shaking his head one more time.

But he began walking. When we finally stepped out into the open, he still hadn't had time to work himself back into a panic, and his expression and movements were as settled as Kor could have hoped. He held his head high, and if this hadn't been a Battleblood-hosted event, he might have smiled.

Which was good, because the moment we were visible, the crowd went wild, Battleblood hosts or no.

Now I was definitely having flashbacks to the Solstice speech, especially with all the dragons trumpeting down on the arena floor and perched on the cliffs above the stadium. At least the thousands of cheering dramá in the stands were in human form, although that was a different flavor of intimidation.

I tried to focus on studying the arena, since Ben had surged us straight here through its daygate, which apparently was just for VIPs. Everyone else flew in or came through the arena's sungate. Yes, this Tournament was such a big deal that it had its own dedicated mountain, complete with its own landing pads, tunnels, chambers, and sun- *and* daygate.

Ben said we hadn't gone far, within a short flight distance, so this must have been another volcanic mountain in the same chain as Mount Krevenyir. Hopefully this volcano was much less active, because, of course, the dramá had made the arena out of its enormous caldera.

Ben and I have way *different paradigms of acceptable risk in structures,* I thought as I eyed the jagged edges of the black peaks all around us and the many tiers of seats hewn straight from black volcanic rock. It looked like an apocalyptic version of the Colosseum—except in good repair and filled to the brim.

At least this caldera didn't have a lava lake. Although I was almost surprised by that. I mean...why not?

This was already the largest structure I had ever seen the dramá make that was exposed to the elements. The main sign I saw of normal dramá security measures was the slight shimmer in the air above the peaks, indicating the presence of one of their clear magic domes—so they weren't entirely throwing caution to the winds. I also realized there was a very practical reason, which even I could sanction, to start the Tournament promptly at dawn: we would want to clear out this arena long before nightfall to avoid presenting a tantalizing target to the Devourer.

But I assumed the importance of letting in sunlight outweighed the dramá's normal reluctance to build and congregate outside. That priority strengthened my theory that the dramá regarded these games with an element of the sacred—as part of their worship of both the Flame Above (the "Sunfather") and Below (their Tree, the "Flamemother").

My speculation was pleasantly distracting as Ben and I approached Lady Yalda, who had just announced us and stood turned to the side to wait, her face still hard as ever.

Sheesh, I sent to Ben. *You would think from looking at her that she hadn't* asked *us to do this, and to be here, now.*

Or rather, demanded.

Ben didn't reply, perhaps hyper-focused on his speech. I felt a pang of guilt for distracting him with such a flippant remark.

We stopped in front of the solid stone balustrade, our respective wings stopping behind us, and the roars and cheers quieted in anticipation.

For the first time, I realized *why* Ben was so nervous. This wasn't about the Tournament. That's just what had brought everyone together like this.

This was Ben's first proper address as King. Judging from the rainbow of colors in the draká below and amá clothing and banners in the stands, this was a sizable microcosm of his entire people. This was the first time he was publicly coming before *all* of them. The first time that so many of them could see and come to know their new Monarch.

What he said next, what he did next, could lay the foundation for his relationship with them—for his entire rule.

When Ben began to speak, he did so normally, but his voice was magically magnified across the arena, and I felt a chill go down my spine at the power of those echoes—and from the sudden strength and surety radiating out of the man beside me. With a prickling awareness, I guessed the reason why: I could almost *feel* his father here again, with him.

In that moment, Ben looked...and sounded...just like him.

"Thank you, all of you." He paused, and perhaps because this was such a multicultural event, he smiled. "As many of you know by now, I am not fond of speechmaking."

A chuckle went around the audience, and he paused again to allow it to fade. "To not disappoint you, I will be predictably brief. Besides, you are not here to listen to me speak. You are here for two reasons, and you have been gracious enough to allow us to combine them. First, you are here for the Tournament."

Wild cheers broke out, and some draká added bugles of agreement to the cacophony. When the uproar died down, Ben continued, sobering.

"A Tournament which is long overdue. We normally celebrate it as part of the Festival of Lights for a reason. The Tournament itself is a symbol of our determination to not just persevere in the face of darkness but to thrive. To excel. To show in our disciplined ferocity our determination to defend our hearths, our families, and our Tree. To bind the Six Realms more closely together—for with each other, and our Tree, we can only triumph. At the Battle of the Solstice, we did precisely that."

This time, Ben did not pause long enough for applause but forestalled it by plunging on. "That battle was the greatest Tournament of our age. But instead of competing against ourselves, we fulfilled its purpose by using our excellence, our ferocity, and our unity to fight off the Second Invasion."

His voice slowed. "We incurred heavy losses that will shadow our flamehearts for years to come. I know this kind of sorrow personally. It is, after all, why I am the one standing before you today instead of my father. Know that I will, for the rest of my life, bear that sorrow with you."

The arena was now utterly silent. I could hear the whistle of the wind across the peaks, and very distant birdsong as the sky lightened to a paler blue.

He paused, taking a deep breath. "Even so, thanks to their sacrifices...we won. Now here we are."

His volume rose, and he lifted his right hand with it. "Let this Tournament remind us this time, more than ever...that *WE ARE ALIVE.*"

Ben clenched his fist and thundered those three words across the arena—and summoned, as if by magic, an uproar greater than all the others. Nearly every draká roared and amá stood up and clapped and cheered and hollered.

Now, as he smiled thinly at them all, Ben looked like himself again...and that was a good thing. I had tried explaining to him so many times that he didn't need to be his father, that he was meant for a different era. Now I finally could put into words why I was right.

Ben was like *them*: born from sacrifice, raised in ever-increasing danger, shaped by the disciplined use of power, and nearly smothered by sorrow—but despite all odds, coming out of it alive and building an ever-greater determination to hope and to laugh and to *live*. Until that zeal for life became a blaze that could not be put out.

That was something that Kavarian, who had ruled in a golden age of peace over them, could never have offered them. Just as the sun set and rose each day in the cycle of life, the old King's death had been at the natural sunset of his era...and the natural dawn of the new.

My eyes stung and my throat tightened as I gazed up at the new King. At *my* sun.

Then, to my surprise, he looked at me. His smile deepened, his golden eyes beginning to glow.

"And we are not just alive. Our greatest act of defiance to the Devourer wasn't at the Battle of the Solstice—it has been every day we have thwarted it since. Every day that we have, once again, begun to thrive. That victory is in no small part thanks to the woman beside me. Her, and her clan, two representatives of which are just behind her. Which leads me to the second reason you are all here...."

He looked back at the audience with a grin. "I don't know if you've heard yet, but I'm going to marry her."

A round of chuckles broke out. My face grew hot. I didn't know whether to be intoxicated by this new Ben that could charm a crowd or infuriated with him because he was using me to do it.

And he wasn't done. He raised his hand, palm up, to me, expression triumphant.

"And so, I formally present to you Sarah Moontouched, White Queen of the Seventh Realm and chosen of the Tree of Ice. My betrothed...and your future Queen."

Another outbreak of cheers, this one surprisingly strong—one of the more boisterous. Particularly, I noted, in the blue-bedecked Starkissed section, but still strong and consistent elsewhere. I felt a hundred things at once: touched and skeptical, flustered and proud, like I wanted to soar and like I wanted to hide under a rock and not come out for the next century.

When the cheers petered out, Ben grinned at them again. "By now I have hopefully satisfied your need for a speech, so I'll close with just this one last thing. It has come to my attention that some of you think I am marrying Sarah for political reasons. I could see why you would think that, since the advantages for us all are uncountable. But...you couldn't be more wrong."

Another round of chuckles.

Ben.... I said uneasily. I didn't know where this was going, but I was certain I didn't like it.

He didn't answer me. Instead, he pressed on to the finish.

"In fact, allow me to prove just how wrong you are with a simple demonstration."

Before I could react, he turned to me. As he cupped the back of my neck and ducked in, he sent, *Kill me later, in private, alright?*

Then he kissed me.

In front of all the Realms.

All *Seven* Realms, if you counted my brother and my *father*.

It wasn't a peck, either. It was a full, passionate kiss that had his fingers digging into my hair and his tongue questing against my lips, with no sign of stopping anytime soon.

Almost the moment our lips touched, a deafening cacophony of cheers and roars broke out, louder and more boisterous than any of the others. It went on and on as the kiss did as well, moment after heart-stopping moment.

The cheers somehow swelled even further as Ben scooped me up and into his arms and crushed me into him.

I...am going...to kill you, I told him savagely.

But I was almost as furious with myself as with him that I couldn't seem to break away. Or stop giving as good as I got. After all, nothing was *making* me wrap my arms and legs around him, or forcing me to dig my fingers into his golden hair.

I know, he said, not slowing down. *Why do you think I was so nervous?*

Because you hate crowds! And speeches!

Well, that too. So, the usual, plus certain death. But worth it for this part, I think.

You are a very strange man.

He finally broke away, panting through his grin, eyes glowing. *Oh, I don't know. I think I'm simply...a man.*

Chapter Seven

MOTIVE

Sarah

BEN WASN'T AS WILLING to consign himself to his fate as he made it sound. Even before the opening ceremony was over, he slipped away with Yvera, ostensibly to get into position for the first event and cheerfully abandoning me to wait out the rest of the ceremony while standing at the back of the balcony.

I had to keep a neutral face for the crowds, but I sent after him with as much force as I could muster with my inner voice, *I know what you're doing, Koriben Sunfilled! And I'm telling you, it's not going to work!*

He pretended not to hear me, not looking back as he and Yvera disappeared through the arch.

About a quarter hour later, the ceremony ended with a dramatic flyover from a wing of the Warflight, led by Yvera flying point with Ben at the center. I had to admit to myself that they were an impressive sight, performing more remarkable aerobatics than I had ever seen human planes manage. I could never tire of watching Ben fly, not when he was at his most glorious.

Even when I was determined to be mad at him.

Finally, the ceremony was over, and Kor led Dad, Michael, and me away to take our seats in one of the private boxes. Meanwhile, another group came out onto the arena floor and performed a fast-paced, drum-accompanied dance while wielding one or sometimes even two flags. They were so mesmerizing that I stumbled on my way to my seat while watching them.

Kor led Dad and Michael to their respective seats on either side of me and then stood next to Dad for the moment, but I presumed from the three seats left vacant on the other side of Michael, those were for him, Ben, and Yvera. Kor and Dad conversed for a bit, and Michael watched with poorly concealed interest.

"Man," he muttered to me after they finished the first dance and began setting up for the next. "These guys are *good*."

"I'm so glad you think so, Rightwing Michael," Kor said, settling into his seat on my brother's other side. "Do you have any experience with banner dancing? Particularly as a martial sport?"

Michael started, perhaps from the fact that Kor had somehow heard him or simply from the shock that Kor had addressed him at all.

"Not personally. I was on the honor guard in college and high school, not color guard."

"Ah, those are your secondary and tertiary levels of education, yes?"

I blinked at that. I was keeping my eyes on the dancers to not disturb the next stage of Kor's plan for winning over my brother, but I was listening closely. So, that detail coming from Kor surprised me. I didn't think I had ever explained our school system to him. But, then again, Kor absorbed and then utilized knowledge like a sponge.

A sponge soaked in nitroglycerin.

"Uh...." Michael said uncertainly. "If you lump middle school and elementary together, I guess."

"We divide our schooling into three segments, on average. Primary is for eight to twelve summers, secondary is for twelve to sixteen, and tertiary is for sixteen to twenty."

"Wait, you start school at eight?"

Kor shrugged. "It's the age that scholars and healers have determined leads to the best long-term educational outcomes. The children have better executive functioning and learn more effectively. Childcare or even schooling can certainly be provided at an earlier age, though, depending on the child's interest or the family's situation."

"Huh," Michael said. I thought he would begin tuning Kor out at this point, but to my surprise, he seemed thoughtful.

Then again, he was the father of a one-year-old, and his wife was a teacher....

"Are there different focuses for the different levels?" Michael asked.

"Certainly. Primary lays the academic groundwork in all the general areas; it's a time for intensive learning and exploration. In secondary, the students begin to specialize, with about two-thirds of their curriculum general and a third their choice. But that is also the age at which we become drakón or not, so that general curriculum is determined by one's Blood manifestation. Drakón, as our greatest warriors and magic workers, have a lot more physical education and magic classes."

"Are they separated from the others?" Michael asked intently.

Kor shook his head and said, "No, and that's deliberate. They must have some classes in common with amón, and they are highly encouraged to socialize and collaborate with them. It helps that only about one in four dramá become drakón."

"Yeah," Michael said. "You can *say* that's how it's supposed to work in theory, but how does it work in practice?"

Kor raised an eyebrow. "We take *blood oaths* when we become drakón. Oaths to protect and help, and not take advantage, of those weaker than us. So, effectively enough that only a few find a way around those oaths—and those cases are taken seriously. And publicly. To be known as an amón-abuser is one of the blackest marks on a drakón's honor possible."

"Huh. So...the social pressure is generally effective?"

"Yes. Trust me, the more troublesome drakón youth save their energy for each other."

I couldn't help but glance to the side at the bitterness in Kor's last words, so I looked in time to see his sapphire eyes soulflare for a moment. I felt a chill of sympathy. Apparently, the greatest danger in school wasn't to be an amón: it was to be the smallest and weakest of the drakón.

As Kor had been, until he became the Tolsyon heir. No wonder he had stuck to his brother so closely.... Almost worshipped him, according to Yvera. When

Kor came to Crownhold for his tertiary, Solim was perhaps the only protection Kor had.

And no wonder Ben's choice of Kor as leftwing instead of Solim had terrified Kor so much. On top of the usual pressures, Kor knew that he would lose his brother's protection. Eventually, when Solim plotted to kill Ben in revenge, Kor lost his brother altogether.

I liked to think that Ben then became Kor's protector—if Kor still needed one, being as powerful and untouchable as he was as the Tolsyon heir. But being sometimes unable to use his powers without being discovered, and being so mentally unprepared to stand on his own, he had probably needed Ben for at least a while. More than he had ever admitted to me.

Michael inclined his head toward Kor; I couldn't see my brother's expression well because his head was tilted away from me, but his leaning in showed he sensed there was more to Kor's words as well.

Kor continued coolly before Michael could ask about it, even if Michael had been intending to, which I doubted. They were both male, after all, and I had noticed that males tended to not talk about weaknesses with each other—especially in public.

"By tertiary, they either choose to continue academics, and the ratio of general-to-specialized is flipped, or they enter a trade apprenticeship. Either way, they are expected to be focused on learning their chosen profession. Quaternary is optional, and only recommended for highly specialized trades, such as scholarship or extended artisan apprenticeships. Or even a second apprenticeship for a multidisciplinary skill set."

"And then...what age are they done again?"

"With tertiary? At twenty."

I remembered that. Once, when we were both talking about school, Ben was surprised to hear that I was still expected to attend four more years. He said he had graduated from tertiary at my age, but then he admitted that was two years early. At the time, I hadn't understood what the rush was—he sounded so exhausted just talking about it.

Now...I wondered if his father's fading flameheart had been the reason; Ben needed to be ready to take over at almost any point. Plus, an active Heir had been desperately needed, given the rising levels of consumed. The dramá couldn't afford to have Ben cloistered in school. So, instead of cheating him of that education, they pushed him harder.

I wasn't sure which would have been better for him, so I wasn't about to judge—especially since Ben had sounded complicit, and surely Avva had been involved in the decision too. But I wondered...and became a bit more anxious about my own child's future.

How quickly a person's thoughts could change, seeing every aspect of life with a whole new set of worries and considerations.

I could understand now why Michael was interested.

Kor continued, "With quaternary, at any year after, but usually no later than twenty-four."

"Huh. And is it all paid for?"

"What do you mean by that, exactly?"

"I mean, is it publicly funded, or does the family have to pay, and if they can't pay, the kid has to drop out?"

"Ah, I see. Well, it's a bit of both. The Tree has declared education as a basic right and public good, so primary and secondary are publicly funded. At tertiary, the families are assessed each year on what they can afford to pay; if that's nothing, the guild or school they choose to join pays instead, with an agreement to teach or use their knowledge in underserved locations for a certain number of years in repayment. Apprenticeships also come with an agreement: the child's labor for training, and for food and lodging if necessary."

"And that works?" Michael asked curiously.

Kor shrugged. "Generally, yes. In some places, better than others. Administration and funding are at the Realm level, so there are variations. Remote holds sometimes struggle to find good teachers or even enough peers. But the Crown funds the largest and arguably the best school at Crownhold, which is available to all and free even through tertiary, and it provides food and lodging starting then. Consequently, children from remote holds often get sent there."

Michael grunted. "That sounds like a recipe for trouble."

"It basically sounds like a boarding school," I said, putting my two cents in before I remembered I was supposed to be ignoring them. "And started at a later age than most."

"Yeah. But those still have their own problems. And send a bunch of country kids to the city? On their own?"

"The children are encouraged to stay with family—if not in Crownhold, then in a hold with a sungate so that they may travel into Crownhold every school day. But you'd be surprised how often extended families make certain at least one trustworthy branch settles in Crownhold, precisely so they can provide a home for the children of extended family to come to. They're called hearthers. If no family hearthers are available, the child is matched with a thoroughly vetted volunteer family."

"Huh. So, more like an exchange program." At Kor's questioning look, Michael explained, "When students from other countries stay with host families in that country."

"Yes, that sounds similar...."

Kor paused for a moment. "Besides the protection of family, the Crownhold Academy is one of the most heavily guarded places in all the Six Realms. We wouldn't allow such a concentration of children there otherwise. They are our most precious resource."

When Michael gave me a look that said, *He's full of it, right?*, I said, "There's likely something to that. They can't have as many children as we can."

Michael paused. "Really? How many?"

"Our average fertility rate is two," Kor said. "You can see why that would be slightly concerning—even during the safest of times."

Michael sat back, looking more thoughtful. "I guess...that would be. And...I guess it makes some of the other things you said sound a bit more realistic, too. Hmm. So, this academy is protected?"

"It's a separate wing entirely, and comings and goings are carefully monitored. Teachers are also held to the highest standards of conduct." Kor smiled. "Trust me, I wouldn't have gone there if it hadn't been one of the best possible schools, and *the* best for my particular interest. And my *mother* wouldn't have allowed me to come unless she had reason to suppose I would be safe."

As safe as a small, sixteen-year-old drakón could be in school. I imagined Kor wouldn't have been better off in another one—outside of Oshal and the prestige his family held there, at least.

"Interesting," Michael said.

That had brought us to the end of the second dance. My brother sat forward at once when he realized the next segment would be using swords, and I think he became oblivious to everything else. Still, he had been engaged far longer than I would have expected. He must have been taking the information personally.

You brought up education on purpose, didn't you? I sent to Kor.

With Michael safely occupied, Kor smirked. *He has a nestling of his own. It was natural to conclude that one of his greatest concerns would be about his son's future—and thus would be one of his greatest sources of resentment toward his current situation.*

I once again had to inwardly shake my head at Kor's uncanny grasp of human nature. If I didn't know better, I would have thought that he had someone on the inside. But that was ridiculous. We weren't a big enough clan for Ben's counselor-spymaster to have *informants* among us.... Right?

Idly, Kor went on. *I don't think I necessarily convinced him to send Tommie to the Academy. But I showed him he has options. And I showed him we are not uncouth barbarians who take little thought for our children's intellectual development.*

Kor eyed the sword dancing. *Despite the Tournament's evidence to the contrary.*

Oh, trust me, Michael doesn't mind this *display of education one bit,* I said dryly. I changed to a serious tone. *Besides, there are many types of intelligence, Kor.*

I inclined my head subtly toward the impressive display of strength, agility, and focus. *This is one of them.*

Oh, I know, Kor said with another smile as he kept his eyes on the dancers. *Speaking of intelligence, though...you haven't told me what you think of Ben's own "performance."* Or asked me a single question about his motives. I'm surprised at you.

I stiffened. *That's on purpose. I know what you two are doing. Or at least what Ben is. He's hoping I won't be able to hold a grudge long enough to get him alone to kill him. Especially not with you around to explain everything for him like you usually do.*

Kor's smile widened. *I have no idea what you mean.*

I rolled my eyes. *So, no, I'm not going to ask you anything.*

Nothing?

Nope. I don't want to hear your explanation. I'm going to let my anger simmer for as long as I can, thank you very much. Especially since you just want a chance to brag about how brilliant you are. Don't think I don't know you were behind everything.

Pity. Because I was going to be singing Ben's *praises, for once. That was all him, just so you know. He showed a true stroke of political genius, both in planning and in execution, and he won't do himself justice explaining himself to you.*

I hesitated.

Fidgeted.

Then finally blurted, *That wasn't your idea? At all?*

Not a bit.

Kor said nothing more, letting his bait continue to dangle.

I held out for about five seconds.

Alright, fine, I growled. If I didn't have eyes on me, I would have folded my arms petulantly. *Spill.*

You are sure *you don't want to—*

Kor.

Very well. He had a laugh in his inner voice. *Like I said, that was all Ben. He wrote his speech himself, only giving it to me after for feedback, and I only made some minor comments.*

Kor's tone turned dry. *Most of which he rejected.*

I couldn't help a slight snort and smile at that. Dad glanced at me, but fortunately, Michael was still too absorbed.

The kiss was also his idea, although I will admit, I brought the problem he needed to address to his attention. But all I did was give him information. He decided when and how to address it. He didn't even tell me that was what he was going to do; he had quite a different, more formal ending to the speech he gave me. So, I was nearly as surprised as you were.

Somehow, I doubt that, I said dryly.

Oh, I was shocked, let me tell you, Kor said, grinning. *I would never have thought he would have had the gall. But I am an extraordinarily pleased leftwing today. Perhaps there's hope for him, after all.*

Yes, yes. But you still haven't explained why.

Ben said so himself, to everyone. Kor's inner voice sobered. *It was because of those rumors he mentioned, although he's not nearly so blasé about them as he pretended. Those rumors are dangerous, Sarah. Especially to you. Ben knows that. And they are strongest here, on Ekrel.*

I felt a sobering chill. *What?*

The most dangerous faction of the Traditionalists is here. Strongshield have their own sizable contingent, but they are far too dutiful and order-loving to make much trouble.

Unlike the Battleblood, I said heavily.

Indeed. And added to that mix, segments of the Battleblood across the political spectrum always held out hope that Ben would eventually choose Yvera as his consort—and that includes our fine Lady over there.

Kor inclined his head to the box directly across from us, where Lady Yalda and her entourage sat. Why we were spaced so far apart, I didn't know. Perhaps it was so that we could more easily glare at each other, as I just noticed Yalda seemed to be doing now.

Then the last piece in her behavior toward me clicked into place.

What? I said, blinking. Trying to keep my face neutral and pretend I hadn't seen her. *She honestly thought he would have....*

You and I both know Ben would never have chosen Yvera, Kor said. *As does anyone who knows the two of them—enough to know what a poor consort she would make, even if Ben were interested. But not everyone knows them like that. Or, in*

Yalda's case, even cares. All that most of the Battleblood clan knew or cared about was that Yvera was their best chance to share the Crown in six generations.

Really? I said, disturbed. *That long?*

Really, Kor said dryly. *Even the* Sunfilled *have produced a Royal consort since the last Battleblood one. Now, that was a controversial marriage, let me tell you.... Actually, no, sorry. Don't let me get sidetracked.*

I smiled thinly. Whatever front he might put on, whatever sacrifices of his very self he might make, Kor was always a historian at heart.

Kor's dry tone was back. *In any case, you can guess why the Battleblood aren't often thought to be* consort *material, though they've had much more than their fair share of rightwing and prominent Warflight positions, so the Crown has tried to soothe them by reminding them of that. But Yvera gave them hope for more, and you can see why. After all, Yvera and Ben have been inseparable since they were hatchlings, and Ben never showed romantic interest in anyone. Add that to Yvera's infamous interest, and well...the facts that the average person would know all seemed to add up to Yvera becoming his consort one day.*

I see, I said heavily.

Then you can imagine what kind of blow it was to the Battleblood when rumors began circulating about Ben's sudden interest in this new young amón woman, one who was potentially a Moontouched Earthren. Many Battleblood refused to believe Ben could be genuinely attached, that he could "abandon" Yvera after all this time. And so, perhaps even before the Moonfair, counter rumors began.

About how Ben's motives must *be political,* I said with a heavy iceheart. I was glad I hadn't heard those rumors before I knew Ben loved me...or I might have believed them.

Exactly, Kor said grimly. *They have only gotten stronger and more dangerous ever since. Some of them paint Ben as a martyr, forced to deny his feelings for Yvera and bow to the political consensus. Others say he is a conniving showman, orchestrating a massive lie to deceive the entire Realms—with, of course, my help.*

Unfortunately, there was something to that. Ben's feelings for me weren't a lie, but Kor, Eskala, their staff, and even King Kavarian took full advantage of his genuine feelings to skillfully weave a romantic narrative to help smooth my and my clan's readmission to the Six Realms. Sophisticated political maneuvering was a double-edged sword...and now we were feeling the other edge.

I didn't blame anyone for not believing our love story. Heck, if I hadn't lived through it myself, I wouldn't have either. I knew for certain that if I'd been a common dramá, perhaps one of the thousands sitting in these stands, and heard some pretty tale about our new King of Flame falling head over heels for the new Queen of Ice, I would have thought it too fanciful to be believed.

At least...until I saw that kiss.

Kor went on. *Those are* political *dangers, targeted at Ben's integrity, and at the integrity of the entire Crown. But Eskala and I expected them, and we're handling them. Right now, they're manageable. In this case, Ben's reputation as a guileless, well-meaning dimtorch who can't act to save his life...is actually saving us. Too many people know Ben enough or have heard of him enough to believe he could abruptly turn into a skillful deceiver. The greatest danger, then, is not to us.... It's to you.*

Ah, I said quietly, finally seeing the catalyst that had made Ben act.

And it's a real danger, Sarah, Kor said quietly, a darker edge entering his voice. His elbows rested on his armrests and fingers interlocked in front of him as he gazed down at the arena floor, examining the performers as if they were chess pieces.

It is not just political, he continued. *There is a dangerous consensus growing in the hardest contingents of the Traditionalist faction that the Tree never meant the Moontouched to return. That you have no place among us any longer. You have your own Realm, of which you are Queen, and there you should stay. Far from our affairs—much less our Golden Crown. They are, essentially, accusing you of invasion.*

Again, I could sympathize with that sentiment. Even *I* didn't understand why the Trees were insisting on creating two Monarchs and Seven Realms. And meanwhile, I was changing things—shaking their views of history, magic, and technology, sometimes to their foundations. I didn't mean to. Sometimes I didn't even want to. But I was.

And now, Kor said quietly, *principally among the Battleblood sect...there have been...threats.*

Oh? I said, unsurprised.

In a way, I had been bracing for this since I came here. Most of the dramá I had met had been so welcoming, I was overwhelmed. I always knew they couldn't represent the entire spectrum of opinion about me—even without Ben's hints that his people had their darker sides, too. I just knew that was the way some mortal minds worked.

I was too different, too new. Too frightening.

If only they could understand the irony.

Nothing concrete, Kor said, voice hard. *Nothing I can follow up with charges. Just vague "what ifs." "What if this new so-called Queen weren't in the picture any longer.... Then things could go back to the way they 'should' be."*

I felt a chill. The way he put it reminded me of how Yvera had described Solim's reasoning to Kor as he tried to get his younger brother to help him kill Ben.

I didn't think Kor's similar phrasing was a coincidence. His face was so controlled, it could have been carved from ice. Only the slightest glow of soulflare belied the fierceness beneath.

In a way, he said with a disturbing coolness, *you can see where they are getting the idea. After all, an assassination is what drove away the Moontouched the last time.*

I sighed, deeply enough that Dad glanced at me again. I just shook my head at him.

I'll tell you later, I sent to him hastily.

Then, to Kor, I said, *And how did Ben handle this information?*

Even before he knew me, Ben had felt needless yet severe ancestral guilt for the death of the last Moontouched Lady, Serona. Similar threats against me would set off more than one of his triggers.

Oh, he was as furious as you can imagine, Kor said. *But as you can see, he is "handling" it rather well.*

I assumed he meant the kiss, but before we got into how exactly they were connected, I wanted one question answered first.

Why didn't either of you tell me?

Because when these latest, most sobering threats began, you two had even bigger problems, Kor said grimly. *First, it was the rock wyrm incursion on Romskal, then the siege on Oshal. Even Ben put it out of his mind, knowing that he had to address the more immediate threats to you and his Realms first.*

I sighed again, acknowledging that made sense.

Besides, Kor said, *Oshal wasn't the place to address the rumors anyway; the Starkissed are your strongest supporters.*

A hint of grudging admiration entered Kor's voice. *But now I can see Ben thought about this more than I had realized, and, all by himself, hit upon perhaps the most effective way he could have addressed it.*

With a kiss? I said, feeling a bit of the heat—both from embarrassment and something else—return.

Oh, it wasn't just the kiss, Kor said, amusement at me mixing with that lingering admiration of Ben. *It was all of it. It was the timing: using such a public podium in the heart of Traditionalist territory, that they couldn't deny him, which he could use to speak before all the Realms.*

Perhaps *that* had been why Yalda had glared at Ben and me like that when we'd approached her on the balcony—and why Ben hadn't answered my surprisingly apropos statement. She *didn't* want us to be there. She only wanted her Tournament, and we were the only way she was going to get it in its proper glory. Yet she feared how Ben would use the opportunity she had to give him to undermine her cause.

And that was exactly what he did.

Kor wasn't finished. *It was also the speech itself, almost the execution more than the words: the way he used all their expectations of him...and at the same time, undermined them. He showed them he was still the genuine, simple young man they had heard of—but also that he wasn't a King to be trifled with, all the same. That he could both fight for them and understand them. Mourn and celebrate with them. He showed them he wasn't an Heir lingering under his father's shadow anymore, nor was he being manipulated by others. He was, well and truly, their* King.

So, my instincts about the importance of that speech had been close. All I had been missing was that undercurrent of danger—political for him, physical for me.

No wonder Ben was so nervous, I murmured.

So was I, Kor said. *I must admit, I had serious doubts that he could pull it off. This is Ben, after all. Or...it was. But perhaps I'm partly to blame. Perhaps it's precisely my low expectations of him that have held him back. Perhaps he has been capable for a while now of more than any of us realized—even him.*

I always knew he had it in him, I said with a soft smile. *If only he gave himself the chance.*

Yes, well, Kor said dryly. *I presume there was some reason you became so fond of him, and he of you. After all, you're the one who gave him that final push to try—and the nerve to follow through, to the very end.*

About the end in particular....

That sealed it all, Kor said with a chuckle in his voice. *So, before you ask, yes—it was necessary, and torched brilliant. Because of its rawness, its simplicity. Because it was so undeniably him. Ben knew he had to prove, as much as was mortally possible, before all the Realms, that he not only chose you, he loved you. That he would not allow history to repeat itself. That whoever touched you would pay in blood tenfold. What better way could he have done that than to show them? In a way that showed joyful confidence to his allies...and a passionate warning to your enemies.*

Ben had said that it had all been worth it, for that kiss. Now I finally realized that he wasn't just talking about fleeting physical satisfaction.

It was worth claiming me in front of the entire Realms. It was worth the success he immediately saw for his sacrifice in the roaring crowds. It was worth the protection he could give me against a danger so nebulous he had few other options to fight it.

If that kiss saved me, it was worth it to him.

Even if I "killed" him for it.

So, of course, finally understanding that...I didn't want to. Not anymore.

As IF SUMMONED BY that conclusion, I felt his pull draw nearer only a few minutes later. Ben and Yvera came into the box and took their seats, Ben glancing nervously my way as he did.

A bit miffed at the unfairness of the universe, I let him sit in silence for a bit, pretending to watch the latest act with cold composure. Then, out of the corner of my eye, I saw Ben fidgeting, hands twisting in his lap, where the crowds hopefully couldn't see his emotional leakage. Yvera leaned over and whispered something to him, perhaps asking what was wrong.

That finally did it.

Not caring if this caused a stir among the onlookers, I stood, went to Ben, and said with a winning smile, "Care to take a quick walk with me, your majesty?"

Ben's eyes widened, the mocking royal style making him think he was well and truly in trouble, as I had intended. He glanced at Kor, as if pleading for reassurance, but Kor just looked back at Ben quizzically, showing no comprehension of what was wrong.

So, I had to forgive Kor for doing exactly what Ben had hoped he would, because Kor played along with me by pretending to Ben that he hadn't.

As Ben looked back at me, he sucked in a breath, then said with an unsteady smile, "Of course."

He stood and took my hand, holding it in an unusually ginger grip as the two of us stepped outside of the box. Guards waited outside, looking at us curiously as we exited.

Four, I noted to myself. Two on each side of the doorway. Two of his and two of mine.

Probably Ben was just making a statement. Maybe.

This way, Ben said in a resigned tone, leading me down a cross hall. *If you're looking for privacy, that is.*

I am, I said archly. Glad he didn't specify for what.

Within a few moments, he led me into what looked like an exclusive refreshment room, judging from the chairs, cushions, and food bar, and he closed the door behind him.

"Sarah," he said immediately, holding up a hand. "I know you're mad, and I know it doesn't make any sense now, but I swear, I did what I—"

"Kneel," I said, pointing to the floor.

"What?" Ben said blankly.

"Kneel," I repeated, pointing again.

This wasn't to intimidate him. If I could have done what I had planned without making him grovel, I would have. He'd done enough groveling for trying to save my life.

Not for the first time, I cursed the difference in our heights. If there was one thing I sorely envied Yvera for, it was that she was so much more his physical match than I was.

Closing his eyes for a moment, Ben kneeled on one knee. Opening them again, he said, "Sarah—"

I cut him off by grabbing his face and pressing my lips to his.

Seemed only fair to return the favor.

Ben froze, but only for a split second. Otherwise, he didn't protest the change in communication methods. He wrapped his arms around me and kissed me back, nearly as intensely but with a slower, deeper heat than he had before.

I knew what that meant: again, this was a statement more eloquent than he could manage with words—and we were discovering an untapped potential there. Except this time, this statement was just for me. It was a heartfelt apology.

He *knew* how much I hated public displays of affection, and that had been the one to top them all. He knew how furious it would make me, potentially more so than I had ever been with him before. And yet, despite all his fears, he had done it anyway.

For me.

Sometimes that was the greater kind of love: not keeping the peace, but doing what *had* to be done, no matter the potential fallout.

And he was right: it had to be done.

So, when we broke apart, panting, I kissed his forehead and gasped, "Thank you."

"For what?" he said breathlessly, blinking.

I smiled. "For loving me enough to let yourself be glorious."

He stared at me for a few moments.

Then, as understanding dawned, his face tensed with fury, and his grip on me reflexively tightened. "That torched *asher*! Kor said.... But he told you everything after all, didn't he?"

I laughed. "He did. And I had forgiven you even before you arrived."

"I'm going to kill him," Ben swore. "I mean it this time. I'm going to put his name on the dueling roster next to mine, and I'm finally going to kill him. Tomorrow. In front of everyone."

Never mind that *I* was the one who had tortured him with the tense wait for a resolution. Maybe Ben thought that was only my fair due.

"That would be a shame. Seeing as he did just save your life—from me."

"That—" Ben cut himself off and just fumed.

I laughed again and pressed my lips to his, curious to see what that fury would taste like. I found it much to my liking.

How long do you think we can stay away? I asked, stepping into him again.

Ben groaned against my lips, even as his hand re-knotted in my hair. *Not much longer.*

Oh well. Let's make the most of it.

Chapter Eight

MEANS

Koriben

The rest of my day was much more pleasant, if a bit dull, since I was expected to sit out the rest of it. But with the way my life had gone for these past few sevendays, I would gladly take a heaping cartload of dull.

With Sarah's anger behind me, I finally could relax and enjoy the performances, which were in large part for my benefit. After all, even these art forms were all part of our battle training and conditioning, and I was their highest martial leader. The first day of the Tournament was almost like a large, elaborate, celebratory parade review. A warm-up, if you will: no stakes, no prizes, just showing off.

Although, to be honest, *every* day of the Tournament was about showing off.

Which was why I was looking forward to tomorrow more than I was going to admit to anyone. If Sarah hadn't forgiven me by then, I had been hoping tomorrow would finally soften her up. Now, though, I could just look forward to the competitions and some chances to impress her. Flame knew I'd had torched few of those. Fate had too often conspired to display me in the worst possible light in front of her. Why Sarah had chosen me anyway, I would never know, but tomorrow, I hoped to fix some of that.

Right now, I could spend the time with her. To no one's surprise but mine, Sarah requested a seating reshuffle when we got back to our box. Not even Kor put up more than a token protest at the ruined order of things, and I think even that was fake. Sarah, seeming to sense the same, ignored him and plopped herself down in the seat next to me, and in that moment, I couldn't have been happier.

Probably just the release of all that adrenaline.

Flame, how glad I was that speech was over. I wouldn't have thought it possible, but that had been worse than the *Moonfair*. At least in the pageant, I didn't have to speak, my actions were predetermined, and I could (and always did) do poorly, and there were no consequences except some laughs at my expense.

This time, I had to not just speak, I had to decide what to say, then memorize and *remember* it. Then I had to perform it perfectly, the entire time, or it would all fall apart. And if it fell apart...Sarah could pay the price.

I could not remember having felt so terrified in my entire life. Only Sarah's heartbeat had calmed me beforehand, reminding me of all the reasons I was doing this. Only Avva's strength and Sarah's support helped me follow through to the end, even giving me the courage to follow my instincts. I had woken up that dark morning with the vague and vanishing dream of the Tree speaking to me. I knew then that I had to change the end and how, but until that last moment, I hadn't thought I would be able to.

But when I had looked down at Sarah, her eyes shining with joyful tears, I knew it was the right thing to do. For her. Even though, ironically, she would be furious at me for it.

There would have been no possible way I could have described to them how I felt about her. Not just because I didn't have the words, but because even if I did, I was certain I wouldn't be able to form them. So, as poor a substitute as that kiss was, it still had seemed sufficient to make my point.

I knew that for certain when everyone settled down again after Sarah and I got back and Kor silently spoke to just me, out of the blue.

Well done, Ben. Well done.

I glanced at him in surprise from where he now sat on the other side of Sarah and her father. He wasn't looking at me and didn't turn even then, but there was a satisfied smile on his face that I knew had nothing to do with the acrobatics display below.

Good reports coming in? I asked cautiously, not sure how to handle a complimentary Kor. It was like approaching a ferocious, cunning rijer who had suddenly turned sweetly docile.

Oh, yes, Kor said with relish, and nothing more.

I left it at that.

Besides, I still wanted to kill him, just a little bit. Partly *because* I was constantly owing him for things like this. It aggravated me to no end that I had him to thank for my relationship with Sarah, for so many more reasons than just today. His help—deliberate or unconscious, enthusiastic or grudging—in bringing and keeping us together was one of the cruelest ironies of my life.

THE NEXT DAY DAWNED bright and clear, and I couldn't remember being more eager for a Tournament. I'd always looked forward to them, but this one would be special. I could feel it. Sarah noticed my happier form of restlessness as we waited for the next opening ceremony to start—one that would be much briefer and require nothing from us but our presence, thank Flame.

Yalda was doubtless just as relieved as I was about that. No doubt furious with me, she had been even more frigid than usual at the feast last night, which put a damper on the atmosphere at the high table. At least the rest of the hall seemed to have a good time, loosening up and getting more boisterous as Battleblood always did the more the drinks kept coming.

Yvera, funnily enough, had adopted my custom of sobriety, even though she went through a brief period when she came of age in which she'd drunk with the best of them. Now, though, she had only one glass of light wine, and she spent much of the evening looking over her drunken kin with expressions ranging from fond exasperation to derision.

You see? Yvera said to me at one point, gesturing with her glass. *This is why I don't drink. A deken ago, they were capable warriors. Now, they're gibbering idiots. If a bolkoth charged down the hall right now, they would be dead.*

That's what the others on duty are for, Yv, I said in amusement, glancing at the guards scattered around the edges and occasionally walking down the aisles.

Doesn't matter, Yvera said with a sniff. *Some would die who otherwise wouldn't have, and they would only have their own torched idiocy to blame.*

I smiled at the memory as I rocked back and forth on my heels while Sarah and I waited.

What's up with you? Sarah asked in amusement, drawing me back to the present.

A fair question, since I was having almost as hard of a time standing still as yesterday morning, except this time for entirely different reasons.

Just excited, I said.

For what?

Before I could answer, we got our cue, and Sarah didn't press the issue once we were resettled out in the open on the balcony.

At *last,* the dawn ceremony was over, Sarah and I were free, and Yvera came up to me, a fierce grin on her face and a light in her eyes.

"Ready for me to crush you into the dirt?" she said.

"You can try," I answered with a grin. "Let's go."

"Have fun...I guess?" Sarah said, looking at me uncertainly. "Is that the right thing to say?"

I laughed. "That works."

I grabbed her chin and kissed her hastily. I wanted to linger longer, certain that the taste of her was bringing me luck, but I could feel Yvera's impatience, piling on top of my own. Besides, we would be the last ones down there. We had to get with our teams and get things moving.

I pulled away with a rueful smile, then I turned and followed Yvera at a fast walk that was almost a jog by the time we got clear of the ceremony attendees.

A half-deken later, I was striding out one of the enormous arches on the arena floor, with Petra as my rightwing. No surprises to anyone there, with Yvera having claimed Ordran, the captain of my elites. Petra was the captain of Sarah's, so it was a sound choice from both a strategic and political point of view.

It was my choice of leftwing that sent a gasp around the arena.

Jake strode calmly at my side, dressed in the strange but beautiful Moon-touched armor, looking as if he had done this ever since he was a twelve-summer, too.

And across the arena, Michael walked out beside Yvera.

This only would have worked if there were a Moontouched on each side. Otherwise, Yvera and everyone else could justly have said I cheated. All was fair in battle, so long as one stuck close enough to a moral code to not lose one's soul. But *games*—games had the strictest moral codes of all. So, from the beginnings of my plan, I knew I needed Yvera's buy-in to include Sarah's father and brother.

She agreed surprisingly quickly when I brought up the idea with her. I thought I would have to wear her down for days, which was why I began as soon as I had the headspace to spare for what was coming. But to my surprise, she grasped the game-changing implications at once, even if she couldn't care less about the political; perhaps it had been the lethally spectacular effect of the lightcannons during the siege of Rosin that had finally convinced her of the need to have the Moontouched on our side.

Then Yvera had, as I'd expected, promptly claimed Michael. Little did she know that had been part of my strategy all along. She would think Michael, sharing her title and the obvious warrior of the two, would be her surest path to victory. Now she couldn't claim any unfairness; there was a Moontouched on both of our teams, and she had had the first pick of them.

So, when Jake led *my* team to victory, she could have nothing to say about it.

Once I had Yvera's buy-in, I'd gone to Sarah. After all, these were her wings and her clan. Though she'd been the least of my concerns, and she proved me right by giving me her blessing at once.

"For what it's worth," she said with a careless shrug. "It's their choice, after all."

She plainly didn't see the importance of the game. I thought that seeing it in action would convince her otherwise, so I saved my breath for kissing her in thanks, then going to find her father and brother.

I discussed the game with Jake and Michael at length, making sure they were confident in their grasp of the rules and the conventional strategies before they made their decision. Michael was instantly all for it, his eyes lighting up with competitive fervor. As I'd expected, the thrill of the sport, and the opportunity to finally go up against me—to, using Yvera's words, "crush" me "into the dirt" himself—was all I'd needed to offer him.

Jake was thoughtful, thinking for long enough that he had his son twitching. Michael understood by then that he could only play if his father did, too, and he looked close to begging. In sharp contrast with the two rightwings, Jake only conceded at the end for the political benefits, which had made Michael throw up his hands in exasperation mingled with relief.

Then I'd sent Michael away to go talk with Yvera, while Jake and I began to strategize. I'd already had some idea of how to use him, but he had helped me refine the plan to perfection, as I'd hoped he would. For the first time, with Jake walking out into the arena by my side, I thought I had a real chance of beating my foster sister at her favorite game.

After seven years of losing to Yvera in front of everyone, oh how I wanted that victory.

Six others trailed behind the three of us, all of them my elites, but one from each of the clans. Across the arena from us, Yvera emerged with her own pick of wings—Michael and Ordran—and elites. It was considered only fitting that the Golden Crown start off the Tournament games, and only fair that they compete against each other.

Except every year before, Yvera's and my face-off had come after Avva's and Alyish's. Yvera and I had just been an afternote, a cooldown for the crowds before the rest of the games began. I hadn't minded; that had made it more fun, lessening the pressure and the sting of defeat. Now that *we* started off, and there wouldn't be an Heir's match to follow us, the stakes were completely different. Avva might have been able to occasionally lose to Alyish without losing face, but I knew that at this delicate stage of *my* reign, I needed that win.

And no way in hellwinds was I going to let Yvera beat me in front of Sarah.

In the center of the arena was our objective and the source of this game's name: a multicolored clutch of giant eggs, even the smallest one larger than my head. They were replicas of draká eggs, created with painstaking craftsmanship to be as exact as we knew how to make them from our records—on the outside. The *inside* of those eggs…was a different story.

The game was succinctly called "kesha," the Drona word for *clutch*.

The rules of kesha were equally simple. After all, the game had its psychological origins from millennia ago, back when draká were a much less civilized race than the kind that founded the dramá. They went through a phase a few thousand years ago in which most of them abandoned their Tree, regressing into a more bestial mentality and becoming prone to fighting amongst themselves.

Given that setting, this was an "abandoned" clutch, whether because of neglect or tragedy. Either way, it represented an opportunity for the other draká: whoever obtained these eggs could raise them as their own, thus adding strength to their clan without having paid the price in resources to create them.

There were only two problems: One, because the eggs had been abandoned, they wouldn't survive for much longer without a nester's heat. The bed of coals they were on wouldn't sustain them forever. The smaller the egg, the more swiftly it would die, but that meant it was worth more points.

Kor and intellectuals like him were always quick to point out that the last bit about "smaller equaling more valuable" didn't fit in with the survival-of-the-fittest mentality of the game's origins, but the rest of us ignored them. One time, I tried countering Kor by saying that was the entire point: we had risen above that mindset by valuing the weakest among us. Kor crushed my triumph at once by snorting with laughter and saying that, if we had become so civilized after all, why were we reenacting a clutch-battle?

Because it was a *battle*. The second problem was that our team wasn't the only one trying to obtain the eggs. Yvera's team had the same objective. There were only so many eggs, adding up to so many points. The winning team was the one to bring the most eggs alive back to their "nester area" (represented by a giant gold circle near our entrance arch, purple near Yvera's) and *keep* them there until all the eggs were gone from the original nest and into one of the others, bringing the end to the game.

Kor, unfortunately, was right, as he almost always was, torch him. What this game lacked in complexity, at least in terms of rules, it made up for in brutality.

There was a reason it was Yvera's favorite team sport.

We walked across the arena floor toward the clutch and each other. Yalda, in drakáform, stood over the clutch, representing the mother—but in reality to make certain both teams behaved themselves until the official start of the game. Otherwise, the arena floor was bare except for the occasional lump of volcanic rock, generally larger than I was, that had been flown in and dropped at random spots around the arena for a bit of cover and variety. It wasn't worth having any other kind of prop. After some matches between Avva and Alyish that I had seen, nothing had remained of even the rocks afterward except scorched, pulverized pebbles.

You know, I thought to myself, a bit too late. *Maybe I should have emphasized the dangers of kesha more to Sarah....*

I'd made them clear to Jake and Michael, while giving them my and Yvera's word that we would do everything in our power to shield them from the worst of it. Both had been strictly instructed to stay away from the main fight, and both our teams were told that they were not to engage directly with the Moon-touched under any circumstances.

Still, I hadn't told Sarah about either the extent of the risk or our precautions, and only now did I realize that might have been a big mistake....

Too late. Both teams reached their designated starting points—a line of dots, one for each of us to stand on, gold for my team, purple for Yvera's—about halfway between each of our nesters and the clutch at the center.

Yalda turned her draká head from Yvera to me, wordlessly asking for our readiness. I couldn't see Yvera across her, which was partly the point, but I nodded.

Then Yalda launched herself into the air in an awe-inspiring burst of power, wings sending waves of dust and rocky crumbles flying in all directions and a vibration through the ground. Now, with the mother having officially abandoned the clutch...the game began.

Predictably, Yvera shot forward. She was always one of the first runners, even though she was more suited to the striker role, which she settled into later. But in the beginning, she couldn't resist the thrill of the first race to the clutch, especially since she knew she was one of the fastest sprinters among us. I'd tried to use that predictability against her in the past but failed.

This time, I hoped for better.

As I raced forward to at least somewhat keep up with my runners, I couldn't help throwing a joke back to Jake.

Hope you're feeling rested.

With it being after dawn, we were going to need every drop of power Jake had left to win this.

He didn't answer, perhaps wisely conserving his energy for his first surge-jump. One second, he was behind me.

The next, he reappeared in a silver blur thirty feet in front of Yvera.

I had warned him that was the minimum amount of space he would need to give her time to halt.

Which she did, eyes going wide, sliding to a stop with one foot forward, body low and back, just feet away from Jake. Then he surged away a blink later.

But the damage was done. Yvera was now at least a hundred feet behind all the other runners, when her team had no doubt counted on her to score a high-point egg before almost anyone else.

You asher! Yvera mentally shouted at me in a rage. I could see her eyes glowing with violet fury even from this distance.

It was a minor victory—by no means the end of the game for her—but it still was sweet.

My move had been a gamble, however. I knew how Yvera had *expected* me to use Jake, and how she would use Michael.

While Jake blocked Yvera, Michael surged straight to the clutch. He was wearing long, thick gloves, which someone must have handed to him at the last second, because he hadn't had them before—I'd checked. Fortunately for me, I seemed to be right that he couldn't safely reach the most valuable egg, even by jump-surging, since that was in the center of the clutch, across the burning sea of coals. Perhaps if it had been night, and he would have had enough energy to sustain flight, *and* if he'd been able to bear the waves of heat that would have surrounded him from all sides as he lowered toward it, he *might* have been able to grab that egg. Not, it seemed, after dawn.

Yvera would have warned him of that. So, he did as she had no doubt instructed him to do and grabbed the smallest one he could reach at the edge of the clutch—which also had the advantage of being the lightest and safest for him to carry.

As it was, I saw him cringe from the heat and stagger from the weight of that emerald egg, especially from how he was forced to hold the burning-hot object away from his body. His armor would shelter him somewhat—Sarah and now Jake had both told me it helped cool them to a greater degree than any of our spellweave creations had so far replicated for Sarah—but he wouldn't want to risk his armor's integrity by clasping the egg to his chest, as would have been the easiest hold for him.

We still didn't know how that clear, white-backed, diamond-hard Moon-touched armor was made, or even what it was made *of*; therefore, we didn't know what exactly it could withstand or how to fix it if damaged. When that armor could save his life one day, it wasn't worth the risk to weaken it for a game—even one as crucial to us both as this one.

I could see what it meant to him again as he spared precious seconds to glance up, find me, and smirk. Then he surged back and out of my sight, perhaps getting almost to his nester circle, for all I knew. That was confirmed a few moments later when a gong sounded from Yvera's side, indicating her team had successfully claimed an egg.

And in perhaps less than half a dek. That surely broke all records and torched them to ashes. Yvera had to be crowing with delight right now, swiftly getting over her pique as she thought she was on the sure path to victory.

Let her think that. I'd made my gamble, and I still stood by it. After all, I knew a quick victory for her at the beginning would also make her arrogant, especially when she had always beaten me before.

Besides, it wasn't enough for me to win. I had to win *thrillingly*. I had to keep my people on the edge of their seats as I proved to them I could beat all odds. I had to give them a *good* game, and that wouldn't happen if I crushed Yvera one round after the other. Then the ending would almost be anticlimactic—hardly even worth staying to the end to see.

No, this had to be close. This had to gradually escalate, one move right after the other until I snatched the victory at the very last second—so that, looking back, when everyone connected the dots, my victory had seemed inevitable, but in the moment, had been anything but.

This had to be *good*.

Of course, philosophizing could only give me so much emotional immunity from her quick win. That still stung, as did the roars of approval for Yvera's team. Luckily, I was also spared whatever look of triumph she was throwing at me by my need to focus on the skirmish that was about to take place as both teams' runners reached the clutch.

There were four primary roles in kesha, not because of a rule (of which, as I said, there were very few) but by pure necessity: runners, strikers, guardians, and nesters.

A runner's sole job was to run for the clutch, grab an egg, run back to the nester, and repeat—for as long as they could put one foot in front of the other...or avoid the strikers. That meant runners were our fastest, most agile warriors with the greatest endurance.

Strikers, as the name implied, tried to stop them—by any means necessary short of intentionally inflicting harm (rule). So that meant pushing, tackling, knocking the egg away from them, or, traditionally, striking.

Strikers carried wooden practice swords that had been coated in enchanted paint that would leave streaks on our armor: purple streaks for Yvera's team, gold for mine. Tackling was alright in a pinch, but the better strategy was for a striker to deal enough "damage" to the runner that a referee would call them out for a healing period—the time it took for the streaks to disappear—or because the runner was determined to be killed outright, in which case, they were out of the game for good.

Technically, we *all* had been given those swords (rule), but as the roles had settled in over the centuries, the runners had stopped carrying them in favor of having their hands free to grab an egg and not limiting their speed or mobility as they ran. Now, a runner only drew their sword as a last resort.

That meant the runners entrusted their safety almost entirely to the guardians. At this point, the guardian's role was self-explanatory.

Equally obvious: I was a guardian.

Oh, I could have made a decent striker. I was a middling runner, as strikers often were (Yvera being an exception), which meant I could have intercepted runners well enough, and with the force I could bring to bear, I knew I'd be an unstoppable opponent, striking out runners right and left. That was the problem. Even in a game, even in *kesha*, when I became perhaps the most ferocious I ever did except in a duel, I couldn't do it. I just knew that if I let myself get into that kind of mindset, I would break people, without even trying to, so I wouldn't do it. Other people knew it too, so no one had tried pushing me into the role.

Besides, not only had guardian been Avva's preferred role, and thus was traditional for the Golden Monarch by now, I had his build for it. As I'd said, I was a decent runner (meaning in the general sense); I could outstrip a champion amón and even most noncombatant drakón, but I was in the middle of the herd among our drakón elites. I simply wasn't built for speed. I was built for power, both physical and magical—and that combination made me the perfect guardian.

This moment, when all the runners reached the clutch, with the strikers not far behind, was one of the ugliest of kesha and one I had specifically warned Jake and Michael to stay far away from. This was when everything could fall apart for my team.

It was my job to see that it didn't.

So, I held back, only keeping up with the runners and strikers as much as was necessary for me to see what was going on and be there to help, but keeping enough distance so I wouldn't be tangled in the fray before I had to be. That marked me to everyone as a guardian, clear as day, but no surprise there to anyone. In that, I had been as predictable as Yvera.

What was doubtless surprising to observers was that I was the *only* clear guardian. Because the roles weren't in the rules, there didn't have to be a certain number of any kind. Generally, there were about an equal number of runners and strikers, so three each. Although sometimes teams changed up the ratio from the outset as part of their strategy, using five runners and two strikers or vice versa. Or they switched roles mid-game to confuse the other team—or from sheer necessity to rebalance as people struck out. Almost always, though, guardians were the fewest aside from the nester, because it was usually considered a waste to spare more than two for the guardian role.

But usually there *were* two, if possible. After all, if there was just one, and something happened to that one, the runners would be left defenseless. Eventually, with only nine players to start with, one guardian would have to suffice when people started striking out, but this was the beginning of the game.

When I had been planning my strategy with Jake and Petra, we knew that at this point, people would hopefully assume two false things, which weren't mutually exclusive: one, since I had included a Moontouched in my nine, I didn't have a team member to spare to help me guard, or two, I was no ordinary guardian, and I was counting on my exceptionalism to carry my team through—or both.

I spared little thought for the audience's or other team's assumptions right now, though. My entire focus had to be on my runners: Starkissed Kvina, Brightflare Eskar, and Peacegrowth Edrik.

Some people might have been surprised to see my entourage's chief healer among my chosen runners, especially if they knew anything about his normally amiable, soothing nature. But he ran like a lightning bolt and was an unexpectedly passionate kesha player. That was how he'd met his new Starkissed wife, Fenra, who was in the same role on the opposite team.

The two of them were the first to arrive at the clutch. They grabbed their eggs and sprinted off without even a glance at each other, which was smart. That meant they got back behind the main groups before the other runners and—most important—the strikers arrived.

The strikers sprinted easily around the nest, which was only about twenty feet in diameter, and headed straight for the other team's runners, easily identified by the ones going for eggs and not holding swords. With single-minded focus, the strikers ignored each other as they crossed paths. With the runners as clustered together as they would ever be, now was the strikers' best chance to get them all out if they could. If they did, that could be the beginning of the end for the other team as they scrambled into roles they were less suited for while facing far superior numbers and skill. That was often a better strategy in the long term than strikers fighting amongst themselves while runners continued to steal eggs under their noses.

Battleblood Edra, Strongshield Lispeth, and, of course, Yvera were the strike team heading straight for my two exposed runners. They were a dangerous trio, especially with Edra, who was a veteran kesha player who had served my father well in many games before. As a King's elite, though, she had been a previously inaccessible choice to Yvera. I knew my foster sister must be ecstatic (secretly, on the inside) to finally fight alongside one of her idols.

Predictably, Yvera took one side, and Lispeth followed her, both homing in on Kvina, and Edra went around the other way, going for Eskar.

All of them timed their attacks for the same moment, hoping to divide my attention and power. A sound strategy, and another reason why having only one guardian was risky.

The strategy's weakness: synchronizing their attacks only made it easier for me to spring up two walls of golden energy simultaneously, instead of having to manage a trickier, staggered timing. True, the shields were identical in shape and thus not as efficient as they could have been. If I'd had the time, I could have made Kvina's shield smaller to save power, because she was stooping to grab an egg at the same time as Yvera was raising her sword to deliver a blow. So, the trio of strikers still won something from their strategy: costing me power. Just a bit more than I would have otherwise spent, but over time, that would add up.

Yvera didn't even follow through on the blow, having expected my shield. She knew my abilities better than anyone else did, just as I knew hers. That was the challenge with us facing off, and what made it such a close fight.

That's why I knew I needed something new. Well, a lot of somethings—Jake only being the beginning. I needed to think smarter, act more ruthlessly.

Part of me had always known I could beat Yvera if I gave it my all. But, just as I had refused the striker role, I had always hesitated, afraid of what I could really do, and what Yvera would do to me if I did it. Now, as King, I knew I couldn't hold back any longer.

Nor could I delude my rightwing any longer, either about the full extent of what I was capable of, or about her own shortcomings. Even if she was my sister.

Which was why the gong sounded two times in quick succession on Yvera's side, indicating an egg had been stolen from her.

I smirked.

Yvera stumbled at that sound, eyes going wide, unable to comprehend how that could be. Only one egg had even *made* it to her nester....

While Edra and Lispeth continued to relentlessly pursue their targets, Yvera stood still for a few costly seconds as she looked past me and saw Jake standing in our nester circle, holding the egg he had stolen from Michael.

Only then did she realize her mistake. She had never changed her initial strategy, not even after she saw me use Jake in a way she did not expect. She had *expected* me to have Jake grab an egg and go back to the nester circle, acting as our nester for the moment, as she had assigned Michael to be.

Flushed with rage at my petty trick and then her early victory, she had never stopped to consider that Jake wasn't tied down protecting an egg like Michael was. She never stopped to look for him. Which left Jake free to use those precious seconds while everyone else had been occupied to steal the egg from Michael.

I hadn't been certain he could. Even though Jake was athletic, Michael was, by Jake's own admission, the fighter of the two of them—the much fiercer opponent. I told Jake not to try for *too* long, to abandon the plan if Michael put up a resistance, but Jake seemed confident. He said he knew his son. My same strategy with Yvera would most likely work with Michael. Michael would ignore his father as a threat and get caught up in watching the action. Jake could then spring up behind him and take the egg before Michael put up his guard.

Which sounded well and good, but I was still concerned. Michael and Jake had agreed to one more rule between themselves: neither of them would surge straight *into* the other's circle. That, they decided, was pushing things too far, because then they could steal eggs from each other with impunity until they ran out of power. That wouldn't be very sporting, and it would take them out for the count very early in the game. Yvera and I agreed.

But that meant that Michael had to be caught off guard enough for Jake to surge right outside Michael's circle, run to him, wrestle the egg away if it was still in Michael's arms or snatch it from where it sat near him if not, and then surge back to our nest before Michael could stop him. I wasn't sure Michael could be *that* surprised, but Jake thought he could manage it.

And so, it seemed, he had.

Yvera stood, stupefied by my second trick, for as long as I could have hoped. Long enough for all three of my runners to make it back safely to the nest circle, where I had always had a designated nester in place, one who *wasn't* Jake: the fiercely protective Battleblood Rovayr.

Yvera had doubtless also assumed I would use him as one of my guardians, and again had not adjusted when I had not. Then again, it helped that I had told Rovayr to remain concealed behind one of the rocks near the circle, so in the furor, Yvera perhaps assumed she had missed him in her scan of the arena, and he must be somewhere in the wings, waiting to help me guard.

Only when the double gong sounded and Jake made it back to our circle with the egg did Rovayr step out from behind the rock to take charge of it. Only then did he shift into drakáform, revealing his intended role. Nesters were the only ones allowed to become draká in this predominantly amáform game, and for a justifiable reason: they had to guard a nest of eggs. So, stealing eggs from another team—though possible—wasn't normally as easy as Yvera had allowed it to be by leaving only Michael as the nester and committing everyone else to the initial fray.

I understood this all from the beginning, because, shockingly, everything had fallen into place exactly as I had planned. Yvera, on the other hand, had to stand still to realize how severely she had underestimated me. Meanwhile, the three gongs went off that indicated my runners had all made it to the nest, and they deposited their eggs in the pile under Rovayr.

Unfortunately for us, three gongs also went off on the other side, so my strike team hadn't managed to take out a runner either, thanks to the skill of Yvera's two guardians: Battleblood Ordran and Sunfilled Korrien. Though I noted with a quick glance that Yvera's Brightflare runner, Verran, had some streaks on his back and thigh, whereas my runners remained untouched. So at least there was that.

Plus, I now had four eggs and Yvera had three. A quick glance in either direction told me I was most likely ahead in points, and that was confirmed a moment later as an announcer gave the tally of the first round: Yvera's team had thirty-one points, mine had fifty-two.

Yvera turned her head slowly to look at me, her eyes burning.

She didn't even bother with words—a bad sign. She just made a slicing motion across her throat.

Yeah...I had always known I might beat Yvera at this game. I also knew that if I did, I might not live for very long after. I supposed I was taking all the risks now.

So, I met my foster sister's eyes...

...and I finally let her see me for who I truly was.

Chapter Nine

OPPORTUNITY

Sarah

"HE'S BRILLIANT," KOR SAID, almost in awe. He was leaning forward, elbows resting on his knees, and his eyes were as wide as I had ever seen them as he gazed down at the arena below. He had a pair of binoculars in hand, but he had lowered them for the moment. "He is torching *brilliant*. He just *blasted* Yvera. He read her like a book...and then threw that book into the fire."

He looked almost shaken, as if he were seeing Ben for the very first time.

"Dad could have helped him," I offered.

Not that I had any doubts about Ben's intelligence—I never had—but I was trying to be nice to Kor. When you grew up with someone, you tended to fix them in your mind, keeping them the same way they had always been. It hurt to have your view of a person shaken like that, to be brought to wonder if you had ever known them. Worst of all, you wondered whose fault it was that you had never seen their real selves: theirs...or yours.

Many of the members of my family had undergone the same kind of shock about me over the few days before the Solstice and our month of isolation after. I wasn't sure of the answer any more than I thought they were. Had I been this way all along, suppressing my potential all this time and living a lie to them...or, over the course of my twelve crucible days in the Six Realms, had I *become* this?

I thought I knew the answer about Ben, though. For as long as *I* had known him, I had known he could pull off something like this.

"No offense, Sarah—your father is a highly intelligent man—but he only just found out about this game's existence, what, *yesterday*? The day before that? This is *their game*. His and Yvera's. No, this has to be Ben. Look at him right now! Look at his face."

Kor was ignoring the fact that he was the one with the binoculars, which he was peering through once again.

"He did this. *Ben* did this. It's written all over his face. Except it's...it's *Ben*."

For the first time since he had arrived at the start of the game, the aged Battleblood sitting on my other side spoke.

"It was long his father's opinion," Alyish said in his deep voice, "that Koriben had a far deeper and more innate grasp of strategy than he ever let on—or perhaps even acknowledged to himself. An opinion that I shared. It was our hope that he would one day balance out Yvera's continued stubborn lack thereof."

I glanced at him and saw no surprise there. Only pride mixed with sorrow on his dark, scarred, clean-shaven face.

Alyish had never said why he had shown up, out of the blue. Even Kor had been startled, which told me Alyish hadn't been expected. Yet neither of us asked, and neither of us protested when the stoic old general took his seat. I assumed that if the old King's rightwing and Yvera's current one was going to be here, this box would be the place for him.

I, and probably everyone else, had assumed Alyish was here to watch his great-granddaughter do him proud. But it wasn't Yvera that Alyish was looking at with pride right now.

"You're not here for her, are you?" I asked softly. "You're here for Ben."

Alyish lifted his eyes from the arena to smile slightly. "Actually, I am here for them both. I consider the two of them to be my two greatest successes...and failures."

There was the source of his sorrow.

"Ben, because you could never get him to acknowledge his potential...."

"And Yvera, because I could never get her to acknowledge her faults," Alyish concluded heavily. "Yes."

"But why *now*?" Kor burst out, putting his binoculars down again as he turned to Alyish. "Seven years. Seven Tournaments, Yvera has publicly beaten him at kesha. Sometimes thoroughly. Why let her do that, if he had *this* kind of potential all along?"

I knew what Kor's unspoken question was, the one that had shaken him so badly—first with Ben's political acumen yesterday, and now with his strategic success today: *Why did Ben always let me think he was an idiot?*

One time could be a fluke. Two times in two days...was a pattern. One even Kor's arrogance couldn't deny.

"Two reasons, I think," Alyish said, returning his eyes to the melee that was resuming down below. He clearly didn't wish to miss a thing. "First, Koriben had that luxury. Now, he doesn't."

Kor scowled at him. "Elaborate, please...sir."

Alyish sighed but reluctantly looked up again, raising his eyebrow. "He was a boy, one who was more scared of success than failure. Failure was comfortable. Failure meant everyone would underestimate him, expect nothing more out of him. In his mind, he could never measure up to his father, so why even try?"

My iceheart clenched for Ben.

"That was why he always excelled as a warrior Heir," Alyish continued. "Because he *had* to. Lives depended on him. He couldn't hold anything back. And that was why he made himself mediocre in almost every other domain: because he *could*."

Alyish gestured at the game going on below. "Kesha has no real stakes for an Heir. Not the kind that were motivating enough for Koriben. Especially not in the face of the second reason."

"Which is?" Kor ground out.

I knew Kor's irritation was because Alyish was making too much sense—his conclusions fitting in too well with what Kor knew of Ben and, therefore, should have seen all along.

Alyish abruptly smiled, a bit of impishness entering his violet eyes for the first time that I had ever seen. "Until a couple months ago, Yvera was the most important female in Koriben's life. He thinks of her as a sister, yes, but how do you think that emotion would have influenced him?"

A random fact popped into my head: that male puppies let their female peers win in their little, harmless tussles, even if the males were bigger or stronger.

Kor groaned, turning his head to put his face into one of his hands. "He would have let her win. With no stakes, with his fear of success, of *course* he would have let his sister win. There was absolutely *nothing* motivating him to truly try."

"Until now," Alyish said, with a wink at me.

"Until now," Kor repeated, lowering his hand and looking down at the game. Another gong sounded at Ben's end: another egg captured. "Because he can't let himself fail any longer."

He gave me a weary, sidelong smirk. "And now he doesn't even want to."

My cheeks grew hot. "Don't look at me. This is all Ben."

"Yes, I think it finally is," Kor said, sitting back and handing me the binoculars. "So, take a good look, Sarah. Because he's doing this for you."

THE GAME BECAME A much tighter match after that, either because Yvera had wised up or Ben was holding back again. Kor and Alyish thought it was a bit of both, but more of the latter.

As Alyish watched his descendant, he said he was hopeful she was finally learning her lesson, but the middle of a kesha game was a bit late to make up for her shortcomings in strategy and leadership.

Yvera was lethal, plain and simple. There was a reason she had been such a good bodyguard for Ben for so long. Whatever task she set before herself to further her team's progress, she usually crushed it. But she couldn't win this game alone—it was a team sport. Not only that, she was her team's captain; she was supposed to be leading them. But her single-minded, reactive mindset and her preferred position as a striker made that difficult for her.

Ben's role as a guardian—in the middle of things, yet a step removed from them—was perfect not just for him but also for a team captain. He was in a much better position to see everything that was going on and direct his team accordingly or step in to assist where needed. He wasn't chasing the glory or the thrill for himself. It was all about the objective and how he could help his team meet it.

"It was why his father also preferred to be a guardian," Alyish said conversationally.

I would never have thought when I first met the terse, all-business rightwing that I would be sitting with him so comfortably, interacting so casually. Then again, right now he was off the clock, and this was a subject he seemed keen on.

I was starting to see why. Even having competed in track in high school, I hadn't been passionate about sports. I had never understood the fervor so many people felt about it. Now I realized sports could sometimes be a microcosm of life, with very real, practical, and important applications.

This wasn't just a game to Alyish. This was a way to train his people in the ways of survival. That's why the results of this match between Ben and Yvera were so important to him, he had come across the Six Realms to witness it. He wanted to see if his students had finally learned their lessons...or could finally teach them to each other.

Because the fate of the Realms might depend on it.

"Oh?" I said, always eager for tidbits about the old King.

"Yes. Kavarian started out as a striker, and he was a wicked good one." Alyish smiled in memory. "But he found around Koriben's same age that it wasn't good enough for *him* to be good. He was the Heir. That meant he always had to lead them—all of them, not just his strike team—and he found he couldn't do that properly as a striker. So, he stepped back—switching places with me, in fact. I wasn't his real rightwing back then, rather his elite captain. But for the game, I was his rightwing. The striker position is actually a good one for a rightwing. See how that's where Koriben has Petra? Strikers need a secondary, reactive leadership."

"A deputy," I offered. "Under the captain."

Alyish paused, perhaps turning the meanings of the English word in his mind. "Yes, that's a good word for it. Or as if the team captain is a general and the strike leader is the captain. Either way, you get the idea. A guardian is good as an overall leader, one guiding the whole team, and the rightwing is good for leading the offensive under them."

"Except Yvera has that reversed," I said, pointing to the male Battleblood standing back from the fight, throwing up purple shields left and right. "Ordran is there, and Yvera is leading the offensive."

"Which can work," Alyish said reasonably. "After all, it always has for Yvera before. But Ordran isn't a match for Ben at his best. Ordran is steadier than Yvera, but too steady. Too slow to react, not decisive enough, especially when it comes to committing others to danger. He makes for a good guardian, soldier, and captain of Koriben's elites, but he's no general."

"Could Yvera be? If she tried?"

Alyish didn't hesitate. "She could be much better. Certainly, she could be better than Ordran, even now. But she'll never be Koriben's match in that sense, and perhaps she doesn't need to be. Yet I've had the most torched time trying to convince her of that, when she thinks she already is."

"She doesn't need to be you, but she thinks she does," I realized. "Just like Ben doesn't need to be his father. There's more than one way to play the game. Put the two of them *together*, on one team, using both of their strengths to their maximum...and they'd be unstoppable."

Alyish smiled at me. Even in this conversation, those smiles had been rare, and I think always would be, but I saw the glitter of approval in his violet eyes. He seemed to think I'd earned it.

In that moment, I wondered if Alyish had come to evaluate a *third* person. I didn't know what kind of test I had undergone over the course of this seemingly casual conversation, but I felt a flicker of relief that I seemed to be passing.

"Oh, there goes the first egg," Kor said, pulling my attention back to the arena floor.

I stared. "What the heck just *happened*?"

A sizable area about midway between the nest and Yvera's goal was now covered in a goopy orange substance. It had splattered far and wide, throwing some spots on a couple of Ben's strikers and one of Yvera's runners, but it had coated one of Yvera's guardians; his Sunfilled-gold scales were now covered in Brightflare-orange goop, and he was spitting it out and flicking it away.

Alyish smiled again as he looked back down, but this time, it was a hard smile that sent goosebumps up my arms.

Kor looked at me. "Well, remember how I said the eggs wouldn't last forever?"

"Yeah."

"*That's* what they do when they die. They explode. What's worse, the substance inside generally has some kind of temporary effect if you're hit with it, depending on the amount. Brightflare eggs slow you down. But if you're hit with as much of any egg as Korrien just was, you're 'dead.'"

I shook my head. Just when I was getting a grasp on things. It felt a bit like the first time I had come to the Six Realms, all over again.

"But Korrien was a guardian, wasn't he? What was he doing holding an egg?"

"Oh, he wouldn't have been holding it," Alyish said. He looked at Kor. "Who threw it at him?"

"Tyri."

"Ah. Good choice, both tactically and politically."

I assumed that was referring to the fact that Tyri was also Sunfilled.

"But Tyri is a striker, isn't she?" I asked.

"The roles aren't set in the rules," Kor answered. "There's nothing saying a striker can't put away their sword for a second and lob a dying egg at someone. It's a common enough play."

"Though usually not as effective," Alyish put in. "Everyone knows to be on their guard when a striker puts away their sword. Ben must have arranged for a distraction."

"Tyri and Koreneth were chasing down Verran, so both Ordran and Korrien were focused on defending him. Plus, Ben was messing with them a bit, throwing some random fireballs. So, while his strikers were rounding the nest, Tyri grabbed the egg. She managed to do it one-handed, since it was so small—kept her sword the entire time, hardly broke her stride. Korrien never saw it coming. So, Ben let Yvera have an egg, but he permanently took out one of her guardians."

"How would Ben have known that egg was about to explode?" I asked.

"It was the smallest one left on the perimeter," Alyish said. "You can see the coals there are dying down. Plus, the eggs can make a whining, hissing sound when they're about to go off, kind of like a tsha kettle. One of his runners could have noticed and reported the sound to him, or he could have even told them to be on the lookout. All it takes is a bit of paying attention, communication, and quick planning when the opportunity arises. Of course, that's torched hard to do in the middle of battle."

I could see now why this would be a real kind of battle—and such good preparation for the deadlier kind. It wasn't just about everyone finding their fit. It was about learning to work *together*.

No wonder the elites were so good at what they did. It wasn't just each of them excelling. It was their unity, forged in these kinds of settings. Ben knew that, and he was taking full advantage of it. Tyri had been impressive, but as Alyish had said, she couldn't have pulled off that maneuver all by herself. Ben's team was functioning...like a team.

Whereas Yvera's....

Korrien stomped off the playing field while Yvera blasted a rock to smithereens to work out her temper. Ben's strikers were the ones to get a bit of splattering from the egg, but even they moved more quickly and cheerfully than the rest of Yvera's team. No doubt they had figured out by now that this would be a different kind of game than any other—and not just because of a couple of Moontouched wildcards.

Who did, indeed, seem to behave like wildcards. Dad especially slipped into pretty much any role as the opportunity arose—grabbing an egg if the nest was vacant but being equally willing to block someone's path or get a tap in here and there. Whereas Michael couldn't seem to find his rhythm, infuriated that whatever he tried to do, Dad could somehow do it better.

I wished Michael could see that his temper was partially to blame; he was losing his cool and burning through his energy, fast, and that wasn't helping him navigate this constantly changing terrain. But Dad's success was also because of Ben's direction. I guessed Yvera was leaving Michael on his own now, whereas I was almost certain Ben was moving Dad around like he would a queen on a chessboard—and Dad, too pragmatic not to let himself be directed when he trusted his leader, obeyed without question.

And you think he doesn't like you, I thought fondly at Ben. Only in my thoughts, though. I didn't dare risk distracting him by sending the words now.

Alyish agreed with my assessment. He watched Dad and Michael with particular interest, delight clear even on his stoic face at the newness they added to his beloved game.

Kor mostly watched Ben, and he'd long ago taken his binoculars back from me to do so. I got the feeling from Kor's interactions with Alyish that Kor wasn't normally this interested in kesha; he seemed to know less about the game than I expected of Kor in almost any other domain. Even now, Kor wasn't engaged by the game. *His* game was watching Ben at work—trying to anticipate what he was going to do, guessing when he was holding back and why.

With more grudging admiration, he finally sat back and looked at Alyish. "He's *keeping* the game close, isn't he? Every time he pulls too far ahead, he holds back."

"That's what it looks like," Alyish agreed with another rare smile.

"He knows that if he wins too decisively, people will become bored, or think him a bully. Or, worse, become suspicious. It would be too drastic a change from before. They would accuse him of cheating. He wants to win, but he knows he has to win in a certain way to *win*."

"Exactly."

Kor shook his head, scowling. I knew what was behind that look.

"Don't be too hard on yourself," I said kindly. "How were you supposed to know something that Ben wouldn't even acknowledge to himself?"

Kor glared at me. "Sarah, I'm his leftwing. It's my *job* to know precisely those sorts of things. How else am I supposed to protect him from his blind spots?"

"Then let this failure be your lesson on your own," Alyish said with a thin smile.

"What?" Kor asked, turning his glare to him.

"You have, in a way, the same problem as my granddaughter. You have tried too hard, and you have been too successful. It has made you arrogant, and that arrogance makes you blind. What is that saying that Eskala keeps telling you?"

Kor settled back and folded his arms in a sulk. I thought he wasn't going to answer, but finally, he sighed and said, "'Keep looking at the world with new eyes.'"

Alyish pointed down at the arena floor. "If you had looked at Ben with new eyes, as Sarah had, you would have seen how much more he had become capable of."

His face softened. "But as Sarah said, don't be *too* hard on yourself. Seeing clearly—ourselves and others—is perhaps one of the hardest things we ever have to do. I learned that the hard way myself—and much later in life, too."

He paused, letting silence fall, as if that was the end of the matter. Alyish let all our eyes wander back to the field before he spoke silently to just me.

Then imagine how rare it is for that clarity of sight to be your strength. *Eskala is right about you. As was Kavarian.*

I glanced at him in surprise, but his eyes were still on the game, looking for all the world as if his entire focus was there. But the corner of his scarred mouth was turned up in the smallest of smiles.

His eyes flicked upward, and that smile abruptly disappeared, killed in a sudden frost. I followed his gaze in alarm and once again saw Yalda across the arena from us in her own box, glaring icy daggers at him—and perhaps shooting more than just a look.

What is it? I sent to him, not daring to move my lips with her watching.

Someone, Alyish replied, *who could use a great deal more clarity. But I am afraid this game will not show her that. I am not certain what will.*

I could tell from his voice and see from the hard look in his eyes that Yalda troubled him.

If *Alyish* was worried....

I felt a chill. When I looked back at Yalda, I saw her glare had turned to me.

Alyish abruptly got up. He stretched and smiled at me.

"Forgive an old warrior his old bones. If I sit still too long, I go stiff—and I am told I am stiff enough as it is."

Contradicting himself, he winked at me. But I noticed he placed himself in front of me, blocking my view of Yalda—and hers of me. It was a small gesture, but the message to both of us was clear: I was protected.

Far from reassuring *me*, though, that only made me grow even colder.

THE END OF THE game came swiftly.

Ben and Yvera were neck and neck in points, and both were down to five core members. Even Michael was out, having been too burned out to dodge a splash from an egg; that was just as well, since he would have been useless to Yvera without any power, anyway. Even Dad was running low, judging from how much he stood still on the sidelines. So, Ben practically had only three teammates to work with besides him: a striker, a runner, and a nester.

Then, eggs started going off right and left, some of them even in the bed of coals; the goo, of course, smothered the coals further, setting off even more eggs as they cooled in a cascading effect of exploding color. I couldn't even keep track of what was going on anymore. Shields, eggs, fireballs, and other forms of magic were going off everywhere in one final push.

Then Yvera emerged from the mayhem, bolting for her circle with perhaps the smallest remaining egg. With her momentum, and no one else near her, and Ben occupied shielding his own runner making a race for his own circle, she appeared to be unstoppable....

Then, out of the blue, with no goo or rocks in sight...she tripped.

Despite that, in an incredible feat of agility, she turned in midair and curled around the egg, cradling it in her chest. She hit the ground with her back, still holding onto it.

To no avail.

The small Sunfilled egg exploded in her arms, coating her violet armor in gold.

A gong rang on Ben's side, indicating his runner had made it in. Then both gongs rang three times, which I assumed meant the end of the game.

Then the announcer gave the final score. Ben's team: three-hundred-fifty-five. Yvera's team: three-hundred-forty-nine.

While the stadium exploded into a roar of cheers and protests, Yvera lay on her back, bleeding gold, and staring at the sky.

Looking as if she couldn't quite believe she had actually lost.

I was shocked too. My heart was still thumping from that last-minute loss. Yvera had had the more valuable egg—perhaps enough to pull her team through. And yet, one mistake....

One very unlikely mistake.

"Yvera doesn't just...trip," I said slowly.

"No," Alyish said. Once again, pride mingled with sorrow on his face as he looked between his mentees. Ben was crossing the color-soaked battlefield to her, shoulders sagging and movements labored, but head held high.

"It was your father," Kor said, gesturing to where Dad stood at the edge of the field. Near the center. Seemingly sitting things out. Seemingly out of power.

But where he would have had a full view of Yvera's end of the arena.

"I was feeling for it, so I noticed a tiny spike of power from him," Kor continued. "My guess is that he used a bit of ice."

Just a bit. That's all it would have taken. Just one slick patch where Yvera wasn't expecting it, or one little lip for her to trip over when she wasn't looking. That would be all.

My breath caught as the implications staggered me. "Why...didn't he do that *before*?"

"Because you never make your most effective play at the beginning," Alyish said. "You save it for the end, when your enemy thinks they have seen all there is to expect from you, when they think you are done. You save it for the moment that matters most."

Ben reached Yvera and crouched down next to her...and offered her his hand.

For a few long, tense moments, Yvera just stared at him, eyes burning even from this distance. But then, she threw her head back and laughed. Still laughing, she grabbed that hand and let him bring both of them up to standing, and then she pulled him in for a hug. When they pulled apart, she shoved him playfully, saying something we couldn't hear.

I looked at Alyish, hoping he could interpret the miraculous transformation I was seeing.

He smiled. "I can't be sure...but I think she just realized that Ben gave her the game of her life."

CHAPTER TEN

ATTEMPT

SARAH

ALYISH LEFT ALMOST IMMEDIATELY after the kesha match was over. He said Ben and Yvera would no doubt find out he had been there, but he wanted to be gone by the time they came back up.

The match had lasted less than half the day, which left plenty of daylight for other events. While the kesha players recovered and showered, and the arena floor was cleared, we watched what we could see from below of draká racing high above us. After the races, they began sparring with claws dyed in paint that left marks just as the swords did.

"What did I miss?" Ben asked cheerfully as he strode into the box maybe an hour later. His hair was damp and tousled, and he had changed into his normal black clothing with gold edging and embroidery instead of his armor. From the egg splatters and scorch marks that had been on his set before, I could guess why.

"Oh, not much," Kor said idly, not even looking up from his tablet. I guessed he was trying to catch up on all the work he had planned to get done during the kesha match. He waved vaguely in the air. "Somebody won, somebody lost. Lots of flapping involved. Nobody died."

Ben raised an eyebrow at his leftwing as he sat down next to me and claimed my hand. "Let me guess: you haven't paid any attention all morning, have you?"

"Oh, I looked up now and then."

I snorted, and Ben glanced at me. I just shook my head. Kor had enough to process without Ben getting further involved.

"Good job," I said simply, rising in my seat to kiss him on the cheek. "I watched the entire time, and I'm proud of you. Very proud."

"Er, thanks," Ben said, going pink.

Still Ben, as he had always been. Just because he could be that intense and incredible when he needed to be didn't mean he was always meant to be. Just like a stiff old general wasn't always meant to be quite so stiff.

EVEN THOUGH YVERA JUMPED back into some of the events, Ben sat out with me for the rest of the day. I thought that was simply his preference, but the next morning, I found out it was because he was saving his strength for that day's main event: dueling.

As in the one-on-one, all-out, melee-mixed-with-magic kind.

While Ben watched the starting sets with as much professional interest as Alyish had watched the kesha match, trading commentary with Yvera as they sized up his potential opponents, I got increasingly queasy as the morning wore on.

I gathered that there was supposed to be some kind of honor code in all of this, but for the life of me, I couldn't figure out what it was, and I was afraid to ask. To me, it seemed like these people were trying to kill each other. No one ever died by the end, but there were concussions, gashes, broken bones, and broken armor—and those were only the obvious injuries. Who knew how many bruises we couldn't see underneath that armor?

Ben was supposed to get involved in *that*? And I was just supposed to...watch?

Ben standing back while he led a team sport, the objective of which was technically nonviolent, was one thing. This...was something else.

Hey, you alright? Ben asked me after a couple of hours, perhaps finally noticing how quiet and serious I'd been.

Are you? I asked.

Why wouldn't I be? he said blankly.

I hesitated. Should I be questioning him right now? He made it seem like his participation was expected, maybe even demanded. He didn't seem to mind that, for once, but still.... What was the point in dumping my concerns on him when he didn't have much of a choice?

I'm...just tired, I said. Given this was yet another morning I couldn't sleep in, that would have been true—without the "just" part.

Ben's eyes narrowed, but before he could say anything, Yvera got his attention again about some maneuver or another that I'd made him miss. That further strengthened my resolve. I shouldn't be distracting him right now. He should be paying close attention to the matches, because something he could observe now could save him later.

I didn't let myself specify what it would save him *from*.

With how big the arena floor was, several duels were always going on at once, with the next set being led out onto the floor the moment their section was cleared and the fires put out and whatnot. I was surprised when duel after duel came and went, and Ben still didn't go down. I wasn't protesting the delay...exactly. But it gave my stomach more time to twist itself into knots.

Then there were only two left.

"So, Mekran or Orsel," Ben said calmly as he surveyed the Battleblood and Strongshield starting off their match.

"Yup," Yvera agreed, legs spread out, hands folded over her lap. "Either one would give you a good fight."

They had been over their qualities many times by now, as those two duelists kept coming up for another round.

I suddenly realized what was happening—and choked.

"Wait. Hold up. You don't have to fight just anybody? You have to fight the *winner*? Of all of them?"

"Well, yeah," Ben said, looking at me in surprise. "Why do you think I haven't been down there yet?"

I ignored that. "Why? Just because you're the King?"

Yvera snorted. "No. Because he's the champion. Two years running."

"Think I can make it a third?" Ben asked her with a wink. Yvera just rolled her eyes.

I reined in my reactions just in time. Ben seemed to care what I thought of his skills, so I didn't want to sound incredulous. "What...does that mean, exactly?"

"The first time?" Yvera waved her hand at the arena. "That he went through all of that and then beat the previous champion. And last year, he beat the challenger. So, he still has the title, and he'll fight whoever of those two wins and tries to take it from him."

I'd always known Ben was a *good* fighter—in fact, one of the best. I just didn't know he was officially considered *the* best.

I didn't know why that floored me so much. I mean, I believed in him and everything...but why would he let himself lose kesha every year, but not this?

Then I realized Alyish had already told me. *That was why he always excelled as a warrior Heir. Because he* had *to.*

Kesha was about demonstrating his ability to *lead* them, which Ben had been terrified of doing. But a simple duel? That showed that he could *protect* them—and that was something Ben had always been willing to pay any price to do.

Only one thing still stumped me.

"Where do you fit into all this?" I asked Yvera.

"Eh," she said with a shrug. "Tournament duels aren't my thing."

I blinked. That made no sense to me whatsoever.

"Meaning," Ben said with a smirk at me, "she wants to beat as many people as possible in as many ways as possible over the course of the whole Tournament, so she doesn't want to risk a knockout injury in a duel."

Oh. Now *that* made more sense. But...the words "knockout injury" did *not* make me feel any better about Ben's participation in this madness.

"I've got a race later, Ben," Yvera whined. "I *like* racing."

Ben shrugged and smiled again at me. "Like I said."

He stood and stretched. "Well, probably time for me to head down there."

"You're fighting?" I asked, trying very hard to hide my alarm. "Already? They're not even done yet."

"Oh, no, not yet. And even after they're done, I'll need to give the winner some time to heal, repair, drink some sundew, and so on. My duel won't be for a deken or two, but I want to get in a good warm-up, maybe even a steam session if I have time."

Yvera looked up at him. "Then I suppose I'll watch these two finish up and report in."

"Much appreciated," Ben said to her with a pat on her shoulder.

Then he turned to me, leaned in, and kissed me, as if he were just going out for an errand. Even though the next time I saw him, he would be walking out onto that arena.

I couldn't help it. When we parted, I asked him, "Are you *sure* you're OK with this?"

"Why wouldn't I be?" he asked, repeating the same question as before with much the same tone and expression of surprise.

I once again struggled to express concern without seeming insulting—and to keep my face neutral for the sake of anyone watching. "I don't know.... Because you don't like...public spectacles."

He snorted in amusement. "Oh, this isn't a pageant or a speech. It's not an act. This is what I *do*, Sarah. This is what I've trained my whole life for."

When I just continued to look at him, he chuckled and kissed me again. "Thanks for your concern, but trust me. I've got this."

To my shock, he winked and then walked away, humming.

As soon as I thought he was out of hearing, I turned to look at Kor, who was watching me with glittering eyes.

I swallowed. "Was that...*Ben*...being *arrogant*?"

"That remains to be seen."

"What?"

Kor smirked. "Well, it's only arrogance if he's mistaken, now, is it?"

I finally relaxed back and rolled my eyes. "And here I was wondering if the two of you had swapped bodies for the day, but Ben would definitely not have said that."

Kor shuddered. "Flame, no. As if I would willingly take part in this barbarism."

"I heard that, you twit," Yvera said casually, her eyes never leaving the duel.

To Kor, I said, "That was very Kor-like. Very good. You're making me feel much better."

Kor grinned. "Then perhaps this is a good time to mention that you're going to have to compete in at least one event."

My stomach plummeted. "*What?*"

His eyes danced. "You're one of the guests of honor. So they're *honoring* you with a place in the Tournament."

I choked. "When were you going to tell me *that*?"

"Oh, right about now. Didn't want to give you *too* much time to panic."

"What on Earth—" I didn't care how inappropriate that exclamation was for me anymore. Or perhaps it was more appropriate than ever. "—can I do that would even remotely measure up in the *Tournament*?"

"Oh, don't get your tail in a knot. I signed you up for a race, since you ran in secondary, right?"

That brought me up short. "Wait. How did you know that?"

Kor scrunched his face in innocent confusion. "Didn't you tell me that? Once?"

I looked away, lost. "I...well, I guess I must have. How else would you know?"

How else...indeed.

I shook myself. "Wait, doesn't matter. Kor, I did fine in track, but I wasn't state level or anything. Let alone *Olympic* level."

"You'll do fine," Kor soothed. "No one expects you to win anything. They just want to see you be a good sport and play one of their games. Yvera can show you the way and get you into position, since she's racing too, remember?"

I choked again. "I have to race against *Yvera*?"

"Pssh, no," Yvera said with a snort. "I'll be in the drakón race, thank you very much. You'll be with the amón."

I put a hand on my heart, suddenly feeling like it might not have to leap out of my chest after all. For some reason, the trial ahead now seemed bearable, because I would be in an entirely different league from Yvera.

Still terrifying as anything. But bearable. Now Ben just had to survive his duel, and maybe we both would see the sunset.

Maybe.

By the time Ben walked out onto the arena floor, I was fit to be tied. At least on the inside. I think I looked alright on the outside. Kor wasn't telling me to fix my expression, anyway.

Unfortunately, Dad and Michael had returned from wherever they had disappeared to while I was getting all that lovely news, and they were back to sitting on either side of me. Dad saw my hands twisting and clenching in my lap and gently laid his own hand over them to bring them to stillness.

"He will be fine, Sarah," he murmured so quietly it was almost a whisper, nearly inaudible over the roar of the crowd.

"'Course he will be," Michael muttered with his arms folded. He was still peeved about yesterday's loss. "That guy is a tank. An untouchable tank."

Perhaps Michael was thinking of one time during the game when he had tried to sneak up behind Ben for a surprise strike, and Ben had not just sensed him coming but had merely pushed him back with a shield. *Gently*. Even keeping Michael on his feet somehow, so that Michael just slid harmlessly backward until he hit the arena wall. Good thing my brother had been too far away to hear me laugh, or he would have never forgiven me. I didn't think he was going to forgive Ben.

The memory helped, tempting my lips to twitch.

"I know, I know," I said, taking a deep breath. "But it's just...hard for me to watch."

"It's just a duel, Sarah," Yvera said, her eyes never leaving Ben as he walked to the enormous golden circle in the middle of the arena. "He's done this hundreds of times."

Which means this time, his number might be up, my cynical side whispered.

Or it could mean he knows what he's doing and will be just fine, I retorted.

I had to have faith in him. Just like he was always having faith in me.

His opponent was a Strongshield who looked at least twice his age, was nearly as tall, and packed even more muscle. What was his name again?

Ah, the announcer helpfully provided it for me: Orsel. I didn't need the recap of deadly facts about him, thank you, but the announcer gave it to me anyway, and with relish. Who he'd learned from, where in the Warflight he'd served and for how long, how many formal duels he'd won: one-hundred-thirty.

The announcer kept things simple for Ben while Ben stood at attention: his name, his title, his duel wins. Two-hundred-five.

I blinked. When Yvera had said Ben had done this *hundreds* of times...I thought she had been exaggerating. And...that was only his *formal* duels?

Then the two of them saluted each other. Orsel put his hand over his heart and nodded deeply to Ben—from this distance, at least, seeming to show every sign of respect. This wasn't some cocky, blustering thug. He was here because of his passion and reverence for the fight, as Ben was.

That...didn't reassure me.

Without further ado, the two courteous warriors began circling, figuring out how to kill each other.

I'd noticed that drakón duels—or this type that I'd seen—didn't begin with weapons. I suppose that made sense, since they could carry pretty much any weapon they wanted with them and draw it at a moment's notice from the ether. There seemed to be some kind of art to waiting until the last moment, choosing the tool for the situation, and using it with lethal force.

The greatest skill, then, was not in wielding the weapon itself, not in strength or in speed, but in being able to anticipate what your opponent was going to do.

That was why Ben had watched his potential opponents so carefully. At first, I thought that would give him an advantage, but then I realized it was only leveling the playing field for him, and slightly at that. The drawback to his being the champion was that everyone else had seen him fight, and often; everyone else knew his strengths, weaknesses, and patterns. Everyone else would be more than prepared to fight him, knowing they would find him at the top. Whereas there would have been little he could have done to prepare himself to fight the unknown challenger.

If Ben was concerned about that fact, none of it showed. In most situations, Ben was as readable as a book printed in a 20-point font. Now, his face was as blank as a wiped slate—almost trance-like in its empty focus. He moved with seemingly effortless grace as he circled, and his hands were open and his shoulders down and relaxed.

Unfortunately, so was Orsel. Yvera was right. This man was going to give Ben a good fight.

That relaxed circling lasted long enough that the crowd became restless, some people booing, but both Ben and Orsel ignored them. If anything, they slowed, continuing at an even more languid pace. In contrast, my heart rate kept going up.

I didn't know who made the first move. Of course it would happen the moment I glanced away to where my hands were clenched in my lap. One second, they were circling. The next, I heard an explosive, crackling sound, and my head shot back up to see the dueling circle filled with roaring flames. I almost jumped up from my seat, but Dad put his hand on my shoulder.

When the flames cleared, Ben and Orsel emerged unscathed, now mere feet apart, protective shields flickering out as they locked swords. Then I realized what the fire had been for: the equivalent of a smokescreen.

How do you get a watching opponent to not know what you're going to do? Make it so that they couldn't see you coming.

Except both had seemed to anticipate the other well enough. In the most intense game of rock, paper, scissors ever, they had both chosen scissors, and now they danced again, but this time with sharpened steel.

For the first time, I realized I had never seen Ben *fight*.

Oh, I had seen him fight as a draká, but each time I had seen that in person, I had been on his back, and not only was my view limited as I tried to hold on, but Ben's priority was protecting me—not on giving his all to the struggle. I had watched him fight for hours represented by a tongue of flame circling over a flame table during the Battle of the Solstice, but details weren't a flame table's forte: the uniform colors of fire, occasional distortions, and chaos of thousands of moving shapes around him hadn't given me a clear view very often.

I had never seen him fight in amáform. I'd seen him prepared to, plenty of times. I'd seen him before and after a fight. But I had never seen the fight itself. Much less when he didn't have anyone to protect, nothing to get in his way—not even himself.

So, I had never seen Ben *fight*. Much less in a familiar form like this that allowed me to understand even the slightest part of the skill, talent, and genius that went into what he did.

How could I claim to know and love him when I had never seen him give his all in his destined and chosen art?

And it was *art*.

I could see that now. There was such *beauty* in the way he moved...a fluidity, a grace, a confidence that I had never seen in him before. As thoroughly as when he changed into a dragon, Ben transformed from the man I knew into another creature entirely. One full of such ferocity, power, and lethality, I felt wave after wave of goosebumps from watching him.

My mind went back to the first time he had brought me to the training room in my hold to teach me how to fight. Without warning, he activated a circle, wound back with the skill of a champion pitcher, and launched a fireball that left scorch marks on my floor and his eyes glowing with deadly power. Before that moment, I had known, theoretically, that he was formidable, but as I told him then in explanation, most of the time, to me, he was simply...Ben. My sun. Not that I ever underestimated him; as I said then, I simply forgot that he was dangerous.

That fire was as deadly as it was beautiful.

Now that duality was on full display, naked as his unsheathed sword and just as sharp on both sides. So much of his energy went into control, restraint, discipline—more than I had ever realized. He kept himself under lock and key for most of his days, and that was for good reason: that kind of fire, uncontrolled and unbalanced, would have been as devastating as the Devourer the fire had been created to fight.

That fire could destroy us.

But right now...right now, he didn't have to hide. He didn't have to hold back. He didn't have to fear. He didn't even have to protect. He could let it all go.

He could *be*.

The memory of his voice echoed in my mind: *This is what drakón are meant to do, Sarah. It's why the Tree made us the way we are.*

And him, as Her King, more than any other mortal alive.

Not just any King—a King unlike any other She had created since the First Invasion and the swearing of the Covenants.

A King for a time of war.

His eyes glowed, even from this distance, even though I didn't think he was using any power. His blankness was gone. He wasn't quite smiling, but there was an intensity to his expression that conveyed a fierce joy, a full presence of being, an *aliveness* I had never seen in him before. Every inch of his skin shone with an inner fire.

He bent over backwards with impossible flexibility and core strength to avoid a swipe of Orsel's blade, and as he rose back up, he *laughed*.

Let this Tournament remind us this time, more than ever...that we are alive.

In so many, far too many ways...this was the very first time I had ever seen the man I loved, the man I'd promised my life to. The sight struck me with the force of a lightning bolt to my core.

I couldn't breathe.

And it wasn't from fear.

SURPRISINGLY, MICHAEL WAS RIGHT, and I was wrong.

Ben was untouchable...and there was nothing any of these duelists could have done to prepare themselves to fight him.

Oh, Orsel gave it a good, valiant effort. The Strongshield was probably better than any single warrior I'd seen fight up to this point, aside from Yvera. Yet no matter what tactic he tried, what weapon he used, what magic he applied, he could never land a blow on Ben. The Golden King seemed to have a preternatural sense for whatever Orsel was going to do and countered it every time—often seeing some opportunity in it for a blow of his own. And his endurance for it all seemed limitless.

Soon, Orsel's scarlet armor was covered in gold streaks, and Ben's golden set only had the occasional collateral scorch mark.

It wasn't long into the fight before even I knew who was inevitably going to win, but Ben seemed to drag out the process. Unlike with the kesha match, this time I thought it was more because he was having too much fun than because he was trying to give a good show. He seemed oblivious to the world outside that circle, unable to care less about the cheers and boos and silences. I assumed his skills depended on an intensity of focus that shut out everything and everyone else that wasn't an immediate threat; now, his unusually blank, tranquil expression at the beginning made sense to me. This was a kind of trance for him—a meditation.

Of the rawest, most brutal kind.

I, too, must have become lost to the world, because I jumped when I felt a tap on my shoulder.

"Hey, Sarah, you coming, or are you dropping out?" Yvera said impatiently, as if this wasn't the first time she'd tried to get my attention.

"What?" I said blankly. My eyes were already drifting back to Ben.

Yvera waved her hand in front of my face, leaning down so that her violet braid spilled down and her scowl filled my sight. "Hey. Race? Running? Ringing any gongs in that pretty head of yours?"

My blood went cold. Well, more than normal, that is.

"Hey, that's my sister," Michael said, straightening.

Never mind that he'd said worse himself in his more immature days. No one *else* was allowed to belittle me.

Yvera rolled her eyes. "I never said it was an *empty* pretty head, did I? Except for maybe right now."

She snapped her fingers in my face, even though she had my full attention now. "Well, you coming?"

"But, but the duel—"

"It's almost over, trust me. Not even Ben can keep this up for much longer, so he'll finish with Orsel soon enough. Your event is right after they clean up from his, so you need to get down there and warm up. Unless you really want to make a fool of yourself?"

I didn't. So, I groaned, took one last look at Ben, and reluctantly stood.

I gave Michael a pleading look. "You'll tell me how it ends, right?"

He snorted. "Sure. Your fiancé wipes the floor with this guy. The end."

"No, I mean *how* he does it."

"I'll tell you if Michael doesn't," Dad said with a thin smile. "And perhaps when I do it badly, he'll start filling in the details."

"Ah, Dad, you're no fun," Michael said with a scowl. Ben wasn't the only one Michael was peeved at for yesterday.

"C'mon," Yvera said, waving at me to follow. "I'm missing the end for you, too, you know. So hurry up before I change my mind."

That finally got me moving. Now that she pointed it out, I was surprised and touched by that kind of sacrifice.

Then again, she'd seen Ben do this "hundreds of times" before.

That made me realize something, though. I wasn't sure whether I dared ask for confirmation, but curiosity burned at me, and since Yvera seemed to be in a helpful mood....

Still, I waited until we were down the hall and out of earshot of even the few elites trailing us before I said quietly, "I think I understand now. That's why Tournament duels aren't 'your thing,' isn't it? You know they're Ben's."

She threw me a scowl, but I was familiar enough with Yvera's glares by this point to know that one lacked true heat.

I thought that was all the confirmation I was going to get, and so my mind had already wandered back to the duel by the time she burst out, "I don't like losing."

I yanked my focus back to the present. "That's...understandable. I don't think anybody does."

"But you know what I hate even more?" she said hotly, staring ahead. "Winning when it doesn't count. When the other person hasn't given it their best. Where is the torching point in that?"

I held back a smile and nodded, even though Yvera still wasn't looking.

"I've fought Ben a lot. In fact, *no one* has dueled him more than I have. So, I figured out fast that he doesn't fight me like he fights others. With me, he holds back. At first, I was insulted. I tried to get him mad, hurt him even, to make him give me a fair fight. But he wouldn't do it, no matter what I did."

Yvera huffed. "I finally realized that he simply couldn't do it. I was too close to him. He just couldn't make himself let it out with me. So...I stopped being mad. And I stopped signing up for Tournament duels. Because what was the point? Ben had to do *something* in the Tournament, something he was good at, and he chose dueling. Which meant if I signed up too, we would inevitably end up fighting each other, and either he wouldn't give me his all, or he would, and he'd torch me in front of my whole clan."

"You wouldn't win, either way," I realized.

"Exactly," she said, and a rare flicker of sadness crossed her face. "So, I stopped signing up. And the year after I first dropped out...he finished second, only losing to the champion. When he was only *seventeen*. He broke a record. And the year after that...he became the champion."

She looked away, letting her braid come between us. "So...yeah. Dueling is Ben's thing."

Again, silence fell, and again, I thought that would be it.

And then, a minute later, when we again were out of earshot of some passer-by, she said quietly, "I told myself that I could always beat him at kesha. That he'd give me a fair fight there, and I could truly win.... Turns out I was wrong about that, too."

There was something so lost about her tone, so unlike the Yvera I'd always seen, that I immediately took my life into my own hands and said, "Yv, that *wasn't your fault*. Ben wasn't trying to deceive you. He simply...couldn't do it. He wasn't ready."

"Yeah...he...told me that. Still hurts, though."

"I bet," I said softly.

"You know what hurts the most, though?" she burst out, as if this had been festering ever since the moment she lay on the field, staring up at the sky, realizing she had lost. Perhaps I was about to find out the reason she had opened up to me at all, at the first opportunity I'd given her.

What? I asked silently, mindful of a group of people passing us.

She switched to her inner voice as well, her tone becoming small and lost again. *What does he even need me for? If he's better than me at...everything.... If he's found someone more important to him than I am...why am I still here?*

I hadn't been expecting my heart to ache for someone over the course of this walk down into the depths of the Tournament arena. Much less for Yvera.

Yv, that's not true.

She cast me a glare, violet eyes soulflaring for one second. *Don't give me that,* Sarah. *Not you.*

She looked away, muttering out loud, "Why am I even talking about this with *you*?"

Because you don't have anyone else, I thought. Ben was perhaps the only friend she had that she could even somewhat bare her soul to...and he was even less suited than I was to helping her now.

It struck me that Alyish may have had a very *personal* reason for making sure I understood what that kesha game would mean to both Ben...and his great-granddaughter. He might have known that if Yvera finally learned her lesson, she would be reeling afterward, no matter what kind of brave front she would put up on the outside, and he wouldn't be able to help her either.

Perhaps I was the only one who could.

Yvera, you said it yourself. Ben can't always let that thing inside him out. It's too dangerous. It has to be contained. Ben can be that kind of warrior only in very controlled or dangerous circumstances, but you can be something so very close all the time. *You don't have his problems, his burdens, his insecurities. He would be dead* so many *times over if it wasn't for you. Because you don't let anything stand in your way, like he does. Because you don't have to be contained.*

Not *entirely* true. She still needed scruples. But I didn't think she was about to go on a mad killing spree just because I said that.

Her steps slowed. Though she was still looking away, making her expression hard for me to see, I took that as a sign that she hadn't rejected what I'd said.

So I pressed on. *As for that other thing...yes, Ben feels...something different for me than he feels for you, but I haven't replaced you in his life, Yv. No one can take that spot. You're something he needs just as much as he needs me: his* friend. *The one who grew up with him, protected him, laughed and fought with him. You two have something I can never share, and gosh, it makes me jealous sometimes. You have no idea how I envy you.*

"What?" Yvera said, startled enough that she spoke out loud, causing a few passersby to glance in surprise.

Well, for starters, who has Ben been talking to this entire morning? *You!* I let a teensy bit of aggravation enter my voice. It hadn't really bothered me...that much. Mostly. But I figured that if Yvera was going to believe me, she needed to see how I was affected, too.

All morning, I repeated. *He had a reason to, because* I *certainly didn't know what to watch for, or how to discuss it with him like you did. There are* so many *things he needs you for and that you can do with him that I can't. You can* duel *him. Yeah, sure, he might hold back, but can you imagine how much practice he'd get fighting* me? *Even if he could bring himself to* try.

Yvera was still silent, but I still thought she was listening. She had never had any qualms about telling me to shut up before.

That's just the beginning! You're so much closer to his height than I am. If I were as tall as you, I could kiss him whenever I wanted! He wouldn't have to bend down, or I wouldn't have to step on something, or.... And gosh, you're gorgeous. *Do you know that? There are people back on Earth who would kill for your figure.*

You...seem to have thought a lot about this, Yvera said slowly, a lighter tone entering her voice.

I felt a flicker of hope. *Of course I have. Yv, I have been jealous of you from the moment I first saw you. I was convinced for an embarrassingly long time that Ben could never possibly be interested in me when he had you standing right there at his side.*

Really? Yvera said dryly, looking back at me for the first time in a while to raise her scarred violet eyebrow at me.

Really, I said fervently. *I tried for him anyway, because I couldn't seem to help myself, but I didn't have much hope.*

She slowly smirked. *Then you were a dimtorch.*

I was, I admitted. *I also didn't know Ben as well as you did. I didn't grow up with him, remember?*

True, she said, with a touch of smugness. Which faded soon after. *If all that's true, why wasn't it enough? Why didn't he choose me?*

I could scarcely believe we were having this conversation, but Yvera was a frank person. Now that I was on her very short list of "People That Could Be Trusted To Not Kill Ben" (the highest honor she could bestow, which I'd paid dearly to earn), I assumed that meant that if she felt like talking with me, she *talked* with me.

I answered her carefully. *You told me this yourself once: he loves you. But...he loves you like a sister.*

I quickly added, *A sister he still needs and loves just as much, even though I'm in the picture now. Just because I love Ben doesn't mean I want to throw away a single one of my brothers and sisters.*

My voice turned dry. *Although Michael tempts me sometimes.*

As did Rachel, but I assumed her name wouldn't mean as much to Yvera.

Yvera chuckled, then sighed. *Yeah...I figured.*

Still hurts, I know, I said ruefully.

Not as much as it did, Yvera said with unusual thoughtfulness.

Before I could ask whether she meant she was already getting over him or that my words just now made that much of a difference, we entered a large training room. I recognized its purpose at once: an indoor track. I supposed there were only so many variations possible in designing a room meant for running around in a circle.

"Huh," I said as I looked around. "Looks like we're the first ones here. Are you sure there was such—"

I was about to say *a need to rush* when Yvera grabbed my arm and yanked me back, just when I was about to step onto the track.

"Shut up," she said flatly.

Yup. She had no qualms about telling me that.

Or...dragging me backward with zero explanation.

"Yv," I protested, stumbling over myself to follow. "What the hell—"

"I said *shut up*."

And then, before my elites could step through, the door we'd come through slammed shut. Lest I hope it was still possible to open, a rim of violet fire ran around its edges, and the gem on the door burned bright. A banging started on the door, to no avail.

Oh.

That was why.

All I'd seen was an empty track, and all I'd thought of was Ben behind me and the race ahead of me. Yvera, ever in the present moment, ever watchful for danger, had immediately seen it for what it was.

A trap.

Yvera whirled around, shoving me behind her, even before someone spoke. Her cold words echoed through the large stone room.

"Give her to me, Yvera. I will make it quick, and your hands will be clean. As they must be, when you are questioned."

My iceheart, already trying to pound its way out of my chest, took another painful bound when I glimpsed from around Yvera the bone-chilling sight of Lady Yalda striding toward us, dressed for battle, carrying a wicked-looking knife, her face and eyes as cold as a glacier.

Yvera's only response was to bring forth her own blade, holding it in front of her with both hands like a shield.

Yalda sighed, as if Yvera were being a petulant child. "Come, girl. Surely you, of all people, can see that this is the way things must be. That boy has made his idiotic determination to marry that chit clear, so we must take matters into our own hands."

Again, Yvera said nothing, and this time, did nothing. She just stood there as before, feet spread, blade up.

And then...she lowered it. "You're...doing this so he won't marry her? Is that it?"

There was an odd note in her voice, one I had never heard before. My iceheart accelerated even more as I heard it, as I watched my best defense—Yvera's sword—lower until the tip touched the ground.

No.

I mean, I knew Yvera didn't *like* me. She didn't like anyone except Ben, as far as I was aware.

But was she really going to...?

"Exactly," Yalda said, smiling.

She had meant the smile to be coaxing, maybe even approving. Unfortunately, it had probably been too long since she'd genuinely smiled, and this one was so brittle, it could have broken with a flick of the fingers.

"You *know* that *you* are the consort the Realms need right now. Only you can balance out the weakness that has entered and festered within the Golden Crown. The boy is a dull fool—surely you know this—but that means we can use him. We, you and I, can right this imbalance. We can save our Realms before it's too late. Everyone knows he is fond of you. Everyone *agrees* the consort crown should be yours by right. It's what you're owed. It's what he, especially, *owes* you."

"He...does," Yvera said slowly, still with that off note in her voice. "He...owes me."

I was frozen with horror now. Something was wrong, terribly wrong. Was Yalda *hypnotizing* Yvera? Was that what was happening? She wasn't herself, that was for certain.

But what should I *do*? If I fought (most likely badly), would that snap her out of it? Or would it make Yvera bring that much-closer sword straight into my heart, doing the job herself? If I left her, tried to surge away to Ben, would Yalda let Yvera go? Or would she kill her, now that Yvera knew too much?

I couldn't do it. I couldn't leave her if that meant Yalda would kill Yvera once I was out of reach. I believed her capable of it now. With those cold eyes of hers, showing a madness breaking out from under the ice, I believed her capable of anything.

Even murdering the granddaughter she was claiming deserved the Golden Crown.

Yvera looked down. "But...what will everyone say? When she's dead?"

"That's why I must take the blame," Yalda said stoically. "You can say you resisted—for you truly have—that you did your duty, but I overcame you. I will then flee to a safehold I have prepared in the Urdek Mountains, where I can live out my exile until such a time as you can arrange my pardon. But I will give you a call scale, and I will guide you from a distance."

"You'd...give me a scale?" Yvera said, and there was almost a tremble to her voice now.

My iceheart sank even further. Was there yet another dynamic at play here? The over-achieving granddaughter, finally getting a scrap of approval from her distant, frigid grandmother? Was Yvera hypnotized or simply extremely conflicted? Hypnotized *and* conflicted?

My hands fisted, nails biting into my palms.

What do I do? I pleaded with my Tree.

I didn't get an answer.

"Of course, I would, darling granddaughter," Yalda said, smiling that brittle smile again and spreading her arms. She took a step forward. "Now, just give that girl to me—"

"No," Yvera said, but her refusal was only petulant. "Give it to me first. Give me the scale, and I'll give you...the girl."

"What?" Yalda said flatly.

"I want the scale," Yvera whined. "You've never given me *anything*. I want it *now*. Or you can't have her."

I blinked. Was Yalda's hypnotism reducing Yvera to the maturity level of a five-year-old?

"Oh, for Flame's sake," Yalda said, producing a violet scale in her free hand. Yvera approached eagerly, like a girl about to receive a piece of candy. "Here you go. Now—"

Yvera moved so fast that I didn't even know what she had done until it was over. In the next moment, Yalda was stumbling back, clutching a stump of an arm gushing hot, violet blood.

Yvera...had never put away her sword. And Yalda had foolishly let her get within range.

"What—you—you," Yalda raged, pain and shock making her beyond coherence for a moment. Her next words slurred, thick with agony. "You *fool*. Don't you see? I'm avenging your mother for her dying for that Peacegrowth wh—"

Yvera kicked her in the chest, sending Yalda staggering, then falling to her knees. "That Peacegrowth *was* my mother, you torched asher. And I'm sure as hellfrost not going to let you kill her son's—my *brother's*—betrothed."

Then Yvera whammed her grandmother with an armored punch to her temple that made Yalda keel over and finally go still.

Yvera flipped her braid and smirked down at Yalda. "Now, I believe that's called *strategy*."

She stooped and began dealing with Yalda's still-gushing limb with brisk, businesslike movements. "Sarah, see if you can get that door open to let the others in and call Kor. He's going to want to get on this—*now*."

I finally unfroze, my brain only now catching up with what had just happened.

I...was alive.

Yvera...was neither hypnotized nor a traitor.

And a Lady of the Six Realms...had gone insane and tried to kill me, and now she was unconscious and bleeding out on the floor, and her hand was lying nearby. Totally separated from her body. I could even see the....

"Give...me a sec," I choked. Then I turned, stumbled, and vomited into a bucket that was among other miscellaneous equipment. The bucket had some things inside it already, but oh well.

Even over my heaving, I heard Yvera's loud huff of exasperation.

CHAPTER ELEVEN

RED-HANDED

KORIBEN

AS LOW ON FUEL as I was after the duel, it only took a few dek of throwing fireballs at a training room wall before I burned dry. No doubt that timing had been intentional on Kor's part.

And on Yalda's.

That sickening realization was enough to make red creep across my vision again, and I had no spark left to spend to drive it back. So, I turned to a punching bag—thank *Flame* that Kor and Ordran had dragged me into a small, well-equipped training room first before giving me the news—and pummeled it with my bare fists until it burst at the seams and the sand spilled onto my boots.

Then I stood still as I could, hands on my hips, eyes squeezed shut, heaving from exertion, knuckles burning, fighting with all my might to rein in my Royal berserk rage with willpower alone. Before it made me do something to an innocent.

When my breaths finally stilled, I opened my eyes and looked at Kor and Ordran, who stood at the other end of the room, guarding the door.

From me, of course. There was another elite outside, keeping anyone from coming in.

"I need Sarah," I said flatly.

I *also* needed to run my sword through a certain Lady's flameheart, but I would not be allowed to do that until after a trial. So, for now, Sarah would have to do.

Kor and Ordran shared a look.

"Ben," Ordran said hesitantly, looking back at me. "Are you sure you're ready?"

I didn't bother with him. He wasn't the one responsible for evaluating my stability. I looked at Kor. "I need to see her. This isn't going away on its own, not completely. I know you've brought her somewhere close by, and that's making it even harder. I *need* her."

Kor sighed, as if he'd been expecting this. Then looked at the sand on the floor, and the fresh scorch marks on the wall. "I was planning on bringing her in here when you were ready, but I should have realized that wouldn't be ideal."

I understood what he meant. Under normal circumstances, Sarah would just blink at the signs of my wanton destruction. Right now....

I could only imagine what she was going through—but trying to imagine it was just making the rage *worse*.

"Please," I begged. "If she can't...if I can't...I'll go, I swear. I just need to see her. With my own eyes."

Of course, I would want more than that, but I would have to satisfy myself with that much if I only caused Sarah more stress.

"Can you control yourself for a few hundred erd?" Kor asked clinically. "As in, expressions and everything?"

I made myself think about that.

"Yes," I said firmly.

"Alright then, come on." Kor rapped on the door, indicating to the elite beyond that we were coming out.

We followed him down some halls and turns—Kor wisely hadn't brought her *too* close—and finally we entered a meeting room, where Sarah sat with Yvera standing guard over her, and her father and brother sitting on either side.

"Ben!" Sarah said, pushing back from the table and rushing out of her seat.

In the next moment, she was wrapping herself around me, and I was lifting her up into my arms and crushing her into me, and almost everything was right with the world again.

Almost.

The red retreated from my mind, leaving me in control, but it condensed into a coal in my flameheart that I knew would not be quenched until I could see that justice was done. Preferably by me.

In the meantime....

"Are you alright?" I asked Sarah, cursing myself for using up all my spark so that I couldn't verify that much myself.

"Fine," she said immediately, no doubt expecting the question. "Just fine."

I leaned back and shifted her in my arms to give her a glare.

"Really," she said, cupping my face. "Just shaken. Just ask Yvera. She's embarrassed on my behalf for my weak, amón stomach."

"It was only a little blood," Yvera said, rolling her eyes.

"Excuse me," Sarah retorted, but her smile was surprisingly steady as she craned her neck to look back at my rightwing. "You chopped off her *hand*. There was more than just 'a little blood.'"

I groaned. Kor had said Yvera had knocked Yalda unconscious, but he had been vague about how, or how she'd gotten to that point. Now I understood why.

Though my flameheart lifted a bit to see Sarah smiling and even joking with Yvera about it now, it also clenched for her. She wasn't a weakling, and she had faced more than her fair share of danger since coming to our Realms, but she still hadn't been exposed to the degree of violence that Yvera and I had. She should not have had to go through something like that. *Any* of it.

I pulled Sarah against me for a moment...then reluctantly set her down and let her go. That was excruciatingly difficult for me, but I had something important to do: I strode over to my sister and crushed her in a hug, which she accepted with stiff stoicism.

"Thank you," I said thickly.

Flame, if she hadn't been there.... I couldn't even think it. Maybe Sarah could have gotten away, or fought her way out, or surged to me, or something.

Or maybe not.

Yalda, after all, had been clever in her madness. That she had somehow hidden it for this long was a testament to that. Her greatest mistake had been thinking she knew her granddaughter—in seeing herself in Yvera. When, in reality, they shared almost nothing in common but blood.

Yvera cringed at my emotional display. "Yeah, well...you would have been even more of a sobbing mess without her, so...there."

That wasn't true. I shuddered to think what I might have done if Yalda had been successful. I might not have lived past the end of my berserk rage, because someone might have had to kill me to end the bloodshed.

It had happened once before, when a Queen's consort had been killed and the Queen couldn't be brought back to her senses. Innocents were dying. Something had to be done. So...her rightwing did it. And that time, the murderers had been consumed. With Yalda being one of our own, one of our *Nobles*....

Repeating history in a way it never should have been again....

But I wasn't about to admit those fears about myself out loud. Especially not in front of Sarah.

I focused on the other untruth in Yvera's words, the one she already knew about.

You can't fool me, I sent to her as I pulled away. I gave her a tight smile through the tears stinging my eyes. *I know that deep, deep down, you* like *Sarah.*

Despite Yvera's declaration to me that she never would.

Ridiculous, Yvera snapped. But she wasn't meeting my eyes, and I heard the off note in her voice that always gave her away.

She was as terrible a liar as I was.

"How could this have happened?" I asked.

With all of us now together, and me calm enough to be thinking again, we all sat down around the table for an impromptu emergency meeting. Sarah's hand in mine resting on top of the table went a long way to *keeping* me calm through this discussion.

"We're still figuring that out for certain," Kor said with a grimace. "I've had my people working on it since nearly the moment Sarah called me, and Eskala and Alyish arrived half a deken ago to take over the situation so Yvera and I could brief you. Still, a lot of things are still uncertain, and probably will be for days. But I assume you want my theory."

"I do." I understood it would be a guess, but I needed *something* now. And Kor was usually right, anyway.

"Then here's what I *think* happened: Yalda's mental decline truly began around the Solstice, when the Tournament was moved and the Second Invasion happened. That's when this Moontouched upstart she'd been hearing rumors about was officially confirmed to exist, to be in a relationship of some kind with you, *and* played such a crucial, lifesaving role in the battle. And Sarah won the loyalty of the majority of the Warflight because of it. That was the last stroke."

"The Warflight's loyalty," I said grimly, clenching Sarah's hand.

"Exactly," Kor said. To Sarah, he elaborated, "It was a loss for the Traditionalists generally and Yalda especially, given how much sway the Battleblood Noble has traditionally had within the Warflight, since the Battleblood contribute the most warriors of all the clans. It might have been the final confirmation her deteriorating mental state needed that the Realms were getting soft, weak—corrupted by Kavarian's decades-long progressive rule."

I hardened. "She would have seen his death as her best chance to halt that 'decline.' She would have seen me as weak, easy to manipulate."

"Especially if you married Yvera," Kor agreed. "That was the justification that Yvera got out of her."

I looked at Yvera in surprise.

"What?" she said, scowling. "I knew Kor would want information. She seemed more than willing to talk, so I let her. I do have a brain, you know."

"Oh, I know," I said hastily. I knew she was intelligent, and she couldn't have escaped being my rightwing for so long without absorbing *something* of what Kor did. She just didn't care. Normally. "That was smart. Thank you."

"She was incredible," Sarah piped up loyally. "Pretended to agree with Yalda and everything."

How well? I sent to Sarah, amused at Yvera's preening.

Um...well, she had me nervous, mostly because I couldn't get what was wrong *with her, but looking back....*

Say no more, I said, suppressing a grin. I could imagine what Yvera's acting "skills" would have been like. If Yalda had known her at all, or had been any less insane, Yvera would never have fooled her.

"So, Yalda finally started breaking down," Kor said grimly. To Sarah, he said, "She's been a spear in the Crown's tail for a while, but just that: a nuisance. That didn't change after the Solstice. If anything, she's been more cooperative since then. I should have seen that as one of the signs, instead of a change of heart."

He scowled.

"Kor," I said with a sigh. "This is unprecedented. A Noble, trying to kill a Royal consort?"

Nobles were Tree-chosen, just like Royals were. Which didn't mean they were immune to moral corruption, especially the kind that power too easily brought, but there were many safeguards in place to remove a Noble if something like this were to happen. Somehow, Yalda had bypassed them all.

"Ellanya—her leftwing—" Kor clarified for Sarah before looking back at me, that scowl returning. "—*told* us that Yalda was acting strangely. Hardly sleeping, eating, that sort of thing. And the threats coming from Ekrel.... Looking back, I can see all the signs, and I *missed* them."

Kor pounded the table with his fist.

To our surprise, Yvera was the one to speak first. "Well, isn't that the way it always is with this kind of stuff?"

When we looked at her, she glared, particularly at Kor. "Why do you think I hate your job so much? Things always seem obvious looking back. Because that's what *happened*. But the future? All maybes, all just as likely. It's a nightmare. I don't know why you aren't as torched mad as Yalda right now from trying. Speaking of...."

Yvera shook her finger at Kor. "What leader in the Six Realms *hasn't* missed sleep these past hellfrosted months? Flame knows you and I have, let alone Ben. I'll bet Fenrith hasn't been sleeping well. He was looking thinner, so I'm guessing not enough food for him, either. And yet you didn't suspect *him* of wanting to kill Sarah—even though she got sick right in front of him. Yalda is smart, Kor. That's the torched truth. Smart enough to throw even you and Eskala off her scent for long enough for her to get close to Sarah, especially with all the other blasted crises we've been facing, one right after the other."

She leaned back, fingering the end of her braid, flicking it in her agitation. "Remember, this is my fault too. I'm in charge of our safety, but even I didn't think it would be Yalda first. Remember, she isn't the only person on Ekrel that has it in for Sarah; those plots you've been chasing and warning me about could still be real. Yalda was just the one who got to her first. We need to just accept that and move on. We've got other things to talk about, then do, to keep Ben and Sarah safe."

Kor stared at her for one long moment, then hardened. "Alright. Yes. Enough about me. In any case, Ellanya knew and reported that something was off, but Yalda had been holding her at arm's length, frequently sending her away on extended assignments. We think something similar, if more severe, happened to her rightwing and Heir, who haven't been seen since Sarah returned to the Six Realms."

"What?" I asked flatly. "I thought Redrik and Emayn were dealing with a rock wyrm nest in Yarmin."

Another oddity, looking back: that the Battleblood Heir couldn't have been spared even for the Tournament.

"That's what we were told," Kor said with a grimace, no doubt thinking the same thing. "Yet I come to find out that it was a harpy flock before that, and a vorpex colony before that. It has been one thing after another for them for the past twenty days, to the point that when we start truly trying to track them down, we find out that no one we can trust has seen or spoken directly with either of them for that long. And they have had the same set of warriors with them the entire time—never going home, never changing out. Yalda hand-picked each of them, and they are loyal to her to the core."

I went cold. "Are they...?"

"We're hoping they're still alive," Kor said wearily. "Yalda mentioned a safehold to Yvera in the Urdek Mountains. We've sent people to comb them for any sign of undocumented habitation, but it's only been about a deken, and, well, they have a lot of sky to cover."

"Looking for what is, no doubt, a carefully concealed shelter," I said, clenching my eyes shut and pinching the bridge of my nose. "So, you're guessing that the Tree revoked Yalda, and passed Her Flame to Redrik, and before Redrik and Emayn could do anything about that, she made them disappear."

"That's what it looks like," Kor agreed.

"Meanwhile, Yalda sends away her leftwing as much as she can and surrounds herself with loyalists, who wouldn't report any signs of madness they might have witnessed."

"Exactly."

That took care of nearly all the most effective safeguards against a Noble's misuse of their power. Oh, cabinet officials could raise concerns to the Crown, but since their Noble had direct control over their appointment—no Tree-confirmation necessary, as was the case with her right- and leftwings—Yalda would have filled them with unquestioning loyalists long ago.

Clan representatives could bring her before the Clansmeet or begin a formal inquiry with enough unity and political backing, but legislative action took much more time than executive—too slow to have made headway in the past twenty days, and that was even *if* they had been given any cause for concern during that time or were even willing to challenge Yalda.

After all, she wasn't beloved by her people, but she didn't need to be. She was competent, resolute, and lethal; those were the qualities that mattered most to the Battleblood. They were also the most Traditionalist clan and thus had seen her as being their balancing force against Avva. Even if the Battleblood Clansmeet had any idea of her mental deterioration, without knowing the full extent of what she was planning, they would have let her be, or assumed her wings and Heir would take care of things if they were truly bad.

Finally, this was a time of danger across the Six Realms. Dangerous times kept political squabbling to a minimum and unity surged to its highest point, and for good reason: it was how we survived. Yalda was—or, at least, had been—a more than competent shield for them. Now would have been the time for her clan to rally around her, not challenge her. They would have written off any signs of madness as simply the strain of sacrifice on their behalf.

Everything had come together to her advantage for this one moment. She had chosen the perfect time to strike, and in her ruthless intelligence, had removed the obstacles in her path with disturbing ease and prevented any others from forming, all the while keeping her madness and intentions from reaching outside her most loyal circle, let alone to the Golden Crown.

There was one more safeguard, however—the one that never should have failed. I felt a surge of resentment, as hot and thick as tar.

"Why didn't the Tree warn us?" I said flatly, lowering my hand and opening my eyes.

"She probably tried, through revoking Yalda and investing Redrik," Kor said dryly.

I waved my hand. "She would have known that wouldn't have been enough. *Why* didn't She get through to someone else? To the mother priestess? To *me*?"

I felt betrayed, the wound cutting deep into my flameheart. The Tree had said that if I did what She asked, She and Her Sister would protect Sarah. Was *this* how She kept Her promise? By keeping me in the dark about the insane bloodthirst that lay at the heart of one of my trusted Nobles?

"Because She knew I would be alright," Sarah said slowly.

I looked at her in surprise. Her face was thoughtful.

"I think...She made *certain* I would be alright. I think She made sure that the one person who would be with me was the one person Yalda thought she could trust—the person who would not only fight Yalda, but *win*."

She looked at Yvera, who fidgeted instead of preening under Sarah's compliment this time.

Sarah looked back at me. "That was Yalda's *only* mistake. Wasn't it? Letting Yvera fall into the trap with me. Thinking she could control her. She should have known better. She was smarter than to take a risk like that. But she did. I wonder if...the Tree was influencing Yalda even in her madness."

"You're saying the Tree *pushed* Yalda to try to kill you?" I demanded.

"No," Sarah said firmly. "I'm saying the Tree knew Yalda was going to try to kill me. So, the Tree made sure it happened in a way *She* could control."

"But why not just *tell* me, so we could have prev—"

I stopped, seeing the answer.

"How could we have proven Yalda's intentions in time?" Kor said quietly. "The Tree's warning to you would not have been justification alone for you dragging a Noble in front of her own Tree for a trial."

Kor was right. That was a safeguard against *Royal* overreach that worked in Yalda's favor: I couldn't bring a Noble to trial without evidence. Otherwise, if I were mad myself or just had it out for one of my Nobles, I could *make up* a Tree's warning to me. Even without the legal hindrance, the political ramifications—especially if I were mistaken—would be enormous. Perhaps enough at this delicate point to cause a schism in the Six Realms.

If the Tree had given me warning, with none of the proper flags having been raised by her own people, it would have been my word against Yalda's. Say I kept the information to myself, and we were only watchful...say I could have pretended for three days that I didn't suspect her (unlikely)...what more could we have done? Maybe tripled Sarah's guard, but that would have made Yalda's plans even more ruthless. If elites *had* been involved, she might have involved more of her own, and people might have died.

"Ben," Kor said reluctantly as he watched all these thoughts go through my mind. "I hate to say this, but...things turned out probably in the best possible way they could have. No innocent, much less Sarah, was hurt. Yalda played her hand, and not only did she utterly fail, but she also gave us everything we need to bring her to justice. Confession, witnesses.... We have even been able to—by some Flame-blessed miracle—keep this disaster contained. People think you, Sarah, and Yalda have stepped out to deal with some Ekrel crisis together. So far, people know something's wrong, but they have no idea what. No political forces are moving against us. Ellanya is giving us her full cooperation. Not even Yalda's loyalists can do anything without revealing they knew of the plot, and my people are making a list of who we might need to apprehend and question as we speak. The Golden Crown has complete control of the situation now, and all the justification we need to hold her in our custody and give her a swift trial."

He sighed heavily, resting his elbow on the table and his forehead in his palm. "I think...Sarah might be right. Yalda *had* to be dealt with, quickly and decisively, before she did further harm to her people or killed her Heir—technically, the real Lord Battleblood right now—if she hasn't already. And...Flame help me, I don't know what better way we could have done it."

"There is one more factor," Jake said quietly, startling us by speaking up for the first time. Mostly, he had listened and watched with those intelligent eyes of his, taking all the information in without obvious reactions or comments. Until now.

"What?" I asked heavily, not certain I wanted to hear it. The tar of betrayal wasn't leaving my chest easily, despite the overwhelming logic of it all.

I didn't want this situation to be *logical*. I wanted to take Yalda's life for daring to take Sarah's, and I wanted to rage at my Tree for letting her try—no matter the reason.

"Trees, as I understand it, know our thoughts, yes?"

I sighed, thinking I knew where this was going, but nodded. "Yes."

"The country I and my family come from has a value that can be summarized like this: the punishment does not come before the crime. There is a very fine balance between preventing imminent disaster and punishing someone for merely their thoughts. It is a hard line to walk, and I am not saying I have the answers here. But what if—Yalda's removal of her Heir aside—she had not fully committed to her course until the last moment? Until we arrived? Or perhaps even this very morning?"

We all were quiet. Sarah was smiling at her father for some unfathomable reason, and Kor was looking at him with respect, but the rest of us weren't meeting Jake's gaze.

"Your Tree then would have known Yalda's thoughts. She would have known whether Yalda was still wavering. She could even have been trying to convince her to turn back. Only She would have known when Yalda would have crossed the point of no return, and that could have been the moment Sarah walked into her trap. Might we then have overstepped, if we had condemned Yalda while there was still a chance for her to be reclaimed?"

"Dad," Michael muttered in exasperation.

I couldn't understand it either. Jake was speaking sense—more than sense, he was saying what was right and just, what I should have known and said myself. But this was his *daughter* that Yalda had just tried to kill. How could he be sitting here discussing fairness and redemption?

Then I saw the tightness of his interlaced hands where they rested on the table, the tension in his jaw, the unusual rigidity in his expression.

He wasn't unmoved. In fact, he was so furious, even *I* could tell he was, now that I was paying attention. He just wasn't pushed to and fro by his emotions, as I was. He was like the steadiest of duelists—able to stand his ground no matter what forces tried to knock him off balance or what taunts were thrown at him. That allowed him to see the situation with astounding clarity, even when it involved his own beloved daughter.

I was in awe.

"She would have been removed either way," Kor said quietly. "The Tree wouldn't have kept her as Lady after what she had done to her Heir, even if that Heir—Lord—is still alive. But...yes, I can see your point. The Tree could have given Yalda a lesser sentence, had she turned from her course. Now, though, both the Tree and the Crown can be fully justified in giving her the full punishment for the crime she finally chose to commit."

"Speaking of which," I said, more eager than I knew I should have been to get on with that punishment. "I'm sorry I got us derailed in talking for so long about what is past and uncertain besides."

I looked between my wings. "You two have done an incredible job so far, both in protecting Sarah and dealing with the aftermath. Thank you. But Yvera is right: some of our hardest work is ahead, that trial foremost among them. Kor, your recommendations?"

"We have the trial immediately, before the day is out. Ideal scenario, we find this new Lord safe and well and get *him* to close out the Tournament. The sooner we can get this over with, the better we can contain the fallout."

I nodded. "Makes sense."

"Speaking of containing, I propose we do the trial before making the announcement about the assassination attempt. We need more proof—and information, if we can get it, especially about the Lord's location and other potential accomplices, but Yalda has been uncooperative thus far. The Tree might get her to talk, or She could tell us where he is Herself."

"Agreed," I said, drumming my fingers on the table. "There's a problem with having a secret trial, though. Even with Ellanya there, all our witnesses are our own—representatives of the Golden and White Crowns. The fallout is going to be bad enough, but with a hushed-up trial, we're going to face accusations of overreach at best, falsification at worst."

Kor nodded, opened his mouth, stopped himself, closed it, and then looked at me with an evaluating expression.

"What?" I said self-consciously, stopping my drumming.

"You make a good point," Kor said smoothly. "So, how would you suggest mitigating that problem?"

I blinked at him. Not only had Kor admitted I was right about something, he was asking for *my* opinion?

"Why are you asking me? Don't you have some ideas?"

"I'm afraid my mind is drawing a blank right now," Kor said innocently. "Overwork, too little sleep. Like Yvera said. My apologies for failing you there."

Sarah made a tiny sound—a cough, laugh, or sneeze, I couldn't tell which—but when I glanced at her, her expression was neutral.

"But you seem to have a grasp of the situation," Kor said. "So, what would you suggest?"

I glared at him, certain he was baiting me into a trap. At the very least, he would dismiss whatever I suggested and then the right course would "occur" to him.

On the other hand, everyone was looking at me, and Kor didn't look like he was going to budge, so I didn't seem to have much choice but to think, then say what I thought. So, I did.

"If we're going to do a trial behind closed doors, I need Traditionalists there as witnesses. No one from the Warflight, because they can be accused of divided loyalties. No one who can remotely be called my ally, actually—but we still think can be trusted to not be torched crazy."

Kor smiled dangerously, and I was certain this was it: the moment he was going to shut me down. Instead, his words gave me an unpleasant jolt of an entirely different kind. "You're right. So, people like...Aldresh?"

The Keeper of Blood, head of the archivists who collected, interpreted, and guarded our precious bloodlines. Not only was he another leading Traditionalist, but he was also known to be no friend to either Sarah or me. Sarah had already had the misfortune of running afoul of him upon first meeting, during her blood registration—for no other reason than existing and betrothing herself to me without the full report on her bloodline being ready. His good opinion of *me* had been doomed from the start, since I was my father's son.

Yet...Aldresh was one of the most *peaceable* of our staunch opponents, known as just an old grumbler glorifying "the old days."

I groaned, putting my face into my hand.

"Yes, people like him."

Chapter Twelve

TRIAL

Sarah

Since they were trying to spare me as much of the burden of being in the Tree of Flame's presence as they could, I entered the Heart Chamber of Krevenyir last, just behind Dad and Michael and arm in arm with Ben. Besides, it seemed to fit their tradition of the highest rank coming last, so none of the gathered audience seemed to think anything of it. They just stood on either side of the paved path as we passed by, expressions ranging from neutral to solemn to—in Aldresh's case—thunderous.

Good thing there weren't many of them, because there wasn't much of a shoulder on either side for them to stand on.

The Ekrel Tree of Flame was, of course, in the center of an enormous cavern, perched on a high outcropping of rock that was in the middle of a ring of—you guessed it—*lava*. (Or was it magma? I could never remember which was which.) There was a stone rim that went around the circular cavern as far as I could see that looked walkable, but the path we were on was the only access to Her and the circular terrace with its central firepit at Her base. The purple flames in that pit, the thousands of burning purple leaves high above our heads, and the glowing lava below were the only sources of illumination in that vast, dark cavern, and the blend of orange and purple light seemed suitably ominous.

Ice help me, I prayed this trial would not take long, because having heat come from *all* sides now was already making my spellweave clothing work in overdrive to keep me at a bearable temperature. If I still sweated, I would have been soaked before we even made it across that land bridge. I could see why Ben, Kor, and Vadya had fussed so much about the length of my exposure.

How are you doing? Ben asked. His glance toward me was casual, but his inner voice was anxious.

I'll live.

I'll try not to let them drag this out. I promise.

His eyes hardened as they drifted toward Yalda, standing straight and stiff on the terrace with her back to us, her arms bound to her sides by a rope that had glowing gold strands in it. The look in Ben's eyes as he gazed at her sent goosebumps up my arms.

It's not fair, I muttered to Ben to distract him. *You didn't have this much trouble being around* my *Tree.*

Kor has a theory about that.

Of course he did. *Being?*

The Tree of Flame is, by nature...intense.

Just like Her King, and the one before him—both in their own ways. And like Her children.

Ah...I suppose that makes sense.

My iceheart thumped as I wondered how that quality in Her and Her children would play out in this trial.

When the verdict was given, they weren't going to just...kill her. Were they?

I was too afraid to ask.

Once we reached the terrace, Ben brought us around to the right side, giving Yalda a wide berth. Yvera and the elites who had been with me already stood across from us on the left side. A saddened Battleblood woman—much younger than I had expected, perhaps in her twenties, and short for a drakón, shorter than even Kor—stood by Yalda and the guards flanking her.

The space across the firepit from them was empty. For now.

Ellanya took a deep breath. Then said, "Our Lady of the Flame. We have come before You now, asking for Your presence."

Even though I was *looking,* fixing my gaze on the spot, I still didn't see Her appear. My eyes skittered to the side for just that one split second, almost against my will. And then, She was there—the naked Woman with coal for a body, floating particles of ash for hair, embers for eyes, and tongues of purple flame for the occasional covering.

Michael started at my side. Only then did I realize that this would be Michael's and Dad's first times seeing the Tree of Flame—either the Tree or Her avatar. This was only my second time, but once before had been enough to fix Her in my memory, even with the difference in flame color. Now I could see what Ben meant: there was an intensity to this Tree that our much slower and gentler Tree lacked.

"*Speak, Leftwing Ellanya,*" the Tree said, Her voice like crackling flames. "*I am here and will hear your request.*"

Yalda stiffened at that, surprised for some reason.

"Thank You, my Lady," the leftwing said with a bow. She rose with a heaviness in her eyes, and she gestured to Yalda as she spoke. "The Queen of Ice and the King of Flame have brought an accusation against Yalda Battleblood. We have brought them before You for trial and judgment."

The Tree turned to...me.

My iceheart raced at feeling those burning ember eyes on me. I panicked, my mind going blank for a second. I had expected Ben to do the talking!

"*Speak your accusation, Queen of Ice. I will hear it.*"

I took several quick, deep breaths that hopefully no one aside from Ben noticed. He clenched my hand tightly in comfort.

"O Lady of Flame," I said carefully. I had been about to say *my Lady,* but didn't know if that was quite right. No one seemed to react to that substitution, so I breathed an inward sigh of relief and continued. "Earlier today, Yalda Battleblood...attempted to take my life."

Gasps and whispers broke out among our carefully selected audience, who had gathered around at the back of the terrace. When my eyes flicked over to them, I saw Aldresh's face go slack with shock. Whatever trumped-up cause he had thought we had fabricated to drag the Battleblood Lady before her Tree, he had not imagined it would be this.

Was it really so unbelievable to these people that a Noble would commit murder? With one of her hands missing, I wasn't certain what Aldresh thought would be the reason, except losing it in a deadly fight with one of us. And who was she most likely to target except me?

Although, as my eyes went back to the Tree, I had to do a double take at Yalda. Hadn't Yvera chopped off her right hand? And yet there it was. Gloved, true, but leaving no obvious sign of a conflict on her. Whether that was an illusion, or a fake hand, or the dramá healers had once again worked miracles and reattached it, I didn't know and didn't have time to ask, let alone think about it further.

"*Have you any witnesses to support your accusation?*" the Tree of Flame said, nothing in Her voice or expression varying one bit from what it had been before.

Uh, yes. You made sure of that, I thought with nervous attitude, but I tried to school my thoughts. There was a reason for this formality. This was the way of justice.

"Yes," I said, gesturing across the fire. "Yvera Battleblood, rightwing of the King of Flame, was there, and came to my defense. The others with her attempted to do the same but were shut out before they could enter."

The Tree turned to Yvera, who stood tall and proud. If she had any qualms about standing as a witness against her own grandmother, she didn't show it.

"*Rightwing Yvera Battleblood, do you witness that what the Queen of Ice has accused Yalda Battleblood of is true?*"

"I do, my Lady," Yvera said calmly. "Yalda confessed her intentions to me and even tried to persuade me to allow it, all so that she could arrange for me to marry the King of Flame instead, then use me as her puppet within the Crown."

"You ungrateful *wretch*," Yalda spat. "I was doing it for you—for your mother, for our Realms!"

Yvera just raised an eyebrow, not dignifying that with a response. Instead, she just looked back at the Tree. "You see? She doesn't deny it."

More shocked whispers from the audience, but this time I didn't let my gaze wander.

Yalda raised her chin, looking back at the Tree. "Of course I don't deny it. Tell them, my Lady. You were the one who commanded me to do the deed—for the good of the Realms."

Stunned silence, all around. Even Yvera blinked in shock.

The Tree's ember eyes flared, and Her voice snapped out like a lashing tongue of flame. "*You are mistaken. You were deceived...and so easily allowed yourself to be so.*"

Yalda stilled, staring. "What?"

The Tree looked around the entire terrace until Her eyes rested on the audience. She raised Her hand, and Her voice rang out, hard and hot. The flames in the firepit surged higher, and the burning leaves above flared stronger. I felt a wave of heat that made me wobble as the power in my spellweave clothing's gems waned and my own limited power instinctively surged to recharge them. Ben threw his hand out behind me to subtly steady me.

"*Heed my warning now, all of you, and heed it well,*" the Tree declared. "*The Devourer does not need to consume you for you to be one of its tools. The more centuries have passed, the cleverer it has become. The greater a hold it has obtained in My Realms, the more its influence has strengthened as well, invisible though it may be to you. The more you turn your hearts from Me, the more you harden yourselves against My touch and My wisdom, the more you leave yourselves vulnerable to the enemy of us all.*"

Ben stiffened. When I'd had this epiphany, I thought I was only just catching up with yet another thing that he had grown up knowing, or I would have told him. Instead, this appeared to be news to him—of the most disturbing kind.

And news to everyone else, who looked among themselves with expressions ranging from discomfort to horror. Aldresh was on the latter end of that spectrum, growing even paler as the Tree's eyes seemed to linger on him.

Then She turned back to Her fallen Lady. "*Yalda Battleblood, My daughter—I say again that you were deceived, by the Devourer itself. For that, I do not condemn you. For your hardness of your heart, I condemn you. For not seeing the inherent evil in what you thought I asked you to do, for not questioning it. For not coming to Me these many months, where I might have corrected you and healed your heart of the darkness whispering ever more loudly in your soul. For that, and for desiring the Queen of Ice's blood of your own accord, I condemn you."*

Yalda trembled. Her face was ashen.

The Tree once again addressed the terrace at large. *"I confirm the Queen of Ice's accusation. Yalda Battleblood sought the life of My Sister's chosen vessel, and for that, Yalda has not been my Lady, not for these twenty days. I revoked her then and invested My Heir. For that, Yalda locked him away, lest he reveal her secret. She further listened to the Devourer's deceit that she still held My favor, that her Heir was lying, greedy for power and seeking to depose her. Never once in those days did she come before Me. Never once did she ask Me if her course was indeed My will. She believed the dark whispers because she wished to. She believed because she refused to accept that the times of old are past—and were never meant to be. That this order, these 'traditions' some of My children have come to hold sacred were only necessary because of the hardness of your hearts."*

Again, Her eyes seemed to linger on Aldresh, who didn't look much steadier than Yalda by that point.

"Know that the only reason I allowed Yalda to make the attempt was so that I could show that her punishment was just, and so I could tell you of the darkness lingering in some of your hearts. I and My Sister protected the Queen, and We allowed no harm to come to her. Nor will We tolerate any such attempts to harm her or her clan again. Nor will I tolerate the hardness of My children's hearts regarding what must be any longer. Let this be your warning."

Her coal lips were almost curling in a snarl. Her voice still was not a shout, but it had enough force to rattle me to the core, and from the looks on everyone else's faces, I wasn't the only one.

Though my iceheart perhaps had more cause than any to race when She pointed to me, still looking around at the others.

"Know this once and for all: this woman is My Sister the Tree of Ice's chosen Queen and one of the keys to your salvation. Know that if you bring harm to her, you bring doom to all. Furthermore, it is Our will that she become your Queen, the true and equal mate of your King. You will obey her as you would obey him, for in Our eyes, they will be—they must be—one."

That made me start. Was She suggesting what I thought She was? That I wouldn't just be Ben's consort over the Six Realms but....

Discussions about that would have to come later, because the Tree scarcely gave us time to catch our breath before She looked back at Yalda, who had sunk to her knees and trembled so badly I thought she was going to fall over entirely.

"F—forgive me, my Lady," Yalda said, voice shaking. "As You said, I was deceived!"

"*You wished to be,*" the Tree said, Her voice dropping in power and volume, a hint of sadness entering Her expression for the first time. "*I gave you every chance to turn back to Me, My daughter. And you refused every one. I can show you no mercy.*"

After an ominous pause, She looked up at Ben. "*King of Flame, come forth.*"

My iceheart began racing, and given the heat all around, my fingers felt absurdly cold as Ben slowly pulled his from them and walked with measured, purposeful steps toward Yalda.

Any hope I'd held out that the dramá didn't believe in the death penalty withered as I watched that walk. It was the stalk of a lion toward its fallen prey.

Ben, I whispered. Even I wasn't sure what I was asking him for. Surely not to disobey his Tree. And yet...was he...could he....

He didn't answer. Everyone else around Yalda—her leftwing and guards—retreated, leaving the trembling woman alone. She flinched when Ben came into her view and stopped in front of her, regarding her for a moment. Then he turned to his Tree.

"I am here, my Lady."

I flinched much like Yalda had. There was something so flat in Ben's voice, so unlike the one I knew.

The Tree raised Her hand, palm facing the ground, fingers spread. "*I have judged this woman, Yalda Battleblood, who once was My chosen Lady...and I declare her guilty of the accusation brought before her, and of holding her Heir and rightwing captive and deceiving her people.*"

She turned Her palm upward. "*I give her now to you to administer justice, as is your right as King and betrothed.*"

I felt a flicker of hope. The Tree had just said "administer justice." Not "kill her." Perhaps Ben would....

Ben bowed to the Tree. Then he brought out a sword, his hand crawling with scales and his nails sharpening momentarily into talons even more than usual to make the weapon materialize in his hand before shifting fully back to human flesh.

I realized, then, that I had never seen Ben kill someone. Monsters who had been trying to kill us both—yes. But not someone I recognized as a person.

I'd learned early on that he had killed people. He hadn't deceived me about that. Yet somehow, I had always pictured him having to do it in the middle of a battle, when he had no choice. He had a choice here. This was a woman, now looking old and frail, tied up and trembling before him.

His Tree had given him a choice...

...and he was choosing this.

He wasn't conflicted about it, either—or if he was, he was hiding it unusually well. His stance was confident, his grip on his sword steady. He didn't have the aliveness that his duel had brought out in him, but he had some of that same stillness, surety.

Ben, I repeated, this time in horror.

As he turned to fully face Yalda, his back still to me, he finally replied, with a hint of sadness in his inner voice that was much like the Tree's. *Don't look, Sarah.*

Until this moment, I had never truly seen him. I had claimed to have seen and known all the darkness there was to be found in him, and yet I had not.

How was I supposed to look away?

As he raised that sword, Dad answered that question for me by pulling me into his chest.

"Don't look," he whispered as he wrapped his arms around me.

I let my father stop me from seeing....

But even he couldn't stop me from hearing.

Chapter Thirteen

SORROW

Sarah

Hours later, I sat on my bed, numb and empty, that moment replaying again and again like a horrible, broken record in my mind.

It didn't help that this was the first chance I'd had to process. Even though I was whisked away shortly after that—trial over, no need to make the poor, sensitive Queen endure any more—I had only been given a short time to rest, and I had immediately fallen into a blessedly dreamless sleep until I was dragged from the comforting arms of oblivion by Vadya waking me to prepare for the Tournament's closing ceremony.

With the Tree's instructions, the searchers had found the safehold Yalda had prepared, where her loyalists were holding the Lord and the rightwing captive. Some fought, some were killed, and some surrendered when the searchers explained Yalda was dead, condemned by her Tree, maddened by her own blindness and deceived by the Devourer.

Though physically leaner and more mentally strained than when he had entered his makeshift prison, the new Battleblood Lord was alive, and he returned and stoically oversaw the closing ceremony. No explanation was given for his sudden reappearance and Yalda's absence. Ben, Kor, Eskala, and Alyish all recommended to Lord Redrik that they delay the announcement of Yalda's execution and his ascension until after the Tournament was over so that its good effects wouldn't be erased by the devastating news, and Redrik had agreed.

Even so, Ben had run his hand through his hair as soon as we were out of sight again, sighed, and murmured to Kor, "Flame, this is *not* how I wanted this Tournament to end."

He'd glanced at me, as if on reflex, and I looked away. Out of the corner of my eye, though, I saw his shoulders sink even further as he walked away. He knew better than to approach me, let alone touch me. He knew that from the moment Dad finally let me go, and Ben's and my eyes met while his sword was still dripping with violet blood.

Perhaps he knew that from the moment he let go of my hand and walked away to become an executioner.

And now here I sat at last, a tray of food on my bedside table that I had hardly touched. Finally alone again, except this time sleep did not save me from memory.

It wasn't that I didn't understand Ben's decision at all. Part of me did, and that was part of the problem.

Should I be mourning Yalda? I didn't even know her—she had gone out of her way to avoid me, interacting with me only when she *had* to. She had clearly been a terrible grandmother and a hard Lady who had given herself to the Devourer's deceptions and deceived her people in turn. That kind of abuse of her position could not be taken lightly. And...well, she had tried to *kill* me. And had imprisoned the rightful Lord; yes, she hadn't killed him (we still did not know why), but I had seen enough of the haunted look in his eyes to know how terrible that captivity had been on him, even just mentally. I didn't ask if anything else had been done to him; I didn't think it was my place to.

All the logical parts of me said that justice had been done.

And yet all the human—yes, *human*—parts of me were screaming away in my head, telling me to feel *something*. To find some sort of injustice in the severity and swiftness of her punishment, to see things as the Sarah I had once been would have seen them, the Sarah that had been an innocent girl exhausted from high school and caring for her younger siblings and fretting about which college to go to. The Sarah who had lived in a society where execution wasn't the norm, even for the highest of crimes.

To be *human* and not...not whatever I had become. Not a Queen who had to be the target of assassination or accuse the assassin before a tribunal. Not the child of Ice who had killed as well.

I had. Even though I had justified it in my mind by telling myself they were just beasts or monsters, all of them trying to kill me. But I had. I was a killer now, too. So, it wasn't like I thought I was any better than Ben, just because I hadn't ever had to kill someone who looked like a person to me.

For the first time, I just wanted to turn back time, to go back to being that girl...even if it meant I would never meet Ben.

And I didn't know *why*. That was perhaps the most terrible thing of all. I didn't know why I was feeling this way—or stopping myself from feeling at all. Alyish had said that clarity was my strength. Dad had called it introspection.

Then why was my soul now a more alien landscape to me than all Six Realms had ever been?

A knock on the door. I looked up, then looked back down. Who else could it be but Ben? I simply couldn't face him yet.

And I still didn't know why.

So, I ignored the knock, hoping he would go away.

A knock again. Then Dad's inner voice. *Sarah?*

I started. Why had I thought it had been Ben? Why hadn't I checked...?

The pull. Which had narrowed down to a thread of what it had once been, almost a whisper. I was unconsciously choking it off, almost to nonexistence. Not entirely, but further than I'd ever done before.

No wonder Ben was staying away from me.

I wondered for a moment what my star looked like in his mind right now. Was it going out?

Sarah? I'm coming in, Dad said, his voice gentle but firm.

Then the door pushed open, with Vadya standing there. She held the door back and gestured for Dad to enter, which he did with a quiet "thank you."

She nodded, only glancing at me with a tight look in her eyes before leaving and letting the door swing shut again. Only then did I realize Dad didn't have the magical authorization to open it. Not that I felt like fixing that. Or felt like doing anything at all—but somehow I doubted that inclination would change when I started feeling again. I was old enough to deny my dad unrestricted access to my bedroom.

Especially the one I shared with....

Dad paused for a moment to just look at me. I stared back at him.

Then the dam broke, and I burst into sobs. He sighed and walked over to me, sat down on the bed and pulled me into his arms, and I cried into him as I hadn't since I was a very little girl, far younger than the one I'd just wished to be again. And yet, what would I give to be her again, too. To have my father hold my small body in his arms while I cried over nothing more than a scabbed knee...and not over a broken heart.

Even now, I still didn't know why it was breaking.

Dad let me cry, not saying anything. He didn't say anything when I soaked his shirt with tears and mucus, or when my sobs finally stilled. He didn't say anything as I sat there, or when I pulled away to find a handkerchief, or even when he handed one to me himself.

I stared at that handkerchief in his fingers. Dad was old-fashioned, but he wasn't the type to just carry around a handkerchief in his pocket. Let alone one with a gold-embroidered border that looked like one of....

"He said you might need it."

Tears flowed, and my throat choked again.

How? How could Ben be so kind and yet....

I haltingly took his handkerchief and used it.

It still smelled like him. As soon as my nose was clear enough to smell again, that warm aroma with notes that reminded me of sunbaked stone, creosote, and juniper flooded my nasal passages and seemed to penetrate my lungs, then my blood, thawing some of the ice there with each inhale.

And that *hurt.*

I lowered the handkerchief, even as I was tempted to keep holding it to my nose like a ball of potpourri.

"Did he send you?" I rasped.

"No. He's in Kor's suite right now, so he simply saw me pass by when I came to check on you."

"What's he doing there?" I asked, surprised. When he and Kor needed to talk about something, Kor always came to Ben's study. Then I realized I knew the answer before Dad said it.

"Presumably, giving you space."

I looked down at the handkerchief I was balling in my hand.

How?

"Why did you come?" I asked hoarsely.

"Because you're my daughter, and you're in pain."

I clenched the ball more tightly. "You haven't come to tell me all the reasons I shouldn't be in pain right now?"

"No, because there aren't any."

"What?" I asked, startled into looking up.

Tears glimmered in Dad's own silver eyes. "You have every right to be in pain right now, Sarah. That woman tried to kill you today. Then you had to watch what Yvera had to do to her to defend you, and what Ben had to do to her to end this."

"Why?" I said, hating how small and lost my voice sounded. I should be stronger than this. Harder. "Why did he do it, Dad? The Tree gave him a choice—"

"No, She didn't, Sarah," Dad said gently.

"She said *justice*, not *execution*."

"What else do you think he could have done?" he said, still in that gentle tone. "What do you think would have happened if Ben had spared her life after the Tree said what She did? He might have undone everything the Tree was trying to do."

"What was that?" I whispered. But I thought I knew. I'd known so many of these things already, even though I couldn't help asking Dad the questions, hoping I would get an answer that would stop making me so....

"She was trying to make as certain as was possible for Her to do that this did not happen again, as faint as the hope of that might be," Dad said grimly. "What

Yalda did has far-reaching implications, beyond even you. It was an abuse of her position of trust and power that has, incredibly, never happened before over the course of their history. That sets a *precedent*. An extremely dangerous one. Once people hear of this, once this spreads and enters their collective psyche, it will become that much easier for it to happen again, because now what was once impossible is not just possible, it happened. The only way to even somewhat combat that is to impress upon their minds the consequences of her actions as well."

Dad sighed and looked down. "We may look at their solution, at its swiftness and bloodiness, and think it is barbaric, but the more I think about it, the more I think it is, perhaps, more civilized than any human justice system on Earth."

"What?" I whispered. This, at least, was new.

"What would a leader in one of our countries have suffered if she had done something like this there? In some of them, she would never have been found out. In others, she would never have been tried. In some, she might have been given house arrest or escaped to another country, and in both those scenarios, she could have lived to paint herself as a martyr and fomented a movement to cause further bloodshed and chaos. Same if she went to prison and was inevitably released some years later. Some countries might have executed her, but simply because she was the loser at the end of a power struggle with another tyrant. And say, in the most 'civilized' scenario you can think of, that she is locked in a prison cell for life, with no chance to do anyone harm ever again...is that really mercy? To let her mind finish its deterioration, now with the added horror of her eyes being opened to what she'd done?"

Dad sighed again. "In this case in particular...I think Ben did the civilized thing—the thing that will preserve *civilization*. The merciful thing. For everyone. The thing that will hopefully save lives and hold together the fabric of their society for years to come...and finally open their eyes to the horror of what the Devourer can do through them, if they aren't on their guard."

Dad let that sink in for a moment. I was looking back down at my hands, at the handkerchief I was clenching inside one.

All those things made too much sense. They fit in with so many of the things I had already known. They had contributed to the numbness I had forced on myself, to try to keep the pain at bay, to tell myself I *knew* why he'd done it. That I, a Queen who had sworn to give my all in the service of my Tree and for the good of all life, shouldn't be hurting like this.

"I thought you said that I had a reason to be in pain," I said quietly.

"You do," Dad said heavily. "Because an innocence that still lived inside you before today is now dead. And because you had an idealistic view of Ben...and now you do not. Even after all you have been through, you still didn't know just how hard a place the world was, and thus how hard Ben had to be to lead in it."

My eyes stung as he finally put into words my pain.

"*Why him?*" I cried out, as if the words had been building up underneath the ice this entire time and now, with it broken, were surging free.

I shook my hand with the balled handkerchief—the symbol of the Ben that I thought I had known, just as crumpled as that view of him was.

"Why did it have to be *him*?" I sobbed. "Why couldn't it...have been Yvera...or the Tree...or *anyone* else but *him*?"

If it had been anyone else, I would not be in this state right now. I suddenly understood that with perfect clarity. If anyone else had been the executioner, I would have been disturbed, but all the rational reasons would have had the settling effect I was immune to now. After all, I had watched Yvera chop off Yalda's hand, and I had only thrown up from shock and then was joking about it with her hours later.

But not him.

Not my Ben. Not my sun.

The kindest soul I knew...who had just killed someone in cold blood in front of me.

"Because he is the King," Dad said softly. "It isn't his fault that you now know what that means. But it isn't your fault that the truth hurts you, either."

"Isn't it?" I whispered. "I'm a Queen."

I squeezed my eyes shut. *I'm supposed to be* his Queen. Their Queen.

"You are not weak, Sarah. You are *tender*. And that is a beautiful, beautiful thing."

I opened my eyes, which were swimming with tears again. "Why?"

"Because your heart is the exact opposite of Yalda's. It is the heart that it would be better if we could all have. You can cry at the death of the woman who tried to kill you. Can't you see how beautiful that is?"

When I looked down, unable to meet the softness of Dad's eyes any longer, he persisted. "You are an incredibly precious thing, Sarah. You can see the world both as it is and believe wholly in *how it should be*. And when the two are so terribly out of harmony, you do not harden. You weep. You mourn the wrong that has been done not to you but to the soul of life itself, and you weep because you know another death does not heal it. And it does not—it only cauterizes it."

"It hurts," I whispered.

"As it should."

"You're not hurting like this. Ben isn't."

"Oh, I wouldn't be too sure of that."

I looked up at Dad in surprise, and he smiled a bit wistfully. "You're more like me than you think, Sarah. I, too, am a bit of an idealist. Only I have had more time to become disillusioned with the world we came from. Perhaps that is one reason I am so accepting of the methods I have seen these people use to preserve this one."

"You're a pacifist," I said slowly, the realization dawning.

"I used to be," he said grimly. "But I haven't been true to that ideal for years now, long before we came here. And then we come here, and...they have something extraordinary here, Sarah. Something I was searching for my entire life but never found. And now that I have found it, I will not see it go the way of Earth. Who am I to say the dramá's methods are inhumane when ours have not made a better world?"

"And Ben?" I whispered.

Dad sighed. "In a way, both I and the people you came from are to blame for some of the disillusionment you're feeling about him now. I raised you to think there is always a nonviolent solution. America raised you to think—at least subconsciously—that a true hero never has to kill to administer *justice*. They only have to lock the villain in a prison. But even those stories are replete with examples of the harm a villain can continue to inflict even from there, let alone when they break free again. Which is the better choice? To sacrifice one hardened life to give justice to the hundreds the villain has killed and save the hundreds or even thousands more tender ones the villain could kill again?"

"How would you know? That they would kill again?" I whispered.

"On Earth, I would have said it is impossible to say. But things are different here. Here, they have someone who knows. And, wisely, they listen to Her."

I opened my fist and stared at the exposed cloth ball in my hand.

After a pause, Dad went on. "But just because Ben understood all of that before that trial even began does not mean he isn't hurting right now...especially for having to do this to you. That is the dilemma a *real* hero faces: how to protect people like you without becoming people like Yalda. How to be hard *and* tender at the same time. Because that is the balance that Ben somehow has to find if he is going to be the King his people, his Tree, and you need him to be."

I fingered the handkerchief...and began smoothing it out on the bed.

"Doesn't that mean I need to become harder?" I rasped. "Like him?"

"I hope not. For all our sakes."

I glanced at him. His eyes were moist again. "You help the rest of us find that balance, Sarah. You, our tender heart. You did that for me today. You're doing that for Ben now. Both of us were a little too eager for justice. You reminded us how hollow it should feel."

"You?" I asked in surprise.

"I said we are alike. Yet there is one significant difference between you and me." He smiled thinly. "I am a father, and today, someone just tried to kill my daughter. That is enough to harden any man."

I blinked at him. "You were the one who was talking about...thoughts and...redemption."

"That was partly to make myself say the words out loud, and partly to justify to myself why Yalda deserved the full measure of justice. I was far from advocating for clemency then, nor do I think Ben did the wrong thing now. It is just that now I am allowing myself to feel the sorrow I should have always been able to feel at what had to be. Because of you. And so, I think...is Ben."

I looked down at the handkerchief. It had smoothed as best as I could make it, with its stickier contents and the creases I'd made. But that could still be fixed. The contents could be washed off, then the creases ironed out, making it as good as new.

It was still his handkerchief. It was still him.

"For what it's worth," Dad said softly, "I don't think you were ever wrong to think of Ben as a hero. He is simply a more *real* one than you ever knew."

I FOLLOWED DAD BACK to Kor's suite. Which was good, because when I saw Dad put his hand on the doorplate and I saw the sapphire gem flash, I realized I might not have access to Kor's suite. Nor did I feel any more need to change that than I did to give Dad access to my bedroom.

As Dad pushed the door open, I caught a glimpse of Ben. He was sitting on a couch in the central room, the one that faced the door. Except right now, he was bowed over, his head in his hands, his fingers digging into his hair.

His head lifted, and when he saw Dad, he rose further, his already distraught expression becoming desperate.

"Jake," he rasped, his voice not sounding much better than mine. "How is—"

Then Ben saw me, and his voice died out. He froze, still with his mouth open, staring at me as if I were a ghost.

Any last lingering inhibitions shriveled to nothing then, at the sight of him like this, having exiled himself to some corner away from me and hurting just as much as I was, if not more. Here was the answer I had been craving all along: how Ben could have done something like that and still be my Ben.

Hard and tender, Dad had said.

Well, that seemed to me like the cruelest state of all. Seemed only fair that I should help him bear it.

I crossed the room to him and offered my hand. "Come back, Ben. Come home."

He stared at that hand, still not moving a muscle.

"Ben," Dad said.

Ben started, then looked at him. Dad was behind me, so I couldn't see his expression, but his voice was kind, yet firm. "It's alright now. She's ready. Go with her."

That was an order, and Ben's frozen mind obeyed. He put his hand in mine, stood, and followed me back to our suite. Even though his movements were stiff and the same blank expression stayed on his face the entire way.

Though he stopped just inside our bedroom, as if finally realizing where he was, and there he stayed, resisting the tug of my hand.

"Why are you doing this?" he said hoarsely, not looking at me.

I stopped tugging and turned to stand in front of him, looking up. He still avoided my gaze.

"Because I forgive you," I said.

His eyes darted to mine, widening again in shock. "*How*?"

I smiled softly. "Because I understand why you did it. And because you are sorry."

Not in the sense that I thought he was admitting that he was wrong and shouldn't do it again. He was *full of sorrow*. He was acknowledging that what he *had* to do...what he had to be...was a terrible thing. The lesser of the evils. Shaped and commanded by his Tree. But still terrible.

It was as simple as that for me...because it meant he was still my Ben.

As if those words had broken a spell, Ben began to cry. At last, he let me lead him over to the couch, and after he sat down, he pulled me into him and held me as his body shook with sobs, and he said, "I am sorry. I am so, so sorry."

MANY MINUTES LATER, AFTER his sobs had long since stilled and his voice had gone silent, after we had sat like that together in softened exhaustion for a while, I whispered, "When was the first time you had to do that?"

"What?" he asked hoarsely.

"Had to...."

"Oh," he said, stilling. He sighed heavily, making me rise and fall with his chest. "I was...seventeen."

Not that much younger than I was. Yet still far, far too young.

"Avva...." Ben swallowed. "He tried to spare me that for as long as he could. But I was in Palla, and a case came up suddenly. Even Lady Maya tried to keep me out of it, but the...the survivor insisted."

"What was the crime?" I asked softly.

I already knew it would be terrible. I wasn't making Ben try to justify himself. I was just trying to understand what he had to go through the first time.

Ben hesitated, then said, "Rape."

He loosened his hold on me, as if afraid that just saying the word would make me cringe from him. But I stayed right where I was, with no change in my breathing or heartbeat. I knew long ago that he would never hurt me like that. Even today, *that* aspect of my faith in him had never wavered.

That seemed to give him the courage to continue. "I...won't go into the details, but...it was bad. Even we mortals could see that he wasn't sorry. That he had done it before, and would do it again if we let him go, that he would be a danger to others, even in prison. He...laughed when the Tree declared him worthy of death."

Ben shuddered. After he had been still for a few moments, he whispered, "That didn't make it any easier, though. I'd killed before—consumed. But he was the first one of *us* I ever...."

"I'm sorry," I whispered.

"No, don't be. If you needed to know this about me, then...then I am glad you asked. Perhaps I should have told you before. I just...I just couldn't bear to have you think.... But that was a mistake. Which made me do far worse to you today."

That wasn't what I had meant, but now was as good a time as any to address this part.

"Ben, I was in shock. And...and I was troubled by how sure you seemed."

But I realized why before he spoke.

"I had to look that way, Sarah. It's part of the whole thing. Her death would have been partly in vain if it didn't deter anyone else. If they thought I was weak. The bad ones need to fear me, and the good ones need to know I'll avenge them. If I could hesitate when my *betrothed* had been wronged, after I showed them all what you meant to me, what might I do when it was one of their spouses, siblings, children? Or themselves?"

"I see that now," I murmured, resettling into him. "I'm sorry it took me so long to."

He laughed painfully. "Sarah, it took you no time at all. I thought...I was afraid...I had finally done it. I had finally done something you couldn't forgive, something that made you think I was a monster. After I first saw that look in your eyes...I was terrified that this was it for us."

There was no point in denying to him that I had been wracked with uncertainty about how I could go on. It was why I couldn't face him, even though I kept telling myself all the logical reasons why what he did was right. But it wasn't enough for him just to be right. Not for trust, for intimacy. Not for me to sit here on his lap like this, laying my ear over his heart, listening to its beat.

"It might have been," I said softly. "If you hadn't been sorry. But you were. And that makes you not a monster. That makes you Ben."

He stiffened.

"What?"

He let out a slow breath. "Flame help me, perhaps I'm an idiot, but...perhaps now is the time for me to mention that I...wasn't as sorry as I should have been. Not...until that moment you asked me not to do it. The second time."

The sadness in his voice when he told me not to look.

"I should have known better by then," he said heavily. "I should have known that killing her was justice, but it wouldn't make things right, whole. But I was so *furious*...."

He put a hand over his face.

"I can understand that," I said calmly. "I can only imagine how I would have felt if Yalda had tried to kill *you*."

Ben lowered his hand. His voice was amused and pained at the same time. "Somehow, I don't think you would have been raging for Yalda's blood."

"I wouldn't be so sure about that," I said, thinking of a bloodlust I'd once had for a certain lish. "But that's getting us sidetracked."

I took a deep breath, choosing my words carefully. "Ben, I knew when I fell in love with you that you were dangerous. That you *had* to be. But, as I've mentioned at least once before, my trust in you was contingent on knowing that you had a tender heart all the same. That if you ever hurt someone, you would feel sorrow. If it was an innocent, you would do everything possible to make amends, and if they weren't innocent, well...you would still feel sorrow. When you could afford to, but you would. And so, you did, because that is who you are. *That* is the man I love. The sorrowful warrior."

Ben was quiet for a long time. But he held me closer, and I took that as a good sign.

Eventually, with a weak attempt at lightness, he said, "Does that mean I'm not allowed to be happy? Don't get me wrong, I'll do what it takes to keep you, but...."

"Absolutely not," I said with a chuckle. "Be as happy as you *possibly* can. Burst with happiness if you can manage it. Just be sad after you have to kill. That's all I need."

"I think...I can manage that. Mostly."

"Mostly?"

"Well, I'm thinking of one necessary execution in particular that I'm going to have a very hard time feeling sorry about."

I sighed. "For Solim, I will grant an exception."

"Oh, good," Ben said cheerfully. "Because I *really* want to be the one to kill him."

I smiled at that. I didn't know why that desire didn't disturb me in the slightest, but it didn't. Maybe because, again, Solim was the one person *I* had wanted to kill.

Then I sobered. "There's one more thing that *I* should clarify now."

"Oh?" Ben said, the cheer leaving his voice.

"I wasn't just in shock or trying to figure out how to trust you again. Part of me was mourning. For me...and for you."

His tone turned uncertain. "For me? Why?"

I turned and rested myself on my elbows on his chest so that I could look him in the eyes and cup his bearded cheeks.

"I was mourning the death of our innocence...and that you had to lose yours so much sooner than I did. So, I have one last confession of sorrow to make: I am sorry that I wasn't there for you that first time, and that I wasn't there after this one. But I'm here now."

Ben's golden eyes glistened, and he swallowed.

"Sarah," he rasped. "You are far too good for me. You know that?"

I smiled softly. What other person could have found this balance that Ben had? Who could be strong enough to survive being both hard and tender?

I didn't think I could have.

"Actually, I think it's the other way around."

Chapter Fourteen

DECISIONS

Sarah

Far too late that night, I realized I couldn't be the only one hurting after the trial, and I tried to make up for my self-centeredness as soon as I could.

The next morning, Yvera came looking for Ben to discuss something with him, but Kor was shut up with him, and they asked her to wait when she knocked. While she did so (impatiently), and while our attendants were busy elsewhere getting ready for us to leave, I saw my chance.

Yvera *looked* alright, pacing with her hand resting on the knife at her hip, her typical hard expression on her face, but I remembered yesterday—how she had concealed her pain about the kesha match so well from all of us under her normal brusque attitude. So, I took a deep breath and came up to her as casually as I could.

Both my knowledge of her character and her glare made me skip the small talk and get straight to it.

"Yvera...are you alright?"

That took her aback, making her forbidding scowl slip. "Yeah. Why wouldn't I be?"

I said as gently as I dared, "Because your grandmother just...."

Yvera raised an eyebrow. Her response was even. "She wasn't my grandmother."

"Yv, I know family relationships can be complicated—"

"No, Sarah, seriously. She was never my grandmother." Yvera rolled her eyes. "I mean, biologically, sure, I *guess*. But even when my biological mother was alive, Yalda was never a grandmother to me. Plus, Avvi—meaning Ben's and my mother—ha, not many people could get on Avvi's bad side, but Avvi hated Yalda. Couldn't stand her."

I blinked. "Really?"

Yvera smirked, folding her arms and leaning against the wall. "Yup. So, I always knew Yalda was ashdust."

I hesitated. "And...it's really that simple for you?"

She shrugged. "Well, yeah. She was a crazy person. Who tried to kill you. And I stopped her. That's it."

I just stared at her. This didn't look fake. I'd heard her fake voice now, and this wasn't it. She truly...seemed to think that way. In her mind, it was that black and white.

"Wow. Um...." I really didn't know what to say or think about that.

Except that this was, perhaps, the clearest example yet of why Ben—and yes, even I—needed Yvera: a rightwing who could see what needed to be done...and just did it, with no looking back.

Ben and I had enough guilty angst to go around.

Yvera turned uncharacteristically thoughtful. "I guess I owe her one thing, though. She helped me realize something. Something I've been a dimtorch for not realizing sooner."

Now I was curious. "What?"

Yvera grinned. "Ben...is my brother."

I stared at her, waiting for the rest. She just looked back, smirking.

After a handful of seconds, I said, "That's it? Just like that?"

"Yup, that's it. Really, like I said: dimtorch—but better late than never, I guess."

She paused, thoughtful again. "Makes me feel bad for kissing him that one time, though."

I felt like she'd sucker-punched me. "Wait. What."

"Oh, I didn't tell you this?" she said in surprise. Then she thought for a moment. "Wait. I didn't. I just told you I told him how I felt. I didn't say how."

"No, you didn't," I said faintly.

She gave another shrug. "Well then, it was back when we were on Yonvey that first time with you. Looking for that moongate. We stopped at that nightshelter, I flew off, and Ben followed me, remember? He told me I could get in one free hit. So...I pinned him down, and I kissed him."

I had to work hard to keep a straight face and not scowl...or burst out laughing. "That...sounds like you," I said in as even a tone as I could manage.

She snorted. "Oh, don't worry. He didn't enjoy it one bit.... I can kind of see why now. I mean...ew. He's my brother."

Her face twisted as if she were tasting something sour.

I took a deep, deep breath. "I don't know what to say about all of that, except, I guess...I'm happy for you?"

Yvera chuckled. "Well, that's good. Seeing as you're going to be my sister."

She pushed off the wall and started walking away, flipping her braid back over her shoulder. "And someday, in more ways than one."

Just when I thought nothing else Yvera could say could surprise me. "Wait. *What*?"

Yvera just pushed open our front door. "Tell my brother that I'm done waiting around for him and he can come find *me* when he's ready."

Then she stepped out and let it swing shut behind her.

Leaving me stupefied.

Then, a memory niggled at me, a little tidbit Kor had once told me, and for the second time in nearly as many minutes, I felt like Yvera had given me a sucker punch.

I have to talk to David, I thought. *ASAP.*

UNFORTUNATELY, MANY THINGS PREVENTED me from calling my brother for that urgent chat, including our preparations to leave and my attendance at Ben's public announcement of Yalda's assassination attempt, trial, and execution and the ascension of Lord Redrik.

After Ben and I took off from Krevenyir's main landing and he began the long, spiraling process of getting our entourage through the sungate, I felt more than the usual relief to depart, and it wasn't just from being able to leave ground zero of the bombshell that we'd finally unleashed.

Only when Ben and I were circling high above everyone else at the top of the spiral did I realize where that added measure came from. It was something that had occurred to me before, but not in the last day and a half at least, and the emotions at finally reaching the end hadn't yet surfaced.

That's it, isn't it? I sent to Ben, during one of the long pauses in between his directions to our entourage. *That's the end of the tour. We're going home.*

Yes, Ben said, echoing my relief and longing to an even greater degree.

He paused, then said, *Technically, Ythra is the last stop. We'll still need to host a feast and dance and everything the night before the heartbinding, but we can take a day or two to breathe before then. There's no need to cater to any Nobles, either in demands or traditions, because it's my Realm. We're just going home.*

Home, I repeated with a happy sigh.

Ben rumbled in his throat—a long, low, rhythmic sound that startled me at first, especially since I could feel the vibrations even through my saddle. Then I realized there was a wavelike pattern to it that was almost like...a cat's purr. I had never heard that kind of sound coming from any draká before, let alone Ben, but I guessed the reason with a laugh.

Something I said? I asked in amusement.

I would have thought the purr was just for his contentment at the thought of going home, but the readiness of his first reply told me his thoughts had already been there, and those thoughts hadn't been enough to bring out this kind of reaction in him. Until now.

The draká purr abruptly stopped, which made me think Ben hadn't even realized he'd been doing it until that moment.

You...called it home, Ben said, risking a glance back at me. I was sure that if he hadn't been a golden-scaled draká, his face would have been beet red by now.

Well, it is, isn't it? I asked in surprise.

It is...to me. I'm just...happy to hear you think it is, too.

Only then did I realize how odd it was for me to call Crownhold *home*. I had only spent a couple of nights there, and only one in the wing I could call my own. I had now spent less time in Ythra, let alone Crownhold, than in any other world in the Seven Realms.

Yet home it was to me. Perhaps because I'd long since accepted that was where home *would* be for me. From when I'd first toured my wing and made my daygate with Ben, to when I relinquished my suite in my family's hold to Rachel, to when I'd cried with Svyer over letting go, to now, I had come to accept that Crownhold was where I belonged. Not just because that was where I could remain with Ben, but because it was my capital, too. The capital of the Seven Realms.

My new home. I felt a rising measure of excitement to finally explore and claim it, sinking my roots deep and far.

Does that mean you'll stay there with me? Ben asked. The question came out in a burst, as if he had wanted to ask it for ages and couldn't help but do so now. Then he began almost babbling to cover his slip. *I mean, you don't have to—the gates make it simple enough for you to travel back and forth if you want to stay in your own Realm, and I'd understand that—I know how much you love it there, I know your family is there, and it's your—*

Ben, I said, keeping my amusement out of my voice. *It's alright. I think this is what's meant to be. Besides...it's what I want. I want to make a life with you, in every sense—and I want to make it there.*

The humming vibrations began again, as if he couldn't help himself for a moment, though he cut them off a few seconds later. I was glad to know he couldn't hear me well right now from where I was sitting on his back, because another laugh escaped me before I could suppress it.

Well, good, Ben said finally, his voice so carefully neutral that I knew he was about fit to burst.

And that made *me* happy.

OUR WELCOME BACK AT Crownhold had a bit of every welcome we'd received in all the other Realms—and that made sense, considering the mix of dramá there to greet us. For once, no clan dominated. Even the Sunfilled were only perhaps a slightly larger fraction than any other.

The draká who trumpeted Ben a welcome home from the moment he first burst through the sungate to the ones who lined up on the landing to greet us had a mix of all the colors: gold, purple, blue, red, orange, and green. The amá who crowded around and underneath them to an unprecedented degree all wore the same variety, if congregating around their own draká.

Cheers, claps, and hollers mixed with draká roars in a deafening wave of sound the moment Ben touched down, which continued while amá rolled a ladder up to his flank to let me down. As I descended, the volume decreased, but only to be replaced by a rising swell of harmony, more voices and instruments joining in with each passing second.

The mood of the song was clear long before I understood any of the words: jubilant, triumphant—joy and hope put into words, drumbeats, and horn blasts, occasionally accompanied by a well-timed roar.

As I waited for the others to rejoin me, I stared out at the exuberant display, trying to discern the words, but I only caught a few here and there, nothing to give me a picture of the subject. Yet every single person seemed to know them and was joining in with laughing enthusiasm, as if the choice of such a song were entirely appropriate to them. Dad and Michael joined me in my staring, though the song weakened for a moment as a sizable portion of the crowd switched their singing voices to cheering when my rightwing and leftwing came to their places at my sides.

What are they singing? Michael asked me, sounding perilously close to being moved.

I don't know, I replied.

I asked Ben the same question when he reached my side and took my hand. His expression was unusually controlled, and his hand clenched mine reflexively, which surprised me. A song this bright and triumphant couldn't be a *bad* thing. Could it?

It's the end chorus to The Daughter of the Moon, Ben said as we began walking down the golden carpet that had been laid down the length of that long aisle, which was already covered in multicolored sparkles, petals, and even leaves. Those now began showering down on us, with a suspicious degree of blue mixed in with the other colors.

The what? I asked, careful to keep smiling and to wave my free hand at the cheering rows, no matter how they bombarded us. I had never seen this many amá crowding around draká. Was this even safe? The draká were having to hold still to avoid any injuries. Although I noticed that for the first time, they spread their wings, resting them on each other's backs in an overlapping canopy that sheltered the amá below from the beating desert sun.

Ben said, *That's the play that they take the pageant from at the Moonfair. After the full-length version, the cast and the audience always sing this together. That's how everyone knows it.*

Oh, I said, my smile wavering for a brief second as I finally realized the reason for Ben's sobriety. Now I shared some of it.

Still, I dared to ask, *What is the song about? I'm barely understanding any of it.*

Ben sighed. *What else? It's about the day that the Daughter of the Moon and Heir of the Sun will unite and rule over them.*

Ah.

I had only one thing left to say, and it wasn't to Ben.

You did this, didn't you? I accused Kor.

The singing *seemed* to have started spontaneously enough, but now I knew better.

I don't know what you and Ben are talking about, Kor said innocently. *The people clearly decided, of their own accord, to remind themselves that despite Yalda's treachery, there is a great deal to hope for right now.*

Right, I said, but now it was with a sigh and a more genuine attempt at smiling for the crowd.

Partly because I'd caught sight of Eskala waiting for us ahead, smiling tiredly at me as she stood next to Alyish. In her eyes, I could see her reminder of her words to me when she set me off on this journey, and of all that I had learned since then.

These people weren't giving *me* honor. They were giving it to the idea of me. They were giving it in thanks to their Tree, and in honor to my own. They were giving it to themselves, to their joy in their own lives and hope for their own future.

Ben and I were only the focal points, the vessels of their hopes as well as our Trees' power. As long as I didn't drink it in, thinking it was for me, I could receive the honor on Her behalf and return it to Her, trusting in Her to help me bear the weight of it. Trusting Her to help me do what needed to be done, for all our sakes.

When I finally stepped in front of Eskala and she kissed my forehead, she whispered, "Now do you understand, dear?"

I nodded, throat tight and moisture stinging my eyes for no good reason.

Yes, I sent to her as she stepped back. *I still don't know* how *I'll bear it. But I'll try.*

Being amón, she didn't have an inner voice, so she mouthed the same thing she had told me before. *That's all our Trees ask.*

REACHING MY WING WAS an intense relief, filled once again with an irrational sense of homecoming, even though I hadn't even stayed there a full day, and now it looked drastically different for being fully furnished and decorated.

Some things had stayed the same, such as the gray central court with its dark, star-filled rotunda; the seven supporting pillars with glowing moons that reflected the phases of their counterparts across the Seven Realms; and the seven-pointed star inlaid in the floor. But now benches and gauzy silver drapery filled now-cozy alcoves around its rim. Plinths displaying fine art or statues occupied smaller nooks, and tapestries of snowy landscapes graced the walls.

And plants—they were everywhere now, from full-blown trees planted in holes that I was almost certain had *not* been there before, to medium-sized bushes in big gray ceramic pots on the back side of each pillar and at other esthetic points, to ivy crawling up every pillar and some of the walls, to planters along the walls and in the alcoves.

Before, the central court had been beautiful, but stark, almost cold. Now it was cool, yet inviting, elegant and refined, yet alive and thriving. The bustling around as my white-and-gray-clad staff got resettled helped clinch the impression. For so long, I had thought I "ruled" over a clan of practically no one.

Now that appeared to be changing before my very eyes.

"You have got to be kidding," Michael said faintly.

I had paused just at the rim of the rotunda, giving my brother and father time to take it all in.

"This...is ours?" Michael said in disbelief.

"Indeed, it is," Kor said with the smallest of smiles.

We had parted ways with Ben and most of his people after we had paraded through the streets of Crownhold all the way to the King's Wing. Yet Kor had postponed his own rest, resettling, and work to help me bring Dad and Michael here, even though I still "remembered" the Queen's Wing's daygate and could have brought them to it myself. Even if I hadn't, Vadya was with us as well, standing at my side, as were a few of my elites, standing back behind us. But now I knew why Kor was here.

He lived for these moments.

"What do you think?" Kor asked, replacing his smile with a concerned look. "Does it not meet with your satisfaction, Rightwing Michael? Not enough silver, perhaps? Or diamonds? We could try adding—"

"No, no," Michael said hastily. Even now, after staying with Kor for nearly a week, he still couldn't tell that Kor was playing with him. His mouth twisted, but he finally gave the dramá the compliment they deserved. "It's...nice. Looks nice."

"It is beautiful, Kor," Dad said smoothly, standing calmly as he surveyed his clan's wing with his hands clasped behind his back. Even though I thought Dad could read Kor well enough, he wasn't going to allow Michael to shame us with his reluctant praise. "Excellently done."

"I'll pass the compliments on to the chief architect and her team. They are the true masterminds behind what you see before you."

"My cousin is being too humble," Vadya said with dancing eyes. "Since his knowledge of the Moontouched was unsurpassed at the time, he provided a great deal of input into the design."

Kor shrugged. "I neglected one aspect, though, which the King suggested himself: the greenery. Or at least, this degree of it."

"Kavarian?" I asked, since he had been the one to sign the funding request in the first place.

"Oh, no, King Koriben," Kor said. Now *his* eyes were dancing as he glanced at me.

I blinked at that. I'd gotten the impression that Ben had involved himself in my wing's renovation as little as possible, seeing as most of it had happened during the month he shut me out.

"It was a last-dek adjustment, but your betrothed insisted," Vadya said solemnly, though her eyes were still bright. "Gwinra was beside herself and has only just barely forgiven him now that she sees the final effect."

Why? I wondered. I appreciated the result immensely, but what had prompted Ben to do it?

Unfortunately, I didn't get much time to guess the answer.

"Speaking of whom," Kor said smoothly as the aged Starkissed amón woman strode toward us, flanked by two assistants. I blinked to see that, in contrast to last time, they all wore white robes with silver accents. More additions to my staff?

"Queen Sarah," Gwinra greeted, much more cheerfully than the last time. "Leftwing Jacob, Rightwing Michael of the Moontouched clan. Allow me to formally welcome you and your clan to your wing. May it serve you well."

"We thank you, Madam Gwinra," I said, putting my hand over my heart and nodding to her. "It is magnificent. I can clearly see why the hold was incomplete when last I saw it. The fulfillment of your vision is breathtaking."

She rose from her own heart-salute and nodded with a pleased expression. "Excellent. Then I hope you will allow me to give you the tour I promised last time, now that your hold is ready to serve you?"

"Of course."

So she did, taking us through many of the same branches and rooms I'd become somewhat familiar with by now after having stayed in so many Monarch's wings, but these showcased the latest innovations in dramá technology, magic, and design, all done with Moontouched comfort in mind. I was impressed, but if I didn't keep constantly reminding myself that this was for the sake of my staff now and generations of my clan in the future, then I would have been more than a little guilty that all of this would have been for just me.

I was sure that the current members of my clan would rarely stay here. As much as Michael gawked and Dad admired, I knew both would be eager to return to their wives and children and the privacy of their own hold as soon as the heartbinding was over.

I got a pleasant jolt when we reached the healer's branch, and I saw my new chief healer directing the final touches to his domain.

"Edrik!" I said in delight, looking at his new white-and-gray uniform and robe. "Did I steal you from Ben?"

"More accurately, I think my wife did," Edrik said with a chuckle and a wink. "I don't think I had much choice in my promotion. Not that I'm complaining, mind you."

He added that last bit hastily at Vadya's smirk, who was no doubt going to report this conversation in its entirety to her right-hand sister, Fenra—the wife in question.

Edrik grinned as he swept his arm over the ward. "Besides, with state-of-the-art facilities like these, I'm the envy of my former superior. Merevya doesn't know whether to feel honored that her tenure with the Golden Crown is being respected or that she's being cheated of the opportunity of her career."

"Either way," I said with mock solemnity, "I promise to do my utmost to ensure that I have as little need of your services as possible."

"That's what every healer likes to hear," Edrik said with another wink. "Though don't try *too* hard. I've been given a birth and a child specialist for a reason."

My cheeks went hot as Michael snorted with poorly contained laughter.

"Getting ahead of ourselves, aren't we?" I said with a cough.

Not to mention optimistic, considering typical dramá fertility. That they were disturbingly close to being right to act as they did was beside the point—they shouldn't have known that.

Vadya answered with innocence radiating out of her. "It is my solemn duty to ensure that my Queen's staff are adequately prepared for any eventuality."

Right. Well, I would just take as much comfort as I could that they were well-prepared for *this* eventuality...and be glad that my father and brother would be gone soon.

AT LONG LAST, DAD and Michael were led away to their own rooms, I was able to slip out of my arrival finery into something more comfortable, and I could shut myself into my study. With a grateful sigh, I sunk into my rounded couch across from the smooth black oval on the wall that Kor had designed to be for my ice-calling magic.

Man, I'd only got to use this study a few times, but how I'd missed it all the same.

I raised my hand and focused my power, making the shiny surface ice over. As usual, I made my ice on the other end appear in the kitchen in our hold, where I caught Lizzy. She brightened at the sight of me and became shy after I asked her to find David for me.

"Uh, sure," she said, tucking her hair behind her ear. "Um, there was something I've been wanting to talk to you about, though."

"What?" I asked curiously.

I also felt a guilty pang. I was the older sibling Lizzy had turned to the most, for anything from help to comfort to advice...and now she had to go without me. Not only did she not have the strength of power to call me, I wasn't usually available, and I hadn't been as diligent as I should have been at seeking her out when I was free. Even now, I'd called to talk to someone else.

Lizzy hesitated, glancing around. When she looked back at me, she burst out, "Um, I've been talking to Svyer, and she, well, she mentioned that her people normally go to their Trees at twelve. And, well...that's my age."

"Oh," I said faintly. "Um...is that something you're...interested in?"

Lizzy's eyes lit up, and she nodded. "Yes!"

I hesitated, but this time with a pang of sadness. "Are you sure? It could change you, Lizzy. Even more than you've changed now. You could become like the others and me."

I held up a white strand of my hair in a rueful demonstration. "It's more than a change of hair color. You know that, don't you?"

My little sister's face firmed, and she nodded. "I know. And I've thought about it, I promise. I've talked with Svyer and Mom. I'm sure. It's what I want. I want to be like you...if that's what the Tree decides, anyway. I want to do more to help."

"You're a huge help already, Lizzy."

"I know. But this is what I want." She jutted her chin with uncharacteristic stubbornness.

I looked at her with a heavy iceheart. There was no sense in telling her that this was a decision she might regret one day. She was old enough to make these kinds of choices for herself, and she had been given all the information she could to prepare. If this was still something she wanted...then I would be hypocritical to deny it to her.

"Alright," I said. "It sounds good to me. Go ahead and talk with Rachel about when you want to be presented."

Lizzy hesitated, then firmed again. "I want you to do it, Sarah. And I want it to be before your wedding. We're all going to come over there for it—Mom said so—and I want it to be before then. Whatever the Tree decides...I want it to be done."

Now I could see some of her motivations, especially in the timing. She wanted all the confidence she could get before facing the dramá—and she wanted to look like she belonged. That insight troubled me even more, but I couldn't withdraw my approval now. I could only trust the Tree to make the right decision for her...and us all.

I sighed. "Alright. I'll...see what I can do. Given how hectic things might be before then, I can't make any promises, though."

"I understand," she said quickly. "That's all I wanted. I'll go get David."

"Actually, ask him to meet me in the Oculus," I called after her.

"OK!" she said over her shoulder, just before walking out of sight.

I sighed again, but dismissed my ice and recast it, making it reappear in the icy cavern at the northernmost tip of our hold. Then I settled in to wait, since I knew this could be a while. Fortunately, my unpackers had put my language study books and materials in an easy-to-find place, so I could use the time productively.

Or I tried to...but my mind kept fretting about David and now Lizzy.

You have to let them grow up, I reminded myself. *Make their own choices, learn for themselves....*

"Hey, sis," David said cheerfully when he came into view of my scrying ice. His hands were in his pockets, and he strolled up to the sheet of ice I must have been displayed in.

"What's up?" he asked, silver eyes bright with curiosity.

I cleared my throat as I set aside my grammar book. "Hey, David.... Thanks for coming to speak with me."

He chuckled. "Sarah, I know you're our 'Queen' and all that, but there's no need to be so formal about it. You wouldn't be like this if it was a phone call."

"A phone call doesn't require you to drop whatever you're doing and come clear across a hold."

David shrugged, unbothered. "Eh, I was in one of the workshops, so I was nearby anyway."

"That wouldn't be the smithy, now, would it?" I said with a smirk.

Now the flushed heat of his tan skin and his bound white hair made sense.

He was growing that hair out now, which I thought was strange. Rachel had taken it upon herself to learn to cut our hair so we would not turn into "utter barbarians," and she practiced her shears on the guys in our family as much as she could. David must have fought her to keep it long, which was surprising, since he used to buzz it the moment he had to start combing it. Even though he had it pulled back with a headband now, I could tell it must be in a shaggy phase that would be driving Rachel *insane.*

"Maybe," David said with a grin. "But I wasn't doing anything more than tinkering around, otherwise I wouldn't have been able to come."

Still, he was taking advantage of Dad's absence to experiment more than Dad's cautious nature would have allowed.

"Alya is brilliant, by the way," David said with evident admiration. "She's been showing me all sorts of stuff."

"Oh, good," I said, glad for more than one reason. Maybe David wasn't interested in Yvera after all, and I was just reading too much into things. I didn't know why I felt more comfortable with the idea of David being interested in *Alya....*

That was a lie: I knew why. Alya, the amón artificer I'd recommended to Dad and now the newest guest of our hold was, indeed, brilliant—but she likely didn't know a thousand and one ways to kill David. Even if she did, she had too placid a nature to ever be likely to try.

"So, what's up?" David repeated. "I know you're usually busy, so I figure you didn't call just to chat."

I winced. That made me sound like Ben, with Svyer. "Sorry."

"Oh, no worries," he said hastily. "I mean, we miss you and all that, but we know you're doing important stuff."

Ah, David. I couldn't have asked for a more chill brother. Which was yet another reason I didn't want him to fall victim to Yvera.

I took a deep breath. "I heard something recently, and you know how my crazy mind works, seeing connections that might not be there and all that. So, I just wanted to ask...and I know this may seem like an odd, invasive question, considering our family's isolation, but...are you...seeing anyone?"

David laughed. "Oh, is this about me and Yvera?"

Another sucker punch, this time coming from the unlikeliest of sources. "*What*? It's *true?*"

"Depends on what you've heard," he said with another laugh. "We're just talking."

"That," I said, pointing at him. "That says it all. Yvera doesn't just *talk*, David. In fact, normally, she doesn't talk *at all*."

"Yeah, I figured," David said, with a bit of smugness. "Except she does with me."

I took deep, calming breaths, steepling my fingers in front of my face. "Look, David. Yvera is...a very dangerous person."

"Well, yeah. I kind of figured that out for myself, sis." He smiled as he cocked his head. "I went with you all to Greenland, remember?"

"Then why are you interested?!"

"Well, shouldn't that be obvious?"

"If it was, I wouldn't be asking."

David smirked. "Well, for one thing, she's *hot*."

I closed my eyes for a moment. Yeah, I had walked right into that one. What other priority would a seventeen-year-old boy have? Especially one that didn't have access to many girls who weren't his sisters.

I opened my eyes and tried to fix him with a stern older-sister stare. "David, be that as it may, she could kill you in the blink of an eye."

"Reason number two," David said, with a kind of dreamy look I had never seen before on my brother's face.

I threw up my hands. "That *does not make any sense*."

David snorted in amusement. He folded his arms—the muscles of which seemed larger every time I saw him. "Oh really? And what about you and Ben?"

I shut my mouth. Then I folded my own arms and scowled at him. "I'm marrying Ben for a lot of other reasons, thank you. He's got a good heart, for one thing."

David smiled. "And you think Yvera doesn't?"

I shifted uncomfortably. "Ben has a lot more...scruples. For one thing, he wouldn't date someone who is underage."

He rolled his eyes. "I don't think she's going to try sleeping with me anytime soon, Sarah, if that's what you're worried about."

"That is *precisely* one of my worries. Yvera is very...physical."

David chuckled. "Again, I have one retort: Ben."

"Again, scruples!" I cried. "He hasn't even slept with me yet!"

David blinked, then laughed as he lowered his arms. "Wait, what?"

My cheeks were on fire now. I had *not* meant to bring this up with my little brother. "Well...he hasn't. We've decided that waiting is what's best for us. So. There. My point still stands. About scruples."

David wasn't going to be distracted. He was still too amused. "Wait, aren't you guys sleeping in the same room and everything?"

"How do you—" I began hotly, then slapped my forehead. "Yvera. How often do you two *talk*?"

And about how *much*?

"Oh, about every other night now," David said with a wave of his hand. "Just whenever you guys aren't dealing with a crisis. She says it's a nice way for her to wind down after a long day."

I just stared at him. Yvera...winding down?

David smiled and shook his finger at me. "Now, be a good sport and answer my question about your 'sleeping arrangements.'"

I admitted to myself that he did, indeed, volunteer private information and that I should pay in kind if I wanted to keep him talking. "Yes, Ben and I are staying in the same room, but that's just to present a unified front, and because most Royal wings aren't built for two Monarchs. But, for your information, Ben sleeps on the floor. He's been quite insistent on that."

David laughed, hard enough that he bent over, clutching his side. Finally, he gasped, "You have *got* to be kidding me."

"David," I ground out. "I wouldn't lie about this to you."

Too much was at stake.

He shook his head, still chuckling and wiping his eyes. "Yv is going to *flip* when I tell her. She's convinced you two have been sleeping with each other since before you broke up that first time."

Everything he had just said...was disturbing on so many levels, not least of which being that my brother had called her *Yv*. But also, I never told anyone in my family about "that first time." Which meant David could have learned about that only from Yvera.

I wished I could be offended that Yvera thought Ben and I were intimate all the way back then, but...she wasn't the only one, and I'd given Yvera more cause than most, given our rivalry. I'd had no idea at the time that I'd been so convincing.

Though I *knew*, I *knew* I should never have slept in the same bed as Ben while he was in a coma...and leave the door open.

But I addressed only the most urgent thing.

"Don't. You. Dare," I told David, leveling a threatening finger. More than just how cringe-inducing the thought of Yvera knowing that kind of detail about me and Ben was, it was also about this slip getting all the way back to Ben, and him confronting me about it.

A bit of uncharacteristic fire entered my easygoing brother's silver eyes as he smirked at me. "Stop me."

I took several deep breaths. This conversation was getting me nowhere. I need *real* ammunition, something to make David *un*interested.

Then I had it. Or...thought I did.

"Are you aware that Yvera was in love with Ben?"

"Yup," David said, without so much as blinking. "But even you used the past tense just now, so you know she's over it, too."

I winced. Man, I was *terrible* at this.

I didn't know whether David's unflappability was making it better or worse. Anyone else would have probably exploded at me by now, said it was none of my business, and stormed out. At least that would have been...a reaction. Something that told me I was getting to them on some level.

David took pity on me and smiled more gently. "Hey, sis. I appreciate the concern. I know it comes from a good place. I get that you're worried about me, and you've got a point about the age thing. That's why we're taking it slow, and still will for a while."

He chuckled. "I knew from the start that it was going to take me a while to get Yvera even this far. I had to keep coming up with excuses to call her and talk her down until she wasn't mad at me for bugging her."

He shook his head fondly. As if Yvera in a temper was *cute*. I just stared.

He continued. "I don't think she'll be interested in anything more than this for a while, and I'm cool with that. It's what I want for now, too."

I stared at my little brother. But he wasn't so little anymore. In height, muscle, voice, and maturity, he was looking and sounding more like a man every day. That last statement sounded...grown-up.

The thought popped into my head that Ben had killed someone at his age.

Not helpful, I snapped back at myself.

Also became a Tournament runner-up.

Still not helpful!

I swallowed. "Just...please be careful, and I mean that in more than the usual way. By that, I also mean that Yvera has an *astonishingly* large collection of knives."

David smiled kindly at me, as if he were the older sibling in this scenario. "Sarah, do you *really* think she would physically hurt me?"

I didn't meet his gaze. "She pushes Ben around all the time."

Maybe that was the source of my deep-seated anxiety about their relationship, however casual it might be right now. The only person I had ever seen Yvera interested in, she treated like a punching bag.

"Fair point. But Ben is kind of indestructible. I think that's why she's that way with him. But, given she knows I don't heal like they do, or know how to fight like they do, do you really think she'll *hurt* me?"

I huffed, but I had to admit, "No. Doesn't mean she couldn't dump you and break your heart."

"Like Ben did with you?" David said gently.

I winced.

"Sorry, Sarah. I know that was a low blow. And I get why he did it, too. But I had to make my point. It's up to me to decide who's worth risking my heart over, isn't it?"

I groaned, throwing up my hands in defeat. "When did you just...grow up?"

"Oh, I think I started about the same time you did." His smile finally faded, and he became sober for the first time. "I know I haven't gone through everything you have, but this has also been tough on me, you know. First you were missing, then I had to leave behind friends, a crush, school, games, hobbies, my car.... Everything. Right now, I'm kind of stuck here, just trying to figure life out again. From scratch."

"David," I said, aghast.

Of all my family members, he had always been the most cheerful, the most uncomplaining. As far as I knew, he had never said a word to me or to anyone else about his struggles.

He shrugged. "It was hard, but not *that* hard, if you know what I mean. Besides, it wasn't your fault. What was the point of complaining to you about it? You had bigger problems. And there are a lot of perks, especially right now. A lot of cool things to be interested in and happy about. I'm figuring things out, so don't worry about me. Yv just helps with that."

"Just helps," huh? I thought.

For a moment, I thought about telling him that Yvera intended to marry him one day. Then I stopped myself. What was I more worried about, anyway? That Yvera *would* break his heart...or that she *wouldn't*?

Either way, David was right.

He got to decide.

Chapter Fifteen

WARMTH

Koriben

I THOUGHT IT STRANGE how empty my quarters felt when I returned to them. Well, that wasn't true. The emptiness didn't feel strange at all. Ever since Avva had ceased filling those rooms with his warm presence, they had felt like a husk of what they had once been. The hollowing out of them began with Avvi's death and was completed with his—the fading hearthfire of our home at last going out with chilling finality.

The strange thing was how I'd forgotten about that emptiness while I was gone, how it hadn't come to my mind even once in that time. Not until I walked into the King's suite, and it hit me again in a wave.

But that wave wasn't as soul-numbingly cold as it had been before, and definitely not as chilling as it might have been after so long. The reason for that, and for the soft blanket of forgetfulness from before, had the same cause.

Sarah made wherever we stayed together feel *full* again. Meaningful again. For someone who lacked much body heat herself, she made the spaces around her feel remarkably warm and bright.

And she had said she would stay with me. Make a *home* with me.

Practically speaking, where she slept or ate or bathed shouldn't have made such a difference, so long as she came back to me every day; I had tried to tell myself that repeatedly, worried more than I should have been that she would understandably want to return to her beloved hold and family.

Yet her *life* was captured in those small moments of sleeping, eating, and bathing. I now craved those living moments with her more than anything. So, her promise to *live* with me made all the difference. The heat of it held the cold at bay as I moved through those quarters, and it kept the memories of Avva from haunting me at every turn.

Though I considered how much I wanted to settle in. After all, Sarah didn't have to come and stay with me here after the heartbinding; we could just as easily make our home in her quarters—or alternate between both. At first, I didn't care which, so long as she was there, yet the more I thought about it, the more I realized there were many advantages to me settling in her quarters, if she would let me.

The lack of memories, for one.

I would still need to come back here during the day. This wasn't just where I slept at night: the King's Wing of Crownhold was the seat of the Golden Crown. But this set of rooms I had grown up in could just become where I worked, and Sarah's quarters could become where I...lived. With her.

It could be where our lives truly began.

Oh, how *ready* I was for them to begin.

First Olsan, my secretary, and then Kor caught up to me not long after I arrived, but by then I'd had enough wandering through those vacant rooms, and certainly enough remembering and debating. I was ready to be occupied again, and they made certain I was, until well into the evening.

Then I began hearing cheerful voices through the cracked door of my study and smelled wafts of food: meats, vegetables, bread, all made with familiar spices and sauces I could parse out and name one by one, with Avvi's voice in my head.

"What's going on?" I asked Kor in surprise.

He just raised an eyebrow at me. "Dinner, obviously."

My flameheart gave a happy jolt, and I shoved upright in my chair. "Everyone's coming here? Just like before?"

"Well, yes," Kor said innocently. "You said nothing about stopping the communal dinners, so I assumed they were to continue. But if you'd like, I can—"

"Oh, don't give me those ashes, Kor," I said, rolling my eyes. "Of course I want them to continue. I just...hadn't thought about it, and you know it."

Kor smirked. "Good thing you have me to think of these sorts of things, then."

"Thank you," I muttered. But inside, I was already feeling three times better, just hearing that commotion and smelling that food wafting through my door.

Kor seemed to tell that he wasn't going to get much more work out of me, and soon after that, he dismissed me like a bemused schoolteacher.

"Go on, you," he said, shooing. "And close the door behind you. *I* want some more peace and quiet."

"Don't forget about dinner yourself," I teased, but I was already making my way to the door.

"If I do, send food," Kor said, already refocused on the lawyer-drafted charter we'd been reviewing together regarding Sarah's co-rulership of my Realms.

With the heartbinding officially scheduled for the day after tomorrow, and the Trees having finally given us something of Their intentions for the new order of things, there wasn't any time to waste. I hesitated, feeling guilt pulling me back toward my desk.

Then I heard Avva's voice again, telling me about balance. Then Avvi's voice, telling me that dinner together was *sacred*. She didn't let Avva or me miss for anything short of a life-threatening catastrophe.

There will always be more work, she would tell the two of us. *Somehow, the Realms will go on if you stop now. But this night we have together might not come again.*

My eyes stung at the cuttingly prophetic nature of her words. The hearthfire I'd felt rekindle within this place threatened to go out again.

Just at that moment, I felt a mental "knock" at my daygate: Vadya, connected to three others. I recognized the person directly after her immediately and gave permission in almost the same instant. I was closing my study door behind me before I realized what I was doing, in time to see the last of the three Linds emerging from the daygate in my reception room, all led hand in hand by Vadya.

"Now, touch that gem on the side," she instructed Jake and Michael. "Just like I had you do with that other one. After that, the gate and you will be connected, and with a bit of focus, you can come here through any other of our gates. Well, you can come through *this* one only after Ben lets you in."

Sarah's chief of staff winked at me.

Meanwhile, Sarah, already knowing how this worked, had already touched the gem and was making her way over to me, beaming up at me.

Without hesitation, I took her up into my arms and crushed her to me. Just like that, the hearthfire roared to life again, and my guilt evaporated in its heat.

There would always be more work, and the Realms would somehow go on without me finishing it all tonight. But right now, I had my betrothed in my arms and my informal family gathered in my home for food, warmth, and laughter.

And I wasn't going to waste one second of it.

"I THINK WE'RE GOING to need a bigger dining room," Sarah said idly.

We were relaxing together in her suite's sitting room, which was much quieter and more private than mine would have been. She was curled up against me, my arm was around her, and her head was resting on my chest, where it had been ever since we had collapsed here, both exhausted after having finally escaped the dancing that had ensued in the central court of my wing right after dinner.

Apparently, Sarah's dancing lessons had begun a tradition, one that no one seemed inclined to stop after the lessons did. And, of course, they weren't above dragging us and even Michael into the fray. Only Jake had escaped, standing firm with calm authority and giving some straight-faced excuse about how he "learned best by observation." Perhaps there was some truth to it, though from the smallest of smiles that I occasionally caught on his lips as he watched his children—particularly Sarah—I thought he was learning something other than dancing.

I still hadn't asked Jake what he thought of me, but that smile gave me a flicker of hope that he wasn't as resentful of his family's new lot in life as I had feared.

But I made myself refocus on the present, and Sarah's statement.

"Oh?" I asked her, running my hand through her hair.

"It just seems unfair that we can only fit so many in there, and so many people want to come now. We're going to be rotating through them forever, and I'm going to forget everything about them by the time they come around again."

I chuckled. "Sarah, no one is expecting you to memorize everyone's name and their life history overnight."

"*You* know them all."

"Because they either helped raise me, or I grew up with them. People understand it's different for you."

"Well, I still think it's unfair how few people we can fit in."

I kissed the top of her head. "That's what makes it special. How many more can you interact with at the same time? We try to host even more, and it becomes a feast, and that's a different thing."

Sarah sighed. "I suppose."

I chuckled again. "Give yourself time, Sarah. Flame willing, you will be their Queen for many years to come."

I refused to consider any other possibility. Even with the Devourer's impending attack on the Tree of Ice. *Especially* then. There was no other way I could function in the meantime. I would just have to have faith in the Tree's promise that Sarah would survive.

"I guess, when you put it that way...." she said ruefully, shifting into a new position against me. "I suppose you had the easier time of it, only having to memorize the names of my family members."

I felt a flicker of sheepishness. "Er...yes...."

She laughed. "You've forgotten some of them, haven't you?"

"There's just...so many of you."

Twelve. In one *family*, if you counted Michael's wife and nestling son as belonging to the same hearth.

"And you've hardly been able to get to know some of them," she said with a sigh. Then she snorted and pushed away from me. "Though that reminds me...."

"What?" I asked in surprise—then felt unease when she resettled to meet my eyes, propping her elbow on the top of the couch and her chin in her hand, a dry look on her face.

"Were you aware that one of your *wings* is *dating* one of my siblings?"

"Dating...." The translation magic in my blood slowly brought up familiar associations of that usage of the English word in my mind, but Sarah provided the translation before I figured it out for myself.

"*Courting*, basically," she said, using the Drona word.

I froze.

Oh no, I thought. *I am dead.*

And of course, Kor wasn't here for me to kill first, which had been our agreement if ever Sarah found out about this.

Sarah's eyes widened in shock, then narrowed in outrage. "You...*did* know?! Ben!"

She punctuated my name with a slap against the top of the couch with the hand that had been propping up her head. I was in trouble.

I let out a breath and held up my hands peaceably. "Alright, yes. I did. But in my defense, I *tried* to tell him not to."

That took her aback. "Wait, what? You talked to *David*?"

"What? No," I said, before my brain caught up with my mouth. "I was talking about Kor."

Then.... "Wait, *David*? Your *brother*?"

Was courting...one of my wings....

"*Kor?!*" Sarah spluttered. "What *about* Kor? I'm talking about David and Yv...."

Then her eyes widened. I imagined my face echoed the same look of horror as we both put the pieces together at the same time.

"*Yvera*?" I wheezed. "*Your brother* is courting *my sister*?"

Sarah's eyes flashed, silvers soulflaring as she raised a finger at me. "Oh, no you don't, mister. First, we're going to have a good long chat about what you know about Kor and...Rachel, I presume?"

I groaned, putting my face into my hand. "Yes," I said, my answer muffled.

"How?! How are they even...?"

I lowered my hand, but I stared at the floor, not meeting her eyes. "You remember that delivery for your family that Kor put together on...your first night back here? That we delivered in the morning?"

"Yes," Sarah said dangerously. Out of the corner of my eye, I saw that her arms were folded and her eyes were glowing again.

"Well, though I didn't know it at the time, Kor slipped in one of his call scales for Rachel. Addressed to her. With instructions."

"That sneaky *devil*," Sarah ground out.

I didn't know exactly what a devil was, since nothing specific came to my mind as a translation, so I figured it was something truly awful. Yet I wasn't about to defend Kor right now. The madder Sarah could stay at him, the less mad she would be at me.

And she looked *mad*.

My faint hope was dashed when her glowing silvers refocused on me. "How long, Koriben Sunfilled?"

"I told you, since that first—"

"No, I mean, how long have you *known*?"

I winced, closing my eyes. "Er...since...the same day?"

Her voice was flat. "You've known...since the very beginning. And you didn't stop him."

"I tried!" I said, opening my eyes and spreading my hands. "Just like I said, I tried to tell him not to—"

"He's your leftwing! You couldn't just *order* him?"

"Not in something like this! I have no control over my wings' personal affairs, Sarah. Not if they don't interfere with their duties. Nor *should* I."

Never mind that ordering Kor in the first place was always a dangerous business. He would obey me only technically while finding some way to do or get what he wanted in the end. If I had ordered him to cease courting Rachel....

"I guess," Sarah muttered, folding her arms again.

I sucked in a tiny breath of relief at that admission and pressed on. "In my defense, when he seemed determined, I told him that if he hurt your sister, I would kill him."

"That doesn't make me feel better, Ben! You threaten to kill him all the time, but you never do!"

"But you would actually let me that time, wouldn't you?" I said, somewhat hopefully. I was also breathing easier now that her eyes were cooling to their normal silver.

Sarah hesitated. Looked away. Then grumbled, "Yeah, maybe."

"See, there you go," I said, putting some forced cheer into my voice. "I did my mortal best to protect your sister."

"Well, that isn't entirely true," Sarah said with a snort. She looked back at me, eyes hard. "You still didn't tell me."

I stilled. "Er...right. That."

"Why, Ben?" she asked, hurt entering her eyes. "You knew from the beginning, you knew I wouldn't like it, and you still didn't tell me. Why?"

That was what finally pierced me. Sarah's anger was a bit terrifying because it arose so seldom and was almost always well-deserved, but I would take her anger over her pain any day.

That pain made me blurt out the truth. "Because...if he was busy pursuing Rachel, that meant he wouldn't pursue you."

She blinked. Whatever excuse she had been expecting, that had not been it. "What?"

Then she groaned as she understood and put her face in her hands. "Right. This was before you'd proposed."

"And before I knew you would accept," I said with a weak smile. "I had just gotten you back, Sarah. I wasn't about to lose you to Kor."

She rolled her eyes. "I hope you know by *now* that there was never any danger of that, but I can understand why you might still have thought that."

I hesitated. I had avoided telling her this when we touched on this subject before, but...perhaps it was time.

It was definitely time for me to stop being a coward, but also, Sarah...should be certain. She deserved to know everything now, before she took that second and final earring from me. No more secrets.

I took a deep breath. "I had...good reason to think that way, Sarah."

"Ben, we talked about this—"

"He told me," I said flatly. "He told me he loved you."

Sarah became still and didn't move or speak for a few long moments. Meanwhile, my flameheart pounded, wondering what her stillness meant. Was it regret?

"What?" she breathed. "In...in those words?"

I thought back, grimacing. "Well, technically...I guess he said something like, 'Do you think you're the only one who loves her?' But...trust me, from the context, the meaning was clear."

"When?" Sarah whispered, still staring at nothing.

"It was right after the blizzard on Ekrel that first time, and you woke me up," I said heavily. "When everyone left, well...I panicked again. I didn't want to hurt you, but I still didn't know how to just *be* with you. Kor found me, and when he saw me like that, he was furious. I don't know if I've ever seen him so mad at me. He said what I just told you. He said...after having your connection for one day, he didn't know how he was going to live without it. That he was sick of seeing you in pain, and that if I didn't make you happy again, he would take you from me. Then he told me to make my choice and left."

"That was why...." Sarah said, eyes still vacant. "When I came to talk to you...."

"I reacted instinctively," I said heavily. "I couldn't lose you. Not to anyone, but especially not...Kor."

Sarah blinked several times. Though she thawed and began moving, she didn't meet my gaze. "Do you think maybe Kor was...bluffing? To give you that final push?"

"He wasn't bluffing, Sarah. I'd suspected it before, but I could see it in his eyes after that. The way he would look at you. The things he would say. Looking back, I can tell the difference now—between when he was flirting with you just to make me jealous and...after."

I looked at the ground and sighed as I ran my hand through my hair. "Should I have told you about Kor and Rachel? Probably. But did I have a real reason to fear Kor would try to take you from me? Well, he threatened to once, so I thought so."

Sarah didn't speak for a few more moments.

"I...see," she said finally. "Do you think he still...?"

I grimaced. "Beats me. But for what it's worth, on the day he gave Rachel a scale, he told me his 'romantic intentions' had shifted. That's how Rachel came up in the first place."

"I see," Sarah repeated dully.

I swallowed, forcing myself to form the words. "I...also should have told you about Kor sooner. I just...."

"I understand," Sarah said, sinking back against me.

I tried to hide my sigh of relief as I put my arm around her again.

"Does this mean I'm forgiven?" I asked tentatively.

And that you're still decided on me? I thought but couldn't say.

"Yes, you are," Sarah said with a weary chuckle. "I honestly might have done the same thing. And...you're not the first person to tell me Kor had feelings for me."

"Oh?" I said with a start.

"Mm-hmm. Rachel did, just from seeing the two of us together. I just didn't believe her." Sarah sighed. "Figures that she would be right about this sort of thing."

Ah, yes.

I snorted. "And she was still willing to let Kor court her?"

"Apparently. Unless you've heard about them breaking it off?"

"No. Kor keeps bringing her up. Says he's trying to desensitize me to the idea of her or something." I shuddered. "If he marries her, I might finally pick another leftwing."

Sarah didn't sound amused. "Do you think...that's likely? Them getting married, I mean?"

"Only Flame knows. But...." I hesitated, then sighed. "You should know that Kor seems...determined."

"That's what I was afraid you'd say," Sarah said in a small voice. "Just like Yvera with David."

I felt a jolt from the reminder of that gut-wrenching revelation. "Can we talk about *that* now? Since when has your brother been courting *my sister*? And why didn't *you* tell *me*?"

"Because Yvera only just hinted at it to me *today*," Sarah snapped. "And I only got the full story out of David after I got here. I told you basically as soon as I could, so don't you point fingers at me about that, mister."

"Sorry," I said immediately, though my insides were still twisting from an unfamiliar, wrenching mix of protectiveness and anxiety. Both emotions I had felt aplenty...but never in quite this combination before, and never for Yvera. "But...*how*?"

And why *her*? Not that I didn't want my foster sister to be happy, but....

Sarah sighed. "Similar kind of story, apparently. Kor bullied Yvera into giving up one of her scales for Michael and David to share, so they could consult her about rightwing stuff just like Dad could talk to Kor. Kor put Yvera's scale in that same package and...guess who ended up with it."

"David," I said heavily. Michael wouldn't have touched the thing, let alone swallowed his pride enough to ask one of us for help.

"Yup. And David...kept calling her, until they started just...talking."

"About what?" I asked, dumbfounded. "Yvera doesn't just *talk*, Sarah."

Even to me. But, well...I supposed we had little to talk about most of the time, seeing as we'd been inseparable for years. Everything we could say, the other usually already knew.

"That's what I said!" Sarah exclaimed. "Well, to David. But he said she does, with him."

Resentment stirred within me. "So he's somehow entrapping my sister over *scale*?"

"Hey," Sarah snapped, pushing away from me to meet my gaze again. "I think the much greater danger is the other way around, don't you? Yeah, David might have initiated, but he's *seventeen*. Yvera's what, twenty-one?"

"Yvera doesn't *do* courtship, Sarah," I said hotly.

Her eyes soulflared as she folded her arms. "Exactly. She just pins a guy down and *kisses* him."

I cringed, anger dying in the face of my chagrin. "Ah.... She...told you about that, did she?"

Sarah just snorted in response.

I raised a hand. "In my defense, I was *not* complicit in that. At all."

Sarah rolled her eyes. "Oh, don't worry, Yv said that, too. But don't you see how that's exactly my concern when it comes to David?"

"I...see," I said heavily.

It was true that of the two of them, Yvera had the upper hand in both age and lethality. Possibly in experience, too, if she had done as much "practicing" as she'd hinted at to me. Of the two, even I had to admit that she was the much more likely one to push physically. I'd experienced that myself.

"For what it's worth," I said with a sigh, "I gave her quite the talking-to after that kiss. I made it clear to her that was a line she shouldn't have crossed. She even said sorry, in so many words."

Sarah blinked. She'd learned by now how rare that kind of apology was from Yvera. Unheard of, basically. "Really?"

"Really. I think...I *hope* that she's learned her lesson."

Sarah grimaced. "With you, maybe. But she seems to know David *is* interested. I tried to warn David, but...."

She bit her lip. I could imagine how well that conversation had gone—about as well as that kind generally does. And, well...I'd been a seventeen-year-old boy too, once. True, I hadn't been intending to court anyone at the time—or ever—but I knew that if I had been, I wouldn't have let my foster sister talk me out of it.

And I hadn't, when the time finally came. In fact, that was what Yvera and I had argued about at the time she'd kissed me, even more than we had about consent. Yvera had been trying to convince me that Sarah was a danger to me, and I had refused to listen. The fact that I was right in that scenario was beside the point. I'd been in that headspace before. I had wanted Sarah, and I was prepared to fight anyone short of the Trees for her.

"I really don't think Yvera will push him that far," I said. She had a good heart—she did. Then I sighed again. "But...I see your concern, yes. Especially with his age.... I'll...talk to her."

For what good that might do. I still had a duty to try.

Sarah's face relaxed with relief. "Thank you. I know she doesn't always listen, even to you. But if anyone *can* get through to her, it's you."

If you say so, I thought.

I wasn't sure I was the best person to talk to Yvera about this, given her feelings for me. Or...past feelings?

Sarah resettled against me, I pulled her in once more, and I sank back with a weary sigh, sliding my free hand over my face. My mind went back to Sarah's question that had started this whole thing.

"How did *both* of my wings get involved with someone from your family?" I said as I stared at her star-studded ceiling. "It's like we're *trying* to start another inter-clan crisis."

Sarah stilled. "Or...prevent one."

I rolled my head toward hers. "What do you mean?"

"Well," Sarah said slowly. "If my siblings *had* to marry dramá...which ones do you think the Trees would have picked for them?"

I became still as well. Finally, I put my hand over my eyes and groaned again. "Ah, torch it."

This had Their hands all over it. Maybe Sarah and I were fighting fate to keep them all apart.

That should have made me feel better about the whole thing. But it didn't.

"Greenland," Sarah murmured.

"What?"

"All of them went to Greenland with us. Kor and Rachel. David and Yvera. Both of the people who would become my wings, both who already were yours, plus my Heir and her future rightwing. The only one missing was Laura, Rachel's leftwing, but she was already married to Michael, and he wouldn't let her come.... It can't be a coincidence."

Though Sarah didn't sound any happier about that than I was.

For me, at least, it was always a bit discomforting to discover that what I had thought was entirely chance or my choice was neither. At least...not completely. The Trees always let us choose, but...They were disconcertingly good at weaving those choices into Their plans for the survival of all Their children.

It was a very good thing I trusted mine.

I sat up with a groan. "I think...that's enough for me for tonight."

I yawned, beginning to feel my nightly crash coming on, and even though my usual slate of meetings weren't resuming yet, Kor and Olsan would be at me again early tomorrow.

"You're not sleeping here tonight, are you?" Sarah asked, rubbing my back.

I glanced at her and was relieved to see her only smiling at me. If a bit wistfully.

I burned more than I had any right to, given how exhausted I'd been feeling just seconds before. But in that, I had my answer.

"No," I said regretfully, avoiding her eyes just in case mine were soulflaring. "I...had better not. Not now that we have our own rooms again."

"I get it," Sarah said kindly.

I swallowed. Then took a deep breath to cool myself down so that I could talk about this without initiating anything. "But after the heartbinding...I would like to. Sleep here, I mean. From then on. If you don't mind."

I glanced at her in time to see her cock her head in surprise. "You'd want to stay here?"

I looked away again. "Yes. If that's alright."

My flameheart pounded, which was ridiculous. What was at stake *now*? And yet, it felt like something was—something crucial. Maybe it was because she still hadn't given me a final answer about Kor. Probably only because she thought she didn't need to; really, she shouldn't have to, at this point. But my emotions weren't so reasonable. Now, those insecurities might see this as the final sign of her acceptance or rejection of me, in the way that mattered most to me in the end.

I had always known Sarah would need her own space, and that I would have to prove myself worthy to be invited into it—and, most significant of all, be asked to stay there.

That was why I hadn't even entered our suite after I'd killed someone in front of her, and I saw that look of horror and betrayal in her eyes. I had thought I would have to sleep in the Heir's suite that night before she would have *maybe* forgiven me. If ever.

Now...I waited for her answer, flameheart pounding, hardly daring to breathe.

Fortunately, this moment didn't seem to have nearly so much significance to Sarah, and she didn't make me suffer long.

"Oh," she said, in simple surprise. "OK, sure. That's fine with me. I just expected you to want me to go over there, in the King's wing. You grew up there, after all."

I tried to conceal my sigh of relief—and the rush of pleasure, triumph, and, most problematic of all, desire.

I cleared my throat, still avoiding looking at her. "Er, yes, well...you have, indisputably, the best kitchen I've ever cooked in. It would be a shame to let it go to waste."

Sarah burst out laughing, as I'd meant her to. "Oh, I see how it is. Did cooking in that said kitchen just before finally proposing to me clinch the deal?"

"Hmm," I said, glancing at her with a grin. "Maybe."

"So good to know a couple days before our heartbinding that you are marrying me for my kitchen," Sarah said with a smile as she rose to place her hands on either side of my face and press a kiss to my lips. "You know what that's going to cost you, though, right?"

With her cool breath in my mouth now, and my nostrils swimming with her clear scent, and her fingers winding into my hair, I was using all my remaining brainpower to keep myself from crushing her into me. So, my mind drew a complete blank.

"What?" I asked, inwardly wincing at the thickness in my voice.

She withdrew so that our eyes could meet. A tremor went through me when I saw the burning gold of my eyes reflected in hers, and I saw her slowly smirk.

She *knew* what she was doing to me. She knew it, and she was doing it anyway.

And, torch it, seeing that intoxicating confidence in her—in my Sarah—just made me want her more. I was having to clench my thighs with all my might to keep myself from reaching for her. From the sting of healing magic I felt there, I was giving myself bruises.

She erased the smirk and said solemnly, "If you want the kitchen so badly, you're going to have to cook for me in it. Whenever. I. Want."

It was as if she had just described paradise to me. As if the price of admission was...to enter.

I swallowed. "You drive a hard bargain."

"Oh, I know," she said smugly. "But I think you'll take it."

"After difficult, lengthy deliberation...I have decided I will."

"Good," Sarah said. Then she sealed our agreement by pressing her lips to mine.

A moan escaped me before I could help it, and Sarah broke away from me with a laugh. I had to swallow a protest when she slipped away and stood up.

"Well, I trust you to see yourself out, so...warm dreams, Ben," she said with a wink.

She walked away from me without another word or look back, yet there was a slight sashay to her hips that had *never* been there before, which I couldn't help but watch until she was out of sight.

Flame help me, I thought faintly.

If I got any sleep after that, my dreams would, indeed, be warm.

That was the whole torched problem.

Chapter Sixteen

GIFT

Sarah

The next afternoon, I was walking underneath the star-studded rotunda of the Temple of Ice. Lizzy walked beside me, holding my hand, and our family trailed behind us. Everyone was quiet; even the twins were sober, something of the gravity of this moment sinking into even their rambunctious heads.

The first time we had done something like this, none of us had known what to expect. Even I, who had spent the previous eleven days learning what a Tree *was*, and had even heard the voice of one, hadn't yet seen one. Now, all of us had not only seen Her, we knew what was coming. Or...what could be coming, if it was the Tree's will that Lizzy be changed just like the first six of us had that day.

I didn't know what to hope for my sister. On the one hand, I knew she wanted that transformation for herself, and I would be dishonest to not admit that there was something empowering, even thrilling, about receiving this kind of power. But it always came with the heavy price of service to the cause of life. Otherwise, we wouldn't be worthy of it.

I had just learned that more forcefully than ever from, of all people, Yalda herself.

With great power....

How are you feeling? I asked Lizzy silently, not wanting to disturb the quiet or embarrass her in front of the others.

Her grip on my hand, already tight, tightened further. *A bit sick.*

For all her limited power now, Lizzy had been one of the first of my family to find her inner voice, and she helped the others follow suit by proving they could. I took that as one indication that the Tree had already changed *all* of us Linds more than normal. Full amón didn't have inner voices.

Probably a good sign, I told her. *It means you're taking this seriously, as you should. Everything will be alright, though. Remember, She's your Mother. She loves you and only wants what's best for you. Even if She offers you Her gift, you don't have to take it. You can change your mind, then and there. It's better to be sure.*

Lizzy lifted her chin as we came to the large doors that led into the Tree's chamber, the ones emblazoned with Her glowing white outline.

I'm sure, she said.

I looked at her for a moment with a heavy heart. Was this something of what Mom and Dad had felt, when I had made my choice?

I looked back at the doors. Letting go of Lizzy's hand, I stepped forward and placed both of my hands on them, on either side of the crack. I laid them there, exerting no force. Then I laid my forehead on that cool, glowing trunk.

Please, I said to them and to Her. *Admit us. And please do what is best for her.*

The doors creaked and began to swing inward. With practiced ease, I backed up to give them room, and this time, my family knew not to stand too close, so they were already out of the way.

When the doors settled again, I took Lizzy's hand. Probably not a part of the typical ceremony among the dramá, but I didn't care. Besides, that smaller hand was trembling. I gave it a squeeze and began leading us all forward.

There was the now-familiar frosted, root-covered rise; the enormous, snowy trunk over a hundred feet wide and stretching hundreds into the air; the branches that stretched over the entire icy dome of a ceiling, frozen diamond leaves glowing with an inner light; the steps which we climbed; the dais set into the base of Her trunk; the bottomless dark well at its center.

Lizzy and I stopped before that well, and our family lined up around the edges, by the retaining walls on either side.

Once everyone was still, I began.

"Our Lady of Ice," I said quietly. "We, Your children, have come before You to present to You one of our own and ask for Your will concerning her."

"Present her before Me."

How? How could I be *looking*, and not see Her appear? There She was, across the well from us. As if She had always been there...and yet, our eyes had not been open to see Her. Not until that moment.

For the first time in too long, the Tree of Ice appeared in Her corporal avatar before me: a Woman made of ice, with hair that flowed to Her feet, dressed in a simple sleeveless gown of the same material as Her body, with heatless white fires for eyes.

Yet my iceheart still pulsed, not comforted by the long-awaited sight of Her. Was it just my imagination, or were Her eyes dimmer than before? Was Her smile weaker, Her hands wearier as they lifted from Her sides in welcome?

I blinked, pulling myself out of my surprise and worry by reminding myself of my role here. I let go of Lizzy's hand and placed both of mine on her shoulders. Again, I didn't know if this was what I was supposed to do, but the rest of my family didn't know that, so it seemed I was going to be able to make up the rules as I went along. This felt right, though.

"My Lady, this is my sister, Elizabeth Lind. She is twelve years old and has requested the honor of being presented before You."

"As is right," the Tree said softly. *"Come forth, Elizabeth, My daughter."*

Lizzy's head twitched in my direction, but she stopped herself and took a deep breath, returning her gaze to the Tree. When I removed my hands from her shoulders, she took the last couple of steps forward before the well.

"I'm here...my Lady." Her voice was quiet but steady, and my chest swelled with pride.

"I am well pleased with you, daughter," She said, Her voice as gentle as drifting snow. *"Your heart is right before Me, and you are worthy to receive a greater portion of My power. If you should take it, you must swear to use it in the service of others, to defend those weaker than yourself, and do nothing with it that is contrary to My will...or I may withdraw it, even until its absence quenches your life. Even*

if you are faithful, if I should ask it, you must give your life for your Realm and for your Tree."

I felt a chill of horror. No. Surely the Tree wouldn't ask Lizzy to *fight* with us in the battle to come?

Yet what other choice did the Tree have? We might need every defender we could give Her. Especially with Her appearing so...worn.

But this...was my *sister*. My little sister. My brave, bright Lizzy.

Was *this* what my parents felt?

"*Is this your desire?*" the Tree murmured.

Lizzy raised her chin. She wasn't ignorant of that potential implication of her decision, was she? I had warned my family of the Devourer's impending attack right after the Tree had told me.

But perhaps...that was one reason Lizzy was here.

I want to do more to help.

I ached with fear and burned with pride to hear Lizzy say, "Yes, it is."

"*Then do you so swear?*"

"I do."

"*Then accept what I offer, and become,*" the Tree said softly.

A ball of ice about the size of Lizzy's fist appeared in the Tree's hand, burning with an inner white light. She released the orb, and it floated across the dark well to my sister. Lizzy held out her hands, and the ball drifted into them. Her hands dipped under the weight.

By now, Lizzy knew exactly what she was supposed to do. She placed the orb over her heart and let it sink into her chest without a trace.

She cringed, and I rushed forward to support her. Yet, like Rachel's wings and mine, she didn't faint, as Rachel and I did. Bravely, Lizzy didn't even whimper, though she curled into me from the pain. I rubbed soothing circles on her back, and I watched her beautiful brown braid turn to white, from root to tip.

For better or for worse...it was done.

"*You may go, Elizabeth,*" the Tree said gently. "*Rest, then practice well. For you will be needed soon.*"

"She's just a child!" Mom cried.

The Tree's eyes were lidded when they met hers. "*You are all children—and all of you are Mine. As such, I will do what I must to protect as many of you as I can, and whatever sacrifice I ask for the good of all, I pay Myself tenfold. You know something of a mother's sorrow, Maria, My daughter. But you know nothing of Mine.*"

Mom flinched and finally allowed Dad to pull her in for comfort.

"*Now go,*" the Tree said wearily, gesturing toward the gate. "*All of you except My Queen. For I have a word to speak with her.*"

As everyone else began to leave, Rachel sang in my mind, *Somebody's in trouble.*

I had a hard time keeping myself from rolling my eyes in front of the Tree.

Somebody's been keeping secrets, I shot back. I hadn't had a chance to confront her before this. Nor did I have much hope of it doing any good.

I thought that would shut her up, or at least give her pause, but to my shock, Rachel didn't even miss a beat.

I never made my interest in Kor a secret to you, she said as she turned away. *You wanted to keep him, you should have accepted his earring when he offered it.*

I choked. I couldn't believe we were having this conversation with the Tree looking on, but how else was Rachel going to fill the silence as she descended the steps?

He did not *offer me an earring.*

He basically did. And then you crushed his heart. Like a grape.

My hands fisted at my sides. "*Amenable.*" That *was the word he used. He said he was* amenable *to the thought of being my* consort.

Sarah, Sarah. You're so smart about so many things, but this is one thing in which you have so much to learn. Her voice turned teacherly. *When a guy like* Kor *says something like* that, *that means he's crazy about you.*

After a pause, she said with a smirk in her voice, *Fortunately for all of us, he's not anymore. You're welcome, by the way.*

I did not dignify that with a response. Partly because I really thought this conversation needed to end, and partly because I didn't know what to say—let alone feel.

Though I kept facing the Tree, I knew when all the others had left when I heard the gates close behind them. By then, I'd taken many deep breaths and somewhat steered my thoughts toward more focused, reverent paths.

Still, I might have spoken a bit too hastily when I asked, "What is it you wished to discuss with me, my Lady?"

"*A request, a suggestion, and a gift,*" the Tree said, smiling slightly. She knew, of course, where my thoughts had been. That was one of the many unnerving things about dealing with an omniscient Tree.

"Oh?" I said, my cheeks heating. There was no sense in asking the Tree if I should have made another choice. I was still certain of the one I had made, and it was the one that both the Trees had indicated They preferred.

But I saw, more than ever, that perhaps Kor had been right. The Trees had, indeed, given me a *choice*...and a choice wasn't a choice unless it was enticing. Which meant I had to confront something even more troubling at the bottom of all of this, and soon.

But not *now*.

I yanked my thoughts back into the present as the Tree began to speak, still smiling. "*My request is that you perform the heartbinding before the Tree of Flame, for I cannot allow all those who should be there into My Temple.*"

"Of course, my Lady," I said sheepishly, feeling bad that I hadn't even thought twice about *which* Tree we should make our oaths before, nor did I think Ben or anyone else had. Yet the Tree of Ice had just as much right as Her Sister to officiate in the union of Her Monarch.

Her smile widened slightly, no doubt at my thoughts. "*This is My suggestion: there is one more application of your surging ability that you have not yet discovered. For the sake of all, I suggest you do.*"

I blinked. "Um...any hints?"

Her smile deepened. "*Only in My gift to you.*"

She held out a shard of ice in Her palm, about the size and length of a large, thick piece of sidewalk chalk, except as multifaceted and beautiful as a diamond. It looked like any of the hundreds I had cast by now myself, although the light inside was brighter.

She lifted Her hand, and the shard floated out of it, across the well, and to my own palm, which I had raised to receive it. Gravity took hold the moment it touched my skin, and my hand dipped under the solid weight of it. It felt cold, but it didn't burn or stick to my skin like ice normally would have...at least, not like it would have when I was more human. I hadn't handled much ice since then, only cast it, so I didn't know if the difference was in me or the shard.

"What is it, my Lady?" I asked, trying to hide my nervousness. The last time I had held one of the Tree's gifts like this, it had transformed me even more thoroughly than Lizzy had just been transformed.

"*A key*," the Tree said. "*To a safe place We have prepared, in the Seventh Realm. A place where you will be safe enough to not bring anyone else, save your new mate. This, We can promise you.*"

When I just continued to stare at Her, Her icy eyes crinkled with what I swore looked like silent laughter. "*We suggest you use it right after the heartbinding.*"

Ooooh. Right. For that thing that came after....

My cheeks started burning.

"*A gift from Us to both of you*," the Tree repeated, expression softening, turning almost sad. "*A moment of peace and joy, before darkness and pain; a reminder that We are not without compassion; and a final sign to you both: that when We ask something of you, We provide the way.*"

I gripped the shard in my hand and swallowed. "Understood, my Lady. And...thank You."

The very next moment, She was gone. But as I stared at the empty space where She had stood, I felt a cool breeze brush against me, and a ghostlike kiss on my forehead.

You have done well, daughter, She whispered in my mind. *I will say the same to you that I did to your sister: Rest. Have joy in the coming days before the darkness. For I will need you again.*

I closed my eyes and nodded, fighting tears for a reason I couldn't name. "I will do my best."

Though, when Her presence fully withdrew, I thought that taking Her advice would be easier said than done.

Chapter Seventeen

SURETY

Sarah

THE FEAST HALL OF Crownhold was immense, one of the largest single rooms I could remember seeing, filled with row upon row of tables—all of which were packed to capacity.

The commotion when Ben and I entered the grand double doors was like when we had arrived at Crownhold, minus the projectiles—which would have gotten into the heaps of food on the tables, and we couldn't have that, now, could we?

The tables held a mix of all the clans, some grouped together, some not, but all standing, clapping, cheering, and hollering as Ben and I walked arm in arm down the aisle, filling that echoing stone room with the cacophony. Then, just like last time, the song rose again, increasing in strength and clarity with each passing second. This time, I understood the words.

And in the day the Daughter
Walks among us again,
And in the day the Son
Searches and finds her again,
And in the day
They become one again,
Through them, the Tree will heal us,
Through them, the Tree will feed us,

Through them, the Tree will shield us,
Through them, the Tree will brighten us,
Through them, the Tree will bind us,
Through them, the Tree will lead us,
Through them, the Tree will make us new,
And bring us to the dawn.

I felt a chill go down my spine.

Kor, I growled at the drakón behind and to the left of Ben.

That honestly wasn't me, he said in amusement. *Either in the writing or in the instigating, in case you were unjustly accusing me of either.*

This time, I muttered.

If the words seem...appropriate, well, that's not my fault, then, is it?

I wasn't so certain. I had learned by now to never underestimate Kor, so I wasn't dismissing the thought of him someday figuring out time travel and going back and writing that dratted play himself, despite his claim just now to the contrary. That seemed just like him.

For the moment, though, I tried to ignore the crowds and focus on the friendly faces ahead of me.

For the very first time, my entire family had entered the Six Realms and were now on display, sitting at one of the three raised tables at the head of the room, the one to the left of the highest. Kor had to get creative to come up with enough "family" members of Ben's to fill out the right table and balance out the nine Linds at the left one.

Svyer and her parents were at the right table, of course, but so were Eskala, Alyish, Yvera's brother, Aldrek, and three other people I either didn't remember the names of or didn't recognize but who wore Sunfilled gold. Yvera would have been among them, had she not had a place at the highest table. That table was empty, with six settings awaiting Ben, me, and our wings.

Behind the scenes, a lot of work had gone on and was *still* going on to ensure that the entire Moontouched clan couldn't be wiped out in one go. Many of Ben's elites were mine tonight and would be until we saw my family back into our Realm. Ward after protective ward had been cast around the three high tables, ones that would allow only the intended occupants and trusted elites to cross and would block all other people and things, even projectiles.

Ben and I had brought my family straight here through a daygate, and they and the other people who were seated there at the front came in through the doors just behind the high tables. Only Ben and I crossed the full length of the hall between all these people, and there were plenty of wards protecting us as well, cast on the aisle and on our persons. Though Ben nodded and smiled for the crowd, he held me tightly against him, and I knew from the prickle of power I felt around him, like static electricity except hotter, that he was ready to summon a shield at a moment's notice.

Even I was openly wearing my gun, in a tasteful holster that had been seamlessly incorporated into my dress's asymmetric design. It was a warlike accessory for a bride, but then, this was a warlike people. Ben was wearing a sword at his own hip, and not the decorative kind. Both Dad and Michael wore their militaristic uniforms and guns as well, and Michael had a large knife, too.

At last, we reached the table. Ben and I remained standing in front of our withdrawn chairs, but at least we were standing together. Our wings sat down on our other sides, with Kor and Yvera at Ben's left, and Dad and Michael at my right, which divided the head of the room between us and made the family tables extensions of our own.

Three perpendicular columns of tables were on either side of the aisle we had just walked down, and the first row had been reserved for each of the heads of the clans. As everyone sat and began to quiet in anticipation of Ben's speech, I scanned those first six tables, and I was surprised to discover how many faces I recognized or names I remembered.

Lord Fenrith and Lady Hilyan (who were seated at Ben's family table, though, leaving more seats at the Peacegrowth table for other officials); Lady Rowin (no Heir Kindra—I hoped the reason for her absence was to ensure that production went on and not that she was avoiding this); Lord Kolwin and Rightwing Yermi, with as many people packed into their table as possible (there had been a dignified contention as to who would get the honor of sitting there at the heartbinding feast of their *yven'roka*); Lady Winthra, her husband, her children, and her wings, with as many others as they could fit (the only table more packed than the Strongshield's); and a bunch of people at the Sunfilled table I didn't recognize, including the most aged drakón I had ever seen—a dignified, yet warm-looking woman with her golden hair in a tidy bun, dressed in simple robes. The only person I *did* recognize there was Aldresh, and he was looking surprisingly subdued. He sat next to the woman, and she was speaking to him in a kind, yet firm tone. When he replied, it seemed to be in monosyllables, but he appeared to be listening.

Even the new Battleblood Lord was there with a small entourage, and I was relieved to see him looking better—or well enough to put up a good front, and comfortable enough in our presence to wear violet-and-black feast clothing (the black perhaps being a quiet homage to Ben and me) instead of the usual Battleblood armor.

My iceheart warmed to see a similarly clothed, beautiful, dark-haired amón woman sitting close beside him, her arm wrapped around his. As she leaned around him to look at the front, our eyes met and she smiled, dark eyes brightening with unusual warmth for a Battleblood. That was when I noticed the emerald earring in Lord Redrik's ear—which, given his short hair, I was certain hadn't been there before.

My own smile deepened. A Peacegrowth amón and a Battleblood Lord, was it? Well, I was sure there had been stranger combinations, and the two of them seemed to fit. Although now I understood at least one reason for the mental strain I'd sensed in Redrik when he was first released. I couldn't imagine what it would have been like for him to wonder during those weeks of captivity if Yalda had done anything to his beloved; knowing Yalda's prejudices, she would have been an obstacle to their union in her best frame of mind.

Yet not only did the Peacegrowth woman appear to be well, it seemed she and Redrik had wasted no time after their reunion. If one good thing had come from Yalda's treachery and his sudden ascension, it seemed their engagement was it. I would have to catch them afterward and wish them well, but for now, I sent a prayer to the Trees for the Battleblood clan as they marked the end of an old era and the start of a new, hopefully much brighter one.

At last, everyone settled, and the room became as silent as it was going to be, with all eyes fixed on Ben and me, the only ones still standing. I clutched Ben's hand three times in wordless comfort, and he returned the message, knowing I needed it just as much. My iceheart was pounding its way out of my chest right now.

"Thank you, one and all," Ben said with a smile. "Thank you for coming to celebrate this long-awaited moment with us. I know it probably seems like no time at all to you, but it has felt like an eternity to the two of us."

Ben cast me a rueful look, and the feasters chuckled.

Ben raised an eyebrow at them. "You laugh, but it's partly your fault."

That, of course, only caused more laughter.

When that finally died down, so did Ben's smile. "Part of it—too much of it—was my own."

Ben.... I sent. We hadn't coordinated our speeches—deliberately this time. Still, I had a feeling where he was taking this. He just squeezed my hand in a quick plea for trust.

"I am not offering an apology to you but rather an explanation. My first month as your King was not what it should have been, and you were remarkably patient with me. For that, I am grateful—whatever your reasons. The kindest of you may have thought that I was simply grieving, but unfortunately, you would be wrong."

He paused, taking a deep breath. "Grief, I have learned, is a part of living. It is the slow acceptance that we are yet alive and the one we love is not—not in a way that feels like life to us. But during that time, I refused to live, and so I could not grieve. I did not think I was worth the life of the best man I have ever known, let alone the love of the best young woman."

He smiled sadly down at me, gold eyes glistening. "I still do not."

Ben....

He just squeezed my hand again as he looked back across the hall. "But that does not matter to them, and they were patient, too. Patient enough to wait for me to accept that for myself, and to offer their forgiveness and love when I was ready to receive it."

He smiled for a moment in soft wonder. "If you have ever truly felt a love that so surpasses your own worthiness you cannot comprehend it, then you know how transforming it is. I tell you all of this to say that I stand before you as a new being—one that was dead and was brought back to life."

His smile faded. "*Now* I am grieving. I meant it when I said before that I carry a sorrow that I will bear with you for the rest of my life. But when I finally accepted the weight of it, I discovered I was strong enough to bear it. In fact, I was stronger than I ever knew. The one who finally showed me that is the one standing at my side now."

He paused again, swallowing. "I...do not have the words to do her justice. All I can say is that I thank the Tree with every breath that she chose to be there. I could not go on, let alone be the King you deserve, without her. Now, along with that sorrow, I carry a humbling gratitude for a debt I can never repay, given in an act of love I can never deserve. For my father did not just save my life: he also saved hers. For that, he gave me life not just once, and not just twice, but thrice.

"Though I wonder if I can be half the King he was to you, I swear that for his sake, and hers, I will spend the rest of my days trying to be. Moreover, I promise you I will not allow myself to become so dead again. From now on, I will live. For every day the Tree grants to me, I will live—for you, for her, for Avva...for myself...and for the sake of any children we may one day have together. This I swear."

The hall erupted into cheers, the claps echoing resoundingly across the space. My pulse ratcheted up again as I realized my moment had come—and now I had to follow *that*.

When the clapping ended, Ben looked at me, and so did everyone else. I felt the tingle of magic at my throat that indicated Ben had cast the spell that would amplify my voice across that space. I breathed as steadily as I could, but I gripped Ben's hand as if my life depended on it.

"I am fortunate to be the second one to speak, because the briefer I am, the more you will approve, because then you can eat."

It undoubtedly was a well-worn joke even among the dramá, but it still got a round of chuckles.

When they were done, I sobered. "The first time I spoke to you like this was on a much different occasion. You may recall that it was at the Battle of the Solstice, when I stood with you to face the Devourer."

I took a deep breath. "By the next morning, I was full of guilt. Though we survived, as Koriben said, it was at great cost. I thought I should have done more, been more. I thought I had failed you all, and no one more than the King, whom I had already come to think of as a father...and his son, whom I had already come to love."

The silence was absolute.

My voice strengthened. "It has taken me this long to accept that I could not have done more.... How could I have done more? I had not been the Queen of Ice for more than a day and had only been among you for twelve. Until I came to your Realms, I had never fought, let alone killed. My powers were raw, growing, largely undiscovered. I could not have even offered my Blood for Kavarian's; She was not my Tree to give it to. All I could have done was try to save the man I loved, and as many others as was in my power."

I swallowed back the growing thickness in my throat. I avoided looking at the Strongshield table at the front. "One of you told me once that we can never be all that we would wish to be as a leader, for we are only mortal. We can never save you all. All we can do is learn from our weaknesses so that we can better serve the ones who remain."

I let that sink in for a moment. "Some of you call me the Moondaughter. If that is what you need to believe to have hope in these dark times, I will not stop you. But I will only ask you to remember that even the Moondaughter was mortal, in the end. In the end, even she could do only so much. My heart is now made of ice, yet it is breaking at this moment from the fear of losing a single one of you, from the fear of not being enough to save you all...and I must accept that I cannot."

I breathed in, then said more firmly than ever, "But I can promise you this: I will give my all to try. You are not just my people now—you are my family. My brothers and my sisters, my fathers and my mothers. And this man...."

I lifted our joined hands and kissed the back of his. Out of the corner of my eye, I saw Ben's eyes were burning even before I lifted mine to meet them.

"This man, who is far, far better than he would have you believe, who already is the King we need...I would do anything for him. Because from the moment I first saw him, he was my sun."

Ben gripped my hand tightly, eyes glistening even as they burned.

I looked back over the people. "So this is my oath: I will serve you, the ones who are left, with all my might and power. I have already become more than I had ever thought possible for your sake, and for his. If there is more left for my Tree to give me to serve you, then I will take it, until I have become all that it is possible for a mortal to be. Not for myself, but for you. For him. And for the ones who may come after. This I swear."

By now, I knew something of the chance that I took with the raw vulnerability of my speech, and I had run it by Eskala just to be sure. But she approved and seemed to think the gain was worth the risk, and Ben's own rawness had given me the courage to stick to my prepared words. The dramá were going to have to get used to vulnerability in their Monarchs, because Ben and I couldn't be any other kind—not anytime soon.

It seemed both our gambles paid off, because the feast hall once again erupted into applause, many people standing from the force of their cheers. Ben, for his part, asked me silently, *Am I allowed to kiss you now?*

I suppose, I said in amusement, and he bent down at once, cupped my face, and crushed his lips to mine.

It seemed *I* was going to have to get used to PDA, because Ben couldn't be any other kind of partner—and I wouldn't have him any other way.

THE FEAST AND DANCING afterward were a blur of happy memories, tinged with hints of anxiety for my family. On the one hand, we couldn't entirely keep them from the dramá, the best of whom were eager to meet the long-awaited members of the Moontouched clan. Yet our elites had to work twice as hard as normal as the Linds mingled as much as they were comfortable with.

Mom stuck with me or Dad for the most part, though I saw her look longingly toward the dancers, and I finally nudged Dad into taking her onto the dance floor once or twice during the couple songs. Mom didn't seem to care that Dad was as stiff as a board the entire time and that he stuck to a very out-of-place Earthren waltz. It was only the second time I had ever seen my parents dance, the first being *Michael's* wedding.

That was what finally made it *really* hit me.

I'm getting married tomorrow, I told Kor, my inner voice faint with realization.

By a strange twist of fate, Kor was the only one who was with me in our corner of that gilded dance hall, other than elites. Everyone else had drifted away, at least temporarily. Michael and Laura were dancing while Lizzy led a tottering Tommie around to gawk at all the shinies (with elites trailing them both).

David, to no small amount of shock to everyone, not just in our family, was dancing with Yvera; the two of them had been nearly inseparable ever since they left their seats at the end of the feast. Though I'd eyed them at first, Yvera was...restrained around David. Comfortable, but in a way that looked astonishingly like gentleness. It was like watching a bearded, tattooed motorcyclist suddenly go soft and gentlemanly around a dog. If anything, David was the more openly flirtatious of the two, and apart from the dancing, they didn't even touch.

Rachel, surprisingly, hadn't attached herself to Kor in the same way. In fact, if I didn't know better, I would have assumed she thought nothing more of him than of any of the many handsome dramá to whom she was happy to give her attention. Kor received no special treatment; they had only danced together once by my count, and Rachel was off with someone else right then. Kor didn't seem to mind; in fact, he acted with the same indifference. Only when I caught him watching her once with his dangerous combination of enigmatic smile and glitter in his eyes did I think that I hadn't assumed too much after all.

Jonah, Noah, and Abby had been taken to another room with others their age, with Peacegrowth caregivers and plenty of our elites to watch over them. I thought the latter should be given a medal for valor, since the last time I had ducked out to check on them, I had seen Ordran "dying" with all the dramatic aplomb my twin brothers could wish for as they stabbed Ben's elite captain with toy swords. I wasn't certain I approved of the violent nature of their play, but...oh well. For tonight, I let them be.

Technically, Tommie should have gone with them, but Michael and Laura drew the line there. They could leave their son in the care of others tonight for a dance or two, but only if he was in their sight. Lizzy, feeling awkward with only a few people around her age, had volunteered to watch him.

Even Ben had been cornered by Lady Rowin on his way back from the refreshment table, and they were discussing something genially but also seriously over their respective glasses of water and wine. Even as I spoke those words to Kor, my eyes lingered on Ben. That tall, strong, *good* man I was pledging myself to. Who had, over this past month, somehow found within himself the balance between his gentleness and his intensity, his sorrow and his joy, which now lent him a kingliness I had only had glimpses of before.

Indeed, you are, Kor replied. *Any regrets?*

I looked into the cup of water Kor had brought me, which Ben had passed to him when it looked like he would not make it back to me with it soon.

No, I said. *None. But I think there* is *something you and I need to discuss.*

Out of the corner of my eye, I saw Kor's lips twitch. *Ah. I was wondering when you would bring it up.*

Rachel gave you forewarning, did she? I asked.

Kor took a sip from his own chalice—wine, of course, and the darkest variety I'd seen. In the dim lighting of the golden orbs of light—which floated in slow, mesmerizing patterns overhead—the liquid looked almost black.

Well, yes, he said, *but I knew it would only be a matter of time before you figured it out.*

By that, do you mean your courtship of her, or...?

Kor smirked at me, eyes glittering. *Both.*

I frowned at him, squashing my twinge of discomfort. It was time I confronted this...past time. *Alright then, first things first—*

Sarah, Kor said, smirk never wavering as he looked me in the eye, *I have no intention whatsoever of hurting your sister. In fact, I intend to marry her.*

Out of "duty"? I said quietly.

He took another sip, his eyes drifting to the dance floor. *Partly. But only in the same way you are marrying Ben out of "duty." How lucky we are that both of us can do precisely what we would have always wanted to do all along, and call it duty. Quite the coincidence, don't you think?*

Kor didn't dabble in coincidences. I thought for a moment, then sighed. *Your "theory."*

The one he *still* hadn't told me in its entirety, only hinted at it now and then.

He smiled, eyes still distant. *That is part of it, yes. I even told Ben this bit, but he refused to believe me. Even when he stared the evidence in the face.*

He turned his head only enough to look at me sidelong and winked.

What do you mean? I said, feeling a stir of unease.

I found something interesting when I was studying the measures of the strength of the Covenants, Kor said, swirling his wine. *At first, I thought it was just a coincidence or a correlation, but that never sat well with me. Then it happened so often, the same pattern repeating. Whether or not it was a corollary, it at least was a consistent one.*

Kor sipped his wine, his voice and expression becoming serious. *You know what all the most powerful Monarchs had in common, Sarah? The ones who led us from times of struggle into prosperity? Who revitalized, even for just a generation, the strength of the Covenants? The one trait that every single one of them shared?*

What? I said with a sigh.

He smiled thinly. *They all had strong marriages. Unusually strong.*

Really? I said, even though I probably should have seen this coming all along. After all, this was about Kor's grand theory of why the fate of the Realms rested on my relationship with Ben.

Oh, each marriage had its challenges, Kor said, as if I had made a logical argument, *and the couple often had more than their fair share of tragedy. But all the Monarchs in this category I'm referring to pulled through, and it was in great measure because of their consorts. That was when I began studying backward, trying to discover the true common denominator in each of their relationships. What was the secret? Was it in their commitment? Was it in how they met? A certain level of compatibility, or passion?*

Well? I prompted, impatient for him to get to the bottom of this.

It was none of those things, Kor said with a shrug. *They often shared some basic traits, yes. Yet the one thing I was looking for continued to elude me. Even arranged or political marriages, which I thought I could write off quickly, were among the mix. I was baffled, and I was about to give up the search as being fruitless when I hit on an account—of all things—of the moment Kavarian met Nyethra. One eyewitness, whom other scholars had discounted as being unreliable, swore that both of their eyes soulflared the moment they first met the other's—even though Kavarian was only nine summers, with their meeting being three years before his presentation.*

At my confused look, Kor added, *Soulflaring shouldn't have been possible for him before then. That's why that account had been dismissed as only retrospective fancy. As such, only fictional, romanticized narrations use that detail.*

Ah, I said, a queasy feeling in my stomach rising as I started to finally see where he was going with this.

That got me curious, though, Kor said, taking another sip. *It was the one stone everyone else before me had left unturned. So, I started digging. Of course, there weren't any other accounts as detailed as that one of the very* first *moment a current or future Monarch met their future consort. But that finally helped me see one consistent trend: after that first moment, the Monarch, at least, became unusually devoted, unusually quickly. Kavarian, by his own admission, fell for Nyethra from that first meeting and dedicated the next eight years of his life to becoming the man he thought was worthy of her.*

Whatever other trials the couple faced in their own relationship and in life, this one thing remained constant: early and earnest attachment. Almost as if the two had known each other before. Or at least knew from that first moment what could lie ahead for them, together....

Kor glanced at me, smiling. *Sound familiar?*

I shifted but didn't answer. I could hardly deny it, when I had just admitted as much myself in nearly so many words in front of all the Realms.

So, satisfy a scholar and friend's curiosity in one thing, if you don't mind, Kor said, swirling his wine again as he looked over the dancers. *When you looked into Ben's eyes for the first time, what did you see?*

Again, I did not answer...but I remembered.

Hmm, Kor said, as if I *had* spoken. *Fascinating. Ben said the same thing.*

Nothing? I said incredulously.

A nothing that means "yes," Kor said with a smirk, still not looking at me. *You should have seen how flustered Ben was when I asked. Considering it was only the evening on the same day he first met you, when he was still absolutely convinced he could never marry and that to court you was to risk alienating you...that's saying something.*

I stood still for a moment, stupefied. I had thought back more times than I cared to admit to that first moment, so of course I remembered the golden glow of Ben's eyes—never once realizing that mine...might have been glowing too.

Far sooner than they should have.

What does that mean? I said uneasily.

Now there is the question, and for the answer, I can only speculate. Because if there is one, only the Trees know it for certain. This is Their doing, after all.

He grew serious, almost grim. *I am not saying that the Trees* do *or* should *play matchmaker for all Their children. In fact, I believe They do not and should not. But...when it comes to their Monarchs, They leave little to chance—particularly in something so crucial to the fate of the Realms as the Monarch's choice of consort. For that consort could make or break their entire reign—or even the Covenants themselves.*

Why? I asked.

But I thought I knew. My eyes drifted back to Ben.

Perhaps because a heartbinding is the ultimate covenant: the ultimate test of the First Covenant of Belonging and Second Covenant of Power that bind our people together in the ways of life. If a Monarch, the vessel of the Tree's own power and the focus of the Covenants, can keep those Covenants in tandem with another living being, then, well...how could the Covenants themselves not be strengthened? And if their people followed suit, how could they not prosper?

Eskala's words came back to me, her response to my protest at how she could be so accepting of the Tree's declaration that the Queen of Ice must marry the King of Flame, with no further explanation.

Let me just summarize our entire history for you: When we obey the Tree, the greatest guide and protector the Creators have given us, we survive. In fact, we thrive. But when we do not....

I looked at Ben, hardly knowing what to feel.

Kor followed my gaze and smiled gently. *You still had a choice, Sarah. Any number of them. In the end, you chose Ben, time and again.*

I knew that by now. I knew the Trees had left the decision up to Ben and me. In this life...and in the one before. Though Kor was more right than even he knew about the care the Trees had taken with choosing us.

Kor went on. *I can say with perfect honesty now that I am glad. I would not have made you as happy as he does now, and I always knew that part. What I didn't know at the time I gave you a choice was that* you *could not have made* me *as happy as Rachel could.*

His eyes drifted back to the dance floor, to my sister, who had been claimed by yet another partner. Kor smiled, eyes glittering again. *As she does even now.*

Even when she's ignoring you? I said with surprising humor. I hadn't expected it to be so easy to talk with Kor about this—about Rachel or...us.

But he was right. Both of us had made our choices, and both of us were happy with them. To finally talk about this was...a relief. Finally closing that door between us, once and for all...and opening the right one instead.

This felt...right.

That was when I finally had to admit to myself two things.

One, I was just the smallest, tiniest bit jealous of my sister. There had, indeed, been a part of myself that had always wondered about Kor, that had found something enticing about him...and now I could put that part to rest. He would always be important to me, but like Yvera, I had been a bit dim to not realize how for so long: he was meant to be my brother.

Which led to number two: not only was there nothing I could do to stop Kor and Rachel's relationship, but I also shouldn't even try. It was...right. They fit.

Oh, she is not ignoring me, Kor said, smile widening as he brought his chalice back up to his lips. *She is* hiding *from me. That is progress I had not expected to make this early. I am a very pleased man tonight.*

Hiding? I repeated. *And that's...progress?*

It means she feels deeply enough for me that it is now frightening her, in a good way, Kor said casually. *I'm giving her space to enjoy the feeling before I close in.*

When he glanced at me and saw my baffled expression, he chuckled. *Your sister and I will always have a very...different sort of relationship than you and Ben have, Sarah. Don't worry about it. I have everything under control.*

Yes, I said dryly, but I was smiling. *That's the part that worries me.*

Not really, not anymore. I trusted Kor now—with everything. Even my sister.

Judging from his smirk, I knew Kor could tell. *As I said, I have no intention of hurting her.*

He looked back at Rachel, cocking his head as he studied her. *I love her.*

He said the words so casually, as if he were talking about the weather. That, more than anything, finally convinced me he did. Kor often hid his deepest feelings under their opposites. At least I was a good enough friend to have discovered that much a long time ago.

Then...I'm happy for you, I said, and I realized I meant it. *And...I wish you luck. I hope you know what you're getting into. I love her too, but I'll be the first to admit that she's a bit of a handful.*

Oh, I know, Kor said with a chuckle. *But aren't we all, in our own ways? Courtship is about choosing the problems we can live with, for the person who is worth enduring them. You found that out yourself, Tree nudges and all.*

My attention was suddenly caught by the sight of Lizzy and Tommie and...of all people, the Strongshield Lord, Kolwin, who was kneeling in front of Tommie and showing him something small and glittering while he and Lizzy occasionally talked over the little toddler's head. Lizzy's back was to me, so I couldn't see her expression, but she was clutching one arm and shifting from foot to foot.

"Excuse me," I said, my alarm making me switch to my vocal cords as I set down my glass on a nearby tray. "It looks like I have to go rescue my sister."

"From what?" Kor said in amusement, but he was looking at the same thing I was.

"From the coldness of a certain Lord, obviously!"

Kolwin had a good heart, I knew that now, but with his formal, emotionless demeanor, he could unintentionally devastate someone as tender and unsure as Lizzy just by glancing at her.

"He appears to be behaving to me," Kor said, gesturing with the hand holding the chalice. "Look."

I looked again, and this time I saw...that Kor was right. Kolwin had the gentlest expression I had ever seen on his fine-boned, aristocratic face. When Tommie tried to tug that shiny something out of Kolwin's fingers, the Strongshield Lord almost...*smiled.* And when he looked up at my sister....

I gulped. *Kor, in all your research, did you ever discover anything about the Tree doing this...thing with more than just the Monarchs? What about...Nobles?*

Hmm, that would have been my next topic of study, had I had the time, but alas, I did not. I had already wasted enough effort on the greatest paper I'll never be able to publish.

Why? I asked, surprised enough to be slightly distracted from my ever-increasing urge to intervene. Still, I kept my eye on the trio instead of Kor.

Because I have a feeling the Trees don't want us to know about it. Not before we figure it out for ourselves. That would defeat the whole subtlety behind what They are doing. After all, with the full knowledge of it that I had, it nearly didn't work on me.

I was shocked into glancing at him. Kor's eyes were back on Rachel, glittering again.

What? I stammered. *Kor, are you saying that when you saw Rachel...for the first time...?*

Kor was the Tolsyon heir of Flame and thus a pseudo-Royal...and Rachel was the Heir of Ice. How had I not put that together before?

"My, look at that," Kor said, gazing down at the bottom of his chalice. "Empty. I had better go refill it. After all, it's not every night I get to drink like this."

He winked at me and walked away.

I took that as the only answer I was ever going to get—which I had to admit was fair, considering it was the same answer I gave him—and I hastily focused my energy on rescuing my sister from Kolwin.

Whether or not she wanted to be rescued. After all, she was only twelve.

Chapter Eighteen

FOREVER

Koriben

The nights before heartbindings were infamously sleepless ones. The romantics claimed it was because of the couple's anticipation, but that ignored the much more ambivalent feelings of all the others involved and the practical reason: the feasting and dancing traditionally went late into the night, and the heartbinding was traditionally at dawn the next day.

Heartbinding insomnia was not a whim: it was a requirement.

Add in the complexity of protecting and shepherding Sarah's family, and you can imagine how little sleep we got, and how little of that was our choice. Sarah and I were too exhausted by the time it was all over to be anticipating anything other than rest.

Although this final bit *was* my choice, I had to admit. Little did Sarah realize it, but I never left her wing after I helped her surge all of her family to her suite's daygate and bring them to the guest branch of the Queen's Wing. Sarah no doubt thought that when we parted ways in front of the guest branch that I would surge back to my own personal gate and go to bed to get what little sleep I could.

Instead, I walked right back to her suite and went straight into her kitchen, where I began reviewing in the dark what I had to work with while I waited for Sarah to finish up with her family and make her way back to her suite and bed. I knew that if she were paying attention, the connection she felt toward me would out me at once, but I had a hunch that she would be too tired to do so, and it seemed I was right. I watched her star come closer and closer, until it passed through her suite's reception room and deeper in, presumably to her bedroom, where her star settled in one place only a few dek later. Never once did she come near the still-dark kitchen.

I relaxed, grinning once I knew I was in the clear. First step of my surprise, complete. The first two steps, actually, because by then, I had verified that the kitchen was, indeed, as well stocked as Kor had promised, and I would *probably* have everything I needed. It was a little hard to tell from my many Drona annotations all over the English recipe that Sarah had written on my tablet, but the theory was simple enough that I was confident I could pull off something edible. Whether it would be something her family could recognize and therefore appreciate as I hoped they would...that would be the tricky part.

Step three was to get the couple deken of sleep that I still could. I spread out my bedroll right there on the kitchen floor—I'd had worse—and then set out a timekeeper candle. After removing the first peg, I charmed the second one to give me a magical jolt when the candle burned down to its level and the peg fell into its bowl. Then I crawled into bed and lit the candle. I think I was asleep almost as soon as my arm fell back to the ground.

Step four: Wake up to that jolt, like being stung by a spark when touching metal on a dry winter day—except all over the body. Not the most pleasant way to wake up, but it was effective. My instincts had me bolting upright, knife in hand. I groaned as I realized where I was and why, and remembered that it all, including the jolt, was of my own doing.

I'm an idiot, I grumbled to myself as I clambered onto all fours and started putting my things away. *A lovesick idiot. Who wants his betrothed's and in-laws' approval* way *too badly.*

But I was doing it anyway. Which...made me even more of an idiot.

Step five: Turn on the lightgems (now that it was safe enough to do so) and re-examine the recipe as best as I could with my crusted eyes and sleep-deprived brain. It was a good thing I had done the preliminary work of gathering all the ingredients and tools beforehand.

Step six: Measure, mix, and cook those little cakes, flipping them over to brown both sides as Sarah had shown me. All as *quietly* as possible. Sarah normally slept deeply, but I wasn't about to test that now, and I kept a careful eye on her star as I worked. I also made the "scrambled eggs" she and I had made at the same time before. *That* was a dish I was well familiar with, even if Avvi had taught me to add more chopped bits, herbs, and other flavorings than Sarah was used to. Remembering Sarah's surprise at everything I had included, I kept things subtle this time. Nothing too noticeable—just enough to add *some* kind of flavor without screaming that was what I was doing.

Step seven: As Vadya and her staff started trickling into Sarah's suite to get her ready to go, act like I was supposed to be there. Even when Vadya stuck her head into the kitchen and raised an eyebrow at me.

"Well," she said dryly, eyeing the heaps of food I had stacked on one counter. "I guess I can cancel the breakfast delivery."

"Looks like it," I said with as straight a face as I could manage.

"Shouldn't you be going, Ben?" Vadya said pointedly.

I had my own preparations to begin at the Temple of Flame: ritual bathing, anointing, meditation, and so on. Even though I didn't require as much esthetic assistance as Sarah was no doubt going to get, it was still going to take me a while to get ready this still-dark morning; the priests working with me would make sure of that, even if I dodged the barber Kor would no doubt drag into this, too. In fact, I was a bit surprised Kor hadn't called me by now to ask where the torch I was.

"I'm almost done," I said, not looking away from the range. I really was on the last batch, but cooking this many little cakes at once required constant vigilance.

"Ben," Vadya said sternly.

"I want to see Sarah first," I insisted.

Vadya sighed, but she ducked out of the room without further argument. A dek or two later, my star wandered in, wearing the loose clothing she usually slept in and looking confused. Then she stopped and stared at the heaping pile of "pancakes." I hoped it was enough—I had no idea how many of those things her family ate in one sitting, so I had made dozens upon dozens of them, utilizing multiple pans to cook them and filling one of the biggest serving trays available.

Tears came to Sarah's eyes.

"Ben," she said thickly.

Perfect timing. I flipped the last cake onto the tray, turned off the heat disks, and then went over and kissed her, winding my fingers through her loose, deliciously tousled hair.

"I promised," I said simply as I pulled away only enough to meet her eyes.

I hadn't just promised to use her kitchen to cook for her. When I had asked her to teach me a recipe two months ago while she was far from home and uncertain of her way back, it was with the intent that one day I would make it for her and her family, to show them I had at least *tried* to take care of her—and would continue to try until the day I died.

"I know," Sarah said with a sniffle. "But you didn't have to do this *now*."

I smiled and shrugged. "I know. It seemed like the best time, anyway."

In that moment, for that look in her glistening silver eyes, it was all worth it, every sleepless dek. Maybe I *was* an idiot, but at least I was a happy one.

I kissed her again, quickly this time, and stepped back, smile deepening. "Got to go. Let me know if they like them."

Even though now I didn't even care if they did.

Then I surged straight to the Temple of Flame.

"BEN, QUIT IT," KOR said with a sigh.

I tried to still my pacing, but it was difficult. My nerves still insisted on making themselves manifest in a tapping foot and my grip on my sword.

Kor, who was lounging against the wall of the small sandstone chamber where we waited, just rolled his eyes. "You would think you were having second thoughts."

"I'm not," I snapped. The pleasure of my surprise for Sarah and her family hadn't lasted long in the face of all that I'd been forced to undergo since, and the long night hadn't left me with much patience for my leftwing. The rituals had been fine, even calming and centering. Too bad those had come *before* all the dressing and trimming and fussing over me.

I took a deep breath, but when I was about to run my hand through my hair and ruin the barber's careful work of styling it, Kor's warning glare stopped me. I lowered my hand, resentment building. Yes, not much patience left for him at all.

"Then what's wrong?" Kor pressed.

"It's just...everything!" I burst out. "I've been waiting for this moment for so long, and now that it's finally here...I can think of a thousand and one ways it could *still go wrong*. What if the Devourer changes its plans and attacks here, *now*? What if Solim shows up? What if someone *else* tries to assassinate Sarah? What if she trips and falls into the ritual fire? What if she gets up there and says *no*?"

Kor smirked. "I'm going to assume that all of those concerns are in random and not ascending order."

I just grunted, letting him assume.

"Ben," Kor said, sobering somewhat as he pushed off the wall and took a few steps toward me. "We've prepared for this, remember? All those kinds of things, you, Yvera, and Alyish have already been over at *length*."

He couldn't help himself and snorted at the last moment. "Well, maybe not about the saying *no* part."

"No, Yvera brought that one up," I muttered. At Kor's look of amusement, I added, "She didn't even sound hopeful, trust me. She was being serious. Planning for every contingency, you know."

"Ah, to have been in the room at the time," Kor said with a regretful sigh. Then smirked. "Do tell: what's the contingency plan if Sarah *does* say no?"

I gritted my teeth. "I thought you implied that wasn't likely."

"Of course that's not going to happen. But now you've made me curious." He poked me in the chest. "You can't just dangle something like that in front of me and not—"

Fortunately, at that moment, the door opened. As we looked, Vadya peeked her head in and scowled. "Kor, my *dearest* cousin, if you're going to assassinate my Queen's consort, do it on another day besides this one. First, I've put a hellwind of an effort into today, and, second, it will make the legalities of your sentencing simpler. Because then he'll actually *be* her consort."

I wasn't the only one whose temper was short this predawn. That was soothing to hear.

Kor turned to her. "I assume all that is to say Sarah is ready?"

"Yes, so shoo! Out with you."

My flameheart began to pound. I had forgotten that the bride and groom got a few dek alone together right before the ceremony. The devout claimed it was for prayer. That's why Kor was handing me a leaf with a wink as he walked away, and why this room had an altar with a flame bowl in the middle. The romantics made jokes about the moment's other uses, which was probably the reason behind Kor's wink.

The cynics said it was for a last chance to back out.

When Kor was past her, Vadya finally opened the door wide and beckoned Sarah in with a flourish, who entered with a bit of surprise and trepidation that told me no one had explained this part to her. Unfortunately, I was too busy staring to give her much reassurance.

You would think I would get used to this. I had seen Vadya's team work their magic on Sarah so many times by now, you would think I would be past the point at which she could floor me. Maybe her stylists had been holding out. Maybe it was just the day, or the moment, or my torched lack of sleep. Or maybe she really had simply become that much more...*something* in the last deken and a half or so since I'd seen her.

I didn't know. All I knew was that I wasn't prepared to see her like this. Not at all.

Her snow-white hair was pulled up into a cascading updo of voluminous curls, studded with white, glowing diamonds. Silver sparkles graced her cheekbones, eyelids, and delicate collarbone. Her nails were painted silver, and lines of white dots with silver, glittery centers were artfully painted on the backs of her hands. They had left the natural color of her lips but covered them with a gloss that shone.

Her dress...was black. Oh, it had a silver trim, and a white and silver, spear-shaped dotted pattern that rose from her hem and ended in a point midway up the full A-line skirt, repeated on her bodice, and branched off to her shoulders. Her translucent cape had a whitish sheen, and more of that dotted white and silver stitching. And everything was scattered with white sparkles—not enough to be garish, but enough to evoke...

"Stars," I whispered, only realizing I was speaking my thought aloud after I said it. "They made you look like the stars."

Sarah laughed, ducking her head and lowering her eyelashes. "Kor owes Vadya a ruby, whatever that means. He said you wouldn't get it."

"How couldn't I?" I said, baffled. My brain must still have not returned to full functionality, because I blurted, "You're my star."

She just smiled softly and came up to me, laying her hand on the gold symbol on my chest. "And you're my sun."

"Ah," I said tightly, trying not to betray how hot her touch made the skin underneath, even through the fabric and embroidery.

No coat for me this time, or even a cape. For an occasion so solemn and ceremonial as this, the cut of my clothing was the epitome of tradition: a loose, long-sleeved tunic bound only by my sword belt; loose trousers; and simple sandals. The ornamentation wouldn't have been controversial either: a large gold sun embroidered on the center of my chest, with gold trimming and filigree elsewhere. But the black cloth was new for *any* heartbinding, let alone a Royal one.

Yet here we were, both in black for the first time. Together.

"I see what they're doing," I said, looking between us.

Sarah smiled. "Kor had to point out that a star and a sun were *technically* the same thing. Vadya told him that was partly the point. And then told him to shut up."

I chuckled. Vadya's impatience with Kor was making me feel much better.

Sarah's eyes brightened, and she stepped back, holding her foot out to lift the center of her skirt. "Oh, and this was my idea."

I studied the triangle of dots for a moment. I'd missed it at first, with all the smaller dots, and then I recognized the distinctive pattern of the largest ones. It was a constellation.

"Korrien's Spear?"

She nodded, and my throat tightened. "To honor your home?"

"It's not home anymore," Sarah said with surprising ease. "It is where I came from, yeah. But that wasn't the main reason. I was mostly thinking of the night you proposed."

That made my throat tighten further, but this time in a good way, and my flameheart pounded. That didn't seem like the attitude of a bride who was having second thoughts.

"I...see," I said finally.

"So...what are we supposed to be doing?" Sarah asked, looking around the sandstone room. It was small and bare, apart from the altar and bowl, so her eyes immediately rested on that.

"Traditionally?" I said, holding up the leaf Kor had given me. "Praying."

"Oh. OK. What's with the leaf, though?"

"We burn it."

"Oh, right, what else?" Sarah said with a smile.

I shrugged. "It's not necessary for prayer, obviously, but it can be a nice way to focus: something to do, something to visualize, something to give up. And different leaves have different meanings. Not because the difference matters to the Tree, either, but because it matters to us."

"Right," Sarah said thoughtfully as she approached and circled the altar. "It must be about...the ritual of it. Rituals have power because we *think* they do. The key is to connect with the Tree, but because we're mortal, repeatedly doing things in a certain *way* helps us do that better."

I just smiled and shook my head at the wonder of her.

She stopped on the other side of the altar from me and looked curiously at the leaf in my hand. "What does that one symbolize?"

I examined it for the first time. It was dried, as was the ideal, but it still retained something of its former gloss and color, though the color was now a dimmed bluish green. It was about the length of my thumb up to the knuckle and was an oval with slightly jagged edges.

"You know what? I don't...know," I said with a frown, bringing it up to my nose for a sniff. "I don't recognize...."

But at that first whiff, I did, and I lowered it with a rueful laugh.

"What?" Sarah asked curiously.

I came up to the altar and handed the leaf to her. "Tell me if you recognize this."

"Ben, you know I don't know anything about your...." Then she finally *looked* at the leaf, turning it by the small stem in her fingers. She didn't even need to smell it. "Oh. It's...my icemint."

"It is. Which means there *isn't* any meaning attached to it already. Because it isn't even one of our plants. It's one of yours."

Figures *that* would be the leaf Kor would get for us.

Sarah became thoughtful. "I guess that means...we get to choose what it means."

"Seems so."

"What should we choose, then?"

I shrugged. "It's your plant. Seems right for you to decide."

"I suppose.... But I want this to be something both of us want, both of us need." Sarah pondered for a moment, touching the leaf to her lips absently.

I could think of something I wanted and needed with those lips of hers. But I wasn't so sure she wanted the same thing right this moment, and it had nothing to do with a prayer, anyway, so I shoved the impulse aside. Besides, Vadya would turn her ire on me if I messed Sarah up now.

Sarah held the leaf up over the bowl. "How about...a miracle? This leaf can symbolize a prayer for a miracle. After all, it's given us a couple of them already. At least, the whole plant has, flowers and leaves."

A cure for brightfever that had been plaguing the Peacegrowth and for darkmold that had been decimating the Brightflare's crops.

All lighter, more carnal thoughts vanished. My chest tightened and flameheart sputtered...but I said quietly, "I agree."

With only a few days left before the month the Tree gave me was up, we needed nothing more than we needed a miracle, and we needed nothing *less* than a miracle. A miracle that had been promised several times by now, yes—otherwise, I wouldn't even be functioning. But I still had no greater desire, and thus no greater prayer, to offer on that altar than for that miracle.

Sarah let the leaf go, and it floated its way down into the wide-rimmed brass bowl, hitting the narrow bottom with a muted *tick-tick* of its edges against the grooved metal. I held out my hands over the altar, and she put hers in them. I tried not to let my desperation leak into my grip, but I still held her more tightly than necessary. She gave me one squeeze of understanding and smiled up at me, inclining her head for me to do the honors.

I focused my power on that single point, and in the next heartbeat, the leaf was alight, flames eating away at its edges. First, the fire turned them black, then it made them vanish into smoke. As that smoke rose and its cool, sharp scent—so like Sarah's own—filled the room, I closed my eyes and gripped Sarah's hands even more tightly.

Please, I begged. *Don't let me lose her now. Not* now.

Not ever—though I knew that much was asking for the impossible. But most certainly not now. I was almost certain that losing her now, like that...would be the end of me.

A gentle knock on the door almost made me jump. I had entered a place that deep inside myself from the force of my desire. I opened my eyes and looked down to see that the leaf was long gone, with only a bit of ash remaining. I let go of Sarah's hands abruptly.

"Sorry," I mumbled.

"Don't be," she murmured as she withdrew them. "I assume that knock means it's time?"

"Yes," I said with a sigh and a quick estimation at how close Kaldrir was to cresting the horizon.

Sarah rounded the altar and took my hand. "Then let's go. We've waited long enough for this moment, don't you think?"

I attempted a smile, squeezing her hand three times. "Yes, we have."

THE MOMENT THE FLAMES of the Gate of Dawn died, Sarah and I walked through hand in hand. For once, we led the crowd, since only priestesses, priests, and Royals were typically allowed in the Temple Heart at night, when all seven entrances were covered in a fire that was only passable if the Tree permitted.

So, this time, no cheers greeted us as we entered the empty chamber, and the procession that followed us was reverently silent, the only sounds being the rustle of cloth, the click of metal, and the shuffle of sandals on the sandstone floors.

To Sarah's surprise, I stopped soon after the threshold and took my own sandals off, but she followed suit without question, using me for balance as she bent over. I didn't want to disturb the moment by explaining to her that we had never done this before because we had never arrived at *dawn* before, when the Tree's fires were at their lowest and Her chamber at its coolest. It was a gesture of respect that we made when we could without coming to harm, especially during moments as sacred as these; at other times, the Tree never expected it of us.

I only said silently, *The moment the ground gets too hot, put them back on, no matter how disruptive it might be.*

She nodded and slipped her hand in mine again, both of us holding our sandals in our other hands.

I walked forward again, Sarah following, allowing the priestesses and priests behind us to enter and do the same before walking to their posts. Though I didn't look back, I knew that each of the guests in the procession would stop at the threshold and take off their shoes, holding them as they moved on.

Sarah tried to take in the Heart as discreetly as she could, but her awe was clear to me as she did so. She had seen two of the Tree's Daughter-selves before, but this was the first time she was seeing the Tree of Flame in Her oldest, most glorious form.

The Heart chamber was immense, the greatest natural cavern I had ever seen. Yet that immensity was covered by the Tree's enormous branches and fiery leaves above and Her massive roots below. Those leaves were at their dimmest now, but the fires that licked at but never consumed them were still visible. Great cracks spiraling from the center of the cavern's dome revealed shards of the dawn-lit sky outside; the leaves would drink in every drop they could of that sunlight, increasing in intensity until their noon peak, when even I would not want to be in here.

Sarah and I walked down a path set with flagstones that was free from roots and had been carefully swept free of sand and pebbles just last evening. We approached a dais set into Her base, where an unlit brazier, also freshly tended and stocked with coals last night, sat inside a shallow pit in its center.

Flames only lightly licked the Tree's massive trunk, just as dim as the fires above, and the flagstones remained cool to *my* feet, at least, so I hoped they would remain bearable for Sarah for the duration of the ceremony. For now, she didn't walk with any visible discomfort, even though I glanced often to check.

At last, we walked up the steps to the dais and approached the firepit. My flameheart pounded, and I only realized that I had begun to grip Sarah's hand more tightly when she squeezed back in silent reply.

Only a few people followed us up the steps: the High Priestess and two assistants, who stopped at the top of the steps; Sarah's family, who filed around to the right; Fenrith and his small family standing in for my own, who filed to the left; and my wings. Though this time, Yvera joined Fenrith as family, and Kor stopped about six feet behind me and to my left to stand as a witness. Likewise, Jake stopped and stood at an equal distance and angle to Sarah's right.

Otherwise, Sarah and I stood at the firepit and unlit brazier alone.

For dek, nothing happened as everyone in the procession found places to stand. They weren't limited to the flagstone path we had followed from the Gate of Dawn, which was good, because there were far too many people who wished to attend than could have fit on it alone, even if they packed in tightly and the column extended all the way to the gate.

So, as soon as they entered, people broke off from the procession and went any which way, with occasional directions from the Sunfilled priestesses and priests as they picked their way around the Tree's roots to find the best places to stand—which were usually on one of the other six paths that radiated from the Tree like spokes in a wheel to the other six gates. But the people could stand among the roots if they had to. The one rule was that they could not climb onto or over Her roots; they had to move and stand on the stone floor alone, so the practical limit to the number of people who could attend was the amount of floor space available. I hadn't ever seen the Heart at capacity, however—not even on the day I was presented before the Tree and chosen as Heir.

Until today.

Because people kept *coming*. I stood waiting as patiently as I could, but the crowd filing into the Heart chamber never seemed to end. Kor had told me that people had been lining up inside the Temple since before the feast even began last night to be here for this moment, but it was another thing entirely to keep glancing back as subtly as I could and each time see that limitless river of people flowing into the Temple Heart.

I was more than just impatient for the ceremony to finally begin. I grew anxious for Sarah; the only reason she seemed to be doing alright now was because of the chill I could feel radiating from her spellweave clothing and the relative coolness of the Tree just after dawn. The longer this went on, the more likely Sarah would suffer for it. When I got too restless, Sarah would just squeeze my hand. I hoped that meant she was still fine and that she wasn't just trying to placate me.

Fortunately, the artisans behind her cooling clothing had finally realized the necessity of placing the power gems in subtle, easy-for-me-to-reach places, so every time I got too anxious, I shifted a finger up to the center of Sarah's wrist, where one such gem rested, and I would press my finger on it to top it off with power. It was just one crystal, covering one segment of her, but it gave me something to monitor and do, like feeling for her pulse. There was another one on her elbow, and I decided if this went on too much longer and its level got too low, I would find some discreet excuse to recharge her there, too.

After an eternity that was perhaps only a quarter deken (no time at all considering the size of the crowd packing into every available space), a silence settled on the chamber, and when I craned my neck upward, I saw why.

At last, a fireleaf from above had broken off and was drifting down to us, floating in a mesmerizing spiral. Flameheart pounding, I let go of Sarah's hand, since I had been holding hers with my right, and lifted my right hand in a cupping shape to receive the leaf. I kept my hand low, however, so that it was within Sarah's reach.

Sarah had been instructed about this part, so she didn't hesitate to lift her left hand and place it underneath and somewhat crossways to my own, forming another side to the bowl of our hands. Another bride might have exposed more of her own skin, thus providing more room, but we didn't know what that burning leaf straight from the Tree of Flame might do to Sarah, so I was glad to see that she was almost guaranteeing the leaf would fall into my hand.

And so, it did, when it finally drifted into our cupped hands, settling in my palm. The flames didn't hurt me; in fact, they only felt pleasantly warm against my skin. Although I knew that if I had been so blasphemous (and stupid) as to pluck the leaf from the Tree myself, it would have done more than just burn me. The couple of dramá who tried soon after the swearing of the Covenants died when they did so—burned alive like living torches to nothing more than ash.

It was an early but forceful lesson for the previously ignorant humans who had joined themselves to the draká: The Tree's power was *never* to be taken—only given. Usually, to give again in turn.

So Sarah and I tipped our hands and allowed the leaf to fall into the brazier below. The coals ignited at once in a roar, and Sarah winced in the waves of heat that rose from it. I placed my hand on her shoulder for a second as naturally as I could and sent a quick but forceful surge of power into the two gems there, both of which I could touch easily with my spread fingers. As our hands intertwined again and we lifted them over the fire, Sarah gave me a quick clench in gratitude.

Normally, the higher-ranking member of the couple spoke next. Since Sarah and I were equal in rank, it had been a toss-up at first, but after thinking about it, Sarah decided I should speak. She said the Trees had requested we do this before the Tree and children of Flame, and this was my Tree and—for a few moments longer—my people. Since Sarah was firm, I finally agreed, though I hoped no one would interpret this as Sarah being deferential to me.

"My Lady of the Flame," I said solemnly, closing my eyes. "I, Koriben Sunfilled, whom you have called to be your King for a season, and Sarah Moontouched, Queen of Ice, come before You and request Your presence."

"*I am here, Koriben, My chosen King.*"

When I opened my eyes, the Tree's avatar stood on the other side of the pit and flames from us, a golden fire of Her own licking around Her body. Her ember eyes were glowing warmly, and Her lips were pulled in the slightest smile of approval. Again, that smile shocked me, but I tried to not let that derail me now.

"*Speak your request.*"

I took a deep breath as I lowered our arms. We would raise them again in a moment, but now was our chance for a break, and with the need to expose Sarah to as little heat as we could help, I was going to take it.

My voice was rough with emotion as I spoke next. "We have come before You to have our hearts bound as one."

"*As is right,*" the Tree said simply, signaling Her acceptance of the union—a line that was only necessary because this was the marriage of one of Her Royals. Otherwise, She would have made no comment and proceeded with what She said next. "*Present the earrings before Me.*"

Sarah and I brought out our earrings—the other halves of the set we had first put into the other's left ears nearly one month ago—and held them out over the fire, the clear gems glittering in our open palms.

The Tree looked at me first, which I was glad to see. She normally began with the lowest ranking of the couple, so that balanced out my beginning.

"*Koriben Sunfilled, King of Flame, do you vow to cherish this woman as your own flesh, heart, and blood, and cleave to her forevermore?*"

I felt a jolt like a lightning bolt go through me. Out of the corner of my eye, I saw Sarah's family were largely unmoved, but my family, on the other side, stirred in shock. Whispers began hissing around that cavernous space. This was the one ceremony the Tree demanded supreme reverence for and the one in which we normally could give it to Her. It was a testament to the explosive nature of that one change that it finally shattered that carefully maintained silence.

What is it? Sarah asked me in alarm. She clearly didn't remember the words well enough to realize what was different.

I couldn't answer her. I was still too stunned.

That was the usual vow...right until that last word.

Every time before, the Tree had said *for the rest of your mortal life*. Every single time. For all we knew, from the very first dramá marriage She had performed until the one that had taken place just yesterday morning. It was the vow my own parents had taken, and I would dare anyone to find a couple more devoted to each other over the entire course of our existence.

Heartbindings lasted only for *life*. This one. The mortal one. That was taken as a given in our very theology. Oh, there were some romantics or grieving partners that claimed that spirits could still choose to remain together in the next, but the Tree had never confirmed that was true, and the High Priestess had to sadly reiterate that fact whenever she was pressed, no matter how earnest the asker. The Tree had never answered that kind of request, no matter how sorrowful the petitioner. Not publicly, at least.

It wasn't that I wanted to ever part from Sarah, but the shock was still too great for me to even move, let alone speak. I would have thought I had hallucinated that last bit if it wasn't for the whispers and movements around me.

The Tree looked around Her Heart and said, "*Silence.*"

Her voice, though mild, carried as it always did to the furthest reaches of the chamber, and the silence that descended at Her command was absolute.

She raised Her coal-skin hand. "*Before your King gives his answer, I must explain this to you all, for too few of you have recognized the fullest significance of this moment.*"

Too *few*? Had *any*?

And then, out of the farthest corner of my eye, I saw...my leftwing smile. Just slightly, so that I had to turn my head further to be sure, and by then Kor's smile was gone, and he merely looked forward at the Tree with a perfectly neutral, attentive expression. But that in and of itself was telling. If he had been even the slightest bit surprised by this turn of events, his eyes would have been burning from curiosity—yet I saw nothing of the kind.

"From the beginning," the Tree declared, voice ringing so powerfully it made my flameheart tremble, *"when I gave to the draká the First Covenant, the Covenant of the Gates, I knew the hardness of their hearts. Though they had returned to Me for their very survival, I knew I had to prove them. Only when they had sufficiently chosen to keep the First Covenant did I and the Tree of Ice grant unto them the Second, the Covenant of Power. Yet again, I had to prove them, and more than before, for when greater is given, greater must be required."*

The Second Law of Creation. The First being that the Trees only had the power to save us that we gave to them—through our obedience and sacrifice.

"To My sorrow, your forebears hardened their hearts again after only a few generations, and they broke both Covenants in succession. Not only could nothing further be given, what was once given had to be withdrawn. And so, the Covenants slowly withered, only sustained by the increasing faithfulness of your Monarchs and Nobles, and the increasing inclination of your hearts toward Me. Until the time for your redemption came at last, and My Sister of Ice sent this, Her chosen daughter, to you."

The Tree gestured to Sarah. Who, like me, had lowered her hand with the earring for the moment.

"These two who stand before you redeemed and swore anew the First and Second Covenant. In them, and in many of you, I and My Sister are well pleased. Therefore, We are at last able to grant unto you what was your birthright from the beginning: the Third and Final Covenant, the Covenant of Union."

Another lightning bolt to my soul, this one knocking the breath from my lungs. If I hadn't been frozen near solid, I might have staggered.

Another Covenant? A *third* Covenant? There had been *more*?

The Tree continued. *"I showed it to your forebears many times, and yet they would not see, told it to them and they would not hear. They would not understand that it was only because of the hardness of their hearts that I allowed your unions to last for this life only and that I allowed you to part in this life at all. Now...hear Me."*

She paused as She gazed around the chamber, eyes burning. Then She raised both hands, palms up. *"We now grant unto you all the Third Covenant, the Covenant of Union—the Final Covenant which I and My Sister have prepared for your deliverance from the jaws of the Devourer. From this moment forth, you may choose to take this Third and Final Covenant for yourselves, allowing your unions to last beyond this mortal life and into the next, but know that I will annul those unions only for the most grievous of reasons. And I must not—and cannot—annul it for these two, the first and the chosen. For they represent you all."*

She turned Her gaze back to me. *"And so, I ask you again, Koriben Sunfilled, King of Flame: do you vow to cherish this woman as your own flesh, heart, and blood, and cleave to her forevermore?"*

With painstaking slowness, hardly able to believe this was truly happening, I raised my earring with my left hand and pricked the first finger of my right hand with the earring's tip. A moment later, a gold light blossomed in the clear gem until the gold filled it with its radiance. I then presented my earring again to Her.

I was shocked to hear how steady my voice was. "Thus I vow."

The Tree of Flame looked at the woman at my side. *"Sarah Moontouched, Queen of Ice: do you vow to cherish this man as your own flesh, heart, and blood, and cleave to him forevermore?"*

Sarah pricked her own finger, just as I did, and held the glowing white earring out to the Tree. "Thus I vow."

"Then join the earrings before Me."

Sarah and I clasped our hands holding those earrings, careful not to spill them. After the earrings were safely pressed between our palms, the ritual fire roared up, encasing our joined hands.

This was the part I had been most anxious about, for Sarah's sake. But though she stiffened, and I did likewise, she didn't appear to be in pain beyond that, and when the flame retreated, I thought I saw and felt...frost covering her skin, as thoroughly as a glove, but I couldn't be certain since it dissipated a moment later.

Only one thing seemed for certain: her hand was far colder than it had been before.... Or was mine hotter?

"*The Trees of Ice and Flame have witnessed this vow,*" the Tree declared.

So perhaps there had been Ice involved after all.

"*You may place the earrings.*"

I slowly turned and kneeled on one knee before Sarah. It was the order we had agreed on before, even before we knew it would be the order in which the Tree would address us.

Only *now* did my fearless bride tremble as she stood over me and brushed back my hair to reveal my right ear. Her eyes glistened, silvers burning. She took the cushion-bandage out of her pocket and positioned it and the sharp needle of the earring on either side of my earlobe, taking excruciating care with the positioning.

Her eyes darted to mine, and I smiled encouragingly. She glanced away and took a deep, steadying breath. Then she pierced through the skin.

I held myself still through the initial pain and stinging thereafter. It helped that she got it all the way through in one go this time; I could feel that much, even before she removed the cushion and screwed the cap over the tip. I supposed this time she knew it was better to not hold back.

She then kissed my forehead, signaling she was done.

I stood, feeling my innate healing already at work to close the wound around the earring. The stinging had already stopped. I could only hope that the gift I shared with Sarah would heal her just as quickly. I was traditionally forbidden from doing anything consciously to speed the process along, other than to sanitize the wound.

She turned her head as I had done for her. I brought out my own cushion and brought both it and the earring to her right ear. Fortunately for her, *I* was stabilizing, perhaps with the return to the expected. Though something inside me still trembled every time I let myself think too deeply about the added significance of what this meant. Sarah and I couldn't let even heartbindings remain unchanged.

I took a lot more care with positioning the earring than last time, making as certain as I could that it was centered in her earlobe. Then, with a small sigh at having to cause her pain like this, I pressed the earring through.

She too stayed still, which helped me feel better, even though I knew she could also just be putting on a front for my sake—and for everyone else close enough to see, of course, because we had an audience this time. I was once again staggered by how large that audience was, now that I had more freedom to look around. I had never seen the Temple Heart *this* full.

Now I understood why the Trees had wanted it to be.

Once I was done screwing on the earring's cap, sanitizing the wound, and putting the cushion away, I tenderly took Sarah's head in my hands and kissed her forehead slowly and softly.

Only now that the shock was thawing was my flameheart beginning to thump from the quiet wonder of it—wonder that was rapidly being surpassed by an even greater emotion. The first waves of joy crashed through me that portended the tsunami to come.

Sarah was mine, and I was hers...

...forever.

Just dek ago, I had wished for the impossible...and I had been granted it.

When Sarah tilted her head up to meet my eyes, I could see the burning of my own reflected in hers.

When I let go, we turned back to the Tree. Our hands found each other's again, without even looking.

The Tree of Flame raised Her right hand, and the ritual fire roared higher. "*The Trees of Ice and Flame have witnessed this union. From this moment forth, the Seven Realms are one. The peoples of Ice and Flame are one. And the King of Flame and Queen of Ice...are one. Forevermore. And what I and My Sister have now declared to be one, let none divide asunder.*"

She gazed around the room, ember eyes burning. "*Else you risk a final shattering that will bring about the ruin of all.*"

CHAPTER NINETEEN

UNION

SARAH

THERE WERE FAR TOO many people to make a path for us to leave, and Ben wasn't about to let me endure the ever-increasing heat long enough for the Tree's chamber to empty, so we decided within moments after Her avatar had vanished that Ben would surge me and my family out of there. Not the traditional exit, but we hoped the people would forgive us, understanding that accommodations had to be made when children of Ice were involved.

Yvera just as quickly approved. She was eyeing the masses of people, who were stirring from their stupor of shock and didn't look in a hurry to depart. We didn't yet know what their collective reaction would be to the revelation of a Third Covenant, but even enthusiasm could be dangerous with a crowd this large.

For the same reason, the High Priestess approached us during our rapid discussion and almost shooed us out of her temple.

"Go on with you both," she said with cheerful sternness. "Let *me* handle this. It's why I'm standing around here, after all."

"Mother Tivien," Ben said in dismay, for the first time seeming conflicted.

"Oh, don't you worry about me, son," she said with a wink and a matronly pat on Ben's cheek. She pointed at Yvera. "Even if the Tree's and my own priestesses' protection wouldn't be enough, you're leaving me this one. Now go!"

Gather round, I sent to all my family, making the final decision for both of us.

They began crowding around me and Ben at once. In fact, Abby broke away from Lizzy and took a flying leap at Ben, giggling with glee as he reflexively caught her.

"You're my brother now," she declared as he settled her on his hip. She parted his hair and touched his new earring reverently, as if she fully understood its significance—that it literally bound Ben and me together by blood.

"I always knew you would be," Abby said sagely. "Now I have *five* brothers."

"Yes, I suppose you do," Ben said with a distracted smile as he watched the others crowd around. "Lucky you."

He wasn't being sarcastic. To a dramá, that was an impossible number of brothers—a bounty Ben could have only dreamed of when he was her age.

"Don't tell the others," Abby whispered loudly, "but I think you're my favorite."

"I heard that, you munchkin," Michael said with a grin as he gestured the last person into the huddle and joined it himself. "You only think that now because he hasn't had a chance to tick you off yet."

"Ready, Sarah?" Ben said hastily, forestalling Abby's pouting protest.

I swiftly but securely lashed everyone together with my power. Even with this many people, it wasn't hard to do, with ties already between all of us as strong as they were.

"Ready."

Ben took us away.

AT LONG LAST, I watched my parents step through the fires of the crowngate, and I sagged against Ben for a moment.

I thought she'd never let me go, I moaned to him silently, since, unless Rachel had closed the doors already, they could still hear us.

Most of my family members had given me brief, sometimes awkward hugs and good wishes before going through the gate, but Mom clutched me to her for what felt like a full minute, sobbing. Eventually, Dad had to gently—yet firmly—pry her off me. Since Mom got wind that Ben and I would some-how honeymoon in the Seventh Realm, she couldn't seem to understand why our family couldn't just clear out a space in our hold, letting us stay with them for that time. Honestly, it was like she didn't even understand what the concept of a honeymoon *was*.

She wasn't ignorant of how special this was for me, either. She'd given me "the talk" too many times over this past month, with me having to reiterate each time that Ben and I were waiting, and with her expressing surprise that our resolve still lasted and yet adamant approval each time. As much as Mom had been understanding all these years of most of us kids following Dad's agnostic path, she couldn't help her religious roots.

And yet, a bit paradoxically, marital intimacy was *too* natural a thing to Mom, so natural that she couldn't comprehend why I would want miles between me and anyone else except Ben when I experienced it for the first time. It was so natural a part of life to her, why wouldn't I be comfortable exploring it while being surrounded by family? Just like I was fine with eating or sleeping or hanging out at home. She saw this as me cheating her of the best time off I'd had in a month, the most precious opportunity she had left with me before I settled into another world and life outside her own.

I was going to have to spend some serious time with her after everything was over to make up for this.

Maybe we should.... Ben said hesitantly.

Nope, I said at once, straightening. *That is still an absolute no. Besides, this is the Trees' gift to us, remember?*

Right, Ben said with relief.

You're going to have to get used to saying no to my mom, Ben. And to Abby, for that matter.

It had been just as hard to pry Abby away from Ben as last time. Especially with Mom making her offers, Abby couldn't understand why we didn't want to come stay with them for a few days. Because she had a true claim to innocence,

I didn't blame *her* in the slightest for her pleas. Even when she finally pouted at me, whirled around, and stomped through the gate.

I know, Ben said with a sigh. *She just looks at me with those big eyes of hers, and....*

I get it, I said ruefully. I was a sucker for those eyes, too. They were the reason I was wandering around our neighborhood creek, looking for Abby's macaroni necklace, when the Tree of Ice opened a wildgate to dump me into the Six Realms.

"Well," I said out loud, deciding we had probably given Rachel enough time to close the doors. Even so, I circled around the gate to the back of that chamber as I pulled the ice shard the Tree had given me out of my pocket.

(A wedding dress with *pockets.* Dramá tailors were *amazing,* and I would sing their praises until the day I died.)

"Ready to give this a try?" I said, holding it up. It hadn't melted in the slightest since the moment the Tree had given it to me. Even so, Ben couldn't stand to touch it for more than a second or two. He swore it felt like normal ice to him—or even colder.

"Have you figured out how?" Ben asked curiously as he followed me.

"I have an idea, at least," I said, turning it in my hand to grip it like a writing utensil, with the slanted tip pointed downward.

It was the shape and size that had given me the idea: it looked like chalk.

That's how I used it, scraping it back and forth over the back wall of the circular crowngate chamber, and despite how it had appeared as hard as a diamond before, the ice smeared across that surface just like chalk—if a frosty, slightly glowing version.

"That looks promising," I said as I continued to swipe back and forth.

"It does," Ben said.

I knew better than to think that the surprise in his voice came from a lack of faith in me. It was his now-familiar wonder as I kept throwing all the rules he knew out the window.

I outlined and then began filling in a rectangle about the size of a small door. If this *did* become a door, it would be a tight fit for Ben, but he'd survive. I didn't know how long this shard would last, so I wasn't taking chances. If I had more left over at the end, I could make it bigger.

By the end, I was glad I had limited myself, because the chalk ice ran out just as I was filling in the final bottom corner a few minutes later.

I stood up from my kneeling position, Ben helping me with the awkwardness of that feat in my voluminous dress. (There were limits to what even dramá tailors could do, though the beauty of their work in this case was totally worth it. This skirt alone was every girl's dream. I didn't mind giving Ben an excuse to touch me, either.)

We both stood back and waited, but nothing happened. It felt right, but incomplete.

"I think it needs power," I decided finally, so I walked forward and placed my palm in the center of that rectangle and pulsed power through the frosted surface. The moonstone lines in the chamber flared in response, and pure ice spread out from my fingers and overtook the frost, filling in every bump and crack in that rough sandstone surface until it was a smooth pane of solid ice. The ice completed itself when I removed my hand, creeping over the print my hand had left until it was no more, and the ice was entire.

Then, just as with my scrying ice, colors came into being on that smooth, frozen surface, forming a crystal-clear image of another place.

It was a hallway, pitch black for the first second, but beginning to be illuminated even before the image had fully formed by more moonstone lines lighting up with the presence of my magic on the other side. Still, that short hallway was pretty much all there was to see, other than a door with a glowing white tree at the end.

I reached forward and placed my hand on the ice, but unlike the ice curtains within my moongates, there was no give to it. It was still as solid as ever, for all the world appearing and behaving just as my scrying ice normally did.

"Hmm," I said thoughtfully, stepping back again.

"What was that other thing your Tree said?" Ben asked as he put a hand on my shoulder. "About surging?"

"She said that there was an application of my surging ability I hadn't discovered yet, and this shard was Her only hint...."

Scrying ice? But what did that have to do with surging? Scrying ice didn't let me enter another place, as I'd just proven; it just let me see it.

Then it hit me. It was so *obvious*.

"I'm an idiot," I said, hitting my palm to my forehead.

"Sarah, you are *not* an idiot."

"Then tell me how I could have *possibly* not figured this out before," I said, gesturing with both hands to the ice. "Ben, I told you this myself: *I can surge anywhere I can see.*"

And now I could see this place that the Tree wanted me to surge to, more clearly than any high-definition screen or photograph could have managed.

Ben looked at the ice.

"Oh," he said. "*Oh.*"

We both stared at the ice as we processed the Realms-shattering implications of what I could now do...and had been capable of all along.

I sighed and gave another wave at the ice. "Like I said: idiot."

"Don't you dare call yourself that again," Ben said, snapping out of his daze. "None of the others figured this out either, remember? Not even Jake, or Kor."

"I wouldn't rule out Kor," I grumbled. "Not until we ask him. After all, who else predicted *the Third Covenant?*"

Kor's grand theory, out in the open at last. The greatest paper he would never publish—because by now the entire Seven Realms *knew*. Well, not about the whole matchmaking thing. But the existence of yet another Covenant was the real reveal, the prediction that would have given him a Nobel-Prize equivalent in Covenantal theory...if he had ever been allowed to make it publicly known.

Really, he'd been an astonishingly good sport about the fact that the Seven Realms might never know just what kind of genius he was.

Ben hesitated, then shook his head. "No, Kor *can't* have figured this one out. It would have been too useful an ability for even him to keep quiet. He wouldn't have been able to resist getting you to use it for *something*."

"Good point...."

In fact, that was probably the most convincing point Ben could have made, the one that finally made me feel a tad better. It was one thing for Kor to keep the Third Covenant a secret so long as he could keep carefully nudging Ben and me along toward the altar, but something like combining surging with scrying...would have been way too useful, at so many points. All the applications during the siege of Rosin, his clan's capital, alone....

"Even the smartest people miss things," Ben said. Then he added, "And you're one of those smartest people, Sarah."

"Thank you," I said with a growing smile. "And while we're on the subject, I think you are, too."

Ben flushed and looked away, coughing. "Anyway, sometimes we're not *meant* to figure some things out until a certain point. Like the Third Covenant. Or...this."

He waved his hand at the ice. "If the Tree of Ice wanted you to know about it before, She could have told it to you before or given you Her hint before. But apparently, She wants you to know about it *now*. So don't let me hear you call yourself an idiot again for not figuring out something that you—that *all* of us—weren't ready to know."

"If that's the case," I grumbled, "then why did the Tree let Kor figure out the Third Covenant?"

But I knew the answer before I even finished speaking, and I nearly slapped my palm to my forehead again.

"Torch me if I know," Ben muttered, running a hand through his hair.

I sighed. "It's us. We're the reason why."

"What?" Ben said blankly.

"Face it, Ben: how much of our relationship right now do we owe to Kor?"

How many times had Kor helped me understand Ben, forgive him for his mistakes, or anticipate his needs? How many times might Kor have done the same for Ben, with me? Despite how aggravating his own "matchmaking" was, I had to admit how critical Kor had been to our getting to this point. Or, at least, getting here so soon and so happily.

When Ben just scowled, I wearily stated the obvious for both of us. "The Trees needed someone who *knew* how important our relationship was, someone intelligent and capable enough to make sure it survived. Someone...like Kor."

Now we both knew why Kor had been so dang determined to see us married—for the good of the Realms, just as he had always claimed. And...yes, because he was our friend and wanted us to be happy. As much as he may pretend otherwise.

That should have tipped me off long ago, given Kor's habit of hiding his greatest emotions behind their opposites.

"Anyway," I said, shaking myself out of my thoughts. "That's all assuming that I've guessed right, that I can even do this. No way to find out for certain until we try."

Ben chuckled as he threaded his fingers through mine. "Oh, I think you can. I'm starting to think you can do *anything*, so this seems more than manageable for you."

"Well, let's get going before I run out of power," I said, weariness sinking in again.

Scrying required a constant stream of energy, so while we had been speculating, I had been maintaining the ice with my reserves, which were limited considering how the day was waxing on and how little rest I'd gotten lately.

Or food. My stomach growled, Ben's heavenly pancakes and eggs long since used up, so I hoped Ben either had food in his ether storage or the Trees had stocked the larder in this place. If not, I supposed we could always go find some (considering how much of the Realms might be at my fingertips now), but I was ready to just be alone with him. Never mind a honeymoon; at that moment, I just wanted *privacy* and *rest*.

I lashed Ben to me—noticing how very little power it took now; less power than ever, in fact—and said, "Ready?"

"Ready," Ben said, not a hint of anxiety about what I was about to attempt in his voice.

He really believes I can do this, I thought in amazement. *Not just believe—he already accepts it as fact.*

I hoped I was right. I couldn't bear disappointing him now.

"Then here goes," I said, taking a deep breath.

Using up a precious amount of my remaining reserves (I truly hoped there was food on the other side), I began to glow. Then I turned us into streaks of silver light...

...and we rematerialized in the moonstone-lit hallway.

I stood there for a moment, frozen, then began looking around.

Without letting go of Ben, I turned and looked back at the ice panel behind us. Though it might *seem* like a doorway, it was just another sheet of ice displaying another image, with no physical connection to the chamber we had left whatsoever. That much was obvious the moment I dismissed the ice and it melted to nothing, revealing nothing but a dead end behind it.

"I...I did it," I said blankly. "I surged...to somewhere I saw in ice."

Ben laughed, tugged me back, bent down, and pressed a quick kiss to my lips. "Knew you could," he said, eyes and smile warm when he pulled away.

"Get back down here," I teased. "I think I deserve a bit more than a peck, don't you?"

"Oh, you most certainly do," he agreed lightly, giving my hand a squeeze. His eyes soulflared for a moment. "But I'm afraid if I do anything more, I might not be able to stop, and this isn't exactly the kind of place I wanted us to...."

"Ah," I said, heat growing in my face. "Right. Ahem. Well, let's see what we've got here, then, shall we?"

Avoiding his eyes, I led him forward down the short hall and to the door with the glowing white tree. I pressed my hand to its trunk, power flowed from me into the door, the glow increased in luminosity, and I felt a magical release, like a popping of ears with a change in elevation.

"That was a time seal, wasn't it?" I asked, glancing at Ben.

"Time seal?" he said, face scrunching in confusion.

"Like those that were in my hold, over the storage rooms and whatnot."

"Oh, you mean the seals against decay," Ben said, face relaxing.

"Right. Time seal. That's what I guess I started calling it in my head."

"*Decay* seal, more likely," Ben insisted. "Nothing has control over time itself, Sarah."

Something about that struck me as not being quite right, but I had no idea why that was, or why I had long since given those seals the label of "time" in my head—or why that *still* felt like the best description to me.

In any case, it was a theoretical discussion I wasn't interested in getting into right then, because I officially had a headache coming on. I wanted food, sleep, and Ben. Right now, in that order. That could change, but that was where I was at.

I pushed open the door, and Ben and I stepped inside.

It was…well, it was a bit like my former, "special" room in my family's hold, except a much smaller version, and one that seemed to blend in much more dramá-like things.

The center was a sunken seating area around a raised firepit, already filled with coals; in my room, that had been a fountain and ring of mossy plants. Just as in my room, these built-in couches were furnished with white, comfy-looking square cushions (more of that mushroom memory foam), but this time with a few thick, golden-brown furs artfully tossed over them. On the left side of the room was a cozy reading nook lined with books, with a nest formed by a bowl carved into the rock and more white foam, and filled with golden cushions and more furs. I wanted to collapse, then curl up inside it at once.

On the other side, where Ben's eyes had been drawn, was a small but tasteful and functional-looking kitchen, equipped with the technological blend of Earthren and dramá appliances found in my family's hold. That was the biggest difference so far: my room didn't have a kitchen at all. Ben drifted from me and began poking around, his expression starting out hopeful and turning appreciative with every small discovery.

I stayed where I was and continued examining, my eyes falling on the space across from the door. Just as in my former room, that was the sleeping area. The bed was just as ridiculously enormous, or even more so, and the comforter was still white, evoking a giant cloud, but the rug underneath, the pillows above, and the enormous curtain behind were all…gold.

Then the reason for the difference hit me—triggered by, of all things, the colors.

White...and gold.

My former room, which I had given up to Rachel when Svyer had moved in, had a lot more...blues. White and blue, that had been its theme, with some gray or black thrown in, especially in the bathroom. The space had been cool, occasionally dark, but always restful, its themed nooks intellectual, artistic, or magical. I had assumed that the intellectual, bookish parts, like the reading nook or writing desk, were for the person I already was, and that I was someday meant to grow into using the arcanist or artisan corners. But when I gave the room up, I realized it hadn't been made for me. Despite my acceptance of my status as Queen, the size and opulence still had never sat quite right with me. It wasn't...me. But it *was* Rachel. And the other things....

White and blue.

That room had been made for Rachel...and Kor. I wanted to smack myself again. I had deliberately kept Kor away from that room, and now I knew why: it fit him like a glove. I could just *see* him in it, writing away at the desk, or immersed in some kind of new prototype in the arcanist corner.

I wryly thought to myself that if Kor had seen the room he could have shared with me, he might not have given me up so easily. In fact, he probably *had* seen it plenty of times by now, at least through a scale. After all, where else would Rachel have talked to him? Knowing Rachel, she gave him the grand tour as soon as she took up residence, just to show it off.

It was a good thing I knew by now that he wasn't trying to marry Rachel just for her title or her room. At least...not entirely.

But *this* space...this could only have been designed for me...and Ben. There was my reading nook, there was Ben's kitchen. The dark gray walls were for me, to balance out the brightness of the white and gold. The firepit in the center was for him, the couches were for both of us to snuggle and talk just as we liked. This smaller, simpler, cozier suite suited both of us, giving us just what we needed and no more.

And it invited a sense of warm *togetherness* that my former room had lacked. Even that reading nook was big enough for Ben to join me in, and that kitchen had a bar for me to sit at while he cooked, and for us to eat at together.

Kor was right: he and Rachel would always have a very different relationship. One that would probably be nauseatingly passionate while they felt like being together (I could already feel myself gagging preemptively), but also one that would require them to spend a lot of time pursuing their own interests, giving each other space. That would not just work for them—that was what they needed.

Ben and I needed something very different: to be together, as much as we could. When the two of us *wanted* to be apart, something was wrong. It wasn't a better kind of relationship, just as this wasn't a better room, objectively speaking. It was just different. It was...us.

"Hungry?" Ben asked with a grin, interrupting my epiphany as he put a bowl of nuts and fruit he must have found somewhere on the bar.

"Oh, *goodness yes*," I said immediately, happy to forego deep thoughts in the face of instantly available nutrition. I made a beeline for the bar and was working on one of the easier nuts even before I'd fully settled onto the barstool.

"I like this," Ben said appreciatively as he ran his hand over the bar counter. He glanced at the stools as well, so I knew he wasn't just talking about the stone surface.

"Earthren thing," I said, just before stuffing nut meat into my mouth. "It's called a bar."

He blinked, then motioned with his hands. "Like a long metal rod?"

I laughed. Sometimes the way the translation magic worked between us was funny. If there wasn't a direct analogy, the magic would try to come up with the next best thing. "No, like a place where a bartender stands to give drinks. Er, not that I've been to many bars. Or had many drinks...."

I may have been old enough to marry without permission, in the USA or the Seven Realms, but in the US, at least, I still couldn't legally drink, and my parents hadn't been the type to skirt that kind of rule. Or any rules, for that matter. Or drink much themselves.

Ben grinned as he continued to poke around the kitchen. "By that, I assume you mean alcohol. For all this being a 'bar,' though, I see your ancestors knew better than to stock it with intoxicants."

"Oh, no, when it's in a kitchen, it just refers to the type of counter," I said quickly, working on another nut. "One you can sit at like this."

He shook his head with a chuckle. "So many uses for one simple word."

"Oh, Drona has plenty of those kinds of words," I said dryly, thinking of my language lessons. "Take *yven*, for example."

Their word for *blood*.

"I suppose you're right," Ben said distractedly, clearly not that interested in a linguistics discussion.

I grinned. "What's your assessment, master chef?"

"It will do," Ben said with a smile that let me know he was more than pleased. "It's smaller than your other one—I mean the one in your wing—but it has the new things from your hold's kitchen. The cold box, for one."

He lifted the lid in demonstration, not even looking inside, and closed it only a moment later. Presumably, that meant he had already found it.

"Also," he said with a satisfied expression, "it's got more than enough food to last us a sevenday, let alone a couple of days."

"Great," I said, cheeks going hot.

I didn't say what we were both thinking at this point: just him and me, for at least two solid days, with no one else, not even Kor or Yvera, let alone a whole contingent of elites, and nothing to threaten either of us, no way for anyone to get to us, and no reason for us to leave. Not even for food.

He cleared his throat and turned his back to me to poke around in the cupboards across from me, even though I knew he had already been through them. "Er, I'd packed that much food anyway, just so you know."

"Oh, I'm sure," I said hastily. "Um...speaking of things that you packed...this dress is pretty and all, but...."

It wasn't the kind of thing that you could just crash into bed in. At least not comfortably.

"Oh, right," Ben said hastily, bringing out my bags and setting them on the floor just outside the kitchen.

"Thanks," I said, grabbing a fruit from the bowl and then rounding the bar to grab a bag with the other hand. As I straightened, I decided I needed to buckle up my courage and clarify something. "Um, I'm feeling tired right now, so I was thinking of changing into something comfy and taking a nap...."

"Of course," Ben said hastily, going red. "I wasn't...er, that is, I knew that...well, you're normally asleep right now."

He took a deep breath, and his voice grew firm. "And I've made you get up at or before dawn far too many mornings lately. And you've been exhausting yourself all morning."

I let out a breath of relief. I was looking forward to this time with him, but I wanted to fully enjoy it. Adrenaline would no doubt wake me up and give me a boost, but I'd lived my life too much by adrenaline lately, and I knew what kind of crash came after. I didn't want our first time to be about me just pushing through.

Ben seemed to tell. He shook his head at me and then leaned in to kiss my forehead before stepping back, giving me a stern look. "Sleep as much as you want. Seriously. That's an order."

"Yes, your majesty," I said with a chuckle, hoisting my bag. I wandered over to our bedroom, where I figured I would find the entrance to our bathroom, and so I did.

When I came back out, face scrubbed clean, hair blessedly loose and de-pinned, dressed in my dramá equivalent of pajamas, Ben was, predictably, cooking something in the kitchen.

"Smells incredible," I said as I wandered over to the bed. "Save some for me for later."

"Oh, er, I'm almost done," he said sheepishly, looking between me and whatever was loudly sizzling in his pan.

"Don't worry about it," I said firmly. I pushed the comforter back and then crawled onto that puffy white cloud. "There's something homey in the sound. It's comforting."

More than just comforting. It was the sound and smell of a space that Ben lived in, and even though we had only been here less than half an hour, that made it *home*. More than the room I'd given up to Rachel ever had been. More than my wing that I'd spent a few nights in had been.

"By the way," I said as casually as I could. My genuine yawn as I pulled the covers over me and snuggled in helped, I thought. "You're welcome to join me when you're done. I *know* you didn't get much sleep last night either. Less than me, even."

"Thanks. Er, I should probably call Yvera, though…. You know, let her know we made it, and that I wasn't assassinated on the way. And she or Kor can pass the message to your family. About you being alright, I mean. Not sure whether they care about my potential assassination…."

I smiled to myself, eyes drifting closed. "Whenever you're ready."

Then I was out.

HOURS LATER, AFTER I'D woken up to discover Ben with me, and he had woken too, we came together for the first time.

It took a bit for us to get to that point, though. We had to get over our initial shyness and awkwardness after spending so long holding back from each other, not to mention our inexperience.

The biggest obstacle, though, was Ben's fear of hurting me, but he eventually worked through it after I showed him as best as I could how much I trusted him and *wanted* this—and finally, of all things, by him entering his battle trance, the mindset he'd cultivated long ago to be fully present, get out of his own way, and do whatever needed to be done.

Far from being repulsed by the change in him, I was thrilled. I had lost heart when I first saw him fight. I thought that was a place I could never enter with him, much less fight as an equal with him. I had despaired that he could never be so alive, so free…with me. I couldn't have been more wrong—and I'd never been happier to be so.

Just as Ben had anticipated his opponent's every move in the duel, he knew me, had watched me, and had touched me enough by now to know what I needed from him—even before I did. He only had to realize that himself...and give himself permission to do so.

Just as the dueling ring brought together his lifetime of training and his innate talent, in a forum that gave him rules, structure, and honor, and allowed him to unleash himself without bringing any innocents to harm...now, all his healing training, all his classes on anatomy and physiology, all his massage practices, all his mother's and cousin's instruction about females, and most of all, his incomparable instincts for how to move and observe and interact with bodies all came together inside him in that one instant, and I was blown away.

When it was over, I was perfectly happy to lie underneath Ben for a minute or two while the scattered bits of my breath and mind came back to me. No matter how much more difficult it was to catch that breath with his dead weight crushing me into that cloud, I craved it all the same. It was more than the fact that he was the ultimate heated gravity blanket. Ben's utter exhaustion meant that he had given his all: power, will, and body.

That was, perhaps, the most precious gift he had ever given me.

So, I held out as long as I could, long after my pulse slowed and my muscles somewhat resolidified...but then some parts of my body started to go numb.

Ben, I said silently, not wanting to risk there being a breathless edge to my voice.

He made a sound that communicated he was conscious, but only just. More reason to address this now, I supposed. Before I was trapped.

You're...just a bit heavy.

Just a bit. How many pounds did a seven-foot-six drakón male made of pure muscle *weigh*, anyway?

For the first time since Ben had entered his battle trance, he stiffened. In the next second, he was flailing onto his back and off me, gasping, "Sorry! I'm so sorry!"

You're fine, I soothed. But I still used my inner voice as I slowly and subtly expanded my lungs to their full capacity again.

He moaned, covering his face with his hands. He mumbled something that I was sure was another apology.

Don't worry about it. I'm fine.

He lowered his hands, looking at me tentatively. Red was creeping over his neck and face again, as if he had only just realized what we had done. His eyes kept drifting down from my face and shooting straight back up.

"Do you need me to cover up?" I teased. Strange how I felt no need to, even completely uncovered as I was now. Yet I didn't feel exposed. I felt safe, free...loved.

Practically speaking, though, there was no part of me Ben hadn't seen at this point.

"Ur, no—not unless you want to," he stammered.

"Then look all you want," I said easily. "I don't mind, Ben."

"You don't?" He cleared his throat. "I mean, you never seemed comfortable with nudity before...."

"That's with other people. You're not other people. You're my Ben."

First my dragon, then my sun, now...my husband.

He glanced meaningfully down at his bare chest and back at me.

It was my turn to clear my throat. "That was me being attracted to you. Far more than was permissible at the time. I thought you had figured out that much."

He smiled crookedly. "Well, I did, but I thought there was more to it than that."

"Nope." I turned onto my side to face him. "With you, that was absolutely all there was to it. So, am I free to ogle you all I want now? If I give you permission to do the same?"

He chuckled. "Seems fair."

"Excellent," I said, letting my eyes drift freely back to that chest. "Because if you'd said no, that would have made life pretty difficult."

He laughed and turned onto his side as well. His eyes also drifted, now with bold curiosity...and the occasional golden flare of his eyes.

He lifted his hand tentatively. "May I...?"

"Of course."

He began tracing me with a featherlight touch, something close to awe coming over his face.

I softened my voice, not wanting him to think I was making fun of him. "You would think you hadn't just gone over every inch of me."

"That was different," he said, a bit of pink creeping back again. "That was for you."

And this was for him. This slow, soft, almost reverent exploration. Almost as if he were a cartographer sketching out the lay of the land that he had just blazed through. Making it real in his head that I was now...his.

When I felt a bit of his power trickle into me through that touch, I raised an eyebrow. "You're ready for another round already?"

He blushed again. "Just...checking."

Ah, I saw now. "No broken bones or missing appendages?"

He scowled at me. "This isn't a joke, Sarah."

"Sorry," I said contritely. "You're right, it's not."

He sighed. "I did my very best not to hurt you, but I think I *still* bruised you. I just healed most of it as I went along. I'm...making sure I didn't miss anything."

"You realize that you'll probably heal anything that's left just by being with me, right?"

"Maybe," he said, clenching his jaw stubbornly. "But I want you whole *now*."

I smiled softly.

He sighed. "What?"

"You. Being you." I traced that bearded jaw, feeling the golden hairs brush against my fingertips. "I love you, you know. Every single part of you."

Ben stopped his tracing and swallowed.

I sighed. "You *don't* have to say it, Ben. You just *showed* it to me, in incredible detail. If that wasn't love...then I don't know what is."

"But why can't I say it?" he whispered, expression agonized. "Why does it get even *harder* each time I try? I used to be able to. It was hard, but I could. Now...."

He closed his eyes.

"Maybe it's because each time you try, you've come to love me more."

He opened his eyes and smiled thinly. "While that's true, it doesn't...feel like that's the reason."

"If there's an answer, you'll figure it out someday," I said with a soft smile. I cupped his face in my hand. "But even if you never do, I won't mind. Whatever way you *can* tell me you love me, that will be more than enough."

He sighed heavily. "You deserve better."

"I think we've been over this," I said, risking a gentle tease. "I believe I made it clear that simply wasn't possible."

He huffed, grasped me behind the neck, and came onto my pillow to kiss me, slowly yet passionately. By the time he pulled away, my lips were burning.

"There," he said with a crooked smile. "Did I make my meaning clear?"

I swallowed, flushing all over with the heat only he stirred in me now. "Hmm. I'm not sure I caught that. Must have been the language barrier. Could you try again?"

He chuckled and partially rolled over me. Not enough to crush me like last time, but certainly more than enough to turn that warmth into a full blaze. Especially with his lips adding more kindling with every second.

When he pushed up a minute or so later, his eyes were burning, and I saw from the reflection that mine were too.

"About that next round...." he rasped.

"That's a definite yes," I said breathlessly.

"Good." Then he recaptured my mouth, and he showed me how much he loved me once again.

For the first time, I realized how dangerous it had been for me to marry the son of the Sunfilled King of Flame and the former Peacegrowth Heir. If only Yalda had realized what a lethal combination that was.

It had created a man who was as tender as he was ferocious, and all the fiercer for that tenderness. A man who could lead armies to battle and sing a little girl to sleep. A man who could kill and mourn, cut and heal, cry and laugh. A man with such power and yet such control. A man who could love me with all of his heart of flame without breaking my heart of ice. A living fire that could never be put out, that did not consume itself in its inferno.

Much like a Tree of Flame.

CHAPTER TWENTY

MIRACLE

KORIBEN

THOSE TWO DAYS WERE the happiest of my life thus far, and not just for the obvious reason. It was the first time I could remember in far too long—years, at least—in which I had had nearly two full days back-to-back in which I could just *rest*, with no duties, meetings, crises, or even scale calls interrupting that precious time.

Still, I might have been at a loss at what to do with that much time on my hands, let alone in such isolated circumstances, if it hadn't been for Sarah. She was the essential ingredient that made whatever we did perfect.

The Seven Realms had somehow been reduced to just that one shelter, its population to just Sarah and me, and the entire course of time and history to just those two days...

...and I couldn't be happier.

In fact, I nearly burst with the emotion. Sarah kept laughing at me because I couldn't seem to stop smiling. Or whistling. Or singing, especially when I was cooking for the two of us. *That* was my second-favorite activity, and Sarah soon protested that as much as she loved my cooking, she couldn't imagine how we were going to eat everything I was making for us.

We also filled our time in other ways. Sarah's second-favorite pastime was for us to snuggle in the reading nook while we went over Avva's sketchbooks, or while I read to us out of the limited selection in my personal "library" in my ether stores and she tried to follow along. The few books that were already on the nook's shelves were blank, meant to be decorative.

Or so I'd thought, but then the next morning, when I woke up, I caught Sarah writing in one while sitting at the bar. After I got up, freshened up in the bathroom, and then went to her and kissed her, I asked her what she was writing, and she admitted she was starting a journal.

"I want to remember this. Everything, really. But especially this."

At my alarmed look, she laughed. "I'm not including certain...details. Don't worry."

"Oh, good," I said with a grin as I went around the counter and into the kitchen to start our breakfast. "Then write away."

"I've always had a journal," Sarah said with a sigh as she looked back down at the book. "I wrote in it almost every night. It helped me think, and cope. I had a whole small chest full of them in my room."

At my questioning glance, she explained, "The only way to keep something private in a family that big—at least one like mine—was to keep it under lock and key."

"Makes sense, I guess," I said, ducking to grab a pan.

"I was so proud of that chest," Sarah said sadly. "Filling it with a new book each year was like filling it with my life. I thought I could give it to my kids someday."

When I came up, I became still as I suddenly realized the reason for her sobriety. My throat and chest tightened.

Those journals were long gone now. Not just out of her reach, or the reach of prying siblings. They had gone up in smoke, along with her former home—her former *life*.

"Sarah," I said, aghast. I set the pan down as softly as possible, not wanting it to make so much as a click against the range.

"Not your fault, Ben," she said calmly.

I swallowed. Only Sarah, of all her family, would say such a thing.

Now I felt another flash of guilt. Here I was, having an obligation as first Heir and now King to keep a personal record of my life, yet I had written as little as I could help and felt no regret over the scant records I'd lost in the various tablets I had broken. (I was the despair of the Archivists Guild long before I started wearing black or courting a Moontouched Queen.) And even without a duty to do so, Sarah had kept a faithful record, and she had lost it all.

Life was torched cruel sometimes.

"Sarah, if I could give those books back to you…."

In that moment, I would have cut off a finger.

"I know, Ben," she said with a smile. "Don't worry about it. I still have the most important things in life. But these empty books…and this fresh start…and the thought of a child all made me realize that maybe it was time to start again."

I started moving about the kitchen again, thinking for a long moment about how I wanted to phrase my question. "You're…writing with the intent of giving it to our child?"

I wasn't sure how I felt about that. Sarah could do whatever she thought was best, of course, but I wasn't sure how much I would want them to know about *my* life. Especially the past two and a half months of it. Somehow, that seemed even more cringe-inducing than the thought of finally being pinned down by an archivist to give a public record of it.

"Of course," Sarah said. "What's the point of going through all of this, learning these things, if we can't help make things easier for them someday?"

"We went through it and learned those things because we had to," I said dryly.

"And they'll have to go through hard things too, Ben. If there's just a chance I can make it even a bit easier for them, if I can show them that *we* went through the same things and survived…then I'm going to do it."

My throat tightened again, and I was glad to have my back to Sarah right now as I gathered ingredients.

We have to survive *first, Sarah,* I thought.

And we needed to *have* that child, or, for some inexplicable reason known only to the Trees…she might not. And if she did not….

My mind flicked to the pact I'd made with myself late last night, while I was holding Sarah as she finally succumbed to sleep. That was the only way to finally calm my flameheart enough for *me* to sleep, since my heart had felt like it would extinguish from the thought of losing her. Every day, the thought seemed more unthinkable, but that life-changing first day of being heartbonded to her had finally pushed me over the edge.

So, in the darkness, what felt like deken after Sarah drifted off, I came to a resolution, which I presented to the Tree. Not because I was giving Her an ultimatum—history had taught me that was a bad idea—but because I felt like it needed to be out in the open between us. As the Tree of Flame's chosen King, I thought it only proper to inform Her that if my wife did not survive the battle to save Her Sister...I would share her fate.

I shook myself out of that dark thought before turning back, determined not to let Sarah see it within me. My resolve, combined with knowing that Sarah was mine forever, had finally brought me a fatalistic calm unlike any I had experienced before, which had distilled over the night and crystallized in my flameheart by the time I woke up. Which meant I could bring myself back into the present moment and smile at her with astonishing ease.

Whatever came, I still had today with her. If today was one of the last days of our mortal lives, well...all the more reason to make the most of it.

So, I rounded the bar, captured her face, and kissed her, slowly and luxuriously. It wasn't long before Sarah put down her pencil and twined her fingers through my own hair.

"I thought...you were making breakfast," she teased breathlessly when I began trailing kisses down her throat and the exposed parts of her collarbones and shoulders.

"Hmm, but are you hungry yet?" I murmured against her skin.

Sarah gasped when I ran my tongue over a sensitive spot, and her fingers tightened in their grip on me. "Er...no. That's definitely a no."

"Then breakfast can wait," I said, scooping her up off her stool and carrying her back to our bed.

After all, cooking was only my *second*-favorite activity now.

As I'd DETERMINED TO do, I made the most of every moment. They consequently slipped through my fingers like sand, but I let them go, not even trying
to hold on to them. Either Sarah and I would have more days like this, or we
would not. If not, I would die content—so long as I died with her.

Sarah made even death seem like an adventure.

So I was happy, even in our last few conscious moments as I held her while
we snuggled late that second night on the bed of cushions I had made for us in
front of the floor-to-ceiling window. Sarah had wanted to fall asleep watching
the stars, and so I made it happen. Technically, with the curtains fully open,
we could have seen the stars just fine from our bed, but we both agreed that we
had spent enough time there, and there was something cozy and secluded about
being together in that oval between the closed curtains and the slanted window.
As if nothing existed outside the two of us and the stars.

Of course, we first made productive use of this new makeshift bed, and now
we lay tangled together, able to give the stars more of our attention. Sarah was
on top of me, her face turned toward the window as she watched the colorful
ribbons of light play out in the sky.

"We call them the Northern Lights," she said wistfully. "At least, in the
northern hemisphere of Earth. I suppose we don't even know if this is in the
north or south of this world."

"It feels like the north to me," I said quietly, playing with her hair.

Sarah chuckled. "Oh, that's right. I forgot that you drakón have internal
compasses."

"Yes. So, unless this Realm is completely reversed in polarity and axis rotation
from mine, I believe this place is in your Realm's 'north.'"

I idly debated whether to tell her something else I had guessed from observing
the sun, the moons, the stars, and the magnetic pull I felt inside: that I was
fairly certain we were near her family's hold, perhaps even within a different
slope of the same mountain. Perhaps there was even some connecting passage
between the two, but Sarah and I hadn't ventured out into the entrance hall

again to investigate. Far from feeling trapped, both of us seemed content with our isolation from the rest of the Realms, and I wasn't about to spoil that for Sarah now.

"What do *you* call them?" she asked.

I cast my eyes on the ethereal ribbons for a moment, but only a moment. While they had enraptured Sarah, I had scarcely let my gaze leave her. The lights would continue for at least a few days longer. Sarah—at least as she was now, in this beautiful, precious mortal form—might not.

"The Promise of Light," I said.

Sarah craned her head up to look at me. "That sounds like it has a story behind it."

"It does."

And so, as I played with her hair, I told her the tale: how the Sunfather had once punished His children for their disobedience to the Flamemother by cursing them to years of winter, and when they had finally repented and turned back to the Tree, She had pled on their behalf by presenting Her Husband with locks of Her own hair, which He accepted and then threw into the sky as a sign forever after that all winters from then on would end.

"Ah, so that's why you're so interested in my hair right now," Sarah teased.

"It's...one reason," I said with a slow smile, winding those long, thick white strands around my fingers and watching the colors from outside play out on them. Even unclothed and unadorned, I didn't know if Sarah had ever been more beautiful to me.

She *was* my Promise of Light. My spring after the eternal winter my life had been ever since Avvi's death—or perhaps even before that, perhaps from the moment I knew I would have to become Heir to save my people. And she was the sign to everyone, everywhere, of the end of the Trees' wrath and the dawn of a new age.

"It's interesting, though," Sarah mused, still watching the rivulets in the sky. "You guys call it the Promise of *Light*. Not the Promise of *Flame*. Normally you guys seem all about fire. And it's supposed to be the Tree of Flame's hair, after all."

I paused as I thought through the tale again. Then, careful not to disturb her position on top of me, I raised an arm and summoned my nursery primer to my hands. I didn't let myself think too deeply about why that was in my ether storage instead of on my shelf in my room.

Avvi had taught me to read from this book.

My hands were much bigger now than they had been then, bigger than even hers; they dwarfed that little, worn book. Even trying hard not to think about the memories, tears stung my eyes at the sight.

"What are you doing?" Sarah asked curiously, turning over onto her back to see what I was holding up. As she did so, she slid off me somewhat, which I had been trying to avoid, but I was satisfied when she settled into the crook of my arm.

"I'm looking up the tale," I said, raising my other hand so I could turn the pages. "At least the version I was taught."

"This was yours?" Sarah said, voice almost reverent. "When you were a boy?"

"Yes," I answered, voice thick.

I came to the story and read through it swiftly, only looking for keywords and studying the illustrations for a few long moments each. Only a few dek later, I closed the book and put it away, lowering my arm.

"What is it?" Sarah asked.

She didn't even have to see my face to know I was thinking.

"It never says 'the Tree of *Flame*,'" I said quietly. "Just 'the Tree.'"

Even the illustrations of the Tree were...vague. Blurred almost. The colors off.

"Is that normal in that book?"

"No." I'd flipped briefly to another couple of stories to confirm. "In all the others, it mentions Her specifically, at least once."

We both were quiet for a long moment. Sarah looked back at the lights.

"It could just be a coincidence," she offered.

"Could be," I agreed.

Another pause, shorter this time.

"Is there...a Tree of Light, though?" Sarah asked, as if she couldn't help it.

"Not that I know of...but that means very little. The Tree doesn't tell us about other Trees and Their children. Only that there is no end to the Creators' creations and thus no end to the need for Her Sisters to guard and tend them."

"Then the only reason you even know about Ice is because..."

"...we're partly Her children, too."

"I hadn't thought of it that way before," Sarah said thoughtfully, twining her hand in mine and raising them both to examine in the shifting light. "That you're descended from both Ice and Flame. Just like I am."

"Just like you," I said softly, looking at those joined hands.

I had needed that reminder. We focused so much on our differences that it was easy to forget we had far more in common than we did not. And yet, what differences we did have were so breathtaking, so spectacular...so lifesaving.

It was those differences, working in harmony, that had saved my people so many times now. If only it would be enough to save hers, too.

"Do we have to leave?" Sarah whispered, finally asking out loud the question we had both avoided for this long, but that had always been at the back of our minds.

"No."

"But we will," she said with a sigh.

"Yes."

Because that was who we were: the King and Queen of our people and the primary protectors of the Trees who had given us so much. Even I had to admit now that the Tree had given me everything that made life worth living. For the first time, I could see that maybe, just maybe, She was not asking for too much for me to lay it all on the line. Even Sarah.

So long as She did not ask me to live without her.

But as my eyes drifted to the Promise of Light in the sky...I realized I had faith that it would not come to that. Doubt and fear still existed, wrestling with that faith. But faith was growing stronger the longer and tighter I held onto it. Perhaps that was the true reason behind the peace and joy of that day—not fatalism. Faith.

In that moment, sheltered as the two of us were in the very palms of our Trees, with a sign from even the Sunfather Himself wafting over our heads, I...believed that Sarah and I would live.

I knew it would be harder in the morning, when we had to leave this sanctuary, this moment in time. I would just have to try my very hardest to remember, to hold this moment like a candle inside my flameheart and use it to sustain the faith inside when the dark frost came.

I WOKE TO SARAH pulling away from me. Brain still not fully functioning, I held her more tightly for a moment, not ready to let her or the moment finally go.

Ben!

The urgency in her inner voice sent adrenaline and fire through my veins. Even before my eyes opened, I instinctively rolled over her, tensed and ready to shield her from whatever threatened us. But as I blinked and glanced around the small, dawn-lit space between curtain and glass, I didn't see, smell, or hear anything amiss. Not even when I glanced outside the window. Only the normal snowy, mountainous expanse, with this Realm's yet-unnamed sun not yet cresting over a peak.

And yet, Sarah thrashed underneath me, movements sharp and urgent.

"What's wrong?" I asked frantically.

Just get off! Let me go!

I obeyed without thinking, rolling back off her. The second Sarah was free, she rolled over onto all fours, clambered to the edge of the cushions...and began emptying her stomach onto the floor.

For a few seconds, I just watched her heaving, frozen in horror. Then I shot upright and scrambled over to her, holding her steady with one arm and holding her hair back with the other hand, even though the damage was already done. Meanwhile, I sank my power into her, desperately searching for the cause of her upset.

That was when I finally realized how cold Sarah was, and growing colder by the second. And yet there was a heat originating from her abdomen that battled with the cold pouring from her iceheart. A war of powers, with Sarah's body as the battleground, and her stomach was caught in the middle—probably why it was emptying itself so violently now.

I froze in horror once again, unable to comprehend what I was feeling, let alone how to fix it. This wasn't *disease*. It wasn't even an imbalance—not a chemical or hormonal one, anyway. This was pure *magic*. This was like when her powers had awakened, except far worse. Before, she didn't have the heat to clash with the ice.

Where was it *coming from?*

Then I finally traced it to its exact source within her abdomen.

My flameheart began racing. My gut clenched, nausea of my own rising—from a hundred emotions, but prominent among them was the same fear I had felt at her awakening, except this time, far worse. This time...the fear had a terrible companion: guilt.

This time...was my fault.

Not letting myself think too deeply about what I had done, I did the best I could for my wife. I couldn't stop the war inside her, but I could at least try to ease its impact, so I focused on doing just that, threading my power through her body with more care and delicacy than ever before to avoid doing more harm than good.

To my sharp relief, that seemed to help. Soon after, Sarah's heaving slowed and stopped altogether. I knew from all her other vital signs that wasn't just because her stomach was now empty. I was gradually calming her systems, and moreover, the weave of my power seemed to form a kind of buffer for her between Ice and Flame. Slowly, the cold of her own power retreated into her heart, like a weary warrior relinquishing the fight to a trusted ally.

Sarah coughed a couple of times, spat to clear her mouth, and then rose and sunk back against me with a moan. For a dek or two, we just sat there while she stopped trembling, and I made certain the worst was over before finally withdrawing my power.

"Sorry," she rasped at last, looking at the mess. The closest cushion had splatters, and the puddle on the floor was seeping toward it.

Self-loathing pulsed through me, now allowed to run free with Sarah stabilized. "Don't you dare say sorry."

She turned and craned her neck to look at me. "Ben...."

"Come on," I said, scooping her up and getting to my feet.

I knew her intelligent mind would have at least an inkling of what had happened, even if she didn't have the definitive proof I had. That meant whatever she said next would be to try to make me feel better or even happy, and I was determined to feel neither. Perhaps it was selfish of me, but I had caught the first glimpse of how selfish I had been to ask her to do this. Just so I could keep her.

I couldn't handle Sarah trying to comfort *me* right now.

As I pushed my way out of the curtains and carried her to the water-room, I said as evenly as I could, "You get clean and comfortable. Leave me to deal with the mess."

If only I could fix what I had done to her so easily.

By the time she emerged from the water-room—clean and dressed, with her hair damp—I had long since finished. The cushions were gone, the curtains were thrown open, and the area smelled strongly of vinegar, which was the best cleaning solution I had on hand. I'd figured it was better than the smell of bile.

I was in the kitchen, making bread. Wasteful, perhaps, since we shouldn't stay long, not long enough for the dough to rise, let alone bake. But short of a practice room to work out my temper, I'd settled for dough that I could pulverize. Plus, I figured the flour would give me an excuse to stay away from Sarah, and she from me.

I'd miscalculated on the last part, because the first thing Sarah did was come up behind me and wrap her arms around me. I stilled, bracing my hands on the counter, bowing my head. I took deep, steadying breaths.

I knew I was piling a wrong on top of a wrong by being like this. I knew I was ruining her moment. I knew everything Sarah could say to me. This was supposed to be a good thing. A new life was a thing to be celebrated, aside from how much we needed it. And we *needed* it.

This was precisely the miracle we had prayed for. This was a miracle that would blow everyone away, one the likes of which few people were even going to believe.

Then why didn't it feel like a miracle to me?

What was *wrong* with me?

"Help me understand what you are going through," Sarah murmured.

I laughed hollowly. "Isn't that the question *I'm* supposed to be asking *you*?"

"I think you understand me just fine right now. After all, you must have felt for yourself what...just happened. And why."

"I felt what was happening in your body. Not your mind."

"That is pretty much all there is to it for me. I'm a bit surprised, although I don't know why, since this was exactly what we were expecting. I guess I had expected it to take a day or two more, at least, or maybe I'm just surprised that we *know* so *soon*. So immediately. It's supposed to be days before.... Even morning sickness isn't supposed to start for weeks, right?"

"I don't know," I said quietly. "But that wasn't sickness."

"Right," Sarah said with a sigh. Then, tentatively, she said, "I think...it was because of the dawn. I was already awake, watching the sky lighten. Then the moment it truly got bright...."

Of course. The moment the balance of the powers had shifted against her...and the invading force seized its chance.

Suddenly, I understood what was wrong.

"I feel like I've...hurt you," I whispered, closing my eyes shut.

Far worse than that, though I couldn't say the words out loud. I had tipped the balance of her Blood, thrown her body into chaos, made it a *battleground*.

I felt like I had...betrayed her.

"You didn't, Ben," she said, squeezing me tightly. "You did it for me, remember? You made these past two days the best of my *entire life*."

I bowed my head further, furrowing my forehead and squeezing my eyes even more tightly shut. "It wasn't supposed to be like this."

But what *else* could I have expected? Did I think it was going to be *easy* for the Queen of Ice to bear *my* child? How could I have been so shortsighted?

So terrified of losing her, I didn't allow myself to wonder what the price of living on would cost her. A price Sarah had only gotten just the first *taste* of.

It was happening. Again. The price of my birth. The cycle of sacrifice that led to my existence, the one I had sworn to stop. Except not only had I now broken that oath, this time, I shared in none of the cost. If *only* the Tree had exacted some of my flameheart to create that life. Instead, my wife had to bear the price alone.

Sarah just continued to hold me—as forgiving, calm, and valiant as ever.

"You shouldn't be the one comforting me," I rasped. "You should be *yelling* at me. Pushing me away."

"I think I've said this before, but you do more than enough yelling at yourself for the both of us. This isn't your fault, Ben. At all. Any of it. I wanted it, I chose it. I still want it, and I would choose it again."

"Because you're too good."

"Because it's what makes me *happy*, torch it!" Sarah said, a trace of irritation entering her voice for the first time. "Trust me, I'm being *completely* selfish right now. Because clearly what is going to make *me* happy is going to make *you* miserable for quite a while, if this morning is anything to go by."

I had to laugh weakly at that. I straightened, and Sarah let me go.

"I'm sorry I'm being like this," I said as I resumed kneading. "It's just...it hits a nerve. All the nerves."

"This isn't something you can protect me from," Sarah agreed ruefully.

"No," I said grimly. "Still, I know I *should* be happy. I just...."

"Hey, Ben," Sarah soothed, rubbing my back. "Forget anything to do with what you *should* be feeling, and just let yourself *feel*. Isn't that what you're always telling me?"

I slowed in my kneading. "I suppose.... Still, my feelings have to be ruining the mood for you right now."

Sarah chuckled. "Maybe, but in retrospect, it's very *you*. I think I might have been weirded out if you had been gleefully jumping up and down while I threw up."

She sobered. "Ben, our circumstances are hardly ideal. It only makes sense that if we're to be feeling any strong emotions right now, a lot of them would be 'negative.' And from what I've seen, nothing about parenthood is simple. At no point is it a bed of sunshine and roses. Worry, uncertainty, stress...those all seem like very natural reactions to me."

What about suffocating guilt? I thought.

Sarah let me knead in silence for a few moments. I finally sighed and glanced at her. "You ready to leave?"

"As ready as I'll ever be. But are you?" she asked, examining me.

"I'm ready to stop putting it off."

I hated looming events, the dread that just kept building with no way to stop it. I always preferred to tackle things head on if I could or absorb myself in doing *something* to prepare if I couldn't. If we had the days right, the Devourer's assault on Earth would be tomorrow, but just in case, we had all agreed we would be ready for it to be today. Everyone else had begun preparations in earnest since the end of the heartbinding. It was high time I joined them.

I stowed the dough in the ether (making a stern mental note to myself to remember it was there) and moved to the sink. "Just let me clean up, and I'll pack us up while you eat breakfast."

"Ben, I'm perfectly capable of packing," Sarah said with a smile.

I just gave her a look over my shoulder and pointed a dripping finger at the plate of leftovers I had put together for her before starting the bread dough. Even though I knew food or disease hadn't caused her intestinal upset, I'd still selected the best combination of plain yet nutritious foods I could find to hopefully help stabilize her system further.

She rolled her eyes but sat herself down on the barstool in front of the plate and picked up her fork. "If it makes *you* feel better."

"It will," I said, turning back to the sink.

By the slightest of margins. But on a day like today, I would take what I could. Speaking of which....

"I'm going to call Svyer to meet us in your suite," I said briskly as I dried my hands on the towel.

"What, why?" Sarah asked after a pause to swallow.

"I'm not a professional healer. She is."

Sarah sighed. "Ben...."

I looked at her. As evenly as I could, I said, "Would you prefer it be Svyer or a stranger?"

If we survived, a birth healer would need to be involved at some point—soon—but for today, I would take my cousin. Not only was she Sarah's friend and someone I trusted, but she would also be discreet. The closer we could hold the secret of Sarah's...condition...the better. At least until after tomorrow.

No need for the Devourer to know, either to think it a weakness in her to exploit or a strength to counter. And no need to add to the sorrow in the minds of our people if the battle...went poorly. No matter how I felt, I knew our people were going to see our child's swift conception as nothing less than an unequivocal miracle, the pinnacle of hope for better years ahead. They didn't need that hope to shatter on top of everything else.

"I really don't think that's necessary at this point," Sarah said, cheeks warming.

I took a deep breath. "Probably not, but please, Sarah. For me. I know I'm being..."

"Anxious?" Sarah supplied gently, her cheeks cooling.

"I was going to say something like 'tyrannical,' but thank you for being so kind." Even the hint of a smile that had touched my lips died a moment later. "But today, of all days...I just can't. I just can't lose you. For *any* reason."

"I get it." She took a deep breath. "So, fine. If it will take at least *one* worry off your mind today...go ahead and call Svyer. But...don't tell anyone else today, OK? For today, I just wanted it to be you and me...and now, I guess, Svyer."

"Fair enough." I'd ruined enough of her moment that I owed her that much. "But you know what Kor is going to think of us keeping something like this from him. *Especially* on a day like today."

Before her request, he was going to be my second call.

Sarah snorted. "Kor can deal."

My lips twitched in spite of themselves, and I began packing up in the kitchen, stowing any perishables in my ether stores. I hoped we would be back here soon, especially with the ease granted us by her newest surging ability, and for more than just the glowing memories of these past two days. I felt like this was a kind of haven for us that we would need in the years to come—assuming we survived. But with the decay seal broken, all this food would now begin to spoil, and I couldn't guarantee we would be back before it did.

"Dang it," Sarah said abruptly.

I glanced at her in mild alarm, but she was only scowling at nothing as she poked at her food.

"What?"

She refocused on me, cheeks heating. "When we finally make it public, even if we don't go into specifics about timing...*no one* is going to believe that we only began sleeping together after the heartbinding, are they?"

I barked a short laugh as I saw where her thoughts had gone. "No, they're not. In fact, *some* are going to have a hard time believing that child is mine, even if they assume we began as soon as we met. Only when they see the results of the blood registration for themselves will they be convinced I'm the father. Maybe."

"I'm seeing why these blood registrations are so important," she said grudgingly. "At least for Monarchs."

I raised an eyebrow at her. "I hope that those kinds of assumptions don't particularly matter to you."

If they did, she had a strange way of discouraging them. After all, she was the one who asked me to stay in the same room as her for the grand tour.

"Not particularly," Sarah said, cheeks still warm. "I know people will always talk about us, and I know I'm a lot to blame for those assumptions in particular. It's just...I never thought I'd be seen as the girl who needed a shotgun wedding.

And the fact that it's not even *true*, that we worked so hard to *make* it not true, but everyone will *think* it is...I think that's what really gets to me."

"Girl who needed a what?" I asked in confusion—and a bit of consternation. I still didn't understand what was bothering Sarah, but I gathered she was worried people would think she had acted dishonorably somehow, and that got under *my* skin.

I was distracted from the beginnings of Sarah's flushed answer as I felt something demanding my attention: a voice that was not a voice, calling my name. I sighed, turning and walking away. "Hang on. Yv is calling me. Probably wondering what the torch is taking us so long."

"Don't tell her!" Sarah called after me, voice laced with embarrassment.

Again, I felt a flash of irritation. If this was something Sarah thought was shameful, I suddenly wanted to act like it was the exact opposite. Absurdly, I wanted to tell everyone and act proud and unconcerned as I did so—no matter what I felt.

And yet, that would be too little, too late with the one whose opinion mattered the most: Sarah. I was the one who had begun this cycle of negativity, and she was dealing with me so well that I had to honor the one request she'd made of me. So, I would keep this from even our inner circle as she asked, and I would have to tease out what was bothering her later—and convince her it was nothing if I could.

"Don't worry, I'll think of...something," I said with a tired wave of acknowledgement.

Whatever I came up with, however poorly I lied, Sarah was right. Yvera would swallow that lie a lot easier than she would the truth.

As SHE HAD PROMISED, Svyer was waiting in Sarah's reception room when we arrived. All Sarah had needed to do to surge us there was to make a discreet sliver of ice appear in the reception room for it to give her a good enough view on the ice display on our end, so Svyer was none the wiser. When we both materialized, she perhaps assumed I had done the surging through the daygate.

My cousin went to Sarah right away and hugged her without a word, mindful of the lack of privacy in this relatively public room.

"Well, shall we?" she said as naturally as she could when she let go, inclining her head toward Sarah's study. "I'm sure we have...a lot to catch up on."

"I'll leave you to it," I said with a sigh, letting go of Sarah's hand and waving for them to proceed without me.

"What?" Sarah said in surprise. And was that a flash of disappointment? "I thought you'd want to...talk with her too."

I grimaced apologetically. "My wings are getting impatient. As soon as Kor hears I'm back...."

Sarah sighed as she nodded in understanding. If she didn't want Kor to find out, then she had to let me go. Unlike Yvera, he wouldn't accept any excuse short of the truth.

"I'm sorry," I said heavily, putting a hand on her shoulder. Silently, I said, *For a lot of things, abandoning you now only being the latest.*

Sarah's face firmed. *You're not abandoning me. You're doing what you have to—to protect us. All of us.*

Her hand went to her abdomen, seemingly unconsciously.

I supposed I was, though unintentionally in that last case. It just so happened now that the life that mattered most to me—the one so essential it amounted to my own—was now inextricably entangled with another's. For that entanglement, I had no one to blame but myself. I needed Sarah to survive, which for some torched reason meant Sarah needed it, which meant it needed her—even to her cost. By that convoluted logic, I needed it too, which, in this struggle for her life, made us grudging allies...for now.

I tried not to let Sarah see how conflicted I still was about that tiny new life as I stooped and kissed her.

"Be well," I said as I parted, then fixed my face with a sternness that was only partly teasing. "That's an order."

Sarah smiled slightly. "Yes, your majesty." Then her smile faded. "You too. I can't lose you either, you know."

In answer, I just kissed her again, long and passionately enough that I heard Svyer shifting—either in amusement or discomfort, I couldn't tell and didn't check, even when I pulled away. I didn't even glance away from Sarah before I finally hardened myself and surged away.

Her silver eyes, so deep and piercing, were the last things I saw before she was gone. I tried to fix them in my mind as beacons of hope for the deken ahead.

I arrived in front of my personal daygate, and for one precious moment, I stood alone in my own reception room.

You promised, I told the Tree. *I've done everything You asked, and I have to admit, You've kept Your end up so far.*

As troublesome as that first miracle was.

Just please make sure she survives tomorrow...and all that might come after because of it.

Because, as I was beginning to see, tomorrow might just be the end of one battle...and the start of another. This time, against my very blood.

Chapter Twenty-One

SIGHT

Sarah

"How's Ben doing?" Svyer asked me when I closed my study door behind us.

I sighed as I went to join her on the couch. Yet, as much as I wanted to, I didn't sink back too deeply into the cushions. I knew I would be needed just as Ben was to prepare for tomorrow, and I intended to immerse myself in it all as soon as Svyer's examination was done.

"About what you'd expect."

That was another reason I wanted to get into the thick of things: I didn't want to leave Ben to brood for too long. He would be surrounded by people today, but no one else besides me would have an inkling of what kind of spiral he was in right now, and thus no one else would know to snap him out of it if he got too deep.

Even Svyer only knew a part of the issue, but that was enough to make her echo my sigh and nod as she propped her head in her hand, her elbow resting on the back of the couch. "I figured. He wasn't happy when he described your...episode to me. Today was already going to be a hard day for you both, and that wasn't a great beginning."

"Tell me about it," I said, feeling an echo of the nausea rise again. Just a memory, thank goodness. For now. Though the overturned balance of powers within me had settled ever since Ben did his thing, I knew from the warm, alien energy I felt stirring more within me the more the day went on that I wasn't out of the woods yet.

And wouldn't be for a long, long time to come.

"Well," Svyer said, straightening and turning businesslike. "Enough about him. Let me have a look at you."

She placed her hands on my shoulders and closed her eyes, and I closed mine as well. Not strictly necessary, but it was less awkward for me that way. It also made it easier for me to focus on Svyer's now-unique healing magic as it sunk from her hands and into me: warm like Ben's but with a cool hint at the edges, which came—as did the silver flecks in her emerald eyes and hair—from when I'd somehow given her a touch of Ice when I'd restored her spirit to her body a few weeks ago.

Minutes passed as she gave me the most thorough healing examination I'd ever received—at least while I was conscious. She didn't just examine my abdomen. She methodically probed her way through me from head to toe, seeming not to linger in any one place any longer than the other, taking me in as a whole. Still, when her power approached my abdomen, I felt a flicker of nervousness, but her special blend of Flame and Ice had nearly as settling an effect as Ben's did. In fact, I was surprised when it didn't do more. Or perhaps Svyer wasn't trying to do anything but observe; that's what it seemed like to me when nothing felt changed after she moved on from one part of my body to the next, and the next.

Finally, she withdrew and sat back, her face closed off. I took a few deep breaths and settled back onto the couch with relief, breaking my resolution against getting too comfortable.

"Tired?" Svyer asked.

"I don't know why," I said drowsily. "I didn't do anything but sit there. You're the one who did all the work."

"On the contrary, even a healing examination takes some of your energy as your body interacts with the healer's power. I think...even that much was more than your body wanted to spare right now. It's a good thing Ben's kept you in such good shape, so I wasn't tempted to do anything except observe, or you might have needed a nap before you'd be good for anything else today."

She smiled, but her expression was still serious.

I turned my head from where it rested on the back of the couch to look at her. "What do you mean?"

A troubled look overtook her clinical detachment, tinged with a bit of wonder. "I mean...Ben is right. You're pregnant."

My lips twitched. "Did you not believe him?"

"Well, I didn't *disbelieve* him, but...it came as a shock, I'll tell you that. Especially given the timeline he told me. Even if a professional birth healer is *looking* for the signs, they can often miss them at this stage. I guess I didn't quite believe it was true until I felt it for myself. But there's no mistake. You have *something* inside of you, changing you, throwing your body into chaos, and the only logical explanation is that you're carrying a child of Flame. And for you, the Queen of Ice...that's clearly not going to be a simple task. Even now, your body is taxed with all the changes that are *already* required to keep both you...and it...alive."

I felt a jolt of adrenaline that pushed me back upright. "Is it OK?" I asked urgently, my hand over my abdomen. "Is it in danger?"

Funny that I should care so much already. Surely it was only a few cells by this point—something far, far from having sensation or consciousness. Far from being anything to love or fear for, or to affect or be affected by me. That we were both calling it the equivalent of "it" in our two languages seemed to attest to that fact.

This was only a seed. And yet...it was already *mine.*

I thought Ben had been overreacting when he'd insisted I see a healer, but now I cursed myself for my complacency. Even when I had *thrown up* from the force of having its power ascend inside of me, I hadn't feared for it, hadn't considered how I was such a dangerous host for its formation. I'd just thought that this was what was meant, so of course it would work out fine. The only miracle we'd seemed to need was to have it at all.

Not to keep it.

Why hadn't I thought more about what kind of miracle *that* would take? For a body that was at least half Flame...to survive to term inside Ice.

Svyer hesitated a second too long, and her expression reminded me of when we had first met—only a few months and yet what felt like lifetimes ago—when she discovered I was human and was faced the uncertainty of what that meant, for her people...and for me. That was the only time my kind, frank friend had evaded my questions...or once even outright lied to me.

"Svyer," I said tightly, grabbing her hand. "Don't you dare lie to me. Not now."

She sighed heavily. "I...don't *know*, Sarah. I just don't know. It's too early to tell. All I can see is that your body is under strain, more than it should be at this point, and your energy is low, even for after dawn. Surely you can tell that much?"

I could. I had just pinned it down to other things. "You sure that's not stress? Or lack of sleep?"

"Those probably aren't helping, but you just have so much activity going on down there—" She gestured to my abdomen. "—and most of it is *magical*. As if something else entirely is working on you right now. Changing you. Preparing you for what's coming. In ways no mother has had to be prepared before."

I stilled, letting go of Svyer's hand. For the first time that day, I closed my eyes and looked inside myself. Not observing others making their healing observations. Not me staring at my stomach in wonder during my shower this morning. I looked inward, all on my own.

I had always thought of my power, the power of Ice, my very connection from my Tree, as coming from deep within some quiet darkness inside me: the wholesome darkness that was rich earth, full of potential and cool with nighttime spring, ready to blossom with life at the dawn.

Well, I encountered the same darkness now, which made "sight," even such as it was for me like this, impossible. And yet, I felt stirrings there I had never felt before.

The seed had been planted, and spring, with its dawn, had come. Yet if that sprout was going to survive the many hot days and cold nights that still lay ahead, it was going to need to be protected. And so, beneath the soil, I felt Powers at work, sheltering it, weaving a cocoon of Ice and Flame unlike any other before.

Little wonder, then, that my stomach had an upset when the balance had tipped at dawn this morning. That had been the smallest, most minor of reactions that could have resulted, just a taste of what could have lashed out at me if that buffering cocoon had not already been in the works. Lashed out at us *both*.

In fact...that tiny sprout might never have survived its first frosty night.

I...could have killed it. So easily. So unconsciously. My body, my magic, could have swept out the hot invader as it does any other alien life, and I would have had no more control over its response than I normally did over my immune system. Its tiny candle flame would never have had a chance against my blizzard.

It had to be protected, given some fighting chance. If that protection sometimes tipped the scales against me, well...that seemed more than fair. In fact, it seemed a small price to pay.

Eventually, I resurfaced and opened my eyes, meeting Svyer's.

"Well?" she said quietly.

I swallowed. "I think...you're right."

Svyer sighed, resting her elbow back on the couch and leaning her head against her palm. "Flame, Sarah, I'm sorry."

"For what?"

"For not knowing what to do to help you. For not even *thinking* about this possibility more!" She shifted, scowling in frustration for a second. The look soon faded to regret again. "I thought for sure we wouldn't have to worry about something like this for, well, months at least. If...ever."

Her eyes lowered, and she picked at some lint on the cushions. "There was another reason I had a hard time believing Ben. To be honest, before today, I wondered...if the two of you could even have children."

With her training as a healer and her unmatched experience tending to children of Ice, she would know better than anyone else what our odds would have been.

"I don't think you would have been wrong," I said quietly, putting my hand over my stomach. "Normally. So don't blame yourself. This is beyond any of us."

Svyer's gaze followed my hand, and she frowned. "This is a Tree thing. Isn't it?"

"Yes," I said simply, leaving it at that.

Svyer scowled. "Well, I'm not normally one to question the Tree, but isn't this kind of a bad time?"

I just smiled thinly.

Svyer sighed. "Alright, keep your Tree secrets. If this is Their will, then...I suppose I'll just have to do the best I can to take care of you both. Somehow."

"Thank you, Svyer," I said fervently. "I don't know how I would do this without you. Honestly."

"Oh, if you didn't have me, you'd still have Ben," she said idly, some of her normal good humor coming back in a slow smile. "He seems pretty attentive right now, and I doubt that's about to change."

"But notice Ben still brought me to you," I pointed out.

Now, I was glad. Ben's worry about me had been expected, and so I'd thought nothing of it other than to worry about him in turn. Svyer's professional concern had been like a dose of cold water on my untroubled dreaming, but now I was wide awake and on alert, poised for any sign of danger toward my little one. From others or...from myself.

Hang in there, I pleaded with that little sprout. *I'll do the best I can, but we're a team in this, you and me. You have to hang in there. Please.*

Ben and I had been right to pray for a miracle two mornings ago.

It seemed we were only at the beginning of them.

THE REST OF THE day passed in a blur.

I had been right: I was not just needed; I was essential, since I was the Queen of Ice, and this was my Tree that the people of Flame were preparing to defend. This time, I was not just a symbol standing on the sidelines.

Though I would be in the fight tomorrow, today my role broadly fell into two categories: gatekeeper and voice. My gatekeeper role involved either ushering in or even surging dramá to and around the Temple of Ice. My voice role was to convey the will of our Tree whenever questions rose to that level or were otherwise unanswerable.

Before the heartbinding, the dramá had planned on trickling through the long way once Ben showed up again after our short honeymoon: first through the Crownhold Library on Ythra, then to the back of the Shrine of the Covenants, where Ben would have opened the hidden magical door for them that, so far, only he or I could open, then down the short hallway lit by both moon- and sunstone (we still had no idea what either of those streaks of white and gold *were*), to the crowngate—the freestanding arch in the middle of that circular sandstone room with flames on one side and ice on the other. Rachel would have opened the moongate on her end, allowing the dramá to pass through and into our hold in the Seventh Realm, and Dad and Michael would have supervised their treks through our hold to the moongate at the northern end of it that led into the Temple of Ice on Earth.

It wasn't an ideal route, even ignoring the fact that it was bouncing the dramá across the cosmos to finally get them to Earth. Ben, Kor, and Yvera had been concerned about how to keep the crowngate's location secret with members of the Warflight trekking regularly through the Library; the adults in my family had been concerned about the necessity of a stream of soldiers trekking through our *home*—almost through our living room, so to speak. But as a testament to how far Michael had come in learning to trust and rely on the dramá—and perhaps even more miraculously, trust and rely on our *Tree*—even he conceded with little discussion that we had no other choice.

Until two days ago. Ben and I had only had the bare minimum of communication with the outside world, yet given the strategic importance of the new application of our surging, he had told his wings about *that* much, and we'd left them to pass the message on to my family and figure out what to do with it.

So they had. By the time I showed up in the King's Wing, ready to help, the first phase of the day's preparations—transportation—was already well underway, and far more smoothly and discreetly than we could have previously dreamed. Small groups of about five warriors each congregated in the main court of the King's Wing (which had been closed off from the public for the day), waiting their turn as group by group, David surged them straight into the Temple of Ice's reception chamber.

To split the magical burden, Dad was maintaining the scrying ice, standing by the roughly six-by-six-foot square of it he'd conjured on one of the bare walls. The size of the ice mirror was larger than necessary, and therefore cost more power, but it gave the transporter, David, a good view of where he was surging without having to get in too close. Perhaps more important, its size gave the groups waiting their turn a good view, maybe making what David was about to do to them make a *bit* more sense as they saw David and each of their comrades ahead of them disappear and reappear on the other side of the ice in the Temple's rotunda.

"Honestly, how did we *not* think of this?" Michael whispered with a tired scowl to me when I came up to him to check on how things were going.

I shrugged wearily. "We weren't meant to, I guess," I said, going with Ben's theory. It was the only one that made *me* feel better. From Michael's deepening scowl, though, it didn't seem to do the same trick for him.

Eskala was set up at some kind of logistics center in one nook of the King's court; Kor was nowhere to be seen, but I had no doubt he was in the thick of things somewhere. Yvera was standing at a different command node, one much closer to where we were, as she and her assistants monitored everyone who came into the King's Wing and directed them accordingly. She was the one who had sent me over to Dad, David, and Michael.

I could see for myself through that large pane of ice that Ben was already on the other side. His height and golden hair was, as usual, pretty hard to miss, even at a distance and in a crowd. He seemed to be in the center of the rotunda, overseeing the dispersing of his people on the other side and occasionally conferring with another supremely tall, grizzled, dark-skinned, violet-haired man that I recognized as Alyish.

"Well, go on," David said with a grin, gesturing with his head as he followed my gaze. "You first. I'll surge this next group when you're clear."

He thumbed back at the waiting handful of warriors that stood ten or so feet behind him, just out of earshot from our ad hoc sibling huddle.

"You sure you don't want me to take at least one group?" I said in surprise.

We'd only had this moment to speak to each other because it seemed David was taking a breather and drinking some icemint tea to recharge. Surging this many people, that many times, at this time of day looked to be taking a toll on him from the weary set of his shoulders.

"Sure you even can?" David said with a good-natured wink, nodding his head to the ice again. "With Ben on the other side?"

I stared at him for a moment, then remembered. *Ben* was the whole reason I *could* lash effectively. Even though I could see him just as clearly as if he were in another room in the King's Wing, he was a universe away from me right now. I could feel that much just from the connection between us, thinned to the size and thickness of a suspension cable—one made of the strongest substance known to mortals, but still probably stretched too thin and tight for me to use it to lash anyone else to me.

Then it hit me, what I should have realized the moment I saw anyone besides *me* group surging.

"How can *you* lash them?" I said, gaping.

But I realized the answer even before Michael gave it, while rolling his eyes.

"His new girlfriend, obviously," he huffed, discreetly (for Michael) inclining his head back toward Yvera's command post. I got the impression Michael was put out not because of David's relationship but because his seventeen-year-old brother could be useful in a way he couldn't. Michael was here as Dad's ice-scrying replacement, and that was it.

I looked wide-eyed at David, but he just shrugged and grinned. "We thought it was worth a shot to try it out, so we wouldn't have to rely on just you. So, we did an experiment yesterday, and it worked."

Now Yvera's location—so near the ice—made much more sense. Or perhaps...the ice's proximity to her. It seemed they had wasted no time in planning all of this out around not just our surging ability...but around who could use it to surge others.

I narrowed my eyes. "And by 'we,' you mean Kor, right?"

"Well, I thought of it too," David said. "After Michael told us what finally made the difference for you to lash. It made me curious. And Yv was game."

Yet another person who had learned a lot about the necessity—and benefits—of collaboration with another race. That change of heart was nearly as stunning as the fact that she and my younger brother were developing the same symbiotic bond that Ben and I had.

I was almost miffed at that. We didn't know when our bond had its start, but it was only fully forged after I was kidnapped by consumed and nearly *died* giving Ben nearly the last of my energy, and Ben took on a whole flight of arrel in a berserk rage thinking I *had*. What kind of life-threatening, soul-rending crisis had *they* gone through?

Although, come to think of it...Ben and I had needed quite a bit of...*encouragement* to get that far. David and Yvera seemed to have no such inhibitions.

"Oh?" I said finally, trying not to sound bitter. "Kor didn't want to test the mettle of his *own* relationship?"

Both my brothers just stared at me blankly. Belatedly, I realized that what I'd already come to accept as a given might not be in everyone else's mind—or even as well-known among our family as I'd assumed.

"Kor?" Michael said, nonplussed.

David's expression cleared, and he chuckled. "Oh, you mean with Rachel? I don't think they've gotten that far, sis."

Now it was Michael's turn to gape at David. "Rachel? And *Kor*? You're kidding me, right?"

David raised an eyebrow. "Didn't you *see* how she was flirting with him on the trip to Greenland?"

"Yeah, but that was weeks ago. She's got to be over it now. She always is."

"I wouldn't be so sure of that," I muttered. "At least *Kor* isn't."

Michael's eyes narrowed. "Just what is Kor up to, Sarah?"

"Oh, so you're taking it in stride that David is with Yvera, but—"

David cleared his throat. "You'd probably better get a move on, Sarah. Yv is asking me what the holdup is."

He grinned at me while tapping his head, and when I glanced her way, Yvera caught my eye and raised an eyebrow. Belatedly, I realized this wasn't the sort of discussion for us to have in front of the Warflight, even if we had been huddled together and talking in low tones. Hopefully everyone thought we were talking strategy or something.

I straightened and tried once again to look like the serious and competent Queen I was supposed to be. "Right," I said under my breath. "See you guys in a bit, I suppose. Try not to have too much fun while I'm gone."

"Oh, I think there's little chance of that," Michael said dryly.

I focused my eyes on my destination, as I always did to surge like this, and in a split second I was a silver streak—somehow shooting across the universe, though I couldn't see or feel anything—and popped back into existence in the rotunda.

Technically, if Ben really had been just in the other room, I would have had more than one way to surge to this place, given Ben's presence here. But unlike Ben, I still needed to be within a mile or so of my gates to surge to them; as much as his pull was stronger than any of my gates, and always there even when they went dormant, I doubted I could have surged to him across the universe, as he could to me through his much more widespread network. Besides, even if I'd had both options, surging by sight and ice meant that I didn't have to smack into Ben in front of all those people surrounding him. Seemed more polite—and dignified—this way.

When I began making my way through the crowd to see who was standing with him, I was glad I had. *There* was Kor, and, standing beside him, looking as regal as a princess, was Rachel: hair done up in an attractive yet still sensible braid and dressed in her Moontouched armor, the clear plates and white body suit conforming to and highlighting her tall, curvaceous body to perfection.

As usual, I felt like a drab sparrow in comparison. Vadya had caught me and put my hair up into a bun braid before I'd left my suite, but she'd let me stay in my usual white shirt, black pants, and brown boots, and now I regretted that choice.

If Michael could have seen Kor and Rachel together right then, he might not have been so skeptical about the existence of a relationship between them. There was nothing obvious, but perhaps since I knew the two of them so well, there was something about the way they *stood*. As if they were two dance partners who were waiting on the sidelines now but at any moment were ready to leap into action once their number was called, and they knew exactly which way the other would move as soon as they did so.

It was an acute *awareness* of each other, nonchalant in the extreme yet telling for that very reason.

Ben's eyes flicked to mine almost as soon as I entered the chamber, probably from sensing my star suddenly appearing nearby. Since I now had these kinds of questions fresh on my mind, I wondered how Yvera's and David's bond would feel to them as it developed—if they felt anything at all, since Ben's and mine mirrored how we felt and interacted with our gates as Royals. To me, his pull felt just like the gravitational tug of an active moongate, and I appeared in his mind's constellation chart of all his gates.

However, even with Ben's eyes following me, it was Alyish who greeted me as I approached.

"Ah, Queen Sarah," the grizzled general said with a thin smile. "Just in time."

"For?"

"King Koriben and I wish to get a view of the surface, since that is most likely where the Devourer's rifts will appear. Are you aware of any way to get there?"

"No, I'm not," I said regretfully. "But to my knowledge, we've never tried."

I looked at Rachel, and she shrugged—gracefully, of course. "Not to mine, either. We were just discussing asking the Tree when you showed up."

I cast my eyes down the dark hallway that led to Her chamber. "Has anyone gone in there?"

"No," Ben said firmly. "We've kept everyone in here out of respect for Her. All of them know not to go down that way."

I glanced in the opposite direction, behind us, and saw that the moongate with the white tree on it was shut. Following my gaze, Ben said, "And everyone knows or has probably figured out that's the gate that leads to your hold, but we've kept it shut the entire time we've been here."

I looked around the room, understanding now why it was so crowded. It was an enormous chamber, but....

"We're going to run out of room in not much time, aren't we?" I said.

If the attack was tomorrow after all, it was going to be cramped quarters for these people, especially overnight. Not to mention the lack of sanitation facilities....

"We discovered passages yesterday," Rachel said, making me glance back at her in surprise.

"Really?" I asked.

"Yup," she said, pointing first left then right, in the other two cardinal directions from the passage to the Tree and the moongate. "There and there."

As she said, where there had only been smooth walls before, there were now immense gates swung open where she pointed, revealing dark passages beyond. It was the utter lack of light down those cavernous passages that had made me overlook the recent additions until now.

"What's down them?" I asked, baffled.

"We don't know. Nothing lights up as you go in, so we didn't get far when we checked on our own. Spooky, you know?"

"Leftwing Laura is currently leading an expedition with a small contingent of your elites down one of them," Alyish said with a straight face, ignoring Rachel's superstitious comment. "Without another adult of your clan to supervise the exploration of the other, we decided to leave it untouched for the time being and keep everyone else here until you gave the word."

"I offered to go, but they told me a Royal should probably stay here—representing the Tree, you know," Rachel said cheerfully.

That did leave us rather shorthanded, since I assumed Mom was staying in our hold with Lizzy and the littles. I became thoughtful, testing my instincts.

Then I turned to look at Ben's leftwing, who had been noticeably silent this whole time.

"Kor, how would you like to lead the other expedition?"

His expression remained neutral, but his sapphire eyes gleamed for a moment. "I am willing."

I knew what an understatement that was. To Kor, a scholar of history and particularly the Covenants, the chance to explore the fabled Temple of Ice was an opportunity he could have scarcely dreamed of a year ago. My offer had been like asking a dual specialist in archeology and mythology if they would like to dive through the recently discovered ruins of Atlantis, with the obvious answer being *Try and stop me*.

Perhaps there was another reason the Tree had concealed any other sections until now. If Kor had known they existed, he might never have let up asking about them.

Silently, I teased him, *I can trust you to respect the sanctity of this place, right? No breaking into any secrets or stealing any artifacts....*

Yes, yes, Kor snapped, a flash of irritation going through his eyes. *I'm not an idiot. I know better than to cross a Tree, thank you.*

I knew that too, which was why I was trusting him to wander through my Tree's Temple unsupervised.

Out loud, Kor said, "Do you care who I take with me?"

I shook my head and looked at Ben, who also shook his head at Kor and said, "Pick five of whoever you want and go. Just leave me Ordran and Petra."

"Will do," Kor said, starting off. He clearly didn't have to be told twice.

I couldn't help a final quip as he passed me. "Remember, the priority is to find the way *out*."

"I'm aware," he drawled over his shoulder.

"What's that about?" Rachel asked in amusement.

"Oh, just reminding him of the good ol' times," I said.

"Those were the days," Ben said with a nostalgic sigh.

Rachel raised an eyebrow. "Meaning...all of two months ago?"

"Given what happened in those two months, that's a lifetime, Rachel," I said dryly. I felt like a different person. Several different persons, in fact. Two months ago, I became a Queen. Two days ago, I became a wife. And at some point since....

Partly to distract myself from my self-consciousness at my secret, I asked, "Doesn't it feel that way to you?"

Rachel paused for a moment and then said, "You know, it does."

Alyish sighed. "You kids are making me feel old."

Only Rachel would have the gall to tease a seven-foot, scarred, seasoned warrior like Alyish. "What? A handsome gentleman like you? You can't be over fifty—sixty at *most*."

He rewarded her with a rare, crooked smile. "I am one hundred and thirty-eight, thank you."

Rachel gaped. Apparently I hadn't adequately explained dramá longevity in her hearing. Or perhaps I had, but it had never sunk in. You could never tell with Rachel. She was supremely good at absorbing only the information that was interesting or useful to her in the moment.

A new round of orders being called out at the latest group of warriors to arrive brought my mind back to our current predicament. I frowned and looked back, then around, eyeing how full the room was getting.

"We planned for this, Sarah," Ben said quietly. "Back when we thought we might only have this area to stage ourselves in. They've been warned and prepared."

"Still," I said in a murmur. "This *does* limit the numbers we have to defend with, doesn't it?"

I looked up at Ben and saw in his eyes that he had known this, from the first moment I had told him of the Devourer's plan to attack my Tree. Even with our new surging making the transportation logistics simpler than we'd had reason to hope, this would be a different battle than the last two we had fought together. This wasn't the dramá defending their Tree on their home turf, with their entire Warflight and their normal defenses, retreats, and long-established plans in place.

This was a new world they were venturing into, and even with some kind of idea of what they would face, it was still a limited one, and they were having to improvise with each step of the way. Our numbers would be limited, our defenses perhaps nonexistent, and unknowns were everywhere we turned.

As if reading my thoughts, Alyish said quietly, "From all we have learned since the Solstice, we have reason to hope that the Devourer cannot launch the offensive it did then. All signs point to its numbers being greatly depleted, primarily by the battle and secondarily by every lesser conflict it has engaged with us since."

Ben and I said nothing. We both knew that my family and I were the true targets here. For thousands of years, the Devourer had been content enough to allow humans to multiply, to forget all they'd ever been taught about it and their Tree, and to create the various weapons of their own destruction, raising them like cattle for the slaughter. As long as they leaned more toward the Devourer than their Tree, it was content to let them ripen and not attack the Tree of Ice head on.

The only thing that had changed in this scenario was me. Unbeknownst to the Devourer, the Tree of Ice had been doing its own kind of cultivation, guarding the mixed bloodlines of Ice and Flame until the time had come for the Moontouched to return, this time transformed. Too late, the Devourer realized its mistake in overlooking humanity. Already I had cost it one sore battle on my own, and my father and brother had helped cost it another, while inflicting harm on its very self. It would not let the risk we posed to both its plans and its being stand any longer.

It didn't matter how many forces the Devourer could or could not bring to bear. Its goal wasn't the Tree of Ice. All it needed to return to the status quo was to kill me and my family.

With that single-minded goal...it wouldn't need a large force.

But neither could all my family hide, nor could the dramá focus their protections on us alone. If we tried, the Devourer *would* target the Tree, and if She fell, all life that Earth held would pay the price as the Devourer consumed it. No matter where we were in the cosmos when that happened, the most changed members of our family—the original six and now Lizzy—would die from the loss of Her power in our new hearts.

So here we were, here to defend Her, because our survival was inextricably intertwined with Hers. And now, so were the dramá, because theirs was intertwined with ours. All of us connected, all of us having to stand together...because whatever we did, if we fell, we fell together.

There was one simple solution to this. The simplest and most powerful answer to the heavy dilemma in front of us, that was surely on the minds of everyone who knew the full scope of things at this very moment, from the lowest-ranking soldier here all the way to Ben: If the Tree of Ice was safe, then my family and the dramá would be too...and there was one way to *make* Her safe, for years to come, with only one person having to come to harm.

My life, my blood—freely offered to Her.

It was such a simple solution. Suddenly, with the full weight sinking into me of what I was asking the dramá to do, the risk I was making my family run, I was staggered by it.

This could all end now. All the difficulty, all the danger, all the uncertainty. All the lives I saw gathering around me would be saved, with not one lost. My family would be safe. My Tree would be perhaps not just safe but restored; gone might be the weariness I had sensed build in Her if I offered Her power the likes of which Her children had not given Her in eons. Never mind that I had received that power and that life from Her. I knew now that true power grew in the giving of it. In the sacrifice of it. That if I sacrificed it all to Her, it would return to Her magnified ten-, perhaps a hundredfold.

That was how the little gifts the dramá gave me during my first ten days among them (Svyer's coat, Wikal's whistle, Ben's scale, and so on) had, when I gave them up to the Tree, been enough to infuse the ice leaf with power that, when I gave it up to Kavarian, had healed him of his fading flameheart. When he had given up that fresh and vibrant, newly restored life and power...his sacrifice had been enough to save us all.

I could end this. Now. I could save them all.

And yet, no one was asking me to. To my knowledge, no one had ever asked or even expected Kavarian to. Alyish had led their defense as if with the full, grim expectation that everything depended on them, not their King. That was why Kavarian's sacrifice had come as such a shock to me—no one, especially Ben, had ever mentioned it as a possibility.

Even though they all must have known it might come to that. Especially Ben.

Who was looking at me right now with hard, glowing eyes of molten gold.

I swallowed with some difficulty as I gazed back at him.

I know what you're thinking, Sarah, he said, his inner voice laced with steel. *Don't you* dare.

But, Ben...why is no one asking me to? I asked, glad to use my inner voice, because I was sure my vocal cords would have cracked. *Why is no one even bringing it up?*

Because they can't, Ben said flatly. *It would negate the sacrifice if they did. It must be offered freely—completely. And it must be the Tree's will as well. The Monarch and Tree* must *be in complete alignment, and the sacrifice must be freely offered, or it will not work. So, we've been taught to never assume it, never count on it, never even mention it. Let alone ask for it.*

His eyes flared again. *No one is going to ask or expect that of you, Sarah. Everyone here came because they* volunteered, *knowing the risks.*

I looked around the room again, at the huddles of drakón and amón soldiers, ranging from joking and jostling with each other, to getting as comfortable as was feasible, to standing or sitting looking bored. Some were even trying to catch some sleep while they could.

"All of them?" I whispered out loud. "Volunteers?"

"When the call went out, our quota filled almost within a deken," Alyish said with a thin smile. "Knowing our limitations, we had to send people away."

My eyes stung, and swallowing became difficult again. "Why?"

Ben's eyes flicked around the room for a moment, and then he pointed subtly in one direction. "You see that Sunfilled woman there? Playing gemstones?"

I looked discreetly and saw a middle-aged blond woman sitting with her back mostly to us, playing a chess-like game with gems for pieces. In that moment, she threw her head back and laughed at something her grinning opponent said.

"Yes," I said quietly.

"Her name's Morina. She was among the drakón who pulled back after night fell at the Battle of the Solstice and congregated to make our last stand. Everyone was clean out of energy by that point, and she was bleeding out on the battlefield. She was given up for dead until your starform gave her the energy to heal."

I stared as subtly as I could, iceheart pounding.

"And that Starkissed man over there?" Alyish said quietly, nodding his chin in the opposite direction. "The one helping direct the others coming through?"

I looked and saw, to my surprise, that the light-blue-haired man was wearing the white half-cloak of one of my elites.

"Name of Pathir," Alyish continued. "Former Waterguard, and a torched good one too, but asked to be transferred to your elites after a lightcannon blast drove the Devourer's shadow away when it was ild from him."

"Not everyone here has a story like that," Ben said quietly. "But many do. And many more have friends and family who also owe their lives to you somehow. Even the ones who don't, they've all heard the stories, and know how much we as a *people* owe to you."

When I looked back at him, he smiled thinly. "I'm not saying these people represent the entire Six Realms, but they are among the most loyal to the Crown and the Tree, and now...to you. Because that's the way they are. The best of them joined the Warflight, or the Waterguard, or our elites because of their desire to serve a greater cause than their own, and they stayed because they found it with us."

"And because they stayed, they see firsthand how much we owe to the Tree and Her Monarchs," Alyish finished, holding my gaze firmly. "Whether or *not* those Monarchs give up their lives for us, we know they *live* out their lives for us. Kavarian touched and even saved far more lives than ever died for him, even before his final sacrifice. That is why nearly every dramá of the Warflight would have given our lives for his."

So Alyish, too, had guessed what was on my mind. And he too, although much more subtly than Ben, was discouraging me from making the same choice.

My eyes stung again. How, when it was so simple, could no one here expect that from me? Never mind if half or even most of the rest of the Realms thought differently, more selfishly, how could there be so many people here who would never ask? And never think me monstrous for not offering?

Was I a monster for not making that choice at once? For not ending this *now*?

But then, if I did...the Devourer would not be weakened. Just temporarily hindered in this one goal. How many more lives could I save over the course of a long, faithful life serving my Tree than the ones gathered here today? How much more damage could Ben and I do to the Devourer itself if we were standing at each other's side?

If I left Ben alone, like that....

How would he...and the Seven Realms...fare in the century to come?

Perhaps this was why the will of the Tree and the Monarch had to be in alignment. I could only see the battle *today*, but the Trees could see the entire eternal war against evil and know when we must die...and when we must live.

For the good of all.

Besides, I had one more thing to consider—perhaps the most important thing, in the end: my life was not my own anymore.

I had to keep my hand from reflexively covering my abdomen, but I felt the tiny burning deep inside, growing all the stronger as Earth's sun, Sekinek, rose to its zenith.

That life had entrusted itself to me. Once, it had had a choice, and it had chosen to come to me. Now, it was an unconscious passenger, if its spirit was even with me yet. Either way, the Tree had told me that my child had chosen to *save* my life. Not for me to snuff out my life—and its own—because I did not want to bear the pain of knowing others were going to die for me.

Now *someone* was going to die for me, whatever I did.

Ben had borne that pain almost his whole life. It had nearly suffocated him at times, but he had done it. How?

I couldn't meet his eyes again to ask for the answer.

"All life is ultimately in the Creators' hands, Sarah," Alyish said quietly, his normally gruff voice softening. "Do the will of your Tree the best you can, and no blood will be on your head for this or any other day."

Rachel disturbed the sobriety of the moment with a snort. "'Course not. Sarah, what's got you so serious all of a sudden?"

She tapped me under the chin with a careless grin. "Chin up, sis. We'll be *fine*. How can we not be with all of these big bad dragons here to protect us?"

I just raised an eyebrow at her, since I knew Rachel too well not to know that underneath her bravado, the reality of our situation was sinking in, and she was becoming nervous. She and Kor were so similar in that respect.

"Regardless," I said slowly, "I think it's time I spoke with my Tree."

I finally got the courage to meet Ben's eyes, which were now heavy. "Yes. I think it is."

Following my instincts, I took a deep breath and asked him, "Will you come with me?"

He blinked. "You...want me to? I mean...you think I should?"

"Yes," I said with still surety. "The King of Flame should represent his people before Her, just as I am representing mine."

"Then...yes, I will."

He turned and must have sent a silent command, because a moment later, Petra made her way over to us.

"Yes, King Koriben?" the Brightflare captain of my elites said cheerfully when she reached us.

"You're now on guard duty," Ben said, thumbing at Rachel. "And you can help Alyish coordinate from here."

Petra put her hand over her heart and nodded sharply. "Understood, sir."

"Ah, really?" Rachel said to Ben in a pout. "If I have to have a bodyguard, couldn't you have called over that hot, purple-haired guy from before?"

She gestured to Ordran, who had his back to us as he was directing the setting up of some tables—perhaps the beginnings of another command node.

Fortunately, Petra didn't seem to take offense, and in fact, her professional demeanor broke with a twitch of her lips.

Ben's expression was stony. "Captain Petra is more than capable of assisting you in any way you should reasonably require, Heir Rachel."

He took my hand, nodded to Alyish in a wordless farewell, and tugged me onward, eager to be away. I followed alongside him, fighting a lip twitch of my own.

You either had to laugh at Rachel...or strangle her. I saw which way Ben was currently leaning.

Aren't you glad I gave you an excuse for a break? I said, inner voice tinged with innocence.

Hellwinds, yes, Ben grumbled. *I hope you can forgive me when I say that I have no idea what Kor sees in her.*

I think I can manage that.

BEN'S EAGERNESS, AND THUS his steps, slowed not long after we entered the short, dimly lit corridor that led to the closed doors guarding the Tree's chamber. As we waited for those large doors to open, Ben gripped my hand tightly. I squeezed back three times in wordless comfort, but to my surprise, he did not echo the sentiment. His gaze remained fixed ahead.

Neither of us said anything as we entered the vast chamber and began climbing the frost-covered steps of the rise to the base of the Tree. I realized Ben had not been here since he first let me back in, and he had not approached Her since the very first time for all of us, when I had been invested as Queen and received the leaf that restored his father's flameheart.

I thought of sending him a silent assurance that everything would be OK, but I stopped when I realized the words might sound hollow to him, with him having just caught me pondering the option of sacrifice.

If the Tree said that was necessary, if I took that option, then for my husband, everything would *not* be OK. Especially not after all he had lost already...and all he had sacrificed to ensure I survived.

No wonder he would not look at me now. And yet, his grip never loosened.

To my shock, once the circular terrace came into view, the Tree's avatar was waiting for us. Only once before had She appeared without my call—again, the first time Ben and I had approached Her. Ben started when he caught sight of Her and glanced away. But after a moment, his shoulders set, and he raised his chin, looking directly at Her with an unusually unreadable expression. His grip on my hand tightened for a moment.

The Tree of Ice's expression was even more inscrutable than his as we approached. Her coldly burning, pupilless eyes rested lightly on the two of us, seeming to focus on neither of us overly much, Her hands clasped before Her in dignified repose. With no visual sign of exhaustion, there was an air of weariness about Her I couldn't quite put my finger on. Perhaps I felt more than saw it—and shared in that weariness, to the marrow of my bones.

That fatigue in my Tree troubled me as much as anything else. I had come to rely on the unimaginable power, wisdom, and immortality of Trees more than I would have thought possible a few months ago. I knew They could be killed, otherwise defending Them would not be necessary, and They could not always hold back the Devourer's darkrifts, but I had absorbed an unspoken assumption that They were otherwise infallible. They never got sick, or aged, or worn...did They?

I cursed myself that I had always neglected to ask Ben before, and I wished I could now, but I wasn't certain whether that was a good idea in the moment. If the Tree indeed desperately needed something above and beyond protection, then Ben would know that *I* would likely have to be the one to provide it.

When I glanced at him as we were ascending the last few steps, his eyes were on Her, and they narrowed, studying Her. I took that as confirmation that I wasn't just imagining things, and my iceheart thudded as we crossed the flagstones and came to a stop in front of the well, across from the Tree.

"*Welcome, Sarah, My Queen,*" the Tree murmured, Her voice as the whispering winter wind. "*And welcome, Koriben, My Sister's King.*"

"We thank You, my Lady," I said quietly. As usual, I felt a stilling, hushing effect from being in the presence of the Tree of Ice, the reverence one feels beholding the magnificence of a silent forest encased in snow.

"And we thank You for seeing us," I finished, clenching Ben's hand.

"*For what purpose have you both come before Me on this day?*"

I took a deep breath. "We both, along with our peoples, have come to Your defense, my Lady, and we seek to know Your will."

Ben's grip on my hand had loosened for a short time, but now it tightened again.

"*It is good you have come,*" She intoned. "*Ask what you will of Me.*"

I nodded. "Our first concern is about space, my Lady. The room we currently have to hold the forces that have volunteered to defend You is...limited."

The Tree raised Her hand, its crystalline facets glittering in the light. "*First, I give the people of Flame leave to freely enter the halls of My Temple that I have opened to you. You may use the rooms and facilities beyond the welcome chamber as you see fit. I require only that any door that is still locked to you remain locked, and any passage that is collapsed or inaccessible remain untouched. You may, however, repair and fortify the accessible areas, as you deem prudent.*"

"Thank you, my Lady," I said in relief, with a glance at Ben. He met my gaze with a quick, thin smile. It seemed we would have a bit of breathing room for his people after all.

Although I felt a flicker of sadness at that hint of disrepair. I had seen nothing of the kind in Her Temple so far, yet I had been led to believe that the extent of it was the welcoming chamber and Her own. Now I knew Her complex was more extensive and perhaps had a hint at why She had concealed the rest until now. We Linds would not have had the time, knowledge, or resources to begin restoring Her Temple to its proper glory, and we might have been distracted from more important, lifesaving matters by exploring its depths, not to mention risking our safety or doing more damage.

"*Second*," She continued, looking at Ben, "*though you may bring in crafts-people for such fortifications, they must be gone by dawn tomorrow. Have your people plan—and limit—their work accordingly.*"

Ben nodded firmly. "Understood, O Lady. Dare I ask if that means…"

He glanced at me apologetically, backing up from taking the lead in this interaction with my Tree.

I looked at the Tree, iceheart pounding. I could guess what Ben was about to ask. "…that the attack will happen at dawn?"

To my surprise, the Tree glanced behind us. "*What say you, Jacob, My son?*"

Ben stiffened, letting go of my hand to swerve to look behind us. Rarely did anyone catch Ben off guard—not even Kor, who was an expert at turning up when least expected. Yet, sure enough, Dad was rising the last few steps to the terrace.

Did you *hear the doors open?* Ben asked me quickly and silently.

No, I sent back, just as baffled.

No doubt seeing the confusion on our expressions, Dad said with his usual equanimity, "Apologies for the interruption. Michael took over for me, then the Tree summoned me with ice, and so through Her ice I came."

I glanced back at the Tree, then back at Dad as he came to my side. "If She summoned you, then don't apologize. But why…?"

"*Because it is time your leftwing revealed to you a gift I gave him nearly two and a half moons ago,*" the Tree said.

Two and a half…. Wait, but that would have been while I was still in the Six Realms the first time, with my family having no clue where I had gone other than some pictures in ice, Abby's dream, and Dad's….

Dad met my stunned eyes with his unreadable silvers. "It was during my dream of the Tree. Or perhaps *vision* is a better word. That's what all the rest ever since have been, waking or sleeping."

"The rest?" I repeated. "You've had *more?*"

"The Gift of Sight," Ben whispered, staring at Dad with a much different expression. One much more like awe…with a tinge of chagrin and apprehension.

I looked at Ben, and when he noticed my gaze, he pressed his lips into a thin line. "It's the greatest gift the Tree of Ice bestows on a mortal except Her power. Or, at least, that's what the legends say. Korrien—the chief of the humans who joined the draká, who became the first Sunfilled King—his wife had the gift. That's how we know about it at all."

His eyes flicked to the Tree of Ice, who stood gazing at the three of us with a regal equanimity no mortal could have matched—not even Dad.

"That is much the same thing She told me at the time," Dad said with the slightest upturn of his mouth at one corner. "Minus the historical bit."

"Then it's true?" I asked, looking at Dad.

I tried to conceal the hurt I irrationally felt. It wasn't like I hadn't kept secrets from him during that time, nor even told him everything the Tree told me. Perhaps it was arrogance creeping in—the loftiness of my title finally getting to me as I assumed that I, as the Queen of Ice, should have been told everything of importance to do with my Tree and clan.

I didn't think arrogance was behind all my emotions, but it was behind more of them than I liked, and I tried to quell both my pride and its bruise before it could be known.

Yet Dad's eyes tightened when they met mine again, as if he saw both. How unfair was it that my father was so unreadable yet so good at reading everyone else? Especially me.

"It's true," he said quietly. "You weren't the only one who has never been the same since you left, Sarah."

"What..."

I had been about to ask the much less reverent *What did She do to you?* and stopped myself.

"...*is* the Gift of Sight?"

Instead of answering, Dad looked at Ben, eyebrow raised—as if expecting Ben to know more about his own gift than he did.

Reluctantly, Ben said, "Well, I'd begun to think *you* might have it, Sarah. At least to some degree."

"What do you mean?" I asked, blinking at him.

"At least a few times, you've seen things in ice, haven't you? Things you didn't ask specifically to see? Things that weren't currently happening—like when you saw Solim with Svyer."

"Oh," I said quietly. "Yes. But...only twice. Like that."

I hadn't given anyone the specifics of the time I saw Kor talking to Eskala. I had just told them I had seen things in ice, and given the chaos at the time, that had been good enough.

"Those were both things from the past," I mused. "So, you're right; it wasn't just my ice scrying."

"*Momentary gifts of knowledge, not power,*" the Tree murmured. When I turned to Her, Her eyes were on me, and they looked soft and sad. "*You have enough burdens, My daughter. You do not require any more. Especially now that you have others to share them with you.*"

I slowly nodded, understanding now another source of conflicted feelings. I had questioned for a moment whether I was not worthy of more in the Tree's eyes, if She had given something to someone else that She did not give to me.

"And it is a burden," Dad said heavily, his eyes on me as well. "Make no mistake. Sometimes I question why I ever accepted it."

His lips pulled into a small, crooked smile as he glanced at the Tree, but She seemed not to take his comment amiss. She only nodded slightly to him, as if answering one of his thoughts.

"Why did you?" I asked, but I thought I knew the answer.

Dad returned his fathomless silvers to me, looking older and wearier than he had any right to in his middle age. I wondered for a second how many more hairs of his would have been white by now if the Tree hadn't changed them all to that color already.

"So you wouldn't have to," he said.

I nodded, swallowing as I understood. I *had* thought both times that the Tree had shown such things to me that the knowledge She had given me was, indeed, a burden. They were things I desperately needed to know, and in the case Ben mentioned, my discovery saved his and Svyer's lives. But they weren't pleasant things.

As if reading my thoughts, Dad said heavily, "I don't just see things from the past, Sarah. I also see things from the present...and even the future."

I started at that last admission. "What?"

Dad—my solid, stoic, grounded father, who was as far from being a flighty, temperamental clairvoyant as you could imagine—could see the *future*?

He grimaced. "Possibilities only. I see what truly was from the past, and is from the present, but for the future...just possibilities."

"Why?" I asked, scrunching my face in confusion. My eyes flicked to the Tree. "Don't Trees always know what will happen?"

Wasn't that how They had always planned for our escape from the Devourer? Sometimes that knowledge had made me uncomfortable, sometimes downright furious and mistrusting, but as my trust in Them had grown, I had also come to rely on it.

As Kor had told me, there was a difference between *knowing* something bad will happen and *making* it happen. If They could not prevent the bad thing, Their knowledge allowed the Trees to mitigate the damage, as best as They could while working within Their laws and with stubborn, fallible mortals like us.

Dad gave another small, crooked smile and cast another look at the Tree. "Supposedly, so I do not become frozen with fatalism."

At my blank look, Ben elaborated, "So he knows he can still make a difference. The Trees never take away our choice. Or curse us with even the illusion of lacking it. That's why the Tree rarely gives a glimpse of the future, even to Her Monarch, and declares it set in stone."

His gaze went to the Tree of Ice, hardening.

"Oh," I said, sheepish I hadn't thought of the same thing. Wasn't that supposed to be the major pitfall of oracles—self-fulfilling prophecy? Well, that, and the human tendency to shoot the messenger. It wasn't the oracle's fault if they were the bearer of bad tidings.

Wry humor fading, Dad said quietly, "That was one reason I didn't tell you. I didn't want you to think that the bad things I saw were destined to happen."

"What bad things?" I asked, swallowing.

Dad's eyes flicked to Ben. My husband didn't miss that look, and he said evenly, "You saw a future in which I didn't let you back in."

"*You* did not."

Ben smiled without humor. "Because I would not have been the King for much longer. But my Tree would not have abandoned you, so I doubt you saw a future in which no one did."

Dad nodded. "I did not."

I stood there, stunned, processing for a few moments. So *that* was how Dad had always seemed so calm, so accepting of our family's fate, even when reason said we'd been cast adrift on a new world to struggle for our very survival. Yet that was also why he never assured me that Ben would soften.

Because he might not have. He still had a choice—which he had not yet made.

I shuddered. But that was the terrible—and beautiful—thing about love: it had to be chosen. Not just by one person, but by two. And not just once, but every day, every moment, no matter what pain that moment might bring. Trust had to be at love's foundation, and hope its guiding light, yet there was always still an element of uncertainty, a constant pressing through the dark together—wondering if there would ever be a moment when the other hand would slip away from yours.

The very fact that the hand *could* slip away was what made its continued presence mean everything.

Not wanting to know the answer, yet unable to help myself, I asked, "Who...else did you see open the gate?"

Neither Dad nor Ben looked at me or answered. They weren't ignoring me, though. They seemed to be having some kind of communication between them, either in looks or in silent words.

My guess tipped toward words when Ben blinked, as if startled, and then he broke eye contact with Dad, a bit of redness creeping onto his face, and one of his folded arms raised for his hand to cup his neck. I looked between them, baffled, but only Dad met my gaze, and his eyes were as unreadable as ever.

"The other reason I did not tell you," Dad continued, as if there had been no break in our conversation, "is because it wasn't relevant until now."

I raised an eyebrow. "Wasn't relevant? The fact that you could *see the future* wasn't relevant?"

Dad grimaced. "I cannot see whatever and whenever I want. I can only see what the Tree gives me. Until this point, I have seen little of use in the future."

His face darkened. "In fact, I never saw even a hint of Yalda's plans to assassinate you."

I glanced apprehensively at the Tree, but She did not move or change expression, maintaining Her composed, patient demeanor as we worked out these details among ourselves. She did not appear to see the need to address Dad's comment—perhaps because we had come to the correct conclusions about that already and She did not need to repeat them or justify Herself before us. But neither did She seem to condemn Dad for his lingering tension in that regard. Her eyes only softened when they rested on him.

Something about the understanding in them made me recall Her words to Mom: *You are all children—and all of you are Mine.*

We may rage at Her for allowing harm to come to our loved ones, but...if She could have protected them without violating some higher law or purpose, She would have. All the while, She toiled for our benefit, asking nothing from us but what was necessary for our survival and joy, suffering more than we ever did for our pain.

Sacrificing more than all.

I felt an inward shudder as I saw the first flicker of something too terrible to contemplate.

"But that's changed?" Ben asked intently, breaking my focus before the flicker could fully form in my mind, and I let it go gladly. "You've seen things of use to us now?"

"Yes," Dad said slowly. "I have. And I have begun to understand that..."

His eyes flicked again to the Tree. "...I would not have been able to make sense of it before. Had I not had some...practice. With lesser things."

"Practice?" I asked.

"Discerning the *when* of what I am seeing, for instance," Dad said dryly. "Or did that come naturally to you?"

"Oh," I said with a grimace of understanding. "No, it definitely did not."

I'd had to use context clues, and even then, I was uncertain. I sure hoped Dad had gotten a better instinctual feel for that sort of thing than I had. I could see how bewildering his life would have become otherwise.

Dad's tone evened. "Or focusing, eliminating distractions, or ignoring irrelevant details. Even just walking and talking like a normal human being when a vision could come to me at any moment—or stopping myself from revealing something I should not have known."

"You know, Dad," I said, risking a slightly teasing tone. "That explains quite a lot about you in general. You sure you didn't have this ability before?"

I expected him to raise an eyebrow at me or make some dry comment, but he only gazed at me thoughtfully for a moment before looking at the Tree.

"*Glimmers of My gifts are given to all My children,*" She said. "*Lights meant to guide them through the dark to My harbor. If they heed them, I can give them more.*"

So Dad had. Agnostic as he'd always claimed to be, he'd always clung to that glimmer until it led him to the Tree...and far more than he could ever have bargained for besides.

"What can you tell us?" Ben asked.

Dad looked at the Tree, and She nodded solemnly. "*All that I have given you of what may come at dawn, you may share to help them prepare.*"

Ben looked at the Tree with his most kingly, inscrutable expression. "And after?"

She just gazed back at him without answering.

"Probably useless to you anyway," Dad said with a frown. "Once the battle begins, there are too many factors, too many branching paths. Even with all my practice, I can't make sense of them."

"There is only one future, though," Ben said heavily, eyes still locked with the Tree. "You know it...and You are not sharing it."

For once, Ben sounded like Kor.

"*You have been given Our word, Koriben, King of Flame,*" the Tree said, voice as hushed and gentle as falling snow. "*You can ask for no more. Do not make the attempt, lest you thwart the very future you hope for.*"

There was something ahead for us, something that if Ben *knew* what it was, he would try to stop it...and in trying, he would doom, not save me.

Sometimes, we simply were not meant to *know*. It was the stumbling through the dark that got our feet on the right path—the path we would have never chosen had we been free to see it. Yet it was that hard path that took us where we most longed to go. All we could do was choose to keep focused on that glimmer in the dark, choose to keep our hand in each other's...

...and choose to trust.

Ben took a deep breath, clasped my hand again...and nodded.

Chapter Twenty-Two

ICE

Koriben

THERE WAS NO PATH to the surface. At least, not a traditional one. But Jake led us straight from the Tree's chamber, through the welcoming chamber, and down the corridor Kor's team had entered, until we came to the end of the long, dark hall.

There, Kor was pacing in a small, strange room shaped like the inside of a spiral shell, with moonstone lines in the walls and a similar spiral on the floor that began to glow as we approached.

"Sarah, perfect timing!" Kor exclaimed distractedly as soon as he spotted her coming. He waved her forward. "We've just found a—"

"—moonpath, we know," Sarah said with a twitch of her lips as she strode inside.

Kor deflated a bit. "What? How?"

He then blinked, noticing me and Jake for the first time as we came in. We had also picked up Alyish along the way, who entered last. "How did you even know to *come* here?"

"The Tree," Sarah said simply, leaving it at that for the moment.

"*This* is a moonpath, huh?" I said, turning around in the center of the small, oddly shaped room. The center was the only part of it in which I didn't have to duck. It was also getting rather crowded, and Kor's fellow searchers had vacated to make way for us newcomers. "The kind you and Kor used to find the Ekrel moongate?"

Apparently, with no danger to either of them and very little flirtation on Kor's part. Or so I had been told. Although it once again occurred to me how little both Sarah and Kor had told me about that long night of searching, and by now, that seemed deliberate. Yet I still chose to trust that they had told me what was relevant for me to know, and I still felt that, because I'd been in a self-induced comatose state at the time and had pushed Sarah away the morning before, I was in no position to ask for more.

"Yes, yes," Kor said impatiently to me. Then he switched his focus back to one of his fellow searchers, a Starkissed named Kvina, who was peering in through the door now that she had given way to us.

I recognized her as one of Sarah's drakón elites, and she had the same telltale dark sapphire coloring, curly hair, and brown skin that identified her as one of Kor's *tol'lon* cousins. It figured that he would pick at least one of them to accompany him through his explorations of the Temple of Ice, just as he had maneuvered two others to be Sarah's chief and deputy of staff. *Tol'lon* were as thick as thieves, and nearly as full of secrets and mischief. And, I had gathered over the years since I had learned Kor's secret, they were deeply loyal to him as the Tolsyon heir. Hence why he trusted them with so much—too much for *my* comfort.

Lately, I had added one more detail to my mental list of *tol'lon* qualities to be wary of: they appeared to be interested in all things to do with the Moontouched restoration...and thus with Sarah.

Kor pointed at the closest white streak in the wall and said, "See here, this is the glow. As I said, though, it only starts when a Moontouched approaches."

"Fascinating," Kvina said, eyes shimmering with that *look* that only Starkissed, particularly *tol'lon*, got as she gazed around the now fully illuminated room.

"But how does it *work*?" I asked, hoping to get us back on track. I looked at the spiral on the floor. "There isn't that map from before. Just this...thing."

"I think that map of Greenland was a onetime thing, Ben," Sarah said, coming to my side and taking my hand. "At least, that was unlike the other moonpaths Kor and I encountered. *Those* were exactly like this one. As for how it works...."

She glanced at the doorway, grimacing. "You all will have to be left behind, I think, sorry. Probably not enough room."

An interesting statement, seeing as all of us *could* fit if we didn't care about elbow room. Kor's team had only left to give Jake, Alyish, and me space to examine and maneuver. But I trusted Sarah knew what she was talking about.

"No worries," Kvina said with a shrug.

"You'll...also have to back out of the doorway," Sarah said, this time more pointedly.

Kvina laughed and withdrew, as did the other couple of curious searchers.

"Make note of what you see!" Kor called after them. "I've been dying to know what this process looks like from the outside."

Not enough to be left behind, though. At least not this time.

"Kor, if you recall, the priority here is to get out," I said with a wry smile.

"Yes, but there's no reason not to learn while we're at it." He smirked at me. "After all, the more we know, the safer we should be, right? Or is *safety* no longer a priority?"

I just rolled my eyes.

Sarah took a deep breath, then let out a self-conscious laugh. "Here goes, then. See if you can learn anything new from this, Kor."

She let go of my hand and began walking the spiral on the floor, starting at the center and working her way outward, toward the ending at the door. All the while, power built around her like an invisible storm. She glowed with it, like a lightning bolt of an arrow straining to be released. I saw what she meant about space now, since the rest of us had to occasionally shuffle to get out of her way, especially in the beginning, before Jake, Alyish, and I understood what she was doing and could anticipate her movement.

I was just beginning to see why she and Kor called this a moon*path* when Sarah finally released that built-up power, letting it shoot forth to the small entrance arch to the room...where ice formed a translucent film, just like the kind that covered the interior of one of her gates.

I blinked at that film, and the new scene beyond, replacing the dark hallway of before: what lay beyond was still dimly lit, but there were moonstone streaks in the walls that started to glow from the presence of Sarah's power, showing a cavern that was a mirror image of the one we were in.

Sarah let out a few heavy breaths from the exertion, but she straightened soon with a smile. "That was easier than before."

"I told you," Kor said to her with a smirk as he passed. "You're far stronger now than you could have imagined back then. And this is only the beginning."

She snorted as she followed. Not knowing what else to do, I did as well.

"I also seem to recall you told me that night that you bet a bottle of your best wine that you'd be hiding behind me before a few months were out."

"And so I did," Kor said as he stepped through the ice. His voice warped only slightly from the barrier as he continued, so this film was even thinner than the ones in Sarah's moongates, and that much was also clear from how it parted around him more fluidly. "During the rock wyrm incursion, remember?"

I clenched one hand into a fist at the reminder of *that* episode.

"*Technically*, that wasn't *behind* me," Sarah said as she went through, her words warping halfway through her sentence when she passed over. Not about to let her get far from me now, I wasn't more than a couple of steps behind, even having to duck a lot of the way. "You were right beside me."

I shivered from the cold of the curtain as I passed through. Going through her gates always felt unpleasant, like stepping through a cold waterfall, but now more than ever with the added thinness and fluidity of this type of barrier. You'd think the thicker ice would be worse, but from the way the thicker fractured around me as I went through, less of it *clung* to me than this stuff did.

"Technicalities," Kor said with a dismissive wave. He was already absorbed in studying this mirror chamber, and I joined him. From the center, of course, where I could straighten again.

"What's wrong with a plain old moongate?" I grumbled, casting a look back over my shoulder at the ice film. If there was any other way out of this new chamber we'd entered, the ice was now covering it. Alyish had passed through by then, his face unreadable and violet eyes sharp as he took in the whole experience. This would have been his first time going through one of Sarah's gates ever, let alone a moonpath version. Jake came through last, looking as unflappable as ever, even though I was fairly certain this was his first time on a moonpath as well.

"Probably many reasons," Kor said absently. "But my guess is the primary one is effort. Power. Sophistication. The more I've thought about it, the more I've come to think that moonpaths are the most *primitive* form of gates. Even older than *sun*gates, if this pair is any indication."

"What do you mean?" I asked in surprise.

"Think about it, Ben. The first sungate was built a thousand years ago. But when would *this* one have been built?"

I sighed. "Let me guess: before that?"

Meanwhile, with everyone in this new yet nearly identical chamber, Sarah dismissed the ice covering the entry and revealed the passage that existed beyond. Illuminated by yet more moonstone, the path rose in an upward slope, even as it curved around to the right about fifty feet from the arch, so that seemed promising.

Kor strode forward eagerly, and Jake followed, falling into step with him.

"What makes you assume that?" he asked, interested.

Kor was more than happy to oblige a fellow intellectual. His voice floated back to Sarah and me, who formed the next pair, with Alyish taking up the rear. "By the time the draká made their first sungate a thousand years ago and crossed through it to Earth, the humans of Earth had long since abandoned the Tree of Ice. We know they had to cross a sea and a frozen waste to reach Her, and they found Her Temple already in place, although derelict, much as it is now."

The passage continued in a slow, upward spiral, wide enough to be circling around the moonpath chamber. I could smell a definite change in the air, which became cooler and less stale the higher we went. And the higher we went, the more the walls were carved from *ice* and not rock, reinforced with a silvery metal skeleton that brought to my mind the impression of being in the belly of a giant snake. Been there once, done that, didn't need to do it again, thank you. As our source of moonstone went out, I cast a few orbs of golden light to make up the difference.

And not because I was nervous that the snake would come alive in the darkness.

"If our records are accurate," Kor continued, "the humans and draká left everything in the state it was when they found it, and all logic points to that conclusion as well. They didn't have the time, resources, or inclination to do otherwise. Their supplies were low, the wastes had little to no food or game, and they had to get back to Ythra to support the draká at large. At the time they arrived, neither the humans nor the draká could do major magical workings, so I find it unlikely they could have constructed this moonpath. The records also say that they struggled for a time to find a way in until Thera, the wife of the human leader and the tribe's wisewoman, had a vision from the Tree of Ice that helped her decipher the ritual to enter."

"Wait, what?" Sarah asked, glancing up the passage at her father. "A vision?"

"Yes," Kor said dismissively, clearly eager to get back to theorizing on the fringes of scholarly knowledge that we were literally walking through now. "Thera had the Gift of Sight. That much is well-established."

"Even before she reached the Tree?" Sarah said slowly. "*Any* Tree?"

"That's not unusual, actually. Thera recorded that during periods of waywardness, the Tree of Ice would often bestow the Gift of Sight on a faithful disciple or at least an *inclined* soul to try to bring the Tree's people back to Her. In Thera's case, literally. She had her first vision of the Tree and was given the Gift on the night Korrien finally made the pact with the draká to help them. Her visions were how they even got this far at all."

"To bring Her people back to Her, huh?" Sarah said meaningfully, glancing again at her father, who still did not look back.

"Anyway," Kor said, voice turning eager again, "concrete details are sketchy—probably deliberately—on just what that entrance ritual was, just that it was in a space where the draká could not enter."

Kor laughed, almost giddy now. "Theories have abounded as to why, usually involving some kind of Tree-enforced barrier. Oh, what would I give to see the look on that stodgy idiot Mornith's face once he reads my paper saying that the draká simply couldn't have physically *fit*."

"*Some* of us still fit poorly now," I grumbled under my breath. The ceiling's height was alright at first, but the further we went, the more I had to bow my head, until now I was stooping. Sarah cast me a sympathetic look.

"I think we're almost there," she whispered.

I thought she was right from the fresher smells and the way the ice was getting brighter. I dismissed my orbs one by one over the next few dek as the walls once again glowed, this time with a different light.

Meanwhile, Jake asked, "If they couldn't do magic, how could they have done what Sarah just did to open the moonpath?"

"Sarah, too, opened her first ones before she was fully invested. And, correct me if I'm wrong, Sarah," Kor said more loudly, casting his voice back, "but the moonstone and chamber itself provide at least some of the power, correct?"

"Correct," Sarah agreed. "I'm giving some, but only a fraction of what's going into it. And there's something about it that focuses or magnifies my power, making a little go a long way."

"Another point to my theory about the primitiveness of the moonpath. And by *primitive*, I don't mean *inferior*," Kor added quickly to Jake. "There's something that's remarkably efficient about them—so efficient, so enduring, in fact, that they can lay dormant for *centuries*, completely untended, and a human with just a touch of Ice can wander in and use them. I know you probably can't fully appreciate the significance of that. Sungates, for example, take massive amounts of our energy on a consistent basis and must be carefully tended, much like a bonfire, or they'll not just go out, they'll fall apart and must be remade entirely to become usable again."

Yet another difference between my sungates and Sarah's moongates that I hadn't fully appreciated until that moment. Even though, as King of Flame, I was the ideological guardian of the gates, seldom was I ever called on to tend or power them myself, especially since the Covenants had been renewed while

I was still Heir, so I often took their maintenance for granted. I sighed, hoping Kor wouldn't hear.

As the passage straightened and became so low that even Sarah was now ducking, Kor concluded with relish, "My paper on the moonpaths, particularly as proto-gates, is going to blow large portions of foundational gate theory to smithereens. And that's not even considering the impact they'll have on Early Covenantal Era history. *We have discovered the ritual.* Thera's entrance ritual, plain as day, is a *moonpath.*"

"Kor, are you sure the Trees want you publishing that fact?" Sarah said with a smile as we climbed the final rise of the path to a round stone door about six feet in diameter, with a familiar white, glowing tree etched onto its surface.

"They have to give me *something*," Kor moaned as he came to a stop. "I was *right*, torch it! I was *right all along.*"

"Let me guess," Sarah said as she left my side and walked in between Kor and Jake to get to the door. "You knew, from the first time we discovered a moonpath, that it was 'Thera's ritual.'"

"I guessed," Kor grumbled, folding his arms. "There were similarities with the flowery, metaphorical account. 'Bowels of the earthen sea,' 'white path of eternity,' and so on."

Sarah glanced over her shoulder and shook her head at him. "I don't know whether to be less or more impressed that a *historical account* is how you figured out the moonpath even before I did."

Kor grinned at her, mollified. Sarah *was* impressed, and he knew it. "Anyone who says history isn't useful can feel the bite of my teeth."

"Yes, that's well and good," I said irritably, "but *some* of us are getting sore being barely able to stand in here, so could we get a move on?"

"Sorry, Ben," Sarah said ruefully, turning fully back to the door. She put her hand on the center of the trunk, and the entire tree flared. Slowly, the door ground open, swinging outward a few ild...and stopped.

"The magic's still working," Sarah said with a sigh. "I think it's just...stuck. I could give it more power, but...."

I could see her reluctance in the weary set of her shoulders. Once again, she'd had to get up at dawn, and once again, she'd taxed herself as the day went on, steadily approaching noon.

"Let me through," I said, as I squeezed between Kor and Jake, who both stepped back. I cast a wry look at Kor. "What was that about 'efficient' and 'enduring'?"

Kor raised an eyebrow. "That's in a more-or-less closed system deep underground. There's little that can mortally be done about a thousand years of plain old *ice*."

And it *was* simply ice, or at least deeply packed snow and ice, accumulated around the door over the centuries of disuse. I felt that much for myself as I cast my awareness out like a net beyond the stone. But I also felt something else that made my pulse pound faster with eagerness: sunlight.

It wasn't far now. Practically within reach. All we needed now was a bit of heat and strength.

Delicately, mindful of the sacredness of this place and Sarah's potential irritation with me if I ruined anything, I sent power out along my net of awareness and gradually heated the crusted rim around the door until rivulets of water were streaming down its surface and puddling at our feet. The others backed to the sides to avoid the tiny river beginning to form and run down the passage's slope, and I sighed.

"Sorry."

"It's fine, Ben," Sarah said firmly. "Do what you have to."

Having a good feel for things now, I turned up the heat, and the water poured in more quickly. No doubt it would freeze and make the path more slippery, but we would worry about that later.

Once I felt the way was clear enough, I put my shoulder to the door and gave it a good push, which broke through the last crusted layer, and the magic was now sufficient to swing the door open on its own.

Washing us with blazing light and frigid wind coming down a short, round tunnel.

I controlled my eager impulse to walk toward the sunlight and instead stood back, gesturing for Sarah to lead the way. She came to my side and took my hand with a smile, then led me through the pipe of a tunnel. I felt a shiver-inducing curtain of ancient spells of protection and concealment as we passed the final threshold and into the sun.

It was like a desert in a way, but the coldest one I had ever set foot in. Within seconds, the wind pierced my clothing and seemed to take the chill all the way into my bones. Only the sunlight radiating down on me kept my flameheart from overstraining as it flared to turn up the heat in my blood in compensation. Even so, I slipped my hand from Sarah's to pull my thickest coat out of the ether and shrug it on as quickly as I could, and the other drakón with me, Kor and Alyish, did the same as they stepped out as well.

Sarah and Jake seemed absurdly unaffected by the cold, though Sarah raised her hand to her eyes and squinted against the brightness and wind.

The glare off all that white was, indeed, intense, causing me to squint as well, and the wind carried an endless stream of ice particles that stung my eyes. Between the two forces, I could study our surroundings only with difficulty. Even my Blood-enhanced senses weren't much help here: there was little for me to smell except barren, lifeless cold, and even less heat for me to sense.

The dominant impression I got through my squinting eyes was of stark, endless, white, only broken up by slight, wind-blasted rises like waves in a dune sea; we had come out of one of those waves—one of the largest around, in fact, so that it counted as something of a hill.

And cold. Such cold that my very marrow seemed to freeze, and my breath became labored. For the first time, I began to feel the kind of weariness Sarah must feel in the presence of my Tree.

And this was near *noon*.

I looked down at Sarah incredulously.

"How can you *not* be freezing right now?" I said loudly over the buffeting of the wind.

Bits of ice and snow were coating every line of us they could; I was glad for her black trousers and light brown skin, otherwise with her white hair and shirt, and the coating of snow over everything, she might have blended with her surroundings to the point of becoming invisible—and losing sight of her like that was *not* something I could handle today.

Yet there she stood, seemingly no more uncomfortable than she might have been on a bright, windy day at the beach at Olsdak.

She shrugged in answer to my question, but her face was troubled as she gazed at us three drakón.

Alyish was gazing up in reverent wonder at the sun.

"So this is Sekinek," he murmured, so quietly I was surprised I heard him over the wind. Then, even more softly, he said something to himself, of which I only caught, "—right after all—old friend."

"What was that?" I asked, feeling a chill run down my neck that had nothing to do with the cold.

"Oh, nothing," Alyish said with an uncharacteristically wistful, distant look. "Just thinking about something your father once told me."

I knew him better than to ask for another clarification on what that was. Instead, trying to fight the instinctual clench in my gut, I attempted a light tone. "Don't go senile on me now, Alyish."

He was nearly as much of an uncle to me as my blood one was, and even more of a pillar in my life and, more important now, my reign. Yvera was the rightwing of the King, but to make up for her inexperience, Alyish still shouldered much of that role for us both. I didn't know what either of us—let alone the Realms—would do without him.

His focus returned to the present, and his hard smile as he looked at me was comfortingly familiar. "Oh, you can take that one concern off your mind, young man. When I die, it will be with my sword in my hand and my mind just as sharp."

Who said anything about dying? I thought but didn't quite have the cheek to say out loud.

Not today.

Echoing my darkening mood, Sarah said to me silently, *Ben....*

I looked down at her, my flameheart thumping at her sober tone. She was gazing out over the tundra and then back at our group.

What? I asked.

How are we going to do this? she whispered. *You three can barely stand to be out here. Can't you? And if even* you *are having trouble, at noon....*

I swallowed—painfully, with the cold seeming to have grown shards in my throat. I took her hand again as we gazed out at the world she was born to and the ice she now belonged to, and yet a land that was as foreign and hostile to my kind as my worlds had been to her.

Yet I had not forgotten where Sarah's thoughts had gone the last time the difficulties of what was to come had weighed her down. I was not about to let her wallow in despair now.

We'll manage, I told her firmly, clenching that cold, frosted hand tightly. I forced all my conviction, all my faith, into my next words. *The Trees will provide a way. They always do.*

Though for the life of me, this time, I could not imagine what that could be. And so far...They had not told us.

I glanced warily at Jake, who was also looking out over the landscape, but if he saw something in those frozen wastes more than we did, he showed nothing of it. His inscrutable silvers only glistened in the reflected glare like two enigmatic suns of his own.

I felt like shuddering, but his silent, private words came back to me in that moment, the ones he had given me just dek ago when Sarah had asked him who else he saw let them back in.

You were always the one meant to be King of Flame, Ben—the one most suited to bear that heavy crown, and the one who made my daughter the happiest, in the end. So, thank you for having the strength to choose what you did, and to be what you are.

I could hardly believe his words in that moment and still couldn't now, re-membering. Jake didn't just approve of me and of my marriage to his daughter, which alone was nothing less than staggering. He also thought I was a good King.

I didn't feel strong as I clutched Sarah's hand and shivered in that waste-land. But I would try my best not to fail them now.

THINGS MOVED MORE QUICKLY after that. Since she had seen and could clearly visualize the welcoming chamber, Sarah could summon scrying ice that connected there and surge us all straight back, and we began the real work of settling in.

Given the Tree's explicit permissions, Kor brought in architects, artificers, and constructors at once to do more detailed surveys of the now roughly mapped corridors, branches, and rooms. Within the deken, repairs had begun on the serviceable rooms, and our people were resettling themselves much more comfortably and effectively in the best of them. With Sarah's permission, and her quick check with her instincts, I even brought in another contingent of the Warflight that we'd had on standby, increasing our numbers by a third.

Despite my muted protest, Sarah took over transportation duties from David, insisting that he needed a break. Be that as it may, my preference was to pause the in- and outflux of people after we got the specialists in, rather than have Sarah stretch herself thin the day before the battle, let alone after the morning she'd had. She asserted she was fine, however, and sent a dry comment to me that she wasn't suddenly made of glass just because she was pregnant.

I felt somewhat justified, yet still disturbed, when after one trip back, she grew pale, put a hand over her mouth, and disappeared—without reappearing on the other side of the ice in the King's wing.

No one else was paying enough attention to notice. Her "passengers" had been delivered as normal and were too busy following their instructions to go to their assigned location to look back at her. Everyone else in the Temple of Ice seemed to think she had gone back. Everyone in the King's court seemed to think she was still here in the Temple.

Yet *I* knew where her star should have gone relative to my other gates had she gone back to the King's wing, and she had surged nowhere near any of them.

She was now a lone speck in a dark, uncharted universe in my mind, and I knew what that must have meant.

She had fled to her own Realm.

Flameheart racing, I made some quick excuse to Alyish and Petra and reached for my star, surging straight to her.

I landed in a stumble, nearly knocking Sarah over even as she crouched in front of the toilet in our water-room back in the suite we had left that morning—as she was heaving out the contents of her stomach.

Noon. It had been precisely noon back on Earth.

As it all clicked, I suppressed a groan. Sarah didn't need to hear that from me right now.

Instead, I gently kneeled next to her. With her hair in a braid this time, I had both arms free to wrap themselves around her, partly to steady her against me but mostly to press one hand to her abdomen, throwing my power into the battle raging inside her.

With a grim surety that I was to become practiced at this, I quelled the triumphant uprising of Flame, ordering it with all the authority within me to give ground to Ice. I was probably assigning too much emotion to such an elemental, currently mindless thing, but when Flame finally gave way, it seemed to do so almost petulantly.

You will not *hurt your mother,* I mentally growled at it from between my teeth.

No more than I could help. No more than I already had.

Not after all she had done for us both.

Sarah's heaving slowed, and within moments, stilled entirely. She sunk against me for a dek or two, until her trembling stopped, and then she began stumbling to her feet. I rose swiftly to my own and steadied her, always keeping a hand on her as she lurched over to the sink and spit into it. She chuckled as I wordlessly handed her a cup, and as she filled it with water, she croaked, "I'd hoped you'd find me."

"I'll always find you," I said quietly as I leaned against the closest wall, folding my arms. "There's not a place in this universe you can hide from me."

Even if she took herself from me. Even then, I was determined to share in her sacrifice and follow her across the Flame, and I had the gold earring glittering in her right ear as testament to the Covenant in our blood that we would still be together, even then.

After sloshing water in her mouth and spitting, she said lightly, "You know what I mean. That time, what with me disappearing out of the blue. I thought you might be watching."

I said nothing, only glad that she didn't seem offended by how closely I had monitored her for any sign of weakening.

After swishing and spitting again, she said, "I thought of asking you to follow, but it was coming on so strongly, I knew I couldn't even wait that long."

"You shouldn't have pushed yourself like that," I said softly, hoping that if I said it gently enough, she would finally listen.

She shook her head. I was relieved to see her color returning. "It wasn't that, Ben. In fact, if anything...."

She sighed, setting the cup down and turning around to lean against the counter and put a hand on her belly. "If anything, I was getting stronger," she whispered.

"Stronger?" I said, troubled.

She grimaced. "I think *that* was the problem. I wasn't supposed to be, obviously, but *she* was getting stronger, so I guess I was too. Until noon, when it became too much, and threw us both out of balance."

I raised an eyebrow. "*She?*"

Sarah stiffened a bit, raising her chin. "I've decided to call her a *she* for now. It's only been one day, but I guess I'm already tired of 'it.' I've also never been a fan of how people just say 'the baby' or even 'baby,' like it's a name."

Some of the stiffness left her, replaced with sheepishness. "And, I don't know...I guess it *feels* like a 'she' to me. What about you?"

I was barely dealing with the fact that the seed of life inside of her was real—and mine. Assigning it a gender—giving it a soul—was asking too much of me right now. Sarah seemed to see that after only a moment.

Her expression turned wry. "Alright, forget I asked."

Reluctantly, I said, "If I had to guess, it would probably be male."

She smiled, eyes lighting up, and her pleasure at seeing me at least *try* to play her game made the mental exercise worth it. "Are you just saying that because *you're* male?" she teased.

"That's part of it."

The other part was that I saw too much of myself in the thing. That was the whole torched problem.

Before she could see too much, I pushed off the wall and straightened, coming over to give her another once-over. "How are you feeling now?" I asked as I settled my hands on her shoulders and started sinking my power into her.

"I'll be ready to go back in a moment," she said with a sigh. "Just have a look at my throat, will you? That second time in one day...."

I'd heard the roughness in her voice, which was what made me think to come over. I directed my healing energy there, repairing the damage her stomach bile had done. Good thing I'd focused on the most important thing first, because I was just finishing up when I felt a familiar tug at my consciousness. I sighed, pulling away.

"Kor is calling."

Sarah's cheeks heated. "Oh, right. How many people noticed when we left?"

As I pulled out Kor's scale, I said, "You leaving? Just me. Me leaving? At least Alyish and Petra and a few aides, who knows who else."

I tapped the glowing blue surface, and Kor's scowling face materialized on the scale.

"Ben, where the torch have you gone off to? Sarah's with you, I'm assuming?"

"Yes," I said evenly. "She overdid it and needed a break."

Sarah huffed, and I raised an eyebrow at her to dare her to find a better excuse. She grimaced but said nothing.

Kor, meanwhile, stayed silent, and that made me look back down at the scale. He was studying me, and the background around him was moving. The voices faded away, and the lighting dimmed as Kor stepped into a dark corner.

"Alright, now that I have a bit more privacy," he said quietly, "is something wrong, Ben? Something you should be telling me?"

"No," I said, focusing on the second question to keep my tone honest and even.

Sarah pressed herself into his view, face hot. "Hi, Kor. Really, I'm fine. I just...overdid it. Like he said. We'll be back in a sec."

"Strange, because you don't *look* like you're suffering from the symptoms of burnout," Kor said dryly.

I should have ended the call right then, because Sarah said, "Er, well, Ben's just a good healer, that's all."

Now you've done it, I silently groaned at her.

"Like she said," I told Kor, "we'll be back soon. See you then."

Then I tapped the scale again, this time cutting off the spell that powered the communication magic, and his image disappeared.

"What did I do?" Sarah asked in resignation.

"You can't *heal* burnout, Sarah," I said, softening my tone. "It's magical depletion, and you can't give someone else magic. Well, *you* can, but I couldn't do the same to you."

Reason dictated I shouldn't be able to help her with what really ailed her, either, seeing as my power was the *source* of the conflict inside her—but perhaps that gave me some authority when dealing with it.

"Oh," Sarah said, groaning. "So...Kor knows."

I put away my leftwing's scale. "He knows there's something we're hiding from him, something to do with you. Something at least a bit urgent, from the way we *both* vanished like that when we're needed so much right now, and you know what that means."

"He's never going to let this go until he figures it out," Sarah said with a nod and a sigh.

"As I've told you before...the longer you try to keep something from Kor, the worse it gets."

"I know I should just tell him. It's just...can't *one thing* be private, be *mine,* for just *one day*?"

I sighed and put a hand on her shoulder. "Well, I think you can put him off for a day. Especially today, of all days. He has plenty of other things distracting him for now...but I wouldn't try for much longer after that."

IN THE BLUR OF preparations, night fell too soon—and with the sunset came another of Sarah's episodes of imbalance, the scales of power inside of her painfully equalizing as Ice overtook Flame. One would have thought that would be a good thing, for her at least, but she still experienced the same savage upheaval, as if the Ice inside her were taking revenge on both her and the Flame. This time, Sarah was more worried.

"Is she OK? Do you think she will *be* OK tonight?" she asked me anxiously after recovering enough, as I held her once again as we sat on the floor of our suite's bathroom and I spread my power through her.

I hadn't asked her why she kept coming back here, of all places in the universe she could call her own. Perhaps this one felt the safest to her, and I couldn't argue with that. Though it still threw me every time she used a gendered pronoun.

I answered as evenly as I could. "It's too soon for me to tell anything like that, Sarah. I doubt even Svyer could. What's really affecting you right now is pure *power*."

Though I suspected that power *was* changing her, and not just her hormones. There was a different kind of tissue developing around the lifeform that I'd never encountered before, nor did it feel like the descriptions of normal fetal structures that I was dredging up in my head from my healing and anatomy classes. Then again, I was no healer, let alone a birth specialist, and Sarah was human, at least by birth.

I made a mental note to get Sarah to Svyer again—soon. The foreign cells were only just forming, at a slow enough rate that I reluctantly decided another professional examination could wait. I would not stress Sarah out about it now, not with her current mood and energy level. No changes in her body were going to harm her in the next day or so...and the next day would determine whether they would ever get the chance to.

"Then look at the power," Sarah said, unusually snappish. "Give your best guess. Is my Ice going to overwhelm her? Harm her?"

I took a deep breath. "You seem to have reached an equilibrium again. I would say that no, the...child will be alright for tonight."

Her shoulders sank, and she let out a long breath of relief. When I withdrew my power, she leaned back against me. I wrapped my arms around her and held her for a moment, and we both said and did nothing else for at least a dek or two.

Too soon, she sighed again and shifted forward to stand up, and I let her go. "Do we have to go back?" she said wearily, all the exhaustion of her long, taxing day showing at once.

I had already been thinking along the same lines, so I had an answer ready.

I spoke as I stood. "I don't think so. Let me make some calls to be sure, but everyone is settled in, and we've been over the defense plans a hundred times by now. Practically speaking, there's not much else for us to do but rest. Given the danger to you, and how quickly you can get us there if needed, I don't think anyone would blame us if we got that rest here."

Sarah hesitated, longing crossing her face for a moment as she cast her eyes at the water-room door and the bedroom beyond—at the privacy and rest that she loved so dearly, beckoning to her. I secretly urged her too, for similar, if slightly different reasons: for the safety this isolated sanctuary offered her, partly, but for once, I had an even stronger desire than her immediate safety.

I wanted her to myself tonight. All of her, my star—body and soul. In that moment, I wanted nothing more than to scoop her up and carry her to that bed and make her forget about pain and danger and evil and duty and family and Trees...about anything else except me.

On this, the last night we might have together in this life, I wanted her more than I had ever wanted her before, and for months now, I had already wanted her more than anything. And I wanted her to want *me* just as much—to feel this soul-rending desire that would make her choose me, choose life, over everything.

For a moment, I thought she would.

Then...I watched her face firm, and with a sinking flameheart, I knew what my *sera* would decide.

"No," she said quietly. "We should be there tonight. With them. There will be other nights to leave them behind. Not tonight."

I swallowed. I couldn't help making at least one attempt to persuade her. "Rachel is already spending the night there, remember? And David, Kor, and Yvera."

The rest of her family would retreat to their hold for most of the night, to take advantage of both its safety and comfort, until the time came for the older ones to rise, return, and get in position for the battle. But Rachel—and David as her rightwing—had volunteered to stay in the Temple, and the two of them had been deferentially given one of the smallest of serviceable rooms to themselves. I had deliberately left Sarah's and my final location to be determined, hinting we should wait to see how Sarah was faring and what the threat level to her might be. Sarah hadn't protested the ambiguity, nor had anyone else.

"I know," she said, gaze distant. "But I shouldn't let my Heir take on that burden alone. I need to be there, for my Tree, and our people need us to be there for them. To see us staying with them, enduring the same conditions, sleeping on the floor with them."

Then that was that, and I took deep but hopefully subtle breaths to reconcile myself to her choice. I had given my word to myself when I had let her back in: her choice, her happiness, above everything. Especially if that choice was, in fact, our duty to our people.

She was right: if we lived, there would be other nights. Perhaps those nights would be better than tonight would have been, without all this weight.

"So," I said, as lightly as I could, "does that mean no private room for us?"

Sarah shook her head, finally looking at me with a thin smile. "I think if we'd wanted one of those, we should have asked for it earlier. Sorry. But I really do think it's better if we sleep in the main barracks room. Same conditions, remember?"

I sighed with mock heaviness. "Better for appearances, maybe, but we'll see how much sleep *I'll* be getting tonight, worried about how exposed you'll be."

These were our most trusted elites and warriors of the Warflight, and the most trusted of them would watch us the whole night. I had personally vetted everyone that day for any trace of consumption, as had Kor with his latest method, and they were staying within a Tree's Temple besides. And yet, you just never *knew*....

"True," Sarah said, smile turning teasing. "After your wake-up reaction this morning, I pity anyone who gets close to me with you sleeping beside me. Seems to me like you'll stab first and ask questions later."

"You laugh," I said, raising an eyebrow, "but I *will*."

"Oh, I'm not laughing," she said, smile dying. "I know."

CHAPTER TWENTY-THREE

TIMING

SARAH

SOMETHING FELT FAMILIAR ABOUT making my rounds that night through the Temple. It reminded me of the long nights during Ben's month of absence, when I would pace through my family's hold after everyone had gone to bed. I told myself I was patrolling, making sure everything was well, doing my duty as Queen. In reality, I was wandering like a listless insomniac, haunted by the ghosts of the time Ben and his wings had been there.

This time, there was no self-deception about duty. My rounds were sober, sometimes even heavy or painful as I greeted one person after the other, any of whom might die for me tomorrow. But my steps had purpose, and that made them stronger and surer than my empty wanderings ever had been. No ghosts of the past haunted me now—only a burning in my belly and a stillness settling over my heart.

I checked every room, to see and be seen, to listen, to ask if there was anything I could do. Always, the answer to that question was a no—sometimes grateful, sometimes indulgent, sometimes bemused. Obviously, whatever they might actually require, there were better people than me to help them get it, but I couldn't help but ask; the gesture never seemed to do any harm and usually did some good.

Most of the accessible, usable rooms served some purpose: sanitation, storage, command, communication, and so on. The two biggest rooms had become our barracks and our infirmary. The welcome chamber, once packed with people and equipment, was now left bare to allow the free flow of people. That wasn't just a convenience: the open space might become essential in an evacuation.

All the rightwings from Alyish to David had insisted we plan for such an outcome. In such an extremity, Lizzy was to throw open the gate from within our hold, allowing whatever dramá David and I couldn't surge away (assuming we were even alive) to flee on foot through the gate and into the Seventh Realm. Not even Michael raised a single objection to that plan—not when he could see for himself how many good people were putting their necks out for us. Even though that plan exposed our family to greater risk than ever before: from disease, from a sleeper agent, or even from consumed slipping through and the Devourer finally discovering just where our sanctuary was in the vast universe.

We weren't going to be blindly trusting. We were mitigating the worst risks by having Mom, Lizzy (when she wasn't needed to perform that one duty), and the littles sleeping and spending the day of the battle in Rachel's suite, which was hidden and inaccessible to anyone but her (and perhaps me, if my access hadn't been revoked when I'd passed the suite on to her, but I hadn't tested that and hadn't cared to).

My rounds, as they had before, led my feet that night to finally stop in front of the arched double doors of the moongate. Though before, I had always come to the Ythra gate inside my hold, and I would hastily close it for the night, trying to think as little as possible about what I was doing and the heartbreak of another day without Ben coming through.

This gate was already closed, never having been opened today, and instead of the Sunfilled crest of a three-pronged crown circling a sun, a white Tree glowed softly on its surface. Instead of hastening away, I instead stood still in quiet contemplation, considering the turns my life had taken to bring me to this spot at this moment.

The past two and a half months of my life had been difficult, sometimes excruciating, with the greatest dangers and heartbreak I had ever been through in my nearly nineteen years. Thinking about it all now, I could scarcely believe I had survived.

And yet, I wouldn't take it back. Not a day—not even one of the long, hopeless nights I had spent wandering, when it felt like I was wading up to my neck through sludge and darkness, unsure if I would ever see the light again.

Those nights, and all the other dangerous and painful ones of the past few months, made me into the kind of person who could not just survive this night but be happy in the ones after. The happiness that I had felt these past two days and the even greater kind that I could feel waiting for me just around the corner were unlike any I could have ever *imagined* two and a half months ago.

More than I would have thought was possible to feel.

Part of me wished I could whisper back through time and tell the stressed-out high school senior I had been at the beginning of this year that it was good I was trying hard and learning so much, but that it truly wasn't the end of the world if I got an A minus instead of an A—or even if I got a D. That it didn't truly matter which college I chose. That I and my family were both strong enough for me to go off on my own to start my own branch of our forest.

Part of me wished I could tell that terrified girl who had been strapped to an altar within her first few minutes in the Six Realms that she would not just survive—all her dreams that were so deep she had not even yet dared dream them were within reach, and she had just been put on the path to find them.

And yet...how could she have understood that? How could she have *known*, to the depths of her heart, to the marrow of her bones, as I did now, without learning that for herself? There were lessons I could have shared, ones I hoped to share with my child one day to ease her way, and I pondered them as I felt her flame burn within me. And yet, some lessons I could have learned through no other way than by living them...and choosing to press forward through the dark.

It was the pressing. The uncertainty, the pain, the molding. The choosing...and being chosen. The loving...and being loved. By so many beings—of spirit, of flesh, and of magic.

But none were more precious to me than the one in my abdomen and the one who was making his way to me now with quiet footsteps on the flagstones. I could never have explained to the Sarah of yesterday *why* they were so precious. She could never have imagined them, let alone understood what they could be to her from descriptions alone. She had to discover—and choose—them for herself.

Again.

Ben came to a soft stop beside me, without saying a word. I didn't glance up at him, but I got the impression that he, too, was resting his gaze on the gate, letting me have my moment of quiet and stillness. I found it remarkable that someone who gave a new definition to the phrase "larger than life," someone who could be as deadly as fire and light up a room with his laugh, could also stand with me in my silence and make it more complete for his being there.

Another memory came to me—a better one, though still heavy: the first moment the two of us had stood like this, gazing at the waterfall in my hold's garden, while I contemplated whether to accept the burden of leadership. I had no idea at the time what it meant—no one had even spoken the word *Queen* yet—and yet still I trembled at the thought of accepting. Ben had just stood there with me; even though everything was riding on my decision, even his father's life, he didn't try to persuade me. He just listened to me. He had understood, as no one else could have, the choice I faced, and he had expressed his quiet support for whatever I decided.

I didn't dare ask whether he still felt the same. So much had changed for us both, and we both had been through and sacrificed so much since that point, the question didn't seem fair. Besides...I thought I knew the answer. If our positions were reversed, I wasn't sure I could have even remained silent, as he was now.

Eventually, though, he asked quietly, "Do you think you could sleep now?"

Now, several hours after dark, most of the dramá had gone to bed to be as rested as they could for the battle at dawn. There was no better way to prepare now.

A bit of wisdom I should finally listen to. "I think so. Flame only knows I've had enough early mornings lately."

I lightened my tone. "With you as my bedmate, maybe I'll be able to transition back to a day schedule after all."

I wasn't sure if it was just my imagination, but I seemed to wake more refreshed whenever he slept with me, no matter the time of morning. Since I'd noticed that phenomenon long before he began "sleeping" with me, I suspected it had to do with his imparting his healing energy with me more easily by proximity.

Ben's reply was still quiet, but now it had a grim edge. "I think you will have to sleep whenever your body will let you, night or day."

"Oh," I said, blinking as my hand reflexively went to my abdomen. As usual, Ben foresaw the trouble ahead that I had not: my body's fluctuations, if continued, would *not* be conducive to any regular sleep schedule.

His voice softened. "That's why I think you should try to sleep now, if you can."

"You think midnight might be a problem?" I said uneasily, tightening that hand over my stomach.

"If the pattern holds," he said heavily.

"How long do we have?" I asked, looking down at my dramá-made watch and tapping its interface to activate it.

Ben shrugged. "Here, your guess is as good as mine. This part of Earth doesn't seem far off from Temple time, though." He was referring to his Temple of Flame, which served as their inter-Realm standard and thus was the time my watch was set to.

"Yes, I noticed," I said absently.

Odd, that, with the differences in seasons and latitudes, let alone any more static differences such as orbit or planet size. The Temple of Flame was on the equator of Ythra and had its winter solstice two months ago. The Temple of Ice was in the far north, and the time was in the fall.

Or...it should have been.

I did the calculations rapidly in my head. Then stilled.

"What?" Ben asked, so he must have been watching me more closely than he let on. He turned to face me, looking me straight on.

"Ben.... How much daylight would you say we got here today? Here, at the Temple of Ice, on Earth?"

He paused for a moment. "When I got here, it was maybe a deken or two after dawn, so all told...about fourteen deken, give or take...."

He trailed off as he realized what that meant. We had warned them, Dad and I. We had told them it should be roughly the beginning of October—officially fall, with the days getting shorter, *especially* this far north. Without access to Google or an encyclopedia, and with our ice calls to the most believing of our extended family and friends mysteriously not working, we didn't know *exactly* how short, but....

"That's too much sunlight, isn't it?" Ben said, face hardening as his battle mind engaged, assessing this new information and incorporating it into his schema of the battle ahead. He would leave the *why* to people like me, Kor, and Dad. His mind, programmed to help us survive, leaped to the *what*.

I looked at him in trepidation, and he at me with hard gold, when both of us realized it at the same time: the two-edged sword.

The dramá might miraculously have more daylight than we'd thought they would have to defend us, but *we* Moontouched would have less darkness.

And the dawn, with all the horror it brought, might come sooner than we thought.

"How could we not have noticed?" Kor groaned as he ran both his hands through his short curls.

Ben and I were with him, Yvera, Alyish, Dad, Michael, David, and Rachel, in the small, formerly bare room that, today, began its short life as a storage area and now served another purpose as a cramped, ad hoc meeting room.

"Probably because it's been such a crazy day for everyone," David said wearily from where he was perched on top of a barrel, slumped against the wall. Yvera stood protectively next to him, and her glares before the meeting began seemed to say that this had better not be about anyone asking anything more of him.

"You don't understand," Kor growled. "We live our *lives* by the sun. We're not familiar with Sekinek, yes, but we still should have noticed how long the day was after Jake's warning. *I* should have noticed."

"Kor," I said quietly. "You've been stretched a thousand different ways today. I think you've been more in demand than anyone, even Ben or Alyish. Give yourself a bit more grace for having missed a detail like that on a day like today."

He gave me a hot glare that said, even without an inner voice, that he had not forgotten *one* detail that only his lack of time to even breathe had kept him from prying from me.

"Besides," Dad said, "the lengthened day gave your people necessary strength today, didn't it?"

Kor only huffed, meaning Alyish was the one to answer. "It most certainly did. We accomplished far more in our fortification efforts than we'd hoped."

In fact, we'd sent the builders, architects, and artificers home already. They had accomplished enough to give us what we needed to get through the night, and we figured there was no point in them working right up until the Tree's deadline if we wouldn't have time afterward to make use of it.

Alyish went on, his voice musing, "Relatively few people knew about the probably shortened daylight hours. The rest simply didn't know what to expect and didn't know to inform us of any divergence from that expectation. If any of them thought of it, they must have assumed it is summer here. The rest of us who knew *have* simply been busy, and it's easier to lose track of the hours down here, where we've spent much of our time. Though we've brought over some timekeeping candles, they can't be everywhere, and only one of us has one of those 'watches' to track the deken so conveniently and accurately."

He gestured to my wrist, and I winced. I, of all people, had the least excuse—no less because my intestines seemed to be such a victim of the time of day. But it was my watch that had proved to everyone just now that we had indeed gotten fourteen deken of daylight.

He finished, with no judgment in his voice. "The rest of us have to rely on our memories and impressions, and those, as our scholars have warned us many times, are often distorted."

"But *how*?" Kor demanded. "If we are within Earth's northern arctic circle weeks into this hemisphere's fall, *how* did we get *fourteen* deken of daylight?"

Alyish looked at me. "Did you speak with your Tree?" he asked, voice mild.

I swallowed. "I tried while Ben was gathering all of you. She didn't appear or say anything to me."

Nor had She when I'd come to Her as the second-to-last stop in my rounds for the night, right before I ended at the moongate.

"Then I suppose we are not meant to know the answer," Alyish concluded, face calm.

His words echoed Ben's from a couple of days ago. *Sometimes we're not meant to figure some things out until a certain point.*

Then, oddly, something else he said soon after came to me, with the same discordant feeling I'd felt then.

Nothing has control over time itself, Sarah.

He was right about the first thing, but wrong about the second—I felt that now.

The Tree...had given us more *time*.

I felt the rightness of that conclusion in my very iceheart. I became still, so overcome by the conviction and implications of that insight that I spaced out of the ongoing conversation. Kor was moaning about something, probably cursing the reticence and unilateral actions of Trees. Alyish and Dad were talking in much more pragmatic tones, speaking about the adjustments to our plans. I should have taken part, but all their voices faded to the background as I stared sightlessly ahead.

Nothing has control over time itself, Sarah.

Except perhaps the Tree of Ice. How, I still didn't know. Nor why. Obviously, more daylight helped us today. As did the match between Ythra's Temple time and...

Earth's.

Today, at least, the Temple of Ice and the Temple of Flame were in almost perfect sync with one another, and with the location of my family's hold in the Seventh Realm. Even though they had no logical reason to be.

At the least, that appeared to be a sign—that there was indeed some grand overarching purpose in all of this, that the Trees were in control. One of Them...over time itself.

Which was still nothing less than mind-boggling, no matter how long I sat there with the feeling. I felt an echo of the same incredulity that I felt when Kor had described the gift that the Tree of Flame had given to Her Tolsyon heirs: to surge to the ether, becoming invisible and unsubstantial—practically unstoppable.

Yet to have control over *time*....

"Sarah," Ben said quietly.

I started, even though he was standing right in front of me and had been for at least a few moments, judging from his proffered hand.

"Oh, sorry," I said, flushing. I took that hand and let him steady me as I slid off my barrel.

To my surprise, we were among the last people in the room. Only Dad lingered, and he was studying me.

I blinked. "Where'd everyone go?"

"To get some rest," Ben said. "As should we. We've given our message. Now there's nothing else we can do."

"Right," I said, but my eyes drifted to meet Dad's.

His silvers were piercing, and with a tingle down my spine, I thought he had guessed much the same thing I had. Yet all he said was, "Go on. The mysteries of the universe can wait for one night."

Especially if our Tree can make that night as long or short as She likes, I thought before I could help myself.

I sighed and shook my head. Our Tree would not use a power like that on a whim, and I had no idea what it might cost Her to do so when She had to. The cost and rules that must come with such an ability *had* to be the reason She hadn't used it to ease our way before, right?

Or...had She?

"Sarah," Ben said, with an edge to his voice now.

"Right," I repeated, once again snapping out of my thought spiral.

Ben sighed and clenched my hand. "Safe sleep, Jake," he said to Dad over his shoulder, and he tugged me forward.

"Safe sleep," Dad murmured behind us.

Ben stayed silent as we walked down the near-empty hall lit with night-dimmed lightgems that had been stuck to the ceiling at needed intervals. This time, it wasn't the easy silence of before. As I thought through the past few minutes, I realized I couldn't remember Ben's voice joining in the discussion at any point while I was spaced out, and now I had a guess why.

He had already come to any conclusion they had about what could be done, so instead...he had been watching me.

You're probably wondering what I was thinking about, I sent to him, my inner voice quiet.

Yes, he responded, tone neutral. *Is it something you can tell me, though?*

I hesitated. The glimmer of insight sounded simple on the surface, but it was just so heavy, so monumental—and ran directly counter to what he firmly believed about the universe. I didn't feel any injunction from my Tree not to share, yet I felt like I needed evidence, or at least to have processed it myself for a bit longer, before I told him.

I think, eventually. But not right now. You're right—now, we need sleep.

I figured you'd say something like that, Ben said heavily.

Silence fell between us again, yet it was still uneasy. But at that moment, we reached the "barracks" room, and even inner voices weren't practical while Ben nodded in greeting to the guards as we entered and an aide hurried up to us, gestured for us to follow, and led us to the spot they'd set up for us. My gaze fell over the rows of sleepers and piles of belongings on the floor, the crates and barrels stacked in corners, and portable tables set up along the walls. I wondered what this cavernous room had been used for in its glory days. Now, it looked like a bomb shelter.

One day, I told myself.

One day, hopefully not too far into the future, my clan would grow in numbers, time, and resources, and we would restore our Tree's Temple to what it should be. We would repair the cracks in the floors and walls, excavate the collapsed corridors and rooms, and flood Her halls with light. But for tonight, we gathered here and used this space to defend Her and each other, and that would have to be enough.

The aide led us along the edge of the long, rectangular room. The only lighting was an occasional red gem stuck to the wall, glowing only brightly enough to illuminate the perimeter paths, letting the middle of the room fade to restful darkness too deep for my unadjusted human eyes to penetrate.

About midway down, we came to two pallets in the outermost row that had been pushed together. That combination seemed to be the only accommodation we'd been given; otherwise, our blankets, pillows, and scant, two-foot-wide border space seemed to be identical to all the others around, which was just what I had requested. The aide gestured uncertainly, as if double-checking this was acceptable, and I gave him a smile of reassurance and gratitude. Ben nodded as well, and the aide left, relieved.

As we pulled aside the covers and kneeled, I spotted a familiar purple braid out of the corner of my eye and glanced at our right neighbor. I saw two glints in the dim lighting that told me Yvera's eyes were cracked open and watching.

It's torched about time, she said silently to the two of us.

Then she turned over, putting her back to us.

If Kor was to be at our left, that explained the empty pallet. Who knew what time *he* would allow himself to sleep tonight. When I glanced around, I saw Ordran standing nearby at attention, watching us as unobtrusively as he could. With his back to the nearest night light, I couldn't read his expression, but he nodded to me. I realized there was a cost to my decision to be with them: some people might benefit, but others would get less sleep than they would have if Ben and I had gone somewhere less exposed. I would have to weigh that hidden cost more carefully next time.

Ben and I settled down, and once we got the covers and pillows situated, Ben pulled me against him. I snuggled into him with relief, glad he allowed that much. Even so, when we became still, I sent to him, *Are you mad at me?*

What? he asked, tilting his head more toward me. The shadows hid his expression, but his tone sounded surprised. *Why would I be mad at you?*

I don't know. Something's *bothering you.*

I felt as much as heard him let out a deep breath. *Nothing...that's your fault. Nothing that* should *be bothering me, anyway.*

Can you tell me what it is, anyway? Instead of wondering about "should" and "should not"?

Alright, Ben said. *But I warned you—I know I'm being a dimtorch about this.*

Now who needs to stop worrying about whether his feelings are silly? I teased gently.

He sighed again and held me more tightly for a moment. After a bit of silence, he finally said in a raw, quiet voice, *I want you to choose me.*

I blinked in the darkness. *What do you mean?*

I mean...no matter what happens tomorrow, whatever...sacrifices you're asked to make, I don't want you to make them. I want...you to choose me, no matter what.

I suddenly understood what this was about—with a soft clarity so piercing, I knew it didn't come entirely from me.

Ben didn't just want me to survive, didn't just want me to stay with him. He wanted me to *choose* him, once and for all, above everything. This situation, my Tree's unexplained actions, and maybe even our child were hitting all his nerves, exposing all his only partially healed wounds, bringing out all of his insecurities, all in one day. A dark voice inside him was telling him that all those things would go away, or at least become bearable, if he could believe that in the end, I would put him above everything. As he had so often, from the beginning, done for me.

This entire day, I had done the exact opposite, putting everyone else before him: my family, our people, my Tree, and perhaps most problematic of all, our child. And tomorrow....

There was a part of him that *still* doubted he was worthy of love—and thus doubted that I could love him as much as he loved me. *Need* him as desperately as he needed me. If I did, I would choose *him.*

When I said nothing right away, Ben loosened his hold on me and muttered, *Like I said, I know I shouldn't—*

I cut him off by grabbing him behind the neck and pressing my lips to his. His body responded, pulling me in and moving his lips hungrily against mine.

Even as his inner voice said with a strained edge, *Er, Sarah? Now really isn't the time....*

I slowed and pulled away tenderly, before we'd even lost our breath. He let my head settle back on my pillow, but otherwise he still held me tightly, and his forehead touched mine, expression unreadable in the darkness.

I love you, I said, reaching up to touch his bearded cheek.

How many times had I told him that today? Had I said it even once?

Flame and Ice, how I love you, Ben—and need you, and want you. As I need and want only you.

He let out a shaky breath and tightened his hold on me, crushing me to his chest with one hand and knotting the fingers of his other in my hair, pulling my head in to rest the side of my face against his neck.

Yet I knew I hadn't entirely addressed the problem, that a voice inside him was still saying, *More than anything?*

Yes, I whispered. *More than anything.*

I felt him swallow. *Then why.... Tomorrow....*

I'll do what my Tree asks me tomorrow because *I love you.*

I...don't understand.

What do you think would happen to you if I didn't obey Her, Ben?

He became still. *You...just always seem to do what's right*—because *it's right. Not because you....*

I think you give me way too much credit, I said dryly. Then I repeated in a kinder tone, *What would happen to* you *if I disobeyed the Tree?*

He didn't answer for a long moment. He knew as well as I did the universe-wide catastrophe that could result if the Tree of Ice fell...and even if he and his people fled with their lives intact, they might not be safe for long with a triumphant and engorged Devourer on their heels.

Ben would *not* flee. He would stand with me to the bitter end—and if I rebelled against the Tree's will by even the slightest measure, it *would* be a bitter end. For us both. In trying to save my life, I might well lose it...and his.

We had both known this, and both knew that the other knew it. What I had not known was that Ben was unaware of my emotions behind what I was doing, the *reasons* I was contemplating sacrifice. Those mattered, even if the result was the same in the end. They made the difference between feeling loved...or forsaken.

Ben theoretically knew why his parents were no longer with him, yet any thoughts of their sacrifice being for *him* only caused him pain because he still thought himself unworthy. Too easily, he could tell himself they were thinking of their people and their Tree, of anyone but him. If Ben could have understood—in his heart, mind, and soul—why his parents had died for *him*, and would have if he had been the only being in the universe...he would be a changed man.

I pulled my head back to rest on the pillow again, nose to nose with him, and once again placed my hand on his cheek.

Ben, I said sadly. *I'll follow the Tree because that's my best chance of saving* you. *If I'm going to die tomorrow...I'm going to die for you.*

You...think of it that way? Even his inner voice was raw with emotion. *You're not thinking of...others? Your family?*

I won't lie and say I'm thinking of no one else...but no one else's loss would destroy *me, Ben. No one's but yours. I need you like I need no other. Whatever* *I choose tomorrow, it* will *be you.*

He untangled his hand from my hair and brushed the side of my face with the backs of his fingers, almost reverently. He came forward and kissed me—slowly. So slowly, so tenderly, perhaps more so than ever before. Normally, he scorched me with his kisses. With this one, he caressed me...and gave me the salt of his tears.

When he pulled away, I wondered if he could see the way my burning, wet lips tugged into a thin smile. *So, you see,* you're *not the one being silly or* *selfish right now. I am.*

He snorted softly, the air brushing my face. *Hardly. If you ever* truly *do* *something selfish, it will be because the rest of us have finally become unworthy* *of you. In which case, you won't be selfish, after all.*

I just sighed. Sometimes, the way he saw and believed in me was wonderful. It made me able to do things I thought I could never do, to be what I could never have imagined. Sometimes...it was part of the problem.

After a few moments, Ben's tone lightened, becoming teasing. *So, we gave them a good show of solidarity. Think we can sneak away now?*

I sighed, having heard the undercurrent of hopefulness he had probably been trying to conceal. *Tell you what. After this is over, I will give you my undivided attention for as many days and nights as you want. Whatever you want to do, wherever you want to go, that's what we'll do.*

He had served his people his whole life, until it had nearly destroyed him. Now he was putting everything he had left on the line for my people. He deserved—and they owed—him that much. For the good of all.

That's quite a dangerous promise, he said. He pulled me in closer and began rubbing tantalizing patterns on my back. *What if I never want to give you back?*

I smothered a laugh. *Unfortunately for you, you'll have quite a few people to contend with in that scenario. Our formidable leftwings among them.*

Ben sighed and stopped his rubbing. *I suppose I know better than to cross your father.*

Besides, I said in a kinder tone. *I don't think you could stand a long vacation. I give you five days, tops, before you get restless and need to get back into the thick of things.*

I'll take that bet, Ben said, his grin visible even to me in the darkness. *Five days, at least. If I can stand more and we can finagle more from our leftwings, then we take more.*

I smiled, my chest lightening at just the *thought* of Ben giving himself that much rest, that much time for him to heal and me to love him.

You're on.

I WOKE IN THE middle of the night with a now-familiar wrench in my gut and bile rising in my throat. Ben tightened his hold on me, still not yet conscious enough to remember what was happening, so I had to once again surge away without explanation.

I didn't know why I kept coming back to our suite in the Seventh Realm, except that each time, it felt like the most private, secure place in the universe for me and my child. I needed that feeling of safety at such a primordial level, I reached for it without thinking. I didn't even have to summon an ice image first anymore, the image of where I needed to go was so clear in my mind.

I collapsed in front of the toilet and heaved again.

Nausea was the worst feeling in the worlds, I decided. Even though it passed soon after Ben got working on me, in the moment, the panic, stench, suffocation, and pain of it always felt like a kind of death. Every time.

This time was worse than any other, though, because the bile didn't just burn my throat. It sliced it with cold razor blades. When I blinked open my watery eyes, I saw why.

There...were shards of ice in my vomit. Edged with blood.

I was cold, all over. Far, far too cold.

BEN! I mentally sobbed.

"I'm here, I'm here!" he said hurriedly, even with his voice still thick from sleep, and in the next moment, he was wrapping his arms around me, sinking his power into me.

At first, he focused his power, as usual, on the flux of magic that was making me wretch, but I cried, *No, heal* her. *Focus on* her. *She could be dying, Ben. Keep her alive!*

"Sarah...." Ben said hesitantly. "I don't know how—"

Wasn't it obvious? How could he not see?

Make me warm! Give me Flame!

"Sarah, you're of Ice—"

MAKE. ME. WARM.

A second later, heat filled me from head to toe, as if Ben had dumped me into a hot tub. I sank into those warm depths with exquisite relief, even as the warmth caused my frosted flesh pain. It wasn't just the thaw: Ben was right—I was not meant to be this hot. Ben's warmth was the only kind I could crave or even stand, and even then, he had never risked saturating me with it like this, and I found it was for good reason. He was giving me a kind of fever with it.

Yet I could take the pain. It was a welcome release from the horror that my body could turn against our child. Perhaps she would have been fine, perhaps it was too soon for my Ice to harm her, or protections were already in place for her—but I wasn't about to take that risk.

As my heaving slowed to a halt and Ben's warmth wrapped me like a suffocatingly hot cocoon, I wearily wiped my mouth, spat, and sank back into him, letting him roast me from the inside out as much and for as long as he dared.

Eventually, he said, "I think...she's fine, Sarah. I really do."

OK, I rasped. *You can let the heat go.*

I remembered now what this must be costing him, too. To expend this much power when he was at his weakest.... I gripped his knee—the most accessible part of him to me with me sitting in his lap like this—and sent him a trickle of power in compensation.

"Sarah, I'm fine," he snapped at me, yet there was an exhausted edge to his voice, and I thought it was from more than just a lack of sleep. "Save it for yourself."

"I won't miss this much," I croaked. Painfully, and audibly so, because Ben sighed and put his hands on my throat, refocusing all his power there.

"What in the name of the Flame...." he growled, presumably at the extent of the damage.

There was ice, I said, switching back to my inner voice. *In the vomit.*

Ben became still—dangerously so. I relaxed even more into him, even though that made him shift his hands to keep them at my throat, hoping my calm posture would soothe him in turn. He healed me in silence, not saying a word as his power traced from my throat and down into my chest and stomach.

When his power finally retreated, leaving me feeling whole as ever, I couldn't help asking, "How bad was it?"

"It could have been worse," he said. "The worst of the lacerations were in your upper esophagus. I don't think the shards formed until then."

Even though I probably should have shut my mouth then, my mind was too bleary to keep my curiosity in check. "Interesting. As it passed my iceheart, maybe?"

"Or got far enough away from your Flame-heated abdomen," Ben said darkly.

"She was protected?" I asked, straightening in my eagerness. "The whole time?"

"I think so. There's this kernel of heat down there now that even I'm having a hard time penetrating. You can't feel it?"

"I...guess I can," I said in a daze. Now that I thought about it, and my hand went under my shirt and drifted across the bare skin of my abdomen, I *could* feel a spot that was warmer than the rest. And...a spot that was colder, too....

Probably just my imagination.

I let out a breath. "So, he might have scared me for nothing."

Still, I thanked Ice and Flame that Ben had been there and had done what I asked. Just in case we were wrong.

"He?" Ben asked dryly.

I blinked. "Did I say he?"

"You did."

I rubbed my eyes and groaned. "I'm just tired, I guess."

He grunted. "Or maybe there really *isn't* a gender to speak of, yet, and your subconscious knows it?"

"Not true," I huffed. "She's a *she*. I know it. You'll see."

Ben sighed. "Well, I suppose I shouldn't be arguing with the daughter of a seer."

"That's right," I said. "But most importantly, with your wife."

"True enough—" He cut off and sighed again. "Kor's calling."

"Oh, right," I groaned, shifting off his lap so he could answer. I half crawled, half stumbled to the sink to rinse out my mouth. "I'm surprised it's not Yvera this time."

I spat as quietly as I could as Kor's voice drifted to me through the scale spell, sounding furious. "Ben, what the hellfrost is going on? And don't give us that ashdust about Sarah overdoing it this time."

"Us?" Ben said. "Yv's there?"

"I'm here," Yvera said. I winced. She did not sound pleased, and I didn't blame her. "Tyri woke me when you two disappeared, then I found Kor."

Tyri must have been the elite on watch. It figured that Kor hadn't gone to bed yet, which also explained why he was coherent right now.

"Now," Kor ground out, "give us the truth, or I'm getting Sarah's own wings involved. What's wrong?"

Ben sighed heavily and looked up at me. I turned to face him and said quietly, "Go ahead."

He looked back down at the blue scale in his hands, face grim. "Are you two alone?"

"Obviously."

"Alright, here's the truth," Ben said matter-of-factly. "Sarah is pregnant, at least as of last morning. And there's been...difficulties. Already."

Silence.

"What?" Kor said. "You can't be serious."

"Oh, I am dead serious." Ben's eyes were his hardest gold.

"He's right," I said wearily, sinking down next to him and peering around his shoulder into the scale. "There's really no other explanation, and Svyer confirmed it when we got back."

Only Kor's face was visible in whatever small, dark room they were standing in, but more distantly, I heard Yvera's snort. "Told you so."

Told....

"You knew?" I said incredulously.

"Well, duh." She leaned into view to give me one of her *looks*. "Ever since you two got back, Ben's been acting all weird about you. Even more than usual, I mean. And that second time you disappeared, you looked about ready to puke. I can put things together. But *this* guy thought I was a dimtorch."

She elbowed Kor, hard enough that he hissed and our view wavered for a moment.

"Don't make me cite fertility statistics again," Kor snapped at her. "Especially for *Sunfilled*."

"Which you knew off the top of your head," she said, the eye roll clear from her tone even without a clear view of her now. If *nerd* had been in her vocabulary, she would no doubt have said it then.

Instead, she said, "Besides, Sarah's not Sunfilled."

"No, she's not," Kor said, his eyes resting on me. "She's not even dramá. That's the problem, isn't it?"

My gut twisted in an echo of the nausea. "Probably."

Kor let out a choice curse and ran his free hand through his hair. "Gah, you two. You always have to make things more complicated than they have to be, don't you?"

"Isn't this the part where we're supposed to say 'warm hearth, blessed birth'?" Yvera said dryly.

She was taking this a lot better than I would have thought. She *had* moved on.

"Not tonight," Kor said with a scowl. He looked back at us. "I'll be happy for you two in a few days, but right now.... This could *not* have been more poorly timed."

With Trees involved? Think again, I thought. But that wasn't a discussion I wanted to get into with Kor tonight.

"Look, Kor, I'm going to be fine. So far, Ben's been able to handle it. It's just a bit of nausea now and then."

Mostly. From the glare Kor gave me, I knew he could see my omission written on my face.

He let it go for the moment, grumbling, "No wonder you've been looking pale. Ben, are you getting enough fluids in her?"

"I've been trying," Ben said, giving me a look.

Kor sighed. "I'll...see if I can scrounge up some icemint. That's probably the best thing for her right now."

We'll see, I thought, thinking of the candle flame in my belly.

"Meanwhile, you two get some sleep, if you can," he said. "I assume both of you are ensconced in that 'unknown location' in the Seventh Realm?"

"Yes," Ben said, with the faintest of twitches at the corners of his mouth.

"Then stay there for the rest of the night."

"You don't think we should come back?" I said sheepishly.

"That might be more disruptive than helpful at this point. Tyri woke Yvera and fetched me as quietly as she could, but some people had to have noticed you are gone by now. They can simply assume we've all gone to deal with something important, so you two can get some better sleep in a proper bed—and have privacy if your nausea strikes again. Your...condition is something we want to conceal for another day or two if we can."

I glanced at Ben as an uneasy thought just occurred to me. He looked back at me; from his grim expression, he seemed to think the same thing.

"What *now*?" Kor growled.

"It's just...." I said. "The next time that's likely to happen...is dawn. *Exactly* at dawn."

Kor was silent for a moment, then let out another curse. "As I said, *timing*."

"Alright," Yvera said, much more calmly. "I'll have a word with Alyish. We'll adjust the plans so you're out of view at dawn."

"Thanks, Yv...and sorry."

To my shock, she said firmly, "Don't be. That child could be Ben's Heir, and Flame knows how we need one."

We all stared at her, even Kor.

"What?" she said with another eye roll, folding her arms. "The timing? Really? This has *Trees* written all over it."

Yvera...was far more perceptive than we sometimes gave her credit for. She had instincts as sharply honed as one of her blades and a faith in her Tree that was as straightforward as Kor's was convoluted.

Which made me wonder if she was right about the Heir thing, too. Unseen to either of Ben's wings, my hand went protectively to my stomach, and Ben took my other in his free one and gave it a tight clench. When I glanced up at him, he was looking at Yvera in the scale, and his face was hard.

Yes...this situation was hitting *all* his nerves.

Chapter Twenty-Four

GOODBYE

Koriben

Too few deken later, my timekeeper candle woke me with a jolt. Sarah must have been so exhausted, she didn't even stir, even as close as she was to me.

I relaxed with a deep sigh, then turned my head to look at her in the darkness. I remembered falling asleep on my side, holding her, but as usual, I had fallen onto my back at some point, letting her go. I truly hoped there wasn't some kind of omen there.

I tried to take comfort from the fact that Sarah, far from letting any distance come between us, had snuggled further against me and wrapped her arms around my right one, substituting it for the pillow she usually hugged to her chest.

I gazed at her face for probably too long, thinking all the thoughts I should not have been. With all my might, I fought the desire to hide here with her until the end of time, to let it all go. Everything except her. But I knew what the result of that would be.

If I reneged on all my oaths and duties as King now, I would lose her even more surely than if the Devourer took her—because then, once and for all, I would prove myself unworthy of her. Even if she didn't turn from me, I would turn from her, no longer able to bear that gulf between us—the gulf of my own making, between the man and King I should have been and the monster I made myself into.

I hardly knew what finally decided me in the end. It was an emotion too quiet, soft, and small to be called courage—at least at first.

But when I turned on my side, cupped the back of her head, and softly kissed her awake, when she stirred and then blinked open her eyes to blindly meet mine in the darkness, that candle flame surged into a bonfire that filled my blood and fused itself into my very bones. Then, I knew its name.

It was love.

"I love you," I whispered.

The words came effortlessly. In fact, at that point, it would have been a struggle to contain them. At long last, I knew why they had become so difficult for me to say, to Sarah most of all.

The first time I had told Sarah I loved her, it had been in goodbye, as I held her unconscious body and contemplated going to my death and never seeing her again. Then, again, the second time had been in goodbye, also with her unconscious—except that time, death seemed certain for both of us.

I love you were the last words my father said to me.

On the day of the Battle of the Solstice, Avva caught me as I was rushing out of the command room. It was nearly noon, just before the battle was to begin, and I needed to be in the air with the rest of the Warflight so the shields could activate and seal off the Temple, and I had already delayed more than was right in waiting for Sarah to wake up—in vain.

Too raw from Avva's near-death just that morning, I had not even let myself contemplate the possibility that I could lose my father that night, even though I of all people should have known that was even likelier than my own death. Yet I convinced myself that the Tree could not be that cruel. He and Sarah were meant to be safe. He and Sarah were meant to live. That conviction was the only thing keeping me functioning in that moment as I left them both to go fight.

Even though Avva himself could have been preoccupied, since he was just coming back from his speech, he did not satisfy himself with returning my wave and nod. He grabbed my arm as I passed and made me look him in the eye, and he said with calm intensity, "I love you, Koriben. More than you will ever know."

That was the first time the answering words had ever caught themselves in my throat. Stupidly, immaturely, I had been trying to avoid saying goodbye to him, knowing how Avva's parting words, whatever they would be, would affect me—perhaps even breaking my precarious mental block against thinking of a tomorrow that did not have him in it.

Someone who did not know Avva as well as I did might have mistaken his utter calm for faith that he would be well. I, however, knew it for what it was: he was *decided*. In that moment, I knew—I *knew*—I would not see him again. Not in this life. And yet, I still refused to know.

But the answering words still caught, affected by the subliminal truth I was mightily suppressing. Somehow, I choked them out, because I thought that was the only way he was going to let me go, let me run from him and from the reality he was making me face.

"I love you, Avva," I said tightly, barely meeting his eyes.

Then I pulled away from him and strode away as quickly as I could without looking like the fleeing coward I was.

I had no deeper regret save what I did to Sarah the next morning than how I pulled away and ran from him that day, and I would carry that regret until I could make amends by rushing to him in the next life and throwing my arms around him as I should have done then.

Now, I realized that experience had left me with more than regret. Three such partings in such quick succession gave me the subconscious conviction that to love someone was to lose them, and saying the words out loud was daring the universe to hasten that severing.

For the past two months, the words *I love you* had meant *Goodbye—forever.*

I now loved Sarah more than I loved any mortal alive, and the fear of losing her made saying those words to her more excruciating each time I tried. I could not tell her goodbye. Not *her*.

Only now, with my choice finally, *truly* made, did I realize that fear and love weren't the same thing—that they couldn't even exist in the heart at the same time. Not truly. My fear wasn't fear for *her*—it was fear for myself. It wasn't love—it was selfishness. Now, with my whole body feeling like it was burning with my love for her...I wasn't afraid. Love had been the reason I was so at peace for the two days that I could focus on her.

For the *very first time*, I received an inkling of how Avva could have let Avvi make a choice that would take her from him. How he could be so calm and yet so full of love as he told me goodbye.

To love someone *wasn't* to lose someone. It was to do what was best for them...even if that meant letting them go...

...for a time. But a love like this, shared between Sarah and me, witnessed by Tree and sealed into our very blood by Covenant, was too strong not to bring us back together one day. In that moment, I understood to the depths of my soul that *I could never lose Sarah.*

Not as long as I remained worthy of her.

My Tree, far from being a merciless being willing to sacrifice my heart over and over again for the good of all, had—with far more patience than I deserved—been leading me on the only path that would let me have all my loved ones again. Far from threatening to take Sarah from me, She had *given* Sarah to me...forever.

The only one who could take her from me now...was me. By being so blind, so stupid, so immature as to try to preserve her mortal life at all costs. For seeing this life as the only one there was, and my pain as the only one that mattered. For not loving her enough to let her go.

I always knew, and even believed, that I could trust my Tree. That She only ever did what was right, and only ever asked what was necessary. Yet that knowledge and even that faith weren't enough. I needed to feel it, too, to the depths of my heart, and most important of all, to feel that She *loved me.*

I had not been able to do so for six years. For those six years, that dissonance between my heart and my head had tortured me—and undermined, to a greater degree than I had ever realized, the crucial relationship between the Tree of Flame and Her Heir.

Avvi's death planted a kernel of doubt in my heart that had grown with each subsequent "proof" of the Tree's indifference to my pain, until the doubt became fear—a spiked, choking vine that had nearly strangled me during that month I had pushed everyone out...including Her.

In my final moment of decision to accept Her will, whatever it may be, I finally recognized that it was the vine of fear that was torturing me, not the Tree. As soon as I yanked it up by the roots and threw it from me, love lit up the void it left, first as soft as a candle and then increasing to an inferno forging me anew. Love for Sarah, for my father, for my mother...for my Tree.

Yes, even Her. Because my Tree...loved me. As unworthy as I was. As did everyone else I loved. And because of Her, those ties would never be broken. For that gift, let alone for that love, I could fall at Her feet, and would have if She had appeared in front of me then.

Instead, I promised to do whatever She asked of me...even if that was to let Sarah go.

Was this...what Avva had felt when he told me goodbye?

Was *this* how he could leave me?

Because he loved me?

Because he wanted me to live long enough to understand and feel for myself that kind of love?

Oblivious to the soul-deep transformation I had undergone in the last few dek, Sarah blinked sleepily at me, then smiled. Voice thick from sleep, she responded, "I love you too."

Then she stiffened. "Wait...you said it."

"Yes," I said, my lips pulling into an easy smile.

"That...didn't sound like it was hard for you. Was it?"

"No."

A beat of silence, then when I didn't elaborate, Sarah asked, "Do you...know what made the difference?"

"Yes..." I hesitated. "...but I don't think I can explain."

I was only barely comprehending it in my head and heart, and any words I could think of seemed inadequate or foolish. Even now, I wasn't as good as she was at articulating my feelings and probably never would be.

Not to mention I was embarrassed that it had taken me this long to feel what I should have felt *and* known all along. If I described my epiphany to Yvera, her reaction would be to roll her eyes and say, "Well, *duh*, you dimtorch."

Which was why I never, ever would.

"OK," Sarah said slowly. "Well. Good then, I guess."

After a moment's pause, she said firmly, "But just so you know, I'll still take whatever way comes easiest to you to tell me you love me."

I chuckled, rolled over her, and kissed her languidly—as if we had all the time in the world, and a lifetime of mornings before us, just like this. As I did so, I silently told her over and over again, *I love you. I love you. I love you.*

She responded eagerly, wrapping her arms around me. When I paused in my litany at that latest motion, she said silently, *Do you think we have time...?*

If we make it quick. I pulled away from her lips and began trailing kisses down her neck. *Is that what you want?*

Yes, she said with a groan.

Then the Devourer can wait, I said. Then nibbled at her earlobe. *Assuming there's even anything left of you after I'm done.*

Will you just get a move on, your majesty? she said as she panted.

That royal address used to bother me. More than just the foreign nature of it—we dramá had no equivalent—the word *majesty* seemed like it could never apply to me, and therefore Sarah must have been poking fun at more than just my ignorance of her language and customs. More likely for Sarah and more troubling for me, though, I thought it showed the opposite: that she saw me in an impossibly idealistic light.

Now, those two English words didn't have the same sting they once did. Maybe I'd never be *majestic*, as Avva had been, and as he perhaps was now more than ever. But maybe I could be a better King, husband...and father...than I thought I ever could be.

Perhaps *that* would be the greatest miracle the Tree would ever perform in my life: to make me worthy of the ones who loved me so well.

I chuckled. *As you wish, my star.*

AS SOON AS WE returned to the Temple of Ice, Sarah was pulled into transportation duty once again—this time taking all the gathered warriors to the surface. The shorter distance seemed to help both her and David, as did the nighttime. Shockingly, even though David could only take five or so at a time, Sarah could take three times that number.

"Why do you think that is?" I asked her when I had a spare moment and she was taking a breather.

She shrugged and took another swig from a canteen filled with chilled icemint tea. Kor had shoved four canteens' worth at her when she first arrived, with no other communication than a glare and a snapped, "Drink," before he rushed off again.

I don't know, she said silently, leaving her mouth free to swallow. *It's not about the amount of power, I don't think. If I had to guess, it's because...I already have connections with a lot of them. However small, it seems to help with lashing them to me.*

I just shook my head fondly at her.

What? she said self-consciously.

I don't think you should underestimate the strength of those connections, I said. *I see the way they look at you.*

I found it hard to believe she hadn't either. It wasn't like we were a subtle race in general. Sarah looked away, cheeks heating.

They hardly know me, she muttered.

They know enough.

Whatever good they had heard about her, whatever good they felt for her, not only was it probably true and justified, it was only a fraction of all she was and deserved. Little did they realize she was more of a miracle than they would ever know.

For the most part, I was too much in demand to think, let alone have more of those quiet conversations with her. Then I realized why. At one point, Alyish pulled me aside and asked me, "Have any idea where your leftwing has gotten himself to? That's the second person who's come to me saying he isn't responding to scale calls."

I had one flash of concern. Then, when I glanced around the room, the most likely answer hit me, and I sighed.

Where's the Heir of Ice? I said silently.

Alyish blinked at me, then turned his head discreetly to look for himself.

I don't know, he said grimly. *But I don't see her bodyguard either. Hopefully that means she's just stepped out. Should I send—*

No, I said. *I think I know where they are, and it's best I go get them myself.*

I was loath to take the stomach-churning task upon myself, but on the other hand, I doubted anyone else would have the authority (or gall) to separate the two of them. If Kor was mentally blocking out calls, then he wouldn't hear even mine, which meant going in person.

Alyish blinked at me. *You think they are....*

Even though he was less informed than I was, Avva's sharp, former rightwing caught on to the meaning behind my look, and he cleared his throat. "Ah, well. Then, if you think that is best, I suppose I'll cover for you while you're gone."

As he left, I heard him muttering under his breath, "Now I *really* feel old."

Though I thought I caught a hint of envy in his voice, underneath the crusty irritation.

I grimaced in sympathy as I made my way across the welcome chamber and down the dim corridor toward where I remembered Rachel's temporary room was supposed to be. Alyish's wife died before I was born, and he always served Avva so stoically, without complaint, and spoke about her so seldom that I had never thought until that moment about how difficult that must have been for him—that the very reason he never mentioned her was probably because it was too painful for him to.

If I had to wait over twenty years to be reunited with Sarah...I shuddered and blocked out the thought. Not because I couldn't face it but because now was not the time to. Now was the time to focus.

As I was going to have to remind my leftwing.

Sure enough, when I approached Rachel's bedroom, I caught whiffs of both their scents, twined together and enhanced by the arousal of their magics, and heard quite enough to know what they were about and what dark corner they had secluded themselves in.

I got my final confirmation when Rachel's bodyguard of the deken, Yshra, stepped in front of me and cleared her throat. From the redness of her pale face, now nearly matching the color of her Strongshield hair, it was clear only sheer duty was keeping her here, with her charge fully in her view, and she felt just as duty-bound to warn me what I was stepping into.

"King Kori—"

"Oh, I know, thank you," I said, walking right on past her. Silently, I sent to her, *Sorry about this.*

I approached that corner with caution, careful to avert my eyes, but I saw enough to be relieved that they were both still clothed, at least.

I stopped about five feet from them and cleared my throat. Loudly.

That, of course, got no response. If anything, out of the corner of my eye, I saw Rachel curl even more of herself around Kor, and I had to fight down a gag.

"Kor," I said shortly once I had command of my voice again.

Torch off, he sent me.

I took that as a sign of progress. Still, I hardened my voice to tell him he would not get another verbal warning from me. That next time, I would use force.

"*Kor.* We need you. It's almost time."

Oh, fine.

He pushed off Rachel and straightened, resisting her tugs to pull him back. Whatever words he used to talk her down, he kept them silent and between themselves. As Rachel listened and perhaps replied, she pouted, but I knew Kor had finally convinced her when she let him extricate himself. She scowled at me, silver eyes flashing like daggers for a moment. But when she glanced again at

Kor, who now had his back to her as he walked to me, I saw another flash in them—this time full of a raw, unguarded emotion I knew all too well: a blade double-edged with longing and fear.

Did she honestly care whether Kor lived or died? I had a hard time believing that was possible, but, given she *was* Sarah's sister and the Heir of Ice...I shouldn't assume she didn't have a heart to lose...or to be broken.

When she caught me watching her, her scowl returned, wiping that rare moment of vulnerability from her face, and her hand fell to the gun at her waist. "You'd better take care of him, you royal jerk—or I really *will* shoot a shard through your flameheart this time."

Ignoring the fact that Kor's duty was to protect *me*, I nodded to her. "I'll do my best, ma'am."

I wasn't about to let *anyone* die for me today if I could at all help it—not even Kor. As many times as I'd threatened to kill him myself, I always knew, deep down, that he was one of my closest, dearest friends—at this point, practically a brother. Perhaps...someday he truly would be.

Rachel's scowl deepened, as if she had a hard time doubting my sincerity and was even more furious at me for it.

Kor turned back to her once he reached my side. In an unusually tender voice, he said, "I'll be fine, flameheart. You'll see."

"You'd better," she said, folding her arms with a sniff. "I'm not accustomed to boys dying on me before I can break up with them. I have a reputation to maintain, after all, and it doesn't involve tragedy."

"Hmm, well," Kor said, his usual smirk returning as he blew her a kiss. "Then I'll have to do my best to ruin that reputation in a much *different* way when this is over."

To my surprise, Rachel's cheeks heated, and she seemed to be rendered speechless—something I would not have thought possible before. Kor didn't give her time to recover. He just winked at her, turned on his heel, and began walking back down the corridor. I shrugged at Rachel and turned to follow.

When I caught up, Kor spoke to me silently, his tone taking an abruptly stern turn. *Not. One. Word.*

I wasn't going to say anything, I replied.

I had put Kor through far worse with Sarah. At least he and Rachel had only made me queasy—not jealous or heartbroken. And it wasn't like Sarah and I hadn't had our own...moment...this dark morning. We'd just been lucky enough to have privacy—something that Kor was certain to point out if I tried judging him out loud.

He was silent for a few steps, as if startled I was smart enough not to. Then, as if feeling a flash of guilt he needed to rid himself of, he muttered, *I was intending to say goodbye much earlier than this.*

But it was one thing after another, I assume? I said, not without sympathy.

Worse, he groaned. *I fell asleep.*

I shot him a careful look. He had always claimed ignorance of his quarter-deken-or-so state of utter stupidity upon waking, never seeming to remember what silliness he said or enacted during that time. He believed none of us when we mentioned it. His utter denial of his condition had forced Eskala, upon his ascension as King's leftwing, to take matters into her own hands to vet and prepare his aides to contain his waking nonsense as much as possible. So far, that had been enough to keep the Six Realms from finding out about it.

I'd always had a suspicion about where it had come from.

At Solim's trial, the traitor had been so livid at his brother, Kor, for Kor's condemning testimony against him, Solim had cursed Kor even as the young man cried from his own heartbreak. I had once looked up the trial records to find the exact words, the last ones Solim shouted before he was dragged out of sight and hearing.

May you always be so soft, insipid, and feeble as you are now, O mighty leftwing.

Everyone else had always thought Solim was just saying words, and those were among the mildest he spat at his former brother after his sentencing. Even I thought the same at the time.

But then, after enough mornings being around Kor, I began to think—especially after I emerged from my own haze of grief from my mother's death and the shock of Solim's betrayal. Years went by before I could bear looking up the trial records, but I remembered enough to have long since come to my own conclusions.

Eskala seemed to think my guess was as good as any, however rare true *curses* were these days. There were tales of them from the amá who had come to Ythra from Earth, and it was said that some of them were capable of such dark abuses of power before they were stamped out.

It was possible that someone as intelligent yet twisted as Solim could have dug up the old, dark ways—or, the thought now occurred to me with an inner shudder, have been taught them from the original source. If the Devourer indeed was gaining influence over inclined, hardened hearts, how long could it have whispered its lies into Solim's ears?

The biggest problem with my theory was that Kor wasn't "always" that stupid—*just* for the first fourteen dek or so after waking. The curse as Solim worded it would have been devastating indeed—enough so that I would have had to release Kor as my leftwing, as Solim had no doubt had intended. As unfair as that would have been to Kor, with him not just blameless for his condition but having received it because he saved my life...it would have been crueler to keep him on—and devastating to the Realms.

Perhaps in that, we had our answer, and that was Eskala's addition to my theory: that if Kor was meant to be my leftwing, then when Solim cast his curse, the Tree intervened, just enough to ameliorate his curse to that first fourteen dek of each waking day.

Confused, I had then asked Eskala why the Tree would not have blocked the curse entirely. My father's leftwing and Kor's mentor just shook her head at me with a smile and said there was no way of knowing the mind and ways of the Tree. But her eyes said she had a theory about that, too, and ever since then, I'd tried to guess what it was.

It couldn't be to keep Kor humble—he remembered none of it and thus couldn't be humbled by it. Then perhaps it was for *our* benefit—to remind the rest of us that, as much as he tried to pretend otherwise, Kor was only mortal. Perhaps part of it was to remind *me* what Kor had given up for me.

So, my probe for more information from him now was careful. *You mean you fell asleep at your desk or something?*

No, Kor growled. To my amusement—which I tried hard to conceal—Kor's cheeks were heating. *I fell asleep once I got to her room. We were just sitting on her bedroll, talking, and....*

Ah, I said. *Erm...and what did Rachel think about that?*

She seemed very...confused when I woke up, Kor said, his tone also turning thoughtful. *And...a bit emotional. Have any idea what that's about?*

I have no clue, I said with complete honesty, although I was glad we were using inner voices, because I was trying very hard to fight a laugh. *Kor, you have far more insight into the workings of that unfathomable female mind than I do.*

True, normally. His thoughtful frown deepened. His steps slowed, since we were approaching the welcome chamber. *Ben...I don't talk in my sleep, do I?*

No.... I answered.

Then I thought to myself, *Not in your* sleep, *you don't.*

She acted like I'd said something, then when I couldn't remember what she was talking about, she changed the subject, Kor said in frustration. *She got all...nervous and left. Then, just a bit ago, she pulls me away from everything to say goodbye. It's like I said I loved her in my sleep or something.*

I came to a halt just outside the arch of light from the welcome chamber. *Do...you love her?*

Of course I do, Kor said, as if that was well-established—even though that was the first I'd heard of the advancement of his feelings, and that casual admission stunned me.

That's not the issue. The issue is that Rachel is not *ready to hear those words from me now, and especially not* this *of all mornings. I would have to be an ice-dead idiot to say that to her now...yet I can't help but shake the feeling that I did.*

Then it hit me: one last reason the Tree might have left something of Kor's curse. He hid his true feelings—his very self—from us so often...perhaps She had given us one brief glimpse into his inner world.

Simplified, of course, down to a level that the rest of us could understand. We were probably blessed that the normal state of his brilliant mind
was carefully hidden away.

I...was going to have to have a word with Rachel about Kor's condition,
if this was going any further (which, Flame only knew why, it seemed like
it was)—*before* Kor did something like propose to her during one of his
sleep-fogged states.

But right now, we both had jobs to do.

"Come on," I said out loud, clapping him on the shoulder. "We can talk
more about that kind of stuff later."

"Right," Kor said, shaking himself. "Right, sorry."

I softened. "Kor, you're allowed to be mortal. You know that, right?"

He smirked at me. "Today? I should hope not. After all, I have a promise
to keep."

I sighed. "That wasn't what I meant, and you know it."

I hesitated for one moment. I couldn't believe I was having to consider
this, but if he truly loved her.... "Kor, if you need to stay at her side
today...."

He blinked. It wasn't often I could startle him, but it seemed I'd done
so now. Then his face softened, startling *me*.

"As I told you before, Ben—there was a reason *you* were meant to be
King. Not me."

I shifted, not knowing what to say. Kor got like this with me so seldom,
I never knew whether it was yet another of his tricks or not.

His smirk returned a moment later, making me feel much better. "Of
Flame, that is."

I just blinked at him, then could have slapped my forehead when I
finally put it together. It was a good thing I trusted in Kor's honor and
goodness—and his sincerity if he said he truly loved her—enough that I
didn't feel the need to warn Rachel or Sarah, but I still couldn't help but
raise an eyebrow at the blatancy of his declaration.

"Intending to become the King of Ice one day, are you?" I said dryly.

Kor chuckled and shook his head at me. "Don't concern yourself over it, Ben. 'Let Kaldrir bring forth the morrow.' For today, my place is at your side.... Just know that it might not *always* be."

ALL TOO SOON, I was standing on the frozen wastes of Earth's far north once more—this time with Sekinek yet to crest the horizon.

This time, more than a handful of others stood with me. Through David's and Sarah's combined, valiant efforts, almost all the dramá who had volunteered and gathered to defend another people's Tree were now standing around on that icy plane with me or huddled just inside the tunnel to the moonpath. The rest were still deep within the Temple, positioned to defend any point we thought the Devourer might somehow breach, and not a few of those were inside the Temple Heart with the Tree of Ice Herself, watched over by Her Heir.

Thinking of Rachel made me snort, which, because I was in drakáform, meant a cloud of steam erupted from my nostrils. Sarah touched one of my shoulder scales from where she sat on my back and sent me yet another trickle of power.

Sarah, I sighed. *For the last time, save it.*

But you're so cold, she fretted.

That, I couldn't deny. Even in drakáform, the chill sliced clear through to my bones. Perhaps the drakáform made it worse: my hard scales were all the easier to frost over, providing little to no insulation. We transformed drakón were huddled as closely together as was wise, trying to shelter each other as best as we could from the biting wind.

How did the Seven do this? I thought in disbelief.

The legends had seemed to go on and on about the travails of the seven draká who had gone to Earth to find humans willing to help their people, but now I realized those accounts hadn't done them enough credit. Either the pure-blooded draká had been made of hotter stuff or they had suffered far more and for longer than we were now, and we were miserable. If I didn't know better, I would have thought we had landed ourselves in the frozen wastes of hell.

For the second time, I felt what Sarah must always have endured in the presence of *my* Tree: a bone-deep weariness as the relentless cold forced my flameheart to burn through my already night-depleted reserves at an unsustainable rate.

That must have been one reason the Devourer had timed its attack for dawn. At first, this moment might seem counterintuitive, just as its attack at noon had been on the day of the Dark Solstice. Why would a creature that thrived on corrupted darkness attack at the break of day?

Because its intended victims and perhaps most consequential foes—the Tree and children of Ice—were long past the peak of their power and would only decline from here. And we, the children of Flame, were already weak and getting weaker as we stood here in the cold, and once the battle had begun, the growing sunlight might not replenish our power quicker than we could burn through it—with the children of Ice unable to make up the difference.

Or so the Devourer would hope.

I wondered how differently the siege of Rosin might have gone had the Devourer attacked at dawn. Without the cold and with the sun, we dramá would have been more self-sufficient, but that might have only dragged out the battle further, costing more lives. In the end, when the Devourer decided to finally commit itself to the fight to press for victory, would we have been able to drive it back without the full power of Ice?

Sekinek, already having lightened the sky, inched over the horizon.

Time for me to go, Sarah said quietly, sending me another spark of power—perhaps just so I could feel her touch through my nerveless scale.

Ghosts of my former fears still haunted me, despite my resolve, especially now in the last moments before battle, when the wait was worse than anything.

Stay away, they wanted me to beg her. *Just stay where it's safe...where I can't lose you.*

I put steel into my reply to them. *I will never lose her.*

Then I dismissed the phantoms, sending them to the shadows whence they came. They would be back, but I could already feel they were weaker than before and would weaken further with each time I drove them off.

Then, filling that void with my love for her, focusing on her star in my mind, I said to her, *Come back to me when you can. We will need you.*

I worried about how she would ride out her body's dawn imbalance without me. But this time, Sarah was to surge to her family's hold, where Svyer waited to tend to her. That would have to be good enough, because at least one Monarch of the Seven Realms had to be here the moment the Devourer struck Earth, and that meant me.

I love you, my sun, Sarah said, her inner voice strained. Whether it was from emotion or the effort of holding back her swiftly rising nausea to linger one more moment with me, I couldn't tell. It probably was both.

I turned my head on my long neck to look back at her as best as I could. I thought for certain that her silver eyes glistened from more than just soulflare.

I love you, my star, I said, putting the whole force of my consuming love for her into each word.

Then she was gone in a silver streak of light, almost too fast to even see. In my mind's eye, I watched her star be reborn in the darkness of the cosmos, eons away from me.

For now.

A moment later, Sekinek's gold light at last broke over that white horizon. Then, just as Jake had predicted, black tears ripped the air all around us. Darkrifts, revealing the void beyond them and allowing consumed of all kinds to pour forth from every breach on land and in air. Surrounding us on every side.

NOW! I roared with throat and mind, springing into the air, flames already licking at my maw.

Almost as one, the other drakón with me did the same, launching themselves in every direction. We may have looked like a small, disheartened group huddled in a tight circle against the cold, but in reality, we had positioned ourselves with great care to face outward for this very moment. Warned as we had been by Jake that the Devourer would attempt to surround and overwhelm us from the start, we had readied ourselves to erupt at a second's notice into action, the ones on the outer edges, like me, Kor, and Yvera, rushing forward, while with each inner ring, the drakón angled upward. Now our maws, as one, spewed a combined inferno that exploded outward in a near-solid hemisphere of flame.

As consumed screamed and turned to ghastly charcoal, as the air filled with smoke and whiffs of burned flesh, bone, feather, and stone, as ice melted and even let off clouds of steam beneath us from that wave of heat, the darkrifts closed, the tears of the void dissipating to nothing as the fire cauterized the wounds in the Tree's veil over the world.

They were only the first round of darkrifts. Already, as we scattered in every angle and direction, the Devourer hurriedly created more, sending more of its slaves pouring through. But it had made its first mistake of the battle in committing so many of its resources so soon, for though we were cold and weary, far from being disheartened, we had been resolved, and far from being scattered and overwhelmed, our combined strike coming from a concentrated center had eliminated the first, tremendous wave all in seconds.

Though the Devourer had struggled to subdue the draká and then the dramá for millennia now, though it thought it had learned our every strength and weakness, there was one thing the Devourer could never comprehend, for that truth was inimical to a being which thought only of its own hunger: our greatest strength was not in our size, our might, our wings, or our flame.

It was in our unity.

Our unified Blood, burning in the fires of our changed hearts and fueled by our faith in the One who gave them to us, the One who bound us to Her and to each other into one Tree of Life.

I could only pray that Blood would be enough to save us again.

CHAPTER TWENTY-FIVE

ADVANCE

SARAH

"THANK YOU, SVYER," I rasped—out loud, to demonstrate I could, despite how the strain in my throat weakened my next words. "That's enough."

"Ashdust," Svyer snapped, bending in more closely. I was sitting on the counter in the girls' communal bathroom so that she could heal me standing up. At least, I'd moved there for her comfort as soon as she stabilized me enough for me to stop vomiting into the toilet. It had taken her longer than Ben to do that, so I was just choking out bile by the time she'd managed.

It was a wonder I had even that much left to regurgitate now.

"Your throat—"

"Ben will take care of the rest," I said. As firmly as I could while still being kind, I pushed her hands aside and slipped off the counter.

"In the middle of battle?" Svyer said incredulously.

"Maybe. I never know with his unconscious healing. But if not, after. But I need to get back *now*, *because* he's in the middle of a battle. He needs me."

Svyer sighed heavily. "I can't believe I'm allowing this. For the love of the Flame, you're not well, you're exhausted, you're dehydrated, and you're *pregnant*."

I took a swig of the canteen of icemint tea I had been wearing on a strap slung across my chest. I really hoped I would not be sick of the stuff by the end of this pregnancy. At least the cool liquid didn't seem to bother the candle flame in my belly. "I've been working on one of those."

"That's beside the point, Sarah," Svyer said, folding her arms and glaring emerald daggers at me. "We *don't send pregnant women into battle.* We don't think they're weak—each child is just too valuable to lose. It's counterproductive to our survival."

Perhaps another reason Kor wanted to keep my condition quiet. We hadn't even told my family yet; otherwise, Mom would have been in here sobbing away, and she would have *never* forgiven me for going. Instead, we had arranged for Svyer to meet me here in secret, counting on the fact that all my family members left in the hold were cloistered in Rachel's room, with access to its own facilities.

I felt a flicker of guilt that reinforced the twisting in my gut, telling me to do as Svyer wanted: stay, rest, heal. Hide. After all, that was the selfless thing to do as well, wasn't it?

Perhaps in the short view.

"Svyer, if I don't get back out there, my daughter might lose more than her father. She might lose her future, too."

If not her life—only just begun—if the Tree of Ice fell and took the power of my iceheart with Her.

Svyer's lips twitched despite the grimness we both felt. "You're convinced it's a girl, then?"

"I'm not just convinced," I said mulishly. "I *know.* You'll see. You'll all see I'm right."

Svyer laughed tightly and then pulled me in for a crushing hug.

"You're coming back," she said, voice thick. "You're coming back, and you're going to live forever, and you're going to give me a strong, happy cousin I can spoil to my heart's content. You hear me? That's an order."

"Ordering around your Queen, are you?" I teased, my own eyes stinging.

"If that's what it takes," she said with a sniffle.

It was odd—this could be goodbye for us. Even though I was going into danger to fight for the chance to live…I still might not come back. And yet, even now, our mortal brains had to find some glimmer of light in the situation.

Perhaps having a reason to laugh gave us a reason to live...and hope that, even if we died...we died having *lived*.

WE WEREN'T SURE HOW easy it would be for me to get back to Ben. Safely, that is. We knew he would be in constant motion in the middle of chaos, making either method of surging back to him dangerous. Ben had advised me to use my scrying/surging combination to get into the general area, out in some open space where I wouldn't be hit by anything, and then surge to his back if I could or his heart if I couldn't. I knew from his expression that he was hoping I'd choose his heart. Even now, knowing as he did how necessary it was for me to be with him, he would rather shelter me inside him.

That had its own problems, though, the first of which being that we had never managed that kind of thing for long. Just as the half-form was difficult for him and my "full" form was for me, merging our two beings into one was not just a delicate mental balancing act; it tended to exhaust us both.

And we also had no idea what effect our full heartbinding might have on that kind of unification. Even just our engagement had altered how we merged, judging from the one time we'd deliberately tried it after exchanging our first earrings. *That* had been the most powerful and thorough blending of all, making us think for a few seconds that we *were* one being, until it all started to unravel, and we fell apart.

So even though Ben's preference was clear, he didn't say it out loud, not when we all knew that he and I had better save that card for the moment we would need it most. We all knew when that would be: if...*when*...Solim showed his face.

"If he's even still alive," Yvera had said with a snort when his name came up in one of our planning meetings.

She was no doubt remembering the plague magic spilling over him when I broke the orb containing it. A plague created by the Devourer itself wasn't kind to *any* form of life, even one so corrupted as Solim's. I'd known from the alarm and fury in his eyes that whatever was happening to him as that inky black substance poured down him, it was bad; whatever effect it had was probably the only reason we hadn't caught a trace of him since.

I knew in my gut that reprieve would not last much longer.

Kor echoed my instincts in his reply to Yvera, his eyes as cold and dark as the deep sea. "He's alive. He will be there. With whatever is left of him."

As I frosted over the bathroom wall to get a view of where I was surging, I tried not to think of those words...and failed.

Please let Solim not have come while I was gone, I begged. *Please let Ben not have had to face him alone....*

There was a good reason I was anxious to get back to Ben. Even exhausted, strained, and weakening as I was, I was Ben's best edge against either Solim or the Devourer—and they knew it. Leaving him like that felt like leaving him exposed, defenseless.

To conserve my energy, I had asked my magic for a ground-level view, not wanting to use my lightform to emerge into and hover in the air. That meant the view I got was utter chaos. Drakón in draká- or amáform flew, ran, or bounded around everywhere after consumed creatures. The landscape was a checkered mess of multicolored blood and gore, of ash-dusted snow and puddles of slush and rivulets of meltwater.

The pristine whiteness was gone, turning the land around my Tree's Temple into a brutal mockery of what it had once been.

It will heal, I told myself. I had no idea if it was true, but I had to believe that it was. *If we survive, we will heal it and make it new.*

"You're going into *that*?" Svyer said, her hand settling on my shoulder. Her voice was strained.

I was surprised at first by her reaction, and then by my own. Svyer, for all her dramá blood and upbringing, and her lack of any oaths to do no harm, was still a healer to the core, and by profession and preference, she had never been directly exposed to *this* degree of violence. I was grim, but I had already seen two battles as brutal as this one, and I found my mind cool and detached, taking in the information I needed and not letting me contemplate—or feel—too deeply about the rest.

I had watched the madness long enough to determine that the dramá seemed to have the upper hand for the moment—they were the ones primarily doing the chasing and cornering, and the number of darkrifts, at least from my view, seemed manageable—which most likely meant that Solim and the Devourer had not yet entered the fray. Most important of all, I could feel Ben's pull pulsing with strength and vibrancy, more powerfully than should have been possible from this distance. I felt a tiny release of relief.

But that was it. That was all I could allow myself. For the good of my people, my family, my husband, my child, and my Tree, I had to become something far different from the helpless, naïve girl that had first entered the Six Realms a few months ago.

Was *this* what Ben felt when he entered his battle trance? This sense of...clarity, this razor-sharpness that cut away everything but what was necessary for survival—for protecting the ones you loved.

"Yes," I said with eerie calm.

And before Svyer could protest, I surged. Not just to the other side of the ice—I surged straight back to Ben, slipping right into the saddle I had left. It had almost been easy, feeling the pull through the ice that strongly.

Immediately, I began reattaching the straps to hold me in place; the more I could rely on them to keep me in place, the less energy I would have to spend.

Ah, you made it, Ben said with the same detached coolness I felt. *I would say "welcome back," but, you know, that would make it sound like this was a feast or something.*

As he spoke, he took us through a corkscrew to dodge some flyers and the flames from other drakón chasing them down, and before we even righted, he opened his own maw and blasted a darkrift that opened right in front of us before it even had a chance to spew any consumed.

Yes, I said from my hunched position, flush with his own body to withstand the G-forces and waves of heat he was forcing on us. *This is no feast.*

Although I could eat a few of them, if you like, he said with unusually dark humor. *Would that help? I've always thought the raka might be tasty.*

I blinked, fixing my eyes on the lines in the leather of my saddle inches from my face. I was feeling a bit of an echo of my former nausea. *Er, no thank you. That will not be necessary.*

Shame. But maybe it's for the best. They do *have a lot of feathers. And claws.*

I could have asked what had gotten into him, but just as with Svyer, I thought I knew: Ben was trying to distract himself from deeper emotions, to keep his head clear and his emotions in check. To think only of the present moment and what it might offer or demand.

There was also an added edge to his inner voice. Something deeper. More...feral.

Something Kor had once told me came back to me: *Many drakón become more draká in times of great emotional strain, but the Royals....*

So, the grim clarity I was feeling *wasn't* the source of Ben's battle trance—or not entirely. His partially came from his becoming something...if not more primitive, certainly more straightforward. Something not so inhibited by complicated human emotions. Something much more *savage.*

Right now, my husband was a dragon—body...*and* soul.

I...didn't know what to think about that. Except that now wasn't the time to have a familiar want for him coiling inside me—or to ponder what that heat said about me.

Case in point....

Hold tight, Ben snapped.

That was the only warning I got before he dove. I didn't even look to see why. I just held myself tightly against him and squeezed my eyes against the brain-scrambling pressure until we leveled off. Another roar of flame and wave of heat rolling over me gave me a hint, though.

When I blinked my eyes open, we were rising again, Ben's wings pounding the air so forcefully to gain altitude that they undulated his body.

Ah, I said, as mildly as I could as I continued to hold on tight. *Good to see we aren't fleshy pancakes on the ground.*

What kind of second-rate flyer do you take me for? Ben said with an irritated snort. Fortunately, the wind was blowing in the other direction, sending his smoke away from me.

None, of course. But even first-raters can make mistakes.

I wouldn't risk you like—

Yvera unknowingly interrupted. *Ben, Sarah, you see that? On the horizon, southwest.*

Ben banked and swerved us around to face that direction, and his right- and leftwing followed him in perfect synchronization, our other body-guards only a beat behind.

There were clouds boiling on the horizon—dark, rolling, familiar clouds, creeping across that clear blue sky like a hungry beast inching forward to swallow the light.

Ah, torch it, Ben said, beating his wings to take us higher, out of the main fray, and into an upward spiral. Whatever his direction, his enormous head tried to keep at least one wary, slitted golden eye on the oncoming storm.

I'm surprised he didn't wait until the last dek again, Yvera said dryly.

Well, the battle isn't going as well for his master this time, Kor supplied darkly. *In his condition, he probably would have preferred to stay out of it entirely, but he doesn't exactly get a choice.*

Why the clouds? I said, gesturing even though they perhaps didn't see. I'd never thought of asking when I had the chance before. *Just for the theatrics?*

They seemed like a dead giveaway to me.

Ben snorted, and Yvera said, *Well, this is Kor's brother.*

Not anymore, he isn't, Kor said, smoke pouring from his nostrils. When I glanced back and to the side at him, I saw his draconic lips were curled back to reveal his enormous, pointed teeth, his slitted eye on the purple draká across Ben from him. *And if I hear you say that one more time, you're meeting me in the dueling ring.*

Ooo, I'm trembling in my scales—

Truth is, Ben interrupted, *lish can only appear at full power under certain conditions, darkness being one of them. Also cold, but that part's already taken care of for him here.*

Ah, I said, trying to hide a flicker of unease at the seeming similarity between us. Hopefully just a coincidence. Right?

I suppose that makes sense, then. And I'm guessing he couldn't appear any closer? Because, given the option, I was certain a stealthy backstab would be more his style.

Correct. Not as a full lish. No darkgates period, and no darkrifts big enough here. He could slip through in amáform, but then he'd be stuck out here in his weaker form until he had enough darkness to change.

I see. So, he might as well set the stage from the beginning—and milk the drama for all it's worth.

I said that last bit as white flashes began appearing in the clouds in a stream, like streaks of a glowworm that allowed us to follow its progress through a gray, semi-translucent apple.

What had Kor called them before? Ghost lightning?

Yup, Ben said in a simple, grim reply.

Ben, Kor said, a new edge to his voice. *Are you seeing this? The black at the end of the spectrum?*

Ben swiveled his head back and forth, eyeing the white flashes. I couldn't discern the difference from this distance and with the dark cloud's interference, but I already knew a draká's eyesight was sharper than a human's.

You're right, Ben said, inner voice tense. *That's...new.*

My iceheart pounded. *Not good, I'm assuming?*

I can't imagine it would be. He hesitated a moment, then said reluctantly, *Be ready, Sarah.*

I tightened my grip on his saddle, feeling the lines of the leather and stitching impressing on my skin. *Just say when.*

Don't forget we're here this time, too, Yvera said.

Ben's silence was telling, and I could almost feel him struggling with himself. To allow me to help in such a dangerous battle was one tremendous concession, and probably only possible for him because he could tell himself I would hopefully be inside him for the duration. To also involve his wings, his best and oldest friends....

Ben, Yvera said sternly, knowing what his silence meant just as well as I did, if not more.

Well, it's not as if I can stop you, now, is it? Ben snarled, puffs of smoke coming from his nostrils.

The underlying tension in his voice reflected the clouds that were rapidly closing in. Their shadows would reach the edge of the battlefield within the minute, and Ben broke his holding pattern to head straight for them. He would not risk Solim taking a shot at one of his people first.

No, it's not, Yvera answered.

Ben's voice turned soft. *Just...don't get hurt.* Any *of you. I need you all. For this...and for the after.*

Well, Kor said, *I'm not sure about that firebrand at your right, but I already told you I have* no *interest in dying today.*

As if I would let a soft, book-dusted Starkissed outdo me at anything, Yvera quipped, shooting a ribbon of flame in Kor's direction that had me ducking, even though I only felt the faintest heat. I figured that was the draká equivalent of her sticking out her tongue at him.

Good, Ben said, his whole body tensing as we closed in on the storm wall. *Because if you all die, I'll kill you.*

We love you too, Ben, I said, a smile tugging on my lips. I figured if I was the only one who could say it in so many words, I might as well.

The white flashes roiled for a moment close to the edge of the cloud...then went out.

Now, Sarah! Ben said, maw opening, flames licking at his teeth.

In the split second before I surged into his heart, I saw a dark monstrosity bursting from the cloud, letting out an ear-splitting, blood-freezing roar.

This time, I saw that the formerly white portion around the lish's black-slitted eyes was streaked with tendrils of darkness.

Then, in a silver blur, I was gone.

Chapter Twenty-Six

ATTACK

Koriben

SARAH'S POWER FILLED MY veins mere seconds before Solim let out his first volley of black-tinged ghost lightning from his maw.

Really, ghost lightning was more like static-charged fog, but that wasn't a reason to underestimate it. Though it may have been slower than lightning, it still traveled with explosive speed, like smoke from a volcanic eruption. No doubt Solim was hoping I wouldn't have enough time or the power to block it, but he was wrong. I'd baited him by delaying my merging with Sarah on purpose, and my gamble had paid off.

While my rightwing and leftwing swerved off to either side at my signal, I kept my course straight for Solim and threw up a shield of golden energy between us. Except this time, instead of holding it at a static distance from my body, I threw the shield outward, smashing it right into Solim's open maw.

He let out a garbled roar of rage, and I grinned, baring my teeth and flexing my clawed fingers as I continued to barrel straight for him. All the while, I grew, expanding with the influx of power infusing my every cell.

A typical lish was larger than even the largest King, especially with the way the Devourer's dark magic contorted their bodies. That was one reason they were so devastating, the only creature that could inflict more casualties on us than a wyrm. In the past, it had taken nearly an entire flight of the Warflight to corner and kill one lish—more, if the lish attacked when they had the advantage of night.

Well, not anymore.

By the time I slammed into a dazed, distracted Solim, I was about one and a half times my normal size, by my rapid reckoning, and that was about half a size over *him*.

That's right, I thought, seeing the fear flickering in his eyes. *See how you like being on equal footing with* me, *you torched coward.*

Although perhaps that wasn't fair. After all, a lish almost always had to fight alone.

I did not.

While he and I grappled in midair in a tumbling, precarious balance of flight, I saw a flash of violet, and a second later, Solim threw back his head and bellowed in pain. Enraged, when his neck swung forward again, he aimed a bite for my own, forcing me to release him and beat my wings powerfully to get out of range.

He still had the advantage over me there, hellfrosts take him. The worst harm he could come to by biting me was chipping a tooth on my scales. I, however, would be poisoned if so much as a drop of his darkened blood or saliva got into my system, and who knows what added edge the plague magic that evidently still infected him might give.

So, as much as it made my blood boil to restrain myself from trying to pay him in kind, I would not even try. Yet, with the urge to rend and tear him with my jaws so instinctual it felt like a *need*, I still might have risked it if I didn't have Sarah's life tied to mine right now...and another's tied to hers.

In those split seconds, I felt the first flicker of something toward that new life that wasn't a reflection of my guilt or self-loathing or grudging reliance. Whatever it was, though, there wasn't time to contemplate it.

Solim closed his jaws down on empty air, but he accomplished his purpose in making me let go, because a moment later, he vanished in a black blur, even as a trail of black blood continued to fall like raindrops to the frozen ground.

I let out a roar of frustration, but Kor said sharply, *He's not done with us yet. He's here, somewhere.*

I didn't doubt my leftwing, but I wasn't in a kindly mood.

Do you see where? I said, punctuating my words with a snap of my jaws. I still felt the urge to bite so strongly it was an ache.

I was also ever aware of Sarah's power burning away in my heart and feeding into my blood. That power had not flagged yet, but it was *day*; I didn't know whether Sarah had enough reserves to spare or if she was, valiant as always, giving me more than she could afford to.

No, Kor said as both he and Yvera turned in tight circles to look at every visible darkrift Solim might have surged to.

He could have gone into the clouds, Yvera said grimly. Those were covering the whole battlefield by now and weren't far above our heads. *If he didn't use ghost lightning, we wouldn't—*

Fear and instinct froze my blood—the same kind of premonition I'd felt when I'd seen the Devourer's shadow while I was swimming in the waters around Rosin.

Kor, DIVE! NOW! I roared, pounding my wings to put myself between him and the clouds.

Kor obeyed my order at once—but, as usual, on a technicality. He didn't dive. He simply vanished.

Which was good, because otherwise, he might have been in harm's way anyway as Solim slammed into me instead and, locked together, we fell in a dangerous tangle of wings, claws, and tails. I scraped at him furiously, not even caring to stop our freefall, and he did the same.

Just before we hit, his jaws clamped down on my neck just above my shoulder, fangs piercing deep.

My roar of rage and agony was cut off as I hit the ground, the wind knocked from my lungs, muscles spasming, vision swimming as my head lashed back and hit the ice in turn. Miraculously, my wings seemed alright, judging from the lack of pain in those areas, but in my narrowed vision, I saw Solim raising a clawed hand to fix that oversight.

Then Yvera was there, gushing flame and slamming into Solim with enough force to send him tumbling off me and out of sight. As my hearing gradually returned, I heard their roars, snarls, gusts of flame and snaps of lightning, and felt the trembling through the ground. Heart pounding wildly for fear for my sister, I rolled over the moment I regained the strength.

But that was when I discovered the other reason for my racing starheart.

Power rushed into each puncture wound in my neck, each aching or pulled muscle, each bruise in my head, frantically healing me with impossible speed. Yet even now, I could feel poison seeping back through my blood toward my heart.

Sarah, I choked, hoping she could hear. *Leave me. NOW.*

As I shakily pressed myself to my feet, her response came, in feelings clearer than words could have been: Fear for me. Reluctance to leave. Determination to fight on.

Ever my *sera*, my valiant star.

LEAVE, I begged her, feeling the poison inch closer. Then, unable to believe I was doing this, I said, *Think of our daughter.*

I felt her hesitate one moment. Believing she would finally part from me, I fixed my gaze on Solim, bracing myself to launch at him with nothing more than my own might. I didn't know if death was inevitable for me, but if it was, I was going to die protecting my family.

Then Sarah gave a burst of power. Not just power—she *expanded*, following the paths her power had blazed before her, spreading herself out beyond my heart, racing through my blood, infusing herself into my every cell.

For a moment—one moment—we were one. For that moment, we radiated a golden light of such glory and power, even Solim turned his head, distracted, black-streaked eyes widening.

That moment was enough to burn the poison right out of my blood. That moment was enough for Yvera to lunge in, cutting a swath of dark blood across Solim's chest with her claws. That moment was enough for him to cry in pain and vanish once again.

Then that moment was over.

Sarah, having given her all, collapsed back inward like a dying star, leaving my blood cold in her absence, and my flameheart feeling like ice.

NO, I thought, just as horrified as the first time she had done this. Because this time, it could be the end.

No, no, no, I begged, just as I had then. *Sarah, don't leave me like* that, *don't. Don't.*

Silver streaks flowed from my chest and reformed her on the ground in front of me. Gingerly, I bent my head down over her. I ached to change back and take her in my arms, but even as my whole soul yearned toward her, my instincts kept me wary, hunching over her as every sense strained to detect an approaching enemy. If she was still alive, I wasn't about to endanger her by weakening myself, even for a few seconds.

Kor reappeared in amáform just a few steps from her, emerging from thin air. He stooped and scooped her up in his arms.

I've got her, Ben, he said gently, meeting my gaze. *She's just burned out. She'll be alright.*

I let out a sigh of relief. With my muzzle so close to the two of them, the huge gust of air ruffled Kor's curls and made him squint. Wisps of Sarah's hair that had escaped her braid fluttered around her face. Her nose scrunched in response, and I hoped for a moment that her silver eyes would open so I could see them one more time.

But Yvera was approaching, watching the skies, and elites were landing around us, ready to escort Sarah to safety. Every moment I held her here was another moment she was in danger—and another moment her would-be murderer breathed.

I raised my head, projecting my inner voice to everyone present. *Get her back inside—and stay with her.*

What about you? he asked just me, eyes going to my neck and narrowing in concern.

Poison's gone, I said—to everyone once again, because I could see a green Peacegrowth drakón pushing through the crowd of elites, intent on healing me. *I'm fine.*

Kor's eyes widened at that miracle. Then his eyes darted to Sarah and back to me, and I nodded.

I'm counting on you to take care of her, I said to just him. *Don't let her come back out before she's strong enough.*

Understood, my King, Kor said soberly, projecting his inner voice to everyone. There wasn't a trace of a smirk on his face or in his voice. *She will be safe with me. You have my word.*

I nodded to him again, trusting him to keep it. Then, without a look back, I stepped to the side and moved past him, allowing the elites to surround them both. I walked across the blood-stained, ash-dirtied, melted and refrozen snow toward Yvera.

What are my *orders, my King?* she sent to just me. There was a smirk in *her* voice, and a light in her draká eye. She was never more alive than in the midst of conflict.

Plus, I didn't think my sister would ever be able to call me by my title with a straight face.

I had begun to decrease the moment Sarah collapsed inward. Now I felt the full weight of my normal size and strength settle on me. I tilted my newly healed neck, feeling the tendons stretch as they should with their full range of motion. For good measure, I rolled my shoulders, feeling the ripple of my muscles and scales.

Now, you and I hunt a lish, I said, spreading my wings.

Excellent, Yvera said with relish.

Chapter Twenty-Seven

DARKNESS

Sarah

I DRIFTED AWAKE TO a rocking motion. The restful darkness, the coolness without the bite of the wind was wrong. The smell of Ben's spiced, desert scent lingered in my memory, but it was long gone now, no trace of it in the musty underground air...or in the arms that carried me.

I started fully awake, tensing, and Kor said soothingly, "Easy, Sarah. You're safe now."

He was missing the point so tragically, it was almost laughable—or it would have been, if I didn't feel like crying instead.

"Ben," I gasped, thrashing. The last thing I remembered was *being him*....

Kor grunted, then as he rebalanced on the tilted floor, he said in a drier tone, "He's fine, too. Seems whatever you did, it healed him."

"The wrongness?" I demanded, hardly daring to hope. Yet I stilled, allowing Kor to continue down the twisting tunnel.

I didn't know *what* was going through Ben's blood. While in that state inside him, I only had the haziest ideas about what was happening outside. Any information I gleaned came from Ben's most intense thoughts and emotions, and even those faded like a dream as soon as I awoke. I knew something *wrong* was happening to him, something that made him fear for me and our daughter, but that was it.

"Wrongness?" Kor asked. "You mean the lish poison?"

"*Poison*?" I choked. Although the conclusion was obvious, now that I had more of a mind to think about it.

"Well, yes," Kor said shiftily, now that he saw I didn't know about this bit.

"Care to elaborate?" I growled, fisting my hands against his armored chest.

Fortunately, Petra was just ahead, and she said with forced cheer, "Well, obviously. Getting *any* bit of a lish inside you—blood, saliva, whatever—is bad news. When Solim got his jaws around the King, we were all worried for a bit. But King Koriben insists he's fine, and I have to admit, he isn't acting like he's dying from lish poisoning."

I looked at Kor, and he just raised an eyebrow at me. "Alyish tried to order him back for at least an examination, and he refused, point blank."

My lips twitched of their own accord. I knew from the Battle of the Solstice that if Ben was feeling well enough to publicly defy Alyish, he was doing alright—and now that he was King, he truly had the authority to do so.

Kor continued. "He insists you healed him completely." He paused, then added fastidiously, "Probably more accurately, the energy you gave him enabled him to heal himself."

I sobered at once. "What happened to Solim?"

Kor's eyes darkened. "He fled—again. Surged away into some darkrift or another."

I swallowed thickly. With my mouth as dry as it was, there wasn't much saliva to go down. "And Ben's gone to look for him."

That wasn't a question, but Kor answered it anyway, eyes still dark. "Yes."

"Still no sign of him," Petra said gently when she glanced over my shoulder. "As of the last update from Mevra, at least."

She gestured behind Kor and me. I glanced over his shoulder and saw one of the elites' faces was lit up in the dark tunnel by the multicolored glow of an active call scale, her expression intent as she examined the scene it displayed. The Battleblood drakón glanced up at me to meet my eyes and gave me a brief, reassuring smile before returning her focus to the scale.

I sighed. Now that I was caught up, I could see where this was going. "And now you're taking me back down."

"King's orders," Kor said, giving me a look that dared me to defy them. Again.

I wasn't that stupid. There was a reason I hadn't insisted Kor put me down by now—other than that I had needed answers more than I had needed to protect my pride. I knew I was no good to Ben now. My body felt as limp as a wet towel, and by contrast, my throat and mouth were as dry as a desert. I served Ben best by recovering as quickly as possible.

"Got any tea?" I asked instead.

Kor's lips twitched. He shifted me in his arms to free up one hand, and after a second of shapeshifting, a canteen appeared inside it. "It's a good thing I held back a couple so I could shove them at you as needed, isn't it?"

"Yes," I said with a resigned sigh as I plucked the canteen from his hand. Most of his arms were still supporting me, so he couldn't hand it to me himself. "It is."

The icemint was blessedly refreshing. Even after a few sips, I found myself wanting to slip back into sleep, and without deciding to, I rested my head on Kor's shoulder, and my eyes drifted closed.

It's a good thing we've established he's my brother.... I thought.

That was the last thing I remembered before I started awake again, this time as we entered the glowing spiral cave of the moonpath. I could have been out for only moments, but even so, I felt a guilty pang. Ben was out there fighting for our lives, perhaps encountering Solim without me, and I was *sleeping*?

Rest was one thing, but unconsciousness felt like a betrayal.

"Hey, sis," David said, standing up from his chair at the far end. From his sagging shoulders and weary smile, he didn't look much more rested than I was. His turn as the moonpath operator had clearly been a busy one. With a clench in my gut, I hoped that didn't mean there had been a lot of injured they'd had to evacuate.

"Heard you were coming down," he said with forced cheer.

He held up a glowing call scale in explanation, and I caught a brief glimpse of one of the command centers set up deep within the Temple. The dramá's ability to coordinate with just the magic they had never ceased to amaze me.

"Aw, David...." Feeling sheepish, I wiggled in Kor's arms, finally trying to get him to put me down. "I can activate the moonpath—"

"Oh, no you don't," Kor said sternly, holding me fast. The even floor helped him this time.

"And let you take away my one job?" David teased with a bit more energy. "No thanks."

He turned his attention to the elites and waved them in with a practiced air, pointing to where he wanted them to go as he spoke. "Come on in. Line up along the walls as best as you can, or in the gaps between the lines if you can't. Just don't stand on the glowing spiral, and we should be good."

The half dozen elites filed in and did as he said. Then David walked the spiral, pulling in power as he did so with a furrow between his brows. I watched him from where Kor held me on the sidelines with a mixture of pride and sadness. How quickly and completely our lives had changed. And yet, there was something about watching David work that made me realize something else.

We were meant for this, I thought with a bit of surprise. *All of us. Not just me.*

David had teased me to put on a brave face through his exhaustion, but he had also pointed out a profound truth: he had finally found his place in the universe—in helping and protecting people. He had spent his time in his former life on video games and cars not from a lack of talent or interest in doing something more purposeful but from a lack of expectation and opportunity...and not knowing where to find it himself.

To have wished for him to go back to that safer, duller life was to wish for him to perhaps have never reached his potential. To have never found his purpose.

That was not something to wish on anyone.

David's armor, hair, and exposed skin glowed the more power he collected. When he finally reached the end of the spiral and unleashed all that coiled potential, his silver eyes flashed, and he shone so brightly I averted my gaze.

Do I look that incredible when I do that? I thought in a bit of a daze as I glanced back at my younger brother.

"Go ahead," he said with a tired smile and a wave at the film of ice that had appeared over the cave opening. "You leave first, then the others come in, then I release the spell."

I saw what he meant as Kor took me through, and I saw another small group gathered in the other cavern, looking geared up for battle. I was glad to see that the dramá took full advantage of each expenditure of David's magic, not making him do twice what only had to be done once with a bit of coordination beforehand.

As David had said, as soon as we filed into the second cavern, the other group went into his, and David let go of the power that kept the ice film over the opening. With that gone, the true opening into the Temple appeared.

As Petra and a few others of my elites went through first, Kor said silently, *If you promise to be good and not surge away the moment I let go, I'll set you down.*

I rolled my eyes. *As if you could stop me if that's what I really wanted to do.*

True, but we'll both accomplish our purposes better if you behave, Kor said. *You won't be wasting your energy and needlessly endangering your life, and thus not distracting Ben and endangering his, and I'll be presenting a Queen to the public who is sensibly taking time to recover, yet able to stand on her own two feet.*

He made a compelling argument, per usual. Drat him.

I grumbled, *Alright,* fine. *I promise to be good and not surge away the moment you let go.*

Notice I made no promises about later. Nor did I define what "good" was. The vagueness of Kor's terms seemed like such an obvious oversight, I suspected it wasn't an oversight at all.

That's my Sarah, Kor chuckled, the glint in his sapphire eyes making me think I was right.

As he lowered me to my feet, I snapped, *For the last time, I'm not "your" anything.*

Oh? he said innocently. *Not my friend? Or, inevitably, my sister?*

Seeing as I'd just admitted as much in my exhaustion-befuddled thoughts, I couldn't deny the relationship now. Convincingly, anyway. So, I just turned my back on him without responding and walked away from my most annoying brother with as much dignity as I could muster.

WHEN PETRA LOOKED AT me to ask where to go, I said the command center. I could recover in the middle of that room almost as well as I could in a quiet room by myself. A quiet room would technically be more restful, but it would also isolate me from what was going on. If I was once again going to sit back on the sidelines, it was going to be somewhere where my presence had some symbolic good and where I could know immediately if Ben was in trouble.

So, once again, I found myself in the thick of the "safe" action, with a few key differences. I was sitting down, for one, having accepted with grace the chair that Alyish ordered brought as soon as I reached his side. Along with the chair, I had a side table with tea and a few baklava-like tidbits packed with a wholesome sweetness that made me think they were carefully designed for maximum energy and nutrition recovery. The moment the first one started melting in my mouth, I felt steadier and more clear-headed.

For another thing, the setup in this large, derelict room was much more makeshift than the meticulously prepared command hub in the Temple of Flame. There were no tables with floating astral charts, no data displays, no holograph-like flames portraying the battlefield; either those could not be set up in the time we had or they relied on input devices that weren't established in this world—like trying to use a GPS on a world without satellites. It didn't matter if you had a working device if no data was coming in that it could use.

Thus, the furniture here was lighter, more portable or expendable. Any tables were only surfaces for setting things, writing things down, or hastily drawing up maps to pass on. Or, in Alyish's case, his table was one huge slab of archival stone on which the battle was drawn, and aides were constantly updating their sections according to incoming information.

There were no carved niches in the walls for all the call scales that coordinating a battle of this magnitude required, but the dramá had made do by somehow sticking them directly on the straight, gray stone surfaces. The dozens, perhaps hundreds of scales everywhere combined with the dim lighting meant that stepping into the room had felt a bit like entering a multifaceted insectoid eyeball.

Then I turned around and saw the biggest difference: the ice wall. One entire wall, split into five sections—the portions on either side of the door and three squares above—were dedicated to displaying ice images.

That was Dad's responsibility, aside from advising Alyish now and then on a question of possibilities. Dad stood at the general's side and attempted to show Alyish whatever he asked to see, at whatever magnitude or angle he required.

I was blown away by Dad's cool-headed ability to take whatever terse commands Alyish would shoot at him and translate them into stunningly clear and detailed results. Alyish never thanked him for his displays or advice, but then, Alyish never complained about the limitations and disadvantages of everything else he had to work with. There wasn't time for either gratitude or complaints. There was only time to take what one could and act on it.

Laura also stood by and helped, occasionally adjusting or taking over one section to ease the load on Dad. My guess from her deepening scowls was that she wasn't as powerful or as practiced as Dad was and could not do more. She, of all the six of us original transformed Linds, had been the most reluctant to practice her magic, finding it a distasteful reminder of all she had lost. So, she convinced herself that there was no urgency to gain skill and stamina with it, putting the least stock in the Tree's warnings and in the magic's utility in life.

Now I could see those illusions were gone, and Laura was furious at no one more than herself for her lack of ability to help. She was the most stubborn person I had ever met besides Yvera, but that meant that once she changed course, it was with her whole soul. If we survived this, I doubted any of us would be able to match her for dedication to a magical practice.

With Rachel in the Temple Heart with the Tree of Ice, that accounted for all the original six except Michael, but I soon discovered what he was up to—and yet another reason for Laura's scowls. Michael surged through the ice from the command center to the surface and back to bring messages, to scout, and to be Alyish's most mobile aide—doing whatever he asked and reporting back in for his next assignment when he was done. Even though Michael couldn't lash to take anyone with him, he was still a tremendous asset to Alyish and was currently braving the greatest danger of any of us to be so. No matter how exhausted he looked when he returned, his eyes were bright and alive, fired up with a purpose that was equal to, if more intense than, David's.

I watched Michael's progress through the ice when he was in view, and I absorbed what I could of the general battle—but with most of my family safe as could be expected and even Michael kept from the worst of the fighting, most of my attention was once again fixed on Ben.

Even without a flame table to display his image on a constant basis, he was easy to spot through the ice. There were other golden dragons out there, but none were as large or as deadly. Or, to my unease, as prone to throwing themselves into the fray if needed. Once again, Ben, Yvera, and the bodyguards who could keep up with him acted as the most mobile elite unit of the battle.

Unlike last time, Alyish left him alone, letting Ben direct his own group as he would. I assumed this was at least partly because Ben spent much more of his time circling high above the main conflicts, and I thought I knew why: he was looking for Solim, either actively hunting him or simply warily watching, ready to dive in the moment the lish showed his dark head.

Those were all the impressions I gleaned as I sat, ate, and recovered under Kor's discreet supervision. He acted to all the others as if he were there to be of use as well, and he did in fact field as many administrative questions and decisions as he could for Alyish. But I knew from his occasional meaningful glance my way why he was really here instead of flying at Ben's side.

After about half an hour, I decided I was done being good. I stood up, and Kor's eyes instantly went to mine. I met his gaze evenly.

"I'm going back out there," I said quietly. I wanted to speak the words out loud to invoke the power of my voice...but I also knew better than to start a fight in the middle of the command center. If a fight to keep me here was indeed coming.

Dad's eyes flicked to me, and even Alyish paused in his study of one of the ice displays to glance back at me, lips pressed into a grim line. Laura was gone, having left to swap out moonpath duty with David to give him a break, and David hadn't arrived yet. Michael wasn't there either, and that wasn't by accident. I'd timed my declaration for right after his latest departure. Like I said, I *was* trying to stop a fight.

Kor examined me impassively, then sighed.

"You're as rested as you're going to be while this is going on, aren't you?"

"Yes."

I'd eaten and drunk my fill, despite the constant clenching in my gut, which I knew had more to do with fear than anything with the hours left until noon. My limbs had steadied, and my power had returned, if sluggishly and only to the level it was ever going to reach at this hour.

What I needed most in this moment wasn't rest—it was for my husband to be safe. Since that wasn't going to happen until *all* of us were safe, I needed to be with him, helping him bring about that outcome as much as I could.

Every moment that ticked by without me out there was another moment Solim could strike at him without me to protect him.

Kor shrugged, as if it didn't much matter to him whether I risked my life—which told me it very much did. "Well, I suppose that meets the King's requirements of me. He said to only keep you away until you were strong 'enough.'"

My lips twitched. I wasn't the only one who could take advantage of vague parameters regarding my wellbeing.

While Kor's expression remained careless, his eyes darkened when they met mine again. Silently, he said to just me, *You realize Solim is probably waiting for either you or me to return? That we may do more harm than good by baiting him back into the open now?*

So, there was another reason Kor had remained down here with me instead of returning to Ben. Only now did I have the vaguest memory come back to me, as fuzzy as a dream, of a lish diving through gray clouds at a dark sapphire draká....

I brushed away the nightmarish memory of a memory and returned his gaze soberly. *We can't hide forever, either. Neither can we let him do the same.*

Kor nodded slowly. To his credit, I saw not one flicker of fear for himself in his eyes. Only a momentary tightening of concern for me. *So long as you're aware of the risk you're taking...with your own life and...others.*

His eyes flicked for just one moment to my abdomen.

I raised my chin, trying to hide my clench of guilt. To the candle flame inside, I said, *I'm doing this* for *you.*

I was doing what I felt with all my being was right.

To Kor, I said, *I am.*

Kor sighed. But he walked the short distance to my side and waved Petra over. She approached from where she had waited in a more out-of-the-way location, seeming unsurprised. Then again, I'd made my intent clear to everyone in the room the moment I stood—discreet discussions or no.

"That's it then?" Alyish said evenly, meeting my eyes.

"Yes," I said, with no other explanation, and without a request for permission.

Alyish nodded slowly. "Ice be with you, then, Queen Sarah."

Silently, but to more than just me, Kor said while locking eyes with Alyish, *Brace yourselves. I'm no seer, but I'll wager my best keg of Sever red that our brief lull is about to end.*

Alyish didn't so much as raise an eyebrow. He just looked at Dad for confirmation.

Dad's only answer was to walk over to me and pull me into a hug, holding me tight. When he stepped back, he made me meet his eyes. His own silvers were glistening. My dad *never* cried—so of course I choked up as well.

"Believe in yourself," he said simply, clenching my shoulders. "You have what it takes to survive this. Believe in yourself...and believe in Her."

"Why, Dad," I said with a tremulous smile. "You make it sound like you believe in Her now, too."

He smiled thinly. "Because maybe...I do."

My eyes swam, blurring my view of him. I could only nod, swallow, and step back.

Kor gave me a moment to recover before he asked idly, "So...think you can take us both to the surface? That would save us a bit of time if we can do it right."

Petra grunted, but when I looked at her in concern, she just rolled her eyes and shook her head. "Don't worry about us. He's right, obviously. We can catch up soon enough."

I focused on my connection with Ben, the perpetual pull I felt of his gravity. Even with the miles of space, ice, and stone between us, I judged it was strong enough to draw on for a lashing, and I nodded.

"Yes," I said, clearing my throat.

Kor put his hands on the archival table and pored over its map, glancing occasionally at the ice displays. "Where would you say is a good place for us to emerge, Alyish? Judging from last time, Sarah only needs a second to deposit me before she can surge again straight to Ben's back—is that right?"

He looked at me for confirmation, and I nodded again.

"I'd rather not attempt to take you with me all the way to his back," I said with a grimace. "You're not as *tied* to him as I am, if that makes sense. You won't know how to position yourself as you come out of it, and I don't know if *I* can position you. I'm worried that I'll just drag you into the air along with me like a rag doll and then drop you, or that, even if I can get you into a saddle seat, you'll slide right off before you can grab onto anything."

Kor chuckled, perhaps at the image, even though *I* didn't find it funny. "I figured it would be something like that. I could probably change before I hit the ground, but let's not risk that, shall we?"

I shuddered. "Yes, let's not."

"Then somewhere on land for the first surge?" Alyish said, studying the map. "Alternatively, Koriben could meet the two of you there, saving Sarah another jump entirely."

Kor shook his head, eyes darkening. "Solim will be looking for something like that. No. This needs to be somewhere secure, where Sarah can deposit me quickly and be gone in a moment, and where I can have the seconds I need to change."

Alyish frowned but nodded thoughtfully. "Well, there's the entrance to the tunnel."

He gestured over the spot marked on the map. It had a multitude of symbols around it that I assumed signified fortifications and magical protections, since they had stayed static the entire time I'd been there, other than increasing in an outward-expanding circle.

"It's an obvious location, but it's the most secure point we have, and there're comings and goings that might obscure your arrival."

With an ease that still surprised me, Dad flicked his hand to conjure a pane of ice on a metal sheet sitting on a nearby easel, meant for ad hoc visual needs like this. The entrance to the tunnel appeared from a perspective on the left inner wall, just steps from the open air. If there hadn't been thick cloud cover, we might have seen a stark white line of sunlight on the ground dividing light from shadow.

"Even better," Kor said as he straightened. "If we appear just inside the tunnel, like so, we'll be out of sight."

"The latest group just went down," one of Alyish's top aides said helpfully, consulting her archival and then her wristwatch—one of the new kinds I had inspired. "Barring any sudden medical needs, that area should be clear for at least seven dek."

She glanced at Dad, as if for confirmation, but he only smiled slightly. He wouldn't always answer our questions regarding the future, leaving us to wonder whether he didn't know, couldn't figure it out, or didn't see the need to intervene. In that sense, he was becoming as enigmatic as a Tree.

Kor looked at me. "What do you think?"

I shrugged. "Sounds good to me. Seems like you're the one at greater risk here than I am, so if you're comfortable with it, so am I."

Kor grimaced. "Don't be so certain. I'm the one Solim wants *personally*, but he's no doubt under compulsory orders to prioritize you. The moment he sees you've rejoined Ben...."

His voice turned musing, his gaze distant.

"Kor?" I asked, poking him. I didn't like the look in his eyes. It had too much of the same dark determination from when he'd plotted to sacrifice himself to get me past Solim to the Ekrel moongate.

"Hmm?" he said innocently, coming back to the present.

I knew this wasn't the best moment for me to confront him, so I pretended to let it go. "You ready or what?"

"Ah, yes, of course," he said with a deep nod—the dramá equivalent of a bow. "Ready whenever you are, Queen Sarah. Take us away."

I rolled my eyes. But while I took the couple of steps to come right up to him, I sent to Dad, *Dispel the ice image of the tunnel as soon as we're there. I need to have a private word with Ben's leftwing.*

Very well, Dad answered, unsurprised. He too was watching Kor with narrowed eyes.

I closed my eyes, took a thread of my power, with Ben's connection as the strong center, and looped it around Kor. I opened my eyes to glance at the image Dad had brought up, and without further preamble, I *took* us there.

When we rematerialized in the tunnel's mouth, Kor stumbled, grabbing onto my shoulder for support. I felt a bit smug.

"Try to imagine yourself standing still as you go," I said. "It helps your feet know what they're supposed to be doing when you arrive."

"Har har," Kor said as he straightened and let go, giving me a look that let me know he knew I was echoing his words from a month ago back at him. With some modifications.

"Well, time for you to be off," he said, turning away. "And for me to—"

Kor, I said silently, my tone turning stern. I grabbed his arm and pulled him back into the shadow of the tunnel's mouth. *You're not planning on doing anything stupid, are you?*

He flashed a grin at me. *Why, my dear Sarah, what a question. When have I ever thought of doing anything* stupid?

I clenched my jaw. *You know what I mean—reckless endangerment of your own life.*

What is "reckless endangerment" is you lingering in one place for too long without Ben, he said, the smirk still on his face as he brushed me off. Though his eyes were darkening. *I, however, am only...trying to be as distracting as I can. Take advantage of that by giving me a few moments to get to work, will you?*

Then, before I could say another word in reply, he vanished.

"Kor!" I said in the most savage whisper I could manage, clenching my fists. I suspected he could still see and hear me. I could almost *hear* his ghostly chuckle.

I growled, but two could play his game. Instead of waiting, when every moment counted to warn his King, I felt for Ben once again—then *pulled* myself to him.

When I reemerged in Ben's saddle, he was circling in a level flight path high above the battle. Which meant he had plenty of his attention to give to me.

Sarah, he growled, his head looking back to turn a golden eye on me.

Save it, I said. *I'm as recovered as I'm going to be, alright? Besides, I thought I might give you a heads up that Kor is about to do something stupid to draw out Solim.*

There was a sigh in Ben's inner voice, and his immense head turned forward again so he could begin scanning the ground more urgently. *Of course he is. Where is he?*

I didn't have time to answer, because just at that moment, I felt a wrongness behind me so strong that bile rose in my throat again. It was the same wrongness I'd felt in the presence of former darkrifts when I'd run through the bowels of the mountains with Kor, and a bit of the wrongness I'd felt when the Devourer's shadow had appeared in the grotto where I and the other Starkissed women had been swimming.

Except the arms that wrapped around me weren't shadows—despite the black sleeves and even blacker stains on his hands, darker than the darkest ink. It was the black that absorbed all light...that devoured it.

"So glad you could join us," Solim whispered in my ear, causing every hair on my body to stand on end.

Before I could react, darkness swallowed us both.

It must have been my imagination, because we should have been long gone by then, but I thought I heard the echo of a roar of pure rage and fear.

WHEN WE EMERGED, IT was into a different darkness, yet it was less complete. Somehow, even without a single star visible in the black miasma that surrounded us on all sides, I saw enough to make out rocky, barren ground. Especially when Solim threw me unceremoniously down onto it.

I thrust out my hands just as Ben and Michael had taught me and caught myself with my nose inches from smashing into that unforgiving stone. I felt only rock and grime—not a single bit of soil, not a single drop of moisture. Not a single speck of life.

"There you are," Solim said carelessly. At first I thought he was talking to me, then his next words sent my head spinning. "I've brought you the girl, as ordered."

His tone hardened, turning as icy as the plane we had left. "Now give me my reward."

Then a boot entered my field of vision.

Or...what a boot might have looked like, had it been made of the void.

I looked up.

I should have seen nothing. Nothing but darkness, for that was all it was. And yet, it was a *greater* darkness than the black, barren waste we were in, greater than the miasma around us, that scraped its cold, hungry fingers across my skin.

This blackness stood out against the rest like a reverse sun: a black hole.

And it was in the shape of a hooded man.

Instinctively, I reached for my magic, trying to flee, but I couldn't force it beyond the surface of my skin. The power rose up in my abdomen as usual; it made my body grow cold with it, and yet, I could not get it *out*. It was as if my power was my voice, and I'd been gagged. I couldn't even reach for Ben's pull; I could still feel it there, if faint, but there was something between us.

I was trapped...and frozen with an all-consuming fear as I looked into the faceless void of my eternal enemy.

The voice, when it spoke, made all my hairs stand on end and bile rise in my throat again, and this time, the burning liquid nearly slipped out.

The voice, like its form, was male. And as cold and indifferent as the grave—as the frosted plane I had gathered the dramá thought of as hell.

"So says the incompetent fool who took so long to obey my command."

"You know very well what took me so long," Solim said flatly.

Its voice was as dry as a frigid desert, yet laced with such a furious power that I crouched lower, and out of the corner of my eye, I saw even Solim flinch. "I refer to the many times you have failed to bring her to me in the past. I have waited this long for my hunger to be sated. You, *slave*, may wait a few moments longer."

I didn't dare glance fully away from the shadow-being in front of me to look at Solim's reaction, but I thought I saw him stiffen, especially at the slap of the word *slave*.

The Devourer's avatar crouched, presumably to examine me, for all I could tell from the cocked posture of its faceless hood. I knew better than to think *this* was it in its entirety, any more than my Tree's whole being was the avatar of ice and light that She showed to me. The Devourer's sickly, hungry power was everywhere in this place. It *was* this miasma that had long ago taken and consumed this world, wherever it was in the vast universe. It was a wonder I could even breathe or live in this place, but I felt a tingle of power encircling the three of us that gave me a hint at why. Though the miasma occasionally crossed that threshold, when it did, it was weaker, the dark tendrils that reached through for me only vines, not life-ending tentacles.

The Devourer was holding even *itself* back from me.

Once before, I had been within its power, and it had not harmed me. Though I soon figured out it had waited not out of any mercy or even any interest in me personally but because I was of the most use to it as a sacrifice.

"What are you waiting for?" I croaked, my fingers scraping against the grimy rock, aching for anything to use or even hold on to.

To my shock, it answered, its voice...puzzled. "I am trying to understand."

"What?"

"How, of all beings, it could have been you."

I swallowed, without having any moisture in my throat to go down. "It?"

The Devourer rose, its voice turning to a sneer that sent a shiver of dread down my spine. "The 'mother.' Why, you can barely even be called such in the commonest sense."

Solim smirked. I couldn't help it—one of my hands went protectively to my abdomen. Another wave of bile made its way up my throat, this time mixed with a ferocity I had never felt before in my entire life. I bared my teeth, feeling like a cornered lioness about ready to lash out.

"And yet, I suppose you are," the Devourer said, some of the icy indifference from the beginning reentering its voice. "So perhaps it is for the best that Solim was so incompetent. Now you have more power than ever for me to reap."

I gritted my teeth, so furious that tears formed as crystals of ice in my eyes.

Ice.

Outside my body.

Even bound and trapped, surrounded and outnumbered...I was not as powerless as my captors thought.

Or were meant to think.

Yet I wasn't given long to ponder this tiny triumph. Tendrils of darkness shot out and held me fast, even as the ground rose beneath me, the rising stone raising me to waist-level to the male and male-figure standing by. As the shadow-vines wrestled me flat on my back, despite my struggles with all my might, I felt a wave of déjà vu.

I didn't need to see the knife the Devourer formed out of its darkness to know what was coming. Clearly, it wasn't going to waste any more time, not even on curiosity. As it had said, it had waited long enough.

And yet, with my head now forced to face the sky, I saw the reason I could still see. Though the stars weren't visible through that miasma, that didn't mean they weren't *there*. I could feel them there, feel their light burning through the true darkness of space.

Not because those stars were mine or of my magic—they were Ben's. Because of how the stars interacted with my own—the magic of *divine* darkness, of quiet stillness, of rest, of shoots beneath the soil waiting for the first sign of spring, of night just before dawn reawakens the world. The darkness of the womb, where both mortals and stars were born.

The Devourer was only a twisted mockery—order gone wrong, life turned on its end, and thus forced to consume more and more to keep existing in its defiance of the Creators.

But neither was I *of* divine darkness. That was where my power began, but that was not what it *became*. It rose from within the darkness deep within my belly because that was where the seeds of it were planted. But when it arose from that nurturing soil....

It was light.

Light.

Ben's and my hands twined in the darkness as the northern lights played out on our skin, pondering our shared Blood. How we were more similar than we were different.

Light was what bound both of us together. His was the light of vibrancy, of bonfires in full flame, of life at its peak, just before the fall, when it began to burn up in its own brilliance—the light of the full, mature sun. Mine was the light of beginnings, of new life, of birth...of light emerging from darkness. Of the nebula, the birthplace of stars.

Neither was superior to the other. Each was just a part of the eternal cycle of life, all connected in one glorious thread of light. Life in all its glory, then death, darkness...and new light.

When my power was first awakening, I told Ben I could feel the stars, even through the clouds above our heads. Then I corrected myself as I examined the feeling within me more deeply.

More like...I can feel...the holes of them.

The holes...the divine darkness—the source, but not the *manifestation* of my power. It was the clay on the potter's wheel, the thread in the weaver's loom, the soil in the gardener's beds.

The Moontouched flag: a white star over a dark moon. A *dark* moon. There it was—the hint at the source of the Moontouched's destined power, all along, hiding in plain sight. *And* the sign of what they were to make with it. The truth almost came to me, in that first moment when Kor described it to me, and in several times since, and yet it had slipped away from me each time.

How could I have fallen for the ruse just like everyone else, letting titles and clan names and expectations distract me for so long from the supernal truth that always lay deep within me that I was not born to reflect light...but to *make it*?

To turn darkness into *light*.

Now, knowing which way to look, I knew which way to reach. So, reaching up with all my soul, I lanced through the corrupted miasma to space itself, and I sucked that pure darkness back down and into me.

And exploded with light.

My bonds evaporated like water in an inferno. Both Solim and the Devourer recoiled from me, and its miasma blew back. A mental, inhuman shriek filled my mind, but I didn't even flinch. I was past caring about pain, even my own. I was burning with surety and *rage*, rage against the lish that had taken me, rage against the Devourer that had, from the first moment I entered a new world and life, sent its slaves after me, who thought to claim my Blood and kill my child, my greatest creation of light.

Well, let it just *try*. I was no longer lost and helpless, confused and afraid. I was filled to the brim with power incarnate and primed with knowledge, purpose, and authority. Now, I was a Queen, a wife, a *mother*.

With that combination, light exploded from me with the force of a supernova.

Except this was no death of a star.

It was its birth.

Chapter Twenty-Eight

LIGHT

Koriben

WHERE IS SHE? I raged, roaring with both throat and mind as I smashed an ahglen into the slushy ground with enough force to separate its boulder of a neck from its stony shoulders with a snap and grind of rock on rock.

I was speaking not to the now-deceased ahglen, of course, but to its master, who I knew could hear me through every darkrift and the mind of every one of its slaves—both of which were dwindling in number as we finished them off faster than they could appear. I knew better than to think that meant we were winning the battle at large. The Devourer, having gained its first objective, was merely distracted bringing about its second.

With the blood of my star.

And so, in despair, I *raged*. Fire spewed almost without ceasing from my mouth. I tore through consumed after consumed like they were nothing but gnats against my fury. Not even Kor tried to reason with me or stand in my way this time. No one did. It was all they could do to scramble *out* of my way as I tore and crushed, torched and mauled. Even consumed no longer stood against me or sought me out; instead, perhaps loosened from the grip of their distracted master or so overcome with terror that they broke free, they fled from me. Yet I pursued each as relentlessly and mercilessly as death itself.

All the while, I strained for my star. Yet though I could see her in the distant cosmos, and the continued flickering of her light was the only reason I held onto some semblance of sanity, I could not reach her. For the second time since she became my star, I could not go to her, just as I couldn't when she was trapped inside that dark shield with Solim on Yonvey. Something was once again between us, blocking me off—and that, perhaps, was the worst part of all.

GIVE HER BACK TO ME! I roared as I grabbed yet another ahglen, too slow to escape my wrath. It didn't matter that I knew, I *knew* my shouts were in vain, the raging of a gnat as pathetic compared to the Devourer as these consumed were to me. I still could not contain them. My rage needed words to convey even the smallest part of my pain, and these were the only ones I had.

GIVE HER BACK, YOU HELLFROSTED COWARD, OR I SWEAR BY MY BLOOD I WILL HUNT YOU TO—

And then, just like that, I could reach her, and her star was blazing like a sun. The door between us wasn't open, but it was like she had turned the key.

That was good enough for me.

I mentally slammed my shoulder against the door and burst it open...

...and blazed straight into her heart.

WE WOKE ON A stony table in a dark cloud, a black knife above our chest, ready to plunge into our heart. Far from being disoriented, far from being helpless, we knew exactly what was happening.

And we smiled.

"What—" Solim began, dark eyes widening as he looked at our glowing body, at the mix of gold and silver light shimmering across our skin and wisping out from us like vapor, by turns hot and cold.

That was all we allowed him to get out before we grasped the dark wrist holding the knife above us.

We were wary enough to form a layer of ice over our hand before we did so, which was good, for though the wrist was more solid than mere shadow, it still was not flesh, and the concentration of corrupted darkness within might have tainted us otherwise. Deciding not to make contact any longer than necessary, we shoved the hand aside with a parting gift of fire that made it stumble away, hissing in surprise.

All of us, both the cold and the hot, got a flash of satisfaction from that hiss, but we did not let it distract us. We had another enemy to deal with first.

We rolled off the altar and danced nimbly to the side and backward, turning so our back was to neither enemy. We watched both warily, but it was at the lish we launched ourselves, springing as swiftly as a snake.

He stumbled back, as startled as if we had indeed become such a creature. Our height was a bit of a challenge, but not as much of one as it would have been if Solim had not been a shorter-than-average drakón.

We jumped, and as we wrapped our legs around his torso, we wrapped our hands around his throat, and with a strength that our small, slender fingers should not have possessed, we squeezed.

For the first time, part of us diverged in purpose.

No, the cooler, more levelheaded part said. *Not here. Not now.*

That part was ever mindful and wary of the enemy now behind us, the one we could feel approaching.

We came to a swift agreement. Instead of letting go of our rightful prey, we lashed him to us and dragged him back with us.

We emerged back into clouded sunlight and biting cold with a glorious smile on our lips, our combined light blazing so brightly for a moment that we stunned Solim, who blinked blindly at us as he choked and fumbled with our fingers at his throat.

No. This wasn't nearly satisfying enough. We jumped back down and released him, thrusting him from us as roughly as he had thrown us to the ground just dek—minutes—before.

He stumbled back, wheezing for air as his hands went protectively to his throat.

Now, in the sunlight, we could see how deeply the plague had infected Solim's amáform. No longer did he look anything like his former brother, our friend. His skin had paled, and his veins stood out starkly as black lines against his lightened brown. Even his dark sapphire hair had changed to inky black, just as his irises had done long ago. Black blotches covered his skin, thickest on the hand that had held the orb, but spreading like a disease to other places—at least from what we could see of his exposed hands, throat, and face. He had lost weight and muscle, and as we watched his movements and analyzed our memories, we realized he was weaker than he had been before. Sickly.

Yet we felt not one ounce of pity. We could not afford to. Solim had his chance to turn back, and even at the very last, he had taken us and would have sacrificed us and our child and *enjoyed* it.

It was time to end this evil, at least. Once and for all.

"What...." he rasped, eyes widening as they once again focused on us.

Instinctively, not even questioning whether we could do this, we thrust our hand out and summoned a sword to our grasp.

A small one—one we had not used since we were little more than a hatchling, just learning to spar. Yet we knew we had to be pragmatic. Though magic unlike any we had felt before was rushing through our veins, impossibly strengthening our muscles, bones, and ligaments through power incarnate, there was little we thought we could do at present about the *size* of our current hands, and this blade simply had a hilt more suited to this hand's grip.

Though a shimmer of white scales was growing on the backs of our hands, so perhaps shape-changing wasn't *entirely* out of the question.

We grinned savagely at the lish. We could almost feel our teeth sharpening as we did so, as three sets of horns grew from our skull and poked through our hair and three sets of ethereal, feathered wings emerged from our back.

"So good you could join us," we purred.

Just before we surged forward in a gold and silver blur.

Solim surged away just as quickly in a black blur of his own. We knew even before we thrust our sword through the air he had occupied that he would be gone, and we let out a savage cry of rage.

Yet Yvera shouted in our mind, *He's still here! South by southwest!*

We whirled around, just in time to see Solim next to the closest darkrift, and we saw him surge into it in a black streak, yet he bounced out of it and back into solidity once more.

"*WHY?*" he shouted at the rift, terror mixing with fury in his voice.

We smiled as we understood.

"Didn't you hear?" we called out to him as we sauntered across the bloody mix of slush and snow to him. "'Slave.' 'Incompetent.' 'Fool.'"

Slowly, he turned back to face us as we continued, his face now a hard mask.

"You chose a master who is never satisfied. No matter what it promises, it will always see you only as a means to an end. Now that it seems you can no longer meet that end, it has discarded you."

Our voice lost its taunting edge and became sober. "You had people who loved you, Solim. A mother, a father, a brother, a clan. A Tree who cared for you as Her own. Yet you turned from them all for power and spite. Those were the loves you chose. See how well they serve you now, at the end."

His eyes flashed darkly, and his jaw set. "Indeed. Let's."

He rushed forward in a dark blur, changing as he did so. We just smiled and surged forward as well, calculating our position and our thrust with precision born of experience and instinct—and not a small surge of power from not just one but two Trees, which strengthened and guided our hands as we plunged our sword up and into the lish's newly forming chest, just before its scales hardened enough to block it.

Then, fulfilling a promise that the hotter of the two of us had once made, we sent a burning fire down the blade and *twisted*.

The lish staggered, making a wet, choking sound in its now fully transformed throat. We left the sword in place and surged away before any of its doubly poisoned blood could touch us. Just as well, because a moment later, the lish fell forward through the air where we had been floating, no doubt driving the weapon even deeper.

Then he was still.

We allowed ourselves to drift down to the ground, our white armored boots touching a clear patch of snow with the softest crunch.

The sound should have been too quiet to hear. Only now did we realize that the rest of the battle had ended, and the only sound was once again the whistle of that eternal wind as all the remaining drakón stood still to watch our final confrontation.

Is that...it? a part of us wondered.

But the other, hotter, fiercer part summoned another sword to our hands. One larger and less suited to our current size, but we thought could make do.

Something isn't right, that part insisted.

Then we both realized what it was: the final darkrift...was still open.

We surged back into the air, summoning fire in one fist, but we were too late. Inky blackness that we hadn't seen from our previous angle was spilling from the rift and into the fallen lish.

No, we thought with unified horror. But even as we watched, a moment later, the trail of ink ended, having entered the lish in its entirety. As final proof of that, the darkrift closed, its creator having no more use for it.

The revived lish slowly raised its head. When it blinked its eyes open, no trace of white remained in them. They were only black voids. Even its teeth, when it pulled its lips back in a savage smile, were obsidian daggers.

Its inner voice was a horrifying blend of both Solim's and the Devourer's.

At last.

Chapter Twenty-Nine

TIME

Sarah

The moment we heard its voice, our soul rent in two. Ben pulled away from me, terror and determination mingling in his heart.

No, Ben! I thought, trying to pull him back, to keep this precarious balance together. *You need me, you—*

But the complete union of our minds, hearts, and bodies was so difficult to maintain that the moment we truly began to think separately, the moment we lost our balance on that tightrope, we fell.

The unraveling, hastened by Ben's urgency, was quick. If painful. Within a couple of seconds, we blurred apart and solidified back on the ground as two separate beings. I bent over and clutched my chest, feeling as if my heart had been ripped in two. Ben tensed from the same pain, but he was more practiced in ignoring discomfort in the face of danger. Instead of hunching over or gasping, he stepped in front of me, one foot braced in front of the other, one shoulder angled forward, the other back. One hand fisted, the other clutched his sword.

Yet he did not change. Even as the Devourer rose to its feet, stretching limbs, wings, and tail experimentally. It seemed to ignore us insects for the present as it explored the confines of its new avatar.

Go, Sarah, Ben said, his inner voice strangely calm.

I straightened. *No! I—*

Trust me when I say this is a fight we cannot win—even together.

Tears of fear, pain, and rage stung my eyes. *You promised, Koriben Sunfilled. You gave me your* blood oath.

He did not so much as look back, keeping his gaze fixed on the Devourer. *That's why I'm not forcing you. I'm asking.* Go. Please. *Save the ones you can. Save our daughter.*

I felt like he had punched me in the gut. I bent over once again from the pain and misery. How could he ask this of me?

How could I refuse?

Unfortunately, our moment of respite was over. The Devourer, content with its explorations for the time being, turned its dark, featureless orbs on us.

Ah, it said in satisfaction. *You have divided yourselves for me. Good. As much power as I might have gained from two Monarchs merged into one,* two *deaths are much more pleasing.*

"Well, tough," Ben said evenly. "Because you'll still have to satisfy yourself with just one."

To my surprise, Ben spoke out loud. Normally, a draká's ears would not have heard him over this distance and the whistling wind. Perhaps Ben was counting on the Devourer retaining some enhanced awareness. Perhaps he didn't want to dignify the Devourer with the touch of his inner voice. When I thought about it, even I recoiled. *Receiving* the Devourer's icy, dark voice in my head was enough to make me feel filthy. Sending my own in return....

Just one? the Devourer asked in amusement.

There was something odd about its voice, now that I thought about it. More than just the fact that it mingled with Solim's. There was something more...animated about it. More emotive. Other than a bit of scorn or curiosity, the Devourer had been cold and emotionless when forced to communicate with us mortals. To its immortal mind, we were nothing more than insects—fleeting, small, and meaningless save when we were occasionally troublesome or useful. Once it grew bored with me, it had thrown me onto an altar and was going to sacrifice me with absolutely no ceremony, no more acknowledgment of what it was about to do than an impatient scientist would have given to the bug it was about to pin down in their collection.

This Devourer was much more...engaged.

Sarah, go, Ben pleaded, distracting me from my dangerous preoccupation.

I hesitated, frozen with indecision. I closed my eyes shut—another inexperienced move, but I needed all the focus I could get.

What should I do? I pleaded with my Tree.

Meanwhile, Ben replied out loud to the Devourer, his voice still calm. "Yes, one. Because the Trees promised me Sarah would not die today. So, sorry, I'm all you get."

I opened my eyes, glancing at Ben in agony. Could that *really* have been what the Trees had intended all along? To save me, at the cost of....

The Devourer reared back its head and let out an undulating roar that I assumed was a sickening mockery of laughter.

And you believe *Them?* it said in incredulous delight.

There was something so familiar about it now....

Even in the face of what I have become? it taunted. *Faced with the certain doom of all you hold dear? You're an even greater fool than I ever thought, and trust me, I had an abysmal view of your intelligence before. How Korinth has held himself back from finishing you off himself these past six years, I'll never know.*

I inhaled sharply. From Ben's start, I assumed he'd realized the same thing I had.

The Devourer wasn't just using Solim's voice. Solim...was still very much in there.

His words to the Devourer came back to me. *Now give me my reward.*

Not healing from the plague. Not Kor—or, at least, not directly. Instead, the same thing Solim had always wanted: power. This time...all of it. All there was left for him to receive, so that he could at last rule all the worlds and destroy with impunity all who had ever defied him.

Even if the price was his own life.

A new voice called out, coming from just beyond Ben.

"Perhaps if *you* were just a bit more intelligent, Solim, you would realize that you can either have these two Monarchs behind me...or you can have me."

I choked, but I already knew what I would glimpse when I stepped to the side to see around Ben.

Where, just seconds before, there had only been a few hundred feet of despoiled snow between Ben and the Devourer, now, perhaps a dozen feet in front of Ben, stood Kor.

Once, I had seen Kor stare down Ben while Ben was in full berserker madness, with Ben's drakáform increased to mind-boggling proportions from the power I had dumped into him, while Kor knew well that his friend and Heir was in a state in which he would just as soon kill Kor as a consumed. Even though at the time I was still uncertain whether I could trust Kor, I knew then to never call him a coward.

That was nothing compared to the courage it must have taken to stand between Ben and me...and his former brother, whom Kor knew desired his blood almost more than anything. Who now was not only a lish but had the Devourer's very own power to take it.

And yet, Kor stood straight and tall, chin lifted, sapphire clothes glistening even in the dimmed sunlight, short curls tousling in the wind. His hands were open and empty, with not a sword or dagger in sight. The only armor and weapons he had brought to do battle with his nemesis were his mind...and his gift.

My chest tightened, making it hard for me to breathe as I realized what he was about to do.

Kor, Ben said with silent urgency, taking a step forward.

If Kor replied, it was just to him. To my eyes, Kor did not so much as move a muscle. Yet *something* made Ben hesitate and stand still once more.

Meanwhile, Solim snorted, a sickly black miasma coming from his nostrils. *And what makes you think that, "brother"?*

"Has your power rush made you forget our birthright?" Kor said. "I can still run from you, Solim. While you pillage and devour here to your black heart's content, I can run somewhere where you can never find me. Nothing has changed this day in that regard."

Solim sneered, revealing his blackened fangs once more. *There is nowhere in this universe you can go that I cannot now devour. The more you run, the longer I will hunt you, the more I will destroy everything you have touched, the more blood and suffering you will heap on your head, until I make your life hell.*

"True," Kor said calmly. "But if you refuse my offer and force me to run, I don't intend to run for long at all before I end that life myself."

I closed my eyes for a moment. *Don't do this, Kor,* I thought. But even now, I didn't send the words.

What if this was the only way?

Solim's long neck reared back a bit in surprise. Then he snarled. *What purpose would that serve, you coward?*

"Isn't it obvious?" Kor spread his hands. "What do you want, Solim? What do you want now, more than *anything*? *You* want to be the one to take my life. But first, you want to make me suffer for everything I ever did to steal your birthright, to betray your trust, to take your place, to mock you with my survival, to thwart you at every turn. To build up all that which you would have destroyed for its not bowing down and worshiping the ground you walk on. You want nothing else now more than to do to me all that you believe I have done to you. To make my life, in your words, 'hell.' But you can't do that...if I die first."

He paused, letting that sink in for a moment. No one moved or made a sound. If anyone else could hear what Kor was saying, they would be hopelessly confused. If we survived this, the heavy secret of the Tolsyon heirs would be exposed, if only from the questions people would have—especially if Kor was the one to buy us enough time with his sacrifice.

And yet, Kor was speaking his secret out loud, for anyone to hear.

That, more than anything, convinced me he was deathly serious. This was no trick, there was no brilliant plan to save himself at the last moment. He would have only risked exposing his secret and undermining Ben's authority if he were about to die. The people would figure out that there *was* a Tolsyon heir, but with the only known one dead, and no one knowing who the next was, malcontents would have no figurehead to rally behind.

Kor said dryly, "In case I have not made my point clear to your consumed, Devourer-addled brain, allow me to be explicit: if you choose to claim these Monarchs and this world, I will fly into the stars, fleeing only so long as it takes me to find some solitary place to end my life. And, as an added twist, I'll make sure it's somewhere that will dispose of my body too quickly for you to find even my bones. Thus, you can pillage across the cosmos all you like, Solim. You will *never* find me, and you will *never* have your revenge. This, I do solemnly swear."

A snarl of pure rage escaped the lish's lips before he suppressed it.

Solim shifted, turning his head, struggling with himself for a moment before he snapped, *Do you expect me to be so shortsighted as to take your bait? To trade worlds for so petty a reward?*

He opened his jaws wide, displaying all his teeth. *Do you not get it, even now, Korinth? I am no mere drakón, I am not even a mere lish. No lish before me has ever been able to contain the Devourer's very essence. Now I am the most powerful being to have ever lived. I have transcended mortality itself. I* AM *THE DEVOURER!*

He punctuated that last savage shout with a roar so deafening and powerful, it ruffled Kor's dark sapphire curls. Kor didn't so much as twitch.

"No," he said flatly. "You're still Solim. A petulant, greedy, small-minded mortal whom I once blindly loved and worshiped as a brother, until you yourself disowned me. And I wasn't the only one. That's the most tragic irony of it all, don't you see? Thinking yourself so *intelligent*, so *wise*, you could not see that you had everything you could have wanted, even as you threw it all away. So, yes, I think you'll throw it all away again—for the chance to destroy the one you thought took it from you."

Solim snapped his jaws. *Then* you're *the fool.*

Kor shifted his stance, as if preparing to sprint at a moment's notice. "Is that it, then? You've made your choice? Shall I take myself away?"

The lish shifted back and forth, twitched its tail, flung its neck from side to side, flapped its wings, and snapped its jaws as if biting at invisible flies.

NO! the Devourer's voice roared. *You* idiot *of a slave! Ignore the cursed boy, let him end himself if that's what he wishes, and take the Monarchs, take them NOW! END. THIS.* NOW!

Yet the lish's body did not move from where it stood. Its head swung madly to eye Kor, then Ben and me, then Kor, then us.

Even with Kor's back to me, I knew from his voice alone that his signature smirk was on his face. "You see, Devourer, that is the tricky thing about investing a mortal with your power. Why do you think the Trees are so very careful with whom They choose to give Theirs to? Because, by the Creators' decree, once invested with a Greater Power...the vessels are free to do what they will with it. You grew too confident in your control over the minds of your slaves, forgetting that, if given half the chance, what desires remained in their hearts could overrule even you. Solim may be a fool...but he was never entirely *your* fool. Now that you've given him your power, your only choice is either to let him use it as he wills...or to withdraw it."

I inhaled sharply. Perhaps there *was* one last flicker of hope, one brilliant twist to Kor's plan that saved *all* of us. If the Devourer abandoned Solim, it would have to abandon this battle altogether, to retreat from this world, lick its wounds in its dark corner of the universe, and plot its revenge for another day.

And all of us might live, for at least one day more.

If....

I held my breath, Ben tensed, and all mortals on that frozen land waited to see what the Devourer would choose.

The lish became still. Its eyes settled on Ben and me, its lips curling in a look of such pure hatred and hunger, grown from millennia of consuming and never being satisfied, that I shuddered and Ben took a sidestep back to me, once again blocking me from view.

With *my* view also obscured, I could only assume that in that moment, the lish turned its head back to Kor, because though it spoke in the Devourer's cold voice, it could have only been addressing him.

Swear. Swear by your Tree to give yourself to me, and I will spare this wretched world and the Monarchs who guard it. For today.

Tears stung my eyes, even as they froze on my lashes in the frigid air. *No.*

I shifted once again to see, so I was just in time to glimpse Kor's head and shoulders lower.

Just for one moment.

Then they rose again.

"Ah," Kor said lightly. "But you see, I don't trust *you*, Devourer. Or Solim. There is no authority either of you swears by but your own. So, this is how things will go. I will swear a blood oath to wait for you in the space outside this world. So long as you come immediately to claim me, I, by the constraints of my oath, will allow you to do so. But if you feast instead, or so much as linger, then I will leave and make good on my threat to take my own life. That I will also swear."

The lish snapped its jaws, but after a moment, the Devourer said, *Very well. But know that I will personally make you suffer even more for this insolence, boy, and I know more ways to inflict agony than Solim can fathom.*

"Oh, I'm certain you do," Kor muttered, so softly the words were probably lost to anyone but Ben and me.

Kor, I sent to him, my inner voice a whisper. I didn't know what else to say. I couldn't beg him not to do this. Too many lives were riding on his sacrifice—including my husband's.

Perhaps the words I was looking for were *I'm so sorry.* But I was in such pain I couldn't get them out, even with my inner voice.

He replied without turning, as he summoned a fireball in the air and brought out a knife. His inner voice echoed in a way that told me he was speaking to more than just me. *It's a distraction, Sarah—like I said. Just buying you a bit of time. It's not much, but...it's all I can offer.*

My eyes swam, frosting painfully in the cold. My guess was that he had sent his last words to Ben as well, so I did too. *It's more than enough. More than I can ask.*

Or repay, Ben said.

Kor raised his knife over his hand. His inner voice was teasing on the surface, but another emotion lurked just beneath. *Then if you two have a boy, name him after me, will you?*

He made the cut, sapphire blood spilling across his hand. As he raised his hand over the fireball, he spoke to us again, his voice sobering.

Tell Rachel...I'm sorry.

Is that it? Ben asked hesitantly. *Not....*

Yes, he said sadly. *She doesn't need to be burdened with the rest. Not after this.... I should have known better.*

I choked, and I clenched my eyes shut from the pain of my breaking iceheart.

Then he spoke out loud. "I, Korinth Starkissed, do swear by my blood—"

Kor's fireball exploded into shards of ice—sailing away in every direction but his own.

There was a silver blur, and in a flash, Rachel was standing in front of Kor, with her back to him, facing the Devourer. One of her hands held her gun, which she fixed on the lish. The other waved to summon ice from the ground that formed a solid, semicircular wall of angled, six-foot-high spikes.

"Oh, no you don't," she muttered, presumably to Kor.

Much louder, she said sweetly to the Devourer, "Tough luck, buster. If you want my fiancé, then you're going to have to go through me."

I was staggered for a moment with sheer horror—and so was Kor, judging from his frozen posture, still holding his dripping hand out in the air.

Rachel could not have said or done a single thing worse.

My older sister wasn't stupid. She wasn't. *Really.* She was just *tragically* uninformed.

I had thought Kor was merely being coy about his relationship with Rachel, in his not publicly demonstrating any affection or testing whether they could lash together. Now I realized there was a very good reason he had kept it quiet for so long, and why he had let me go so easily after making his offer.

Solim.

The lish recovered from the shock first, letting out another horrid, draconic laugh.

Is this your betrothed*, Korinth?* Solim jeered. *The* Heir *of* Ice? *Are you* still *dutifully trying to fulfill Tolsyon's prophecy?*

Prophecy? What *prophecy*?

No time, I snapped at myself.

Rachel! I cried at her. *Get out of here! Now!*

From Kor's frantic grab on her arm, I assumed he was urging her to do the same.

You actually love *her, don't you?* Solim said with even greater glee. *Even more pathetic. And you call* me *the fool.*

Without any other warning, the lish opened its maw, black clouds flowing from its mouth, black lightning flicking like sparks deep within its throat.

"NO!" I screamed, spending nearly every last drop of power I had to form a shield of ice in front of my brother and sister. A golden dome appeared around them at the same time, covering a smaller, sapphire one of the same magic. The last I saw of the two of them was Kor pulling Rachel into him as he turned his body to shield her.

Just a split second before lightning and darkness swallowed them whole.

Yet, I felt my shield hold, even as it fractured. I could only pray that meant Ben's and Kor's did as well. Wisely, though, Rachel did not wait for the cloud to dissipate. A silver streak shot as quick as lightning out of the cloud and to the east.

I let out a tiny bit of tension. There was one sibling out of immediate danger, at least.

Then the cloud dissipated...and *neither* of them were there.

I let out the rest of my breath. Kor had used his power to vanish, too. I shouldn't have been so relieved. Now we had our own lives to worry about. But somehow, I felt better, having escaped becoming a monster who would sacrifice her own brother.

NOOO! Solim roared, slamming the frosted ground with one of his forepaws as he threw back his head and bellowed out loud. *You coward, you sniveling, hellfrosted—*

You FOOL, the Devourer spat, taking over his voice. *She took him back with her!*

Back....

Understanding dawned on Solim and me at the same time. I could see it settle over him as he stilled, head turning toward the east. Where...I could feel the power of my Tree pulsing beneath the ice. My eyes widened, and I gasped in horror.

"No!"

But Solim didn't hesitate. He stretched out his wings, crouched, and launched himself into the air.

"What's happening?" Ben asked me tightly. "Where is he going?"

I grabbed his arm. "Ben," I choked. "He's going for the Tree. That's where Rachel took Kor."

Ben's eyes widened with the same horror I felt. Without hesitation, he backed away from me and began running, changing as he did so. I did not go with him. I knew that—even if there were anything Ben and I could do against a Devourer-possessed lish—this time, my place was elsewhere.

Come to me, dear one, my Tree whispered deep within my iceheart. *It's time.*

I, too, turned into a silver blur that shot toward the east.

And down, down through the ice.

"—TORCHING *IDIOT*," KOR WAS raging at Rachel when I materialized. We were all now standing on the circular dais at the base of the Tree. Safe...for about the next five seconds.

I left Kor to handle my sister, even though I wanted to shake her a bit, too. Instead, I scanned the room, looking for the Tree's avatar to direct me, or, failing at that, to see what I had to work with. A couple of the dramá guarding the Tree and Rachel were keeping a respectful distance at the top of the steps, and the rest were strung down the steps and along the small semicircle of flagstones at the base of Her hill. About forty all told, about thirty of them drakón—but not enough room for more than a handful to change, and that was without leaving them room to maneuver. I inwardly groaned. Well, it wasn't like I really thought we could take a Devourer-lish down with numbers alone.

"You have just single-handedly endangered your Tree, *everyone* in the Seven Realms, and *Earth*," Kor cried, waving his hand at the icy ceiling. "Why would you *do* that?"

Rachel just folded her arms and raised an eyebrow at him, cocking her hip. "Because my Tree told me to. Duh."

"Your—" Kor realized what she had just said and abruptly deflated. His next word came out in a choke. "What?"

Even I started and looked back at my sister. Yet, true to form, she didn't elaborate.

Instead, her face hardened, and she punched him in the shoulder. "Also—*what the hell*, Kor! You promised me you'd take care of yourself. You *promised*."

"I—tried," Kor said weakly. "Circumstances—"

"You're not the only one of us who has something to lose here," she snarled at him, poking him hard in the chest. "When I said I'd marry you this morning, it certainly *wasn't* so you could go breaking my heart by playing the hero—*the very same day*."

Kor froze again. "You...said...*what?*"

"Uh, I believe the exact word was 'yes,'" Rachel said dryly. "I'm not repeating *your* own words, because honestly, as far as proposals go, it was pretty dumb, especially coming from you. Even *Ben* must've done better. I'm going to demand a redo once this all is over, just so you know."

Kor stared at her as if she'd just grown two heads. In a choked voice, he said, "I...proposed?"

It was Rachel's turn to deflate. Her voice became small. "You...you honestly don't remember, do you? You were just...sleep talking. *Again*."

She put her head in her hands. "I can't believe I was so *stupid* to think...."

Kor reached for her in alarm. "Rachel, flameheart, no, it's not as if I wouldn't have—if I thought you were ready to—"

She lowered her hands, silver eyes flashing as she pulled away from him. "And why should I trust that, huh? You *still* haven't even told me you *love* me!"

"Because I thought you weren't ready!"

I groaned. "Ugh, Rachel, Kor, I think I know what happened, but I'll tell you later, OK? Now *really* isn't the time, because Solim is headed right—"

Just then, the ceiling shuddered as if from a tremendous impact. Crumbles fell from the ceiling and walls, and the Tree's ice leaves tinkled like a shaken chandelier. Last of all, a shadow crossed over the glowing ice.

Kor slowly looked back at Rachel, his eyes soulflaring. "If we all die because of you," he said in a low voice, "I will kill you."

"Allow me to translate," I said with a nervous smile, iceheart fluttering. "When a guy like Kor tells you something like *that*, that means he loves you."

"Pssh," Rachel said, outwardly recovering somewhat as she flipped her braid over her shoulder. "I already knew *that* part."

I knew my sister too well, though, to not see the trembling in her fingers. She had more of an inkling of how much danger we were in than she let on—and she was just as terrified as we were.

"Er, Queen Sarah?" Kvina, one of the guards at the top of the steps, said hesitantly, eyeing the ceiling.

As the ceiling shuddered again, and cracks formed in the ice, I took one more look at the cavernous room...and at all the people looking to me to give them orders. Or...to save them.

Perhaps it was time I did both.

I looked at Kor, then at Rachel, feeling the first inklings of my destiny rise from the depths of my soul.

"Get them out," I said quietly. "All of them. Everyone that's left in the Temple. Open the moongate and evacuate everyone. Now."

Kor's face fell. He alone seemed to comprehend at once what that meant. "Sarah," he whispered.

"It's too late, Kor," I said kindly. "You won't be able to reason with him—I can feel it. He's too far gone. It's up to me now. I might be able to offer you a bit more than a distraction, but..."

Just then, we heard the faintest roar, filtering down to us all the way through the thick ice. The shadow shifted, and there was a billow of darkness, and a flash of fiery light—of flame.

Ben. He, too, was buying us time.

I swallowed and closed my eyes for one second to send a prayer to both Trees for him.

Then I looked back down at my brother and sister and smiled wanly. "...no promises."

"Sarah," Rachel said, paling. "You're not...staying behind...are you?"

I looked at Kor. "Start the evacuation, Leftwing Korinth. Now."

Kor swallowed, and his eyes flashed for one moment. But he nodded. "Yes...my Queen."

Silently, he said, *Just for the record, I love you too...sister.*

Then, without another look back, he went to the top of the steps and spoke to the guards there, gesturing.

I tuned him out as I turned to Rachel, who was looking at me with the most devastated expression I had ever seen on her face. Tears were pooling in her silver eyes—real tears, not the ones she was all too good at faking.

"No," she said, shaking her head. "No, this isn't the way it's supposed to be. This isn't the way the Tree said it would be."

"*I said everything would be alright, dear one, if you trusted Me,*" the Tree murmured behind me. I whirled around to see Her now standing just on the other side of the well, somehow looking straight and tall yet weighed down with exhaustion. Though She still had the care and strength to smile sadly at Rachel. "*And so it will be.*"

Rachel's face twisted with fury. She pointed at me as she shouted, "It is certainly *not* 'alright' if my sister dies for me!"

"*Then it is alright if* all *die because she does not?*" the Tree whispered. "*If that is what is required to save them?*"

Rachel's fury collapsed, turning into a look of utter betrayal. "You...lied to me. I trusted you. I didn't want to, but I came to trust you. To care.... And all along, you lied to me. You never really cared about me at all, did you?"

"*I did not lie to you,*" the Tree said, voice as soft as the first snow. "*I love you more than you can imagine. All* will *be well, you shall see. Trust in Me just a bit longer, and you shall see.*"

Another slam against the ceiling. Another roar.

Rachel seemed ready to rail again, but I cut in, knowing each moment Ben bought us could come at the cost of *his* life.

"Rachel, please," I pleaded. "Think of the rest of our family who are here. Dad, Michael, Laura, David. Kor. You have to help them. They need you right now. Do it for *them*."

"Please, flameheart," Kor said quietly, coming back to her side. He wrapped his arm around her waist. Out of the corner of my eye, I saw the steps were now empty and the last of the dramá were hurrying out the doors. "Don't make us lose you, too."

Rachel looked down at the floor, her face scrunching with the effort to hold back a sob. She said to Kor, "Do you love me? Really?"

"I do," Kor said with the solemnity of a vow. "By my life, I do."

"Good," she answered tightly as she raised her head, meeting my eyes. "Because I'm going to need you when my oldest, truest friend is gone."

Tears stung my own eyes. I had no idea...she thought of me that way. Gorgeous, feted Rachel, popular wherever she went?

But more insecure of anyone else's true love than I had ever known.

I swallowed and said with difficulty, "It...might not come to that."

The Trees had promised us it wouldn't. Right?

Rachel shook her head. "No promises. Remember? Just...if you die...."

I smiled. "I get it. You'll shoot me."

Rachel nodded, even as she sniffled. "Darn right. Right through your stinkin' iceheart."

My smile strengthened. "I love you too, sis."

She sniffled one more time, then straightened to her full height, raising her chin with a regality I despaired of matching. She nodded to me once, every inch the Heir of Ice...then she and Kor were gone in a silver blur.

The doors began to shut, closing me in alone with my Tree. As I slowly turned to fully face Her, the ceiling shook and cracked again, letting in lines of light and shadow through the cracks. I heard another roar, and this time I knew for certain that it came from *my* dragon. He had to know I was down here; he had to suspect what might be coming.

I worried that would make him desperate.

I bowed at the waist to my Tree. "I'm here, my Lady. What would You have me do?"

I thought, *And please, let's get it over with quickly....*

She smiled sadly at me, tilting Her head. Her voice was tender, almost...wistful. "*My faithful daughter. How I will miss you.*"

My iceheart felt like it was about to pound out of my chest. "What?" I rasped.

Instead of answering, She went over to Her trunk and placed Her hand on its surface. When She withdrew Her hand, a branch grew there before my very eyes. In seconds, it was perhaps half a foot long, with several off-branches and small crystal buds. The Tree placed Her hand at the base of the branch, and it shrunk, then parted seamlessly from the trunk, allowing Her to pull it away and walk back to the well with it.

"*Here, daughter,*" She said solemnly, holding it out to me over the well on outspread palms. "*Take this.*"

"What is it?" I asked hesitantly, approaching.

"*A beginning...*" the Tree said, smiling thinly. "*...and an ending.*"

I stopped in front of the well, raising my hand but hesitating to reach out to take it. "Care...to elaborate?"

"*You will have use of this in a moment. Through it, you will be able to channel My power in its rawest form.*"

"Oh," I said. That made a *bit* more sense.

I gingerly picked the branch out of Her hands, remembering a previous warning that to touch Her skin meant I would have to pass on. I felt odd—almost wizardly—as I held the wand-like stem. Then I felt even more so as the stem grew, and grew, and grew—turning into a full staff of my height, solid and thick. It kept some off-branches with crystal buds near the top, but most of its length was now smooth; its top, however, was one enormous crystal—in much the same shape as one of the buds, but larger than one of my fists.

"*Ready yourself,*" the Tree said solemnly. "*It is time.*"

I gasped, looking back at Her. "Wait, what am I supposed to *do*—"

Then the ceiling shattered.

Immense blocks, larger and more jagged than boulders, crashed down everywhere, taking out my Tree's limbs left and right, with one falling straight for us. Forget a lish, I was about to die in an ice cave collapse!

I reacted by instinct, hoisting up the staff and calling for all the power I had left...and then some.

The Tree's avatar glowed, as did every single one of Her leaves, even the ones scattering like falling stars. I felt a rush of power I had never felt before, not even in starform, not even united with Ben. I, too, glowed like a sun for a moment, and felt as cold as liquid nitrogen. If not for the staff, I might have fallen over from the weight of that *power*.

And not a small amount of it was concentrated in my abdomen.

Then it was over.

I gasped, staggering against my staff as I blinked the spots from my vision.

The silence hit me first: after the crashing cacophony of before, the utter lack of sound was shockingly complete. Had I...died after all?

Then I looked up and saw that the multi-ton block of ice that was about to crush me and the Tree's avatar had...stopped.

As I straightened from my hunched, braced posture, I saw that the ice boulder was fixed in place.

In fact...*everything* in the chamber had stilled. Every boulder, shard, falling branch, and scattered leaf-star.

And there, so horrifying I jumped a little when I saw it, was the Devourer in the midst of it all, diving down through the chaos, claws reaching out, black, hate-filled eyes fixed on us, maw open and ready to consume, black vapor and lightning licking at its jaws....

Frozen.

As if time itself had come to a halt for everything...except me and the Tree. And....

"SARAH," Ben gasped, surging right next to me. Power already swirled around his fists and into a shield, and he braced himself over me with his shield over both of us. But then he, too, saw the semi-frozen state of the world and straightened, blinking.

"What...." he whispered. Even his voice sounded strange—muffled, as if we were in a much smaller space than this cavernous room. Perhaps...we were, if this dais was the only space in which time still flowed right now.

"I think...I broke time," I said faintly.

Ben looked down at me, eyes wide. "You did *what*?"

I shrugged sheepishly. "I know you think nothing has power over time itself, but lately, I've gotten a hunch that you're wrong. I think...the Tree of Ice *does*."

I glanced back at Her avatar, but to my surprise and rising concern, She was gone. I knew Trees were like that, of course—there one moment, gone the next, without any mortal preambles or leave-takings—but something felt different about Her absence this time.

Then I realized what it was. Even when no avatar was visible, Her presence normally saturated the chamber like the most powerful of scents, like a coolness that sunk into your very bones. That presence, though not gone...was diminished.

The only things to change in that chamber besides Ben and me...were the lights of Her leaves and the buds on my staff. The buds were increasing in luminosity, and the leaves...were dimming.

A beginning...and an ending.

"My Lady," I gasped, tears stinging my eyes.

"What is it?" Ben demanded, shaking himself out of his stunned survey of what I, through the Tree's gift of power, had done.

I looked up at Ben with eyes that were overflowing. I could hardly believe my words, and yet, at the same time, as I spoke them, I knew they were true. "Ben...I think my Tree is dying."

He just stared at me.

The tears spilled down my cheeks. I could barely hold back a sob as I said, "She *is* dying. She's giving Her all to do this, Ben. She didn't ask for *my* life. She is giving Her own."

"Oh," Ben breathed, his eyes going to the Tree. My broken, fading Tree.

I squeezed my eyes shut.

You didn't have to do this, I cried at Her in my head. *I was willing. All you had to do was ask.*

I know, She whispered in reply, Her voice softer and fainter than I had ever felt before. *But it was not your time...and it was Mine. This was the way it was always meant to be, My precious child.*

I finally broke into a sob. Without saying a word, Ben pulled me up and into his arms and held me tight. I just cried for a few moments, mourning only my Tree. Then a question came to my mind, and my breath caught.

If it's not my time, then how will I—my family—live without You?

How would Earth?

You will live...long enough. The Branch I gave you... She began, as if with great difficulty. That "branch" was now uncomfortably pressed between Ben and me, since I'd never let go of it. *Take it to...My Sister.*

I inhaled sharply, pulling back from Ben to stare at the growing luminosity of that main crystal bud.

"What is it?" he asked urgently.

I just shook my head at him, keeping my focus inward. Although I whispered my words out loud. "Then there's hope still?"

The Tree's voice carried a trace of tender indulgence. *There is always hope.*

"When do we take it?" I demanded. Ben set me down on my feet. "Now? Before it's too late?"

It is already too late for Me, the Tree said. *I must die to save you all.*

My iceheart sank once more.

But She wasn't finished. *And you must linger a little while...with Me. For when I die...My burden shall pass to you...for a moment.*

That...didn't sound good.

It will not be easy, the Tree agreed, answering my thought. *It will take all you have become. And more.*

"Sarah," Ben said tensely, studying my expression.

But the King...must leave. Now.

Then, as if words had become too difficult for Her or Her time too short, She *poured* the knowledge into me, making it crystalize in my mind in a second.

Oh boy.... My husband was *not* going to like this.

I looked up at him, tears pricking at my eyes again. I cursed myself for that. The waterworks weren't going to make this *easier* for him.

I swallowed. It was difficult, but I wanted to speak out loud for this. "Ben...you have to go."

"What?" he said flatly. As if in defiance, he grasped my shoulders and clenched them.

I struggled for a moment to put my knowledge into words. "It's like...we're in a bubble of time right now. Frozen time. Except the Tree's made exceptions for the three of us."

At a herculean expenditure of power that I would not mention to him right now. But for a moment, I felt a flicker of awe and fervent gratitude that the Tree was being so kind, so good, as to include Ben in this sub-bubble of time, to give me this moment with him now...even as She was dying from the effort.

"I'm with you there," he said. "Well, sort of. To a point. Good enough."

He grimaced. "But what do you mean, I have to *leave*? Without *you*?"

I swallowed again. "That's just the thing—the bubble, it's...going to get bigger. Right now, it's just over this cavern. That's why you weren't frozen when it first began—because you were outside the cavern. You could surge to me because the Tree let you into our time stream. But the frozen bubble isn't meant to stay this small. It's meant to be much, much bigger. She's holding it back now, to explain all of this to us and let my family and your people escape, but...it's going to cover the whole world, Ben. All of Earth is going to become frozen in time."

He stilled. "What? Why?"

"Because of *that*," I said, pointing to the lish suspended in mid-dive for us. I tried not to look at it too closely. "That's not *all* of the Devourer. It's a lot of it, more than it's ever concentrated itself in one place before, but not all. Right now, my Tree is *dying* to trap that chunk of it here, but that leaves the rest of Earth exposed."

"Oh," Ben said, eyes widening as he looked between me and the Devourer. Then his face hardened, and he let go of my shoulders to turn to face it. "Why don't we fight it then, instead? Try to end this portion of it, here and now?"

"You know why," I said sadly. "You figured it out before I did. You just knew, instinctively, that this was a battle we can't win. Because we can't. Not as we are. Not in time. It's not a shadow I can freeze and you can burn anymore. *That's* why it wanted Solim's body so badly, enough that it didn't withdraw from Solim when he rebelled—so Solim's flesh could protect it from *us*. Now, not even with our powers and bodies combined can we obliterate the Devourer when it's like this—not before it consumes us first."

There was a speculative glint in his eyes. "Well, if the Tree can hold it still like that, then I could maybe—"

I pointed to the ground. "We step outside this dais, and we'll be frozen too. We send any power beyond it, it'll be frozen. Same with any weapon. No exceptions. Even *this* much is all the Tree can manage."

"Then what are we supposed to *do*?" Ben exclaimed. Then hardened again. "And don't say—"

"This is the Tree's plan, Ben," I said sadly. "Sacrifice Herself to freeze Earth—*all* of Earth, so the rest of the Devourer can't enter to claim it when She's dead. But that means my family, your people, and you...have to leave Earth. Before you're frozen too."

Ben set his jaw. "What about you?"

I shifted. "I won't be...frozen. But I have to stay, Ben. Once the Tree dies...someone will have to hold the freeze in place, and the only person who stands even a chance of doing that is...me."

"Sarah," he growled, grabbing my shoulders. "You can't possibly be suggesting that you should remain *trapped* here for...for...."

I swallowed, then whispered, "For as long as it takes. Yes."

"How *long*?" Ben demanded.

"I don't know. She didn't say. Just...long enough."

He let go of me and took a step back, his eyes at their hardest gold. "Then I'll stay with you. For however long that is."

I knew this was coming, so I just sighed. "No, Ben. You can't."

"And why not?" he demanded.

"Because once the spell falls to me, it will be all I'll be able to do to keep *myself* from freezing. This time stream around the dais? It's going to shrink to just *me*."

"Then I'll go inside you."

"That won't work either. First off, you'll not make it in time; you'll just freeze. Second, even if you could, we can't hold it that long, *especially* when I need to be concentrating on a very different mental load. Third, as soon as we broke apart, you'd be frozen."

"Then I'll be frozen," he said stubbornly.

I shuddered. "Please. *Please*, Ben. Don't. Don't do that. Don't trap yourself in the *same moment* with the Devourer. You see how it is now. It's maybe a second or two away from us. It could take you in a heartbeat if you let yourself be caught with it. Don't you see? Letting yourself be frozen is *suicide*."

Tears pooled in my eyes again. "Please, on top of everything I'm about to have to endure, don't make me have to watch you for who knows how long, with you frozen one *second* away from being killed. *Please.*"

For the first time, I saw a flicker of hesitation in his eyes. "But...what about you?"

I felt the surety of my words settle into me even before I said them. "I won't die."

"But you'll be *trapped*."

"We don't know for how long. Maybe not long at all."

"And *then* what?" Ben cried, waving his hand at the Devourer. "Then you get to face *that*? *Without* me? How is that *not* suicide?"

I raised my chin, even as the tears streamed down my face. "*I won't die.* The Trees promised. I feel that in my bones, in my heart, Ben, and you know it too. Now that the moment has come to let me go, you're just too terrified to let yourself feel it."

He flinched, pain lashing across his features.

Slowly, he turned his back to me, putting his face in his hands as he took deep, ragged breaths.

Regret flashed through me. "Ben...I'm so sorry. That wasn't fair. That wasn't fair at all, considering what you've been through, what I'm asking—"

"No," he said quietly, lowering his hands. "You're right."

He let out a huff that was half sigh, half bitter laugh as he stared at the floor. "I don't know why I keep trying to argue with you. You're always right."

I swallowed, the tears streaming thickly now. "Does that...mean you can believe in me? That I can do this?"

He put his hands on his hips and chuckled again, this time without bitterness. "Well, when you put it like that...."

He turned around and pulled me into his arms. He distributed my weight so he could grab my neck and tangle his fingers into my hair with one hand, and he gave me a burning, heart-wrenching kiss. I felt the fire of his power seep through every inch of our touching skin and into my very blood, setting it ablaze.

How, how could I be a being of ice and not just *endure* his heat...but crave it? And now, in that moment, more than ever.

Perhaps it was because we were both beings of light.

That seemed so when Ben finally tore his mouth from mine. His eyes were blazing, brighter even than in the first moment our eyes had met.

He touched his nose to mine. Because he was still panting from that kiss, he said silently, *I believe in you. Flame Above and Below, I believe in you. If there's anyone who can do this and live...it's you. I'm sorry I was such an idiot that it took me this long to fully, truly accept that in my heart and my head.*

I smiled at him. I'd recovered my breath enough by then that I said out loud, "For the last time, Ben: *you're not an idiot....* You just love me. A *lot*."

"The smartest thing I've ever done, by far," he said with mock solemnity.

"You know that's not what I meant," I growled, nipping at his lips in revenge.

Oh, I know, he said with his inner voice as he pulled me in for a proper kiss. *And I do. I love you, my* sera, *my star. Flame, how I love you. More than you will ever know.*

This round was much shorter. I think we could both feel our time was coming to a close, the sands trickling through the hourglass as the Tree's power waned. The lights of Her leaves above and scattered around us were almost out, and the bud on the staff that I was *still* holding was glowing like a star.

Ben tore himself away after only a few moments and set me down. Still, his hands lingered on my shoulders, and his expression was agonized.

He swallowed, then said, "For the record, when I say, 'I love you,' that doesn't mean *goodbye*. That means *you're mine, and you always will be, and wherever you go in this universe, I will find you, and I will make you mine again.* Even if that's across the Flame."

"Duly noted," I said with a solemn nod. "Same to you."

I put my free hand over his flameheart and smiled, tears pricking my eyes again. "I love you, Ben. I truly do."

"Glad we established definitions before you said that," he grumbled.

But he put his hand over my own and held it there over his flameheart as his face sobered. "Remember that it's yours. It will be waiting for you...however long it takes."

I nodded, the tears blurring my view of him. I blinked them away as fast as I could, not wanting to miss a second. "Keep it safe for me, then."

I worried about him being without me.

"I will," he said softly. "I swear it."

I smiled through my tears. "Then that's the greatest gift you can ever give me."

With agonizing slowness, he lowered his hand from mine, then stepped back. Blinking back his own tears, he swallowed and said, "Er...how...*do* I leave?"

I laughed wetly, then gestured with my staff toward the well. An ice film formed over it.

"Your turn to fall through the ice," I said with a weak attempt at a joke.

"What?" he said blankly. Then he took a second look at the ice, eyes narrowing. "Wait. I feel something...."

"It's...a wildgate, basically," I explained. "Like the one I first came through. Just before you found me."

"Not so 'wild' then, is it?" he said dryly as he warily approached the rim of the well.

"A bit of a misnomer," I agreed. "But then, we always knew it was the *Tree* that sent me."

"I suppose we did." He hesitated. "So, I just...step onto it?"

"And fall through," I said gently. "Just so you're forewarned. But you'll arrive on Ythra. Promise."

He looked at me, eyes sad. "Did you see it happen? My arrival, I mean?"

"Not exactly. I just...*know* you will."

I tried to hide my anxiety for him in a shrug. I reminded my heart of what my head already knew. Easier said than done, though, when love was involved. Especially a love like this one.

I knew I wasn't the only one with the same struggle as Ben took one last, long, pained look at me. Then he let out a breath and looked back at the ice.

"I don't know how you just...*did* this," he muttered.

"I wasn't given a choice," I said dryly.

"Oh, right." He still didn't look up at me. Yet he still didn't take a step.

"I could give you a push if you want," I teased weakly.

He grimaced. "No thanks."

The light in my staff's bud flared.

"Ben," I said uneasily.

He took a deep breath and nodded. "I know."

He looked at me one last time. "I love you," he said simply.

Then he looked back down and stepped forward and onto the ice. It held long enough for him to get his other foot onto the frozen surface...and then shattered, the well swallowing him within a second.

I couldn't help it. I rushed to the edge with a cry. But he was already long gone, and nothing but darkness remained.

I squeezed my eyes shut. *Please, please take care of him. Let him get back safe, and take care of him.*

He already has, my Tree whispered. *And My Sister will. As will you, when you return to him.*

I took a deep breath. That would have to be good enough.

I slowly turned to face the frozen Devourer. I planted my Tree's Branch in front of me, gripping it tightly with both hands.

Then, after I'd taken three steadying breaths, the bud burst with light.

My Tree died in one last whisper of power, a brush of a cool breeze like a kiss on my forehead...and then the weight of the world fell onto my shoulders.

I gasped, trembling under the pressure. It was a burden of power the likes of which I could never have imagined. This was nothing like being in starform, nothing like being one with Ben. Nothing like what I'd felt when I'd helped the Tree begin this spell. Those were snowflakes compared to this glacier of power.

A glacier that was rapidly melting from my utter inability to contain it.

The dam the Tree had maintained to buy us time burst at once, and the power flowed out of me. I had no choice but to let it do what it would. I could no more control it than I could contain it. I was the channel, that was all. And so, the freezing waters spilled from me, flooding the Earth at a speed of hundreds, perhaps thousands of miles per hour. Whatever the spell touched, it froze, locking it in that moment in time.

I felt each life as it froze—a staggering, impossible number of living beings, far too many for my mind to even comprehend, especially at the speed at which they flashed through my mind. I knew I would be able to remember none of them individually—only themes and impressions of the whole.

One of the most personally significant impressions was that I did not feel any dramá or members of my family get caught in the flood. Somehow, Kor and Rachel had gotten all the others out in time. I had no strength for anything other than relief at that, no portion of my mind to spare to wonder how they accomplished that miracle, or at what all those brave souls thought of being ordered to leave behind their Queen and their King, when they had been so willing to die for us both. I had no capacity to hope Ben was with them now, explaining things to them and reassuring them I would be alright.

Eventually.

The other general sense I got was an outpouring of...love. Pure, powerful love as overwhelming as all the fleeting impressions were. I felt with every fiber of my body, heart, and soul how incredibly *precious* every single life on this miraculous planet was. Every single one. But none more so than my Tree's beloved children, given to Her special care.

If anything of my Tree's spirit lingered in this mortal plane, it was in that love. The love...that only a mother could have for her child.

I understood, now—at least partly. I understood *why* I *had* to be a mother first: so that I could be worthy of channeling that love, of even somewhat containing it, understanding it, comprehending how *necessary* the pain was to save them all.

And oh, it was pain.

Pain greater than I had ever felt before. Pain greater than I could have imagined. The weight of the world was suffocating. My lungs labored vainly to get me enough air to breathe. I clutched the staff with all my might. Fortunately, it seemed to have rooted itself into the ground, because I could not have held it up any longer. Now it held *me* upright, but only just; I still slid down to my knees and collapsed against it, heaving, trembling.

And yet, the pain did not end. It went on, and on, and *on*, as the magic continued to pour across the world, as I felt each life as a flickering light in my mind, as my consciousness shot past it like a meteor.

After only moments, the only question on my mind was, *When will it end? When will it end? When?*

When?

An eternity seemed to pass without it ending. If I still had been able to sweat, I would have been drenched from the agony. In compensation, my very blood seemed to want to come up from my pores to escape the *weight* crushing my very soul.

I thought for a time that my Tree had lied to me. That I could *not* survive this, after all. That She had abandoned me here to die.

Why? I thought faintly. Like a trusting child suddenly shut in the dark, left blinking in bewildered betrayal.

As if in answer, a second later, the weight became almost—*almost*—bearable. When no one else should have been there with me in that void of time, someone else was there.

Knowing I was no longer alone in this space and with this burden made all the difference in the worlds.

My first thought was that my Tree had somehow returned—but no, that didn't feel right. There was a different feeling in the air, one that struck a chord of déjà vu in my mind, but nothing like the presence of a Tree. But who *was* it...?

Then...I felt a touch on my shoulder.

"That's enough, Avvrini," a man said gently. "You have held it long enough. Now it is our turn."

Even through the pain, I gasped at the sound of that voice. It was a baffling combination of Ben's and my father's: Ben's warm timbre, but Dad's sobriety and exactness.

If he hadn't sounded so much younger than Dad....

Then the title he'd given me finally sunk into my agony-befuddled mind.

Mother.

He had called me *mother*. In Drona. Even though the rest of his words were in clear, unremarkable American English. *That* was one reason he had sounded so much like Dad. Ben—the few times he ever attempted to speak my language—retained a Drona accent you could have cut with a knife.

But this young man...

...sounded like me.

My eyes blinked open, but they were still unfocused from pain. Even though I so much *wanted* to turn, I still could not. I was too weak, too weighted.

Still, I managed to choke out, "You're...you're my *son*?"

"I am indeed," he said soberly, even though there was a slight smile in his voice. There it was—my dad in him. That was exactly the kind of overly formal thing he would say in this kind of situation. That inherited quirk finally clinched it in my mind.

I...was going to have a son?

I felt a wash of disappointment that I quickly tried to suppress. Not that, given less suffocating circumstances, I wouldn't have been jumping up for joy and grabbing him in one great big hug. It was just...I had been so certain I had felt a daughter. My little candle flame, my *suki*. I felt a pang that was almost too much to bear at this point from a sense that I had somehow lost a child.

And then, I felt a hand on my other shoulder—a different hand. And a second later, a cheery soprano voice chimed in, "Don't forget about me! Your favorite, most brilliant, most *amazing* daughter!"

I choked a laugh, and tears swam in my eyes from pure, exquisite relief. For a moment, the agony was almost bearable.

I would also have a daughter. Maybe at a later time, but....

Meanwhile, my son muttered, "You mean her *only* daughter."

"Well, yes. But just because you were born a few minutes ahead of me doesn't make you the center of her universe, you know."

I choked. "You're *twins?*"

I was carrying *two* lives inside me?

I wished with all my might that I could turn around, but even if I could, I'd gotten an inkling by now that might be a bad idea. Timey-wimey things and...stuff. Even the paradoxical implications of this very moment were making my head hurt. More than it already was, that is.

As if confirming my thoughts, there was silence for a moment.

"Oops," the young woman said, and I could almost picture her brother giving her a warning glare. "Were we not supposed to say that?"

The young man just sighed. It sounded like a well-practiced sound.

"Oh, come on," she complained with feeling. She let go of my shoulder, and I could just picture her gesturing with both hands. "How was *I* supposed to know that *Avvi* didn't know that yet?"

"If you'd stopped to think about it for one second, you might have," the young man said through clenched teeth. "Seeing as we were only just *conceived. Yesterday.*"

"Oh, yeah.... Uh, ew. Can't believe that we needed *that* detail."

He groaned. "Maybe so you wouldn't spout out things like this. But now I can see why you blocked it from your mind. In any case, that's enough wasting time. Avvrini is suffering, remember? And we have a job to do."

"Oh, right," she said, sheepishness entering her voice again. She returned her hand to my empty shoulder.

"It's alright, Avvrini," he said, gentling his voice to address me. "Like I said, you can let go now. We're here to take over."

I gripped the staff with a frantic need to hold on to the weight, every bit as powerful as when I'd longed to let go. "I can't just let you *have* it," I wheezed. "You're my *children*."

The young man sighed again, but this time his sigh was more patient, as if he had been expecting me to be difficult. "Yes, but as you can no doubt guess, we're also technically about your *age* right now. And together, even more powerful than you."

"And that's sayin' somethin'," the young woman quipped. "'Cause, ya know, in our time, you're—"

"*Sister*," the young man said in tight warning.

"My *age*?" I rasped.

"Yup, nineteen! Our birthday was just yesterday," the young woman said, undeterred. Then she yelped and shuffled, as if the young man had stepped on her toe.

"Does the instruction 'Don't reveal unnecessary details' ring *any* gongs in your head?" he snapped.

"*You're* the one who told her we were her same age!"

"About! I said about! And she could have guessed that much from our voices alone! Besides, how else are we going to convince her that we are perfectly capable *adults* that she can responsibly hand the fate of the worlds off to?"

"Oh, so you're doing a *much* better job at that than I am, huh?"

He moaned. "Avvrini, I promise, we do *not* fight this much normally."

I didn't need the young woman's snort to know not to believe that much. I had siblings of my own, after all.

The young man continued. In his voice, I could imagine him shooting another warning glare at his sister. "We're just a little...tense. As you can imagine. But we can handle this. After all, it's what we've trained our whole lives to do."

"That isn't exactly making me feel better," I said between gritted teeth, closing my eyes again. "What kind of mother am I if I force you two to grow up like *that*?"

Maybe Ben was right. Maybe this was wrong. Maybe I should just hold on until this killed me....

And killed them? Never giving them a chance to even *live*? I wasn't thinking straight....

The young woman clenched my shoulder and leaned in, her voice softening and becoming serious for the first time. "Ah, Avvi, don't think like that. You gave us a *good* life. You truly did. The *best* life."

There was a meaningful pause.

"*Right*, Ri—" she began pointedly. Then, perhaps at a warning glare, she corrected, "I mean, right, *brother*?"

He let out a deep breath, but when he spoke, his voice was soft and sincere. "You did, Avvrini.... The best life."

"But...." I said, tears of despair coming to my eyes. "I can't just...leave you, *my children*, to face the Devourer on your own."

"Oh, we're not on our own," the young man said, and I heard a grim smile in his voice. "There are others waiting to help, don't you worry."

"Including *you*, and Avva," the young woman said brightly. In a loud whisper, she said to her brother, "That's allowed, right? We've more or less said already that—"

"It's fine," he hissed.

"And I didn't mention—"

"That's enough!"

"Then where are all these people?" I asked in bewilderment. "Why's it just you two right now?"

"Oh, you should know that already," the young man said in surprise. "Didn't the Tree tell you? Only those who were here when the seal of time was made can be here before it's broken."

"That's why you had to have *us* before today," the young woman said eagerly. "Get it? We can be here with you *because we're already here with you*."

She giggled as if she had made some brilliant joke. Perhaps she had, but my brain was too befuddled with pain and time paradoxes to follow.

"In more formal terms," the young man said dryly, "we helped you *make* the seal, so we can help you hold and then break it. But...you had best leave first, so your *other* you can come through. Apparently, having two conscious, adult versions of you present is a bit too much for the health of time itself."

"I can imagine," I said, taking a shaking breath as I closed my eyes. My voice trembled from the effort of holding on. "If I'm not abandoning you...if I'm waiting to come through to help you—why didn't you say that from the *beginning*?"

Silence for one moment.

"That...would have been smart," the young man said.

"I'm refraining from commenting," the young woman said.

"That *was* a comment, just so you know," he whispered fiercely.

"Alright," I croaked, eager not to drag this out any longer. "What do I do?"

I could feel my grip slipping on the magic anyway. In fact, I felt just a bit faint and dizzy. If anything, it was a wonder it had taken me this long to reach this point. But then...my children had made me discover strength within myself I never could have found otherwise.

"Oh, first, Ri—er, my *brother*—apparently has a message for you from Avva," the young woman said hastily. "Sorry. But I'm sure he'll make it quick."

"A message?" I said, blinking. I was getting spots in my vision.

The young man cleared his throat.

"Avvrana says to tell you he loves you," he said, using the formal Drona word for *father*. "And for this next part, I better quote him word for word."

His voice became stiff and formal, as if he were reading a scripted part he would very much rather not play. "'Get the hellwinds back to me already, because if I recall correctly, about now, I'm ready to bring Crownhold down on us all.'"

"Wow," the young woman said in surprise. "He wrote that? Also, that's a very confusing mix of tenses and persons. Lemme see that."

"Here," the young man said in exasperation. "Have the thing. *I* never wanted it. But Avvrana thought it should come from me—probably because he thought you would try to make it *funny* somehow."

I chuckled weakly, pressing my cheek against the cool surface of the staff. "That sounds like your father, alright. All of it."

"He also said to be patient with him," the young man said in a more comfortable tone. "He said it's going to take him a bit longer, but he'll learn to love us just as much as you do."

"I mean, what's not to love, am I right?" my daughter said smugly.

I could *hear* the eye roll in my son's voice. "Right."

I closed my eyes and smiled. I could feel myself slipping even further. The pain was fading now, perhaps into numbness. "Good to know."

"That's it, Mom," he murmured, clenching my shoulder. "Let it go. Give it to us."

My iceheart pulsed more strongly for a moment, fluttering with the warmest glow of its brief life. It gave me the strength to raise my head and brought tears to my eyes.

"You called me 'Mom,'" I said thickly. In English. Not the formal *Avvrini*, or informal *Avvi*, or even the formal English *mother*.

Mom.

"Ooo, good call," the young woman whispered. "You know she loves it when you do that. You should have done that before."

"Your critique is noted," he ground out.

He sighed. "Please be patient with us too, Mom."

"You're gonna *love* us, you'll see," she said, a wink in her voice.

"Oh, I already do," I whispered.

Then I finally let the spell go...and took myself home...

...smacking straight into their father, who appeared to be in the crown-gate's circular chamber. Others were with him, crowded into that small space, but I couldn't make them out—my vision was too hazy.

Ben gasped as I collapsed into him, and he clutched me to him. One of his hands held me upright, the other knotted in my hair as if he were determined to never let me go again. I was just fine with that plan.

"Thank the Flame!" he said shakily, kissing the top of my head. "I was about ready to bring down Crownhold."

"So you said," I replied woozily.

Then I fell into restful darkness.

Chapter Thirty

BEGINNING

Sarah

In what I was sure was going to be my typical fashion for the next nine months, I woke to my stomach trying to claw itself up my throat...and I was as cold as ice.

Yet I was so tangled up with Ben, the sheets, the blankets, and something hard, long, and wooden that I couldn't get out of bed this time. It was all I could do to pull myself to the edge and puke over the side. Ben woke with a disoriented grunt and then a deep groan. He crawled over to me and put his hand on my back, sending his power through me.

Even before I was done heaving and spitting, I sent to Ben in a mental gasp, *Is she—*

"Most likely *fine*," Ben said irritably. "As before, I can only assume that she's in this kernel of heat that seems untouchable. Of course, there's also this weird point of cold, too...."

Cold....

Of *course*. One child of Flame, one child of Ice.

How could I not have seen that before?

That was why my body was swinging so wildly between states of power—not just because Ben and I were of different powers, but also the very children in my *womb* were, each one unconsciously striving for dominance, even now.

It was a good thing I loved them, because I already wanted to knock their heads together—and they didn't even have heads to *knock* yet.

My iceheart pounded, too full of the reeling implications of having *two* children to worry about, let alone with such opposing needs, to explain the hot-cold phenomenon to Ben. Fortunately for his peace of mind, he seemed to just shrug it off and focused on stabilizing and healing me. I focused on sinking back into the bed and....

That's when I realized I was still holding the staff.

I gasped and rose onto one forearm.

"What?" Ben began in alarm, but then he followed my dazed gaze to the staff. "Oh. That thing."

"It's still here," I said, my eyes stinging with relief. "I still have it."

"Well, yeah," Ben said, irritation coming back into his voice. "You would not, under any circumstances, *let go of it*. Trust me, I tried, but I was worried I was going to break your fingers if I pried any harder. It was like you'd frozen them to it."

"And good thing," I said fervently. "Ben—this is all that's left of my Tree."

"Well," he said, clearly trying to be reasonable about this. "That makes sense, but you can relax enough about it to put it down, Sarah. If you don't want me to hold it in my ether storage, I can find a safe place for it—"

I shook my head, the knowledge of what my instincts had known all along crystalizing in my mind. "No, Ben, you don't understand. My Tree is *dead* now...except for this Branch."

Ben stilled as he finally understood. I saw his eyes widen as he looked between me and the staff. "You mean...if that thing dies too...."

I swallowed. "I think I'll die. Yeah. And, just as it's keeping me and my family alive right now...I think I'm the only thing keeping *it* alive."

I could feel the steady trickle of power from me into the Branch through my hand wrapped around it. More than that, I felt a now-familiar motherly protectiveness over it that I could hardly find the words to explain to Ben...especially given his conflicted feelings about parenthood right now.

"Oh," Ben said. In the light of the faintly glowing buds, I could see his skin darken with a flush. "Er. Sorry I...."

I let out a breath, sat up, and cradled the staff to my chest. "You didn't know."

He hesitated, then sighed. "Well, I'm apologizing for a bit more than that. It's just that...I thought I was going to lose you...but now we're both alive...and the first thing you do after waking up is fuss about our kid, then a staff."

I stared at Ben for a moment, aghast. Then, maneuvering the staff as best as I could to not hit him, I threw my arms around him.

"Oh, Flame," I gasped. "Ben, you're *alive.*"

He chuckled. "That's a bit more like it." He pulled me in, nuzzling his nose through my hair to my throat and pressing a kiss there.

"So are you," he whispered there, a tightness entering his voice. "Thank Ice and Flame Above and Below."

"You're alive," I repeated thickly. I began to sob as the past half-day of memories hit me all at once.

Ben just pulled me into his lap, manfully put up with me holding a staff at his back and occasionally knocking it into his head, and let me cry as I processed. He spoke only when I would occasionally make out a question.

Yes, my family was just fine.

Yes, Kor and Yvera were too. And Alyish, and most everyone else.

"We had very few dead, all things considered," Ben murmured.

By then, my sobs had stilled, and I'd stopped blowing my nose (one-handedly) with the handkerchiefs he kept handing me, so maybe Ben thought I was ready to handle the worst of the news. Even then, though, he tried to keep things light.

"Your family were heroes. In the evacuation, David got most of the people who were still left on the surface, and Rachel handled all the wounded herself, getting all of them in only two trips. Between the two of them, everyone who couldn't get to the moongate fast enough still got out."

I let out a breath. "That's good. But how many, Ben?"

"How many?" he hedged.

"How many died?" I said softly. "Give me the number."

He sighed heavily. "A little less than forty."

We both sat in silence for a while after that declaration, mourning the loss of that many lives. It was a small number by some standards, but any was still too many. I didn't let myself ask if there were any names I knew, as uncomfortable as it was to let the dread build in my stomach. For this moment, all those lives should be held inside me with equal respect, whether or not I'd come to know them.

"I know it may be hard to believe from your end of things," Ben said with some forced cheer, "but the battle went astonishingly well for us. The Devourer must have either been very distracted, or it truly was coming to the end of its consumed horde. Alyish thinks both."

"That would explain its desperation," I said quietly.

As much as it had acted cold and indifferent when it had the upper hand with me, it must have had a deep-seated existential terror that drove it to take such risks. The battle, for starters, when it couldn't afford to lose any more of its slaves—who weren't just its army but also its food source. Also the whole buildup to that encounter, in which it had wasted more slaves and exposed its shadows to our power. Investing Solim with its power, and refusing to withdraw, even when that seemed by every standard of reason I could think of to have been the more shortsighted choice.

It was as if it had known...that some kind of great reckoning was coming...and it was desperately trying to head it off.

I am trying to understand, it had said. *How, of all beings, it could have been you.... The "mother."*

I hadn't had a chance in that moment to ponder it, but now the word sent a chill through me.

"What?" Ben asked, feeling me tense.

"Ben," I said slowly. "Did Kor explain to you what Solim meant by 'Tolsyon's prophecy'?"

Ben snorted. "Oh, that. Yes, but only after I cornered him—and that took a while, what with all the things we had to handle when we got back, you know. In fact, I only managed it right before he finally sent me off to bed."

"And?" I said, iceheart pumping.

"Well, technically, it's the Tree of *Ice's* prophecy, for one thing."

That startled me. "Oh? But the Tree of Ice was always Earth's Tree."

As far as I had heard, Trees almost never interfered with each other's children.

"Yeah, well, this was at the time that Tolsyon, the Starkissed Lord, was helping the Moontouched escape to Earth, remember?"

"Yes...."

"So, as I understand what Kor said, first the Tree of Flame rewarded Tolsyon by declaring that one of his heirs could become the Monarch of Flame should the Sunfilled ever prove unworthy."

I nodded. "Right. That part, we know."

"Exactly. The part that Kor never told either of us is what comes next. That night...or some night soon after, can't remember if Kor said specifically when.... Anyway, the Tree of Ice came to Tolsyon in a dream and said She also had a promise to give him: that the secret burden of the Tolsyon heirs would come to an end when the last Tolsyon heir became consort to the Monarch of Ice."

I sat with that bombshell for a moment, stunned.

Solim's mocking jab at Kor came back to me. *Are you* still *dutifully trying to fulfill Tolsyon's prophecy?*

Still trying.... Duty.

Kor had been "amenable" to marrying me, and he loved Rachel now, but he *still* made his offers to both of us out of duty.

Both Rachel and I...had been right. When had that ever happened?

"So, Kor," I said faintly, "wants to marry my sister to fulfill this prophecy and *end* the line of Tolsyon heirs."

"Well," Ben said uncomfortably. "He did say that was a *factor*—but also that he really did love her. And, torch me if you want, Sarah, but...I think he actually does."

I sighed. "Yeah...I think so, too."

How lucky we are, Kor said to me, *that both of us can do precisely what we would have always wanted to do all along, and call it duty.*

"There's one more thing, though," Ben said, a different kind of unease entering his voice.

"More?" I said incredulously.

"Just one thing more. Well, as far as Kor told me, but he *claimed* this was the end of *this* Starkissed secret, at least," Ben grumbled. Then his voice sobered. "The Tree of Ice warned Tolsyon that in that day...the Devourer would rise in its might to destroy both our peoples."

I swallowed. "Well, good to know. *Now*."

"Kor made a good point," Ben said wearily. "He said it wouldn't have done any good for him to warn us because, first, a Tolsyon heir *still* hasn't married a Monarch of Ice, and, second, we got the same message directly from the Trees, anyway."

"True," I grumbled. "Still explains a few things about Kor, I guess."

"It does indeed," Ben said dryly. "Especially this next part."

"I thought you said *that* was the last part."

"This is the other half of that last part," Ben insisted. "Because the Tree of Ice apparently offered a bit of hope with Her warning. She said that, at the same time, *three* Monarchs, their *three* Heirs, and their consorts would arise, and if they were united, they could destroy the Devourer."

I stilled. Figures that this would be the greatest bombshell of them all. Greater than a Third Covenant. Greater than the end of the Tolsyon heirs....

"*Destroy?*" I whispered.

Ben was grim. "Kor said that was the exact word in the prophecy. That was why Kor was so intent when you first described having helped destroy a piece of the Devourer's shadow, remember?"

"I remember," I said faintly.

"He saw it as yet another sign that the time had come—the time in which we could destroy the Devourer, once and for all."

The words of a Tree etched themselves into the mind of Her Monarch like they were runes carved into stone. So I could recall, with perfect clarity, every single one my Tree told me when She first spoke to me of the Devourer's coming attack.

There is hope. The Devourer can be defeated. My Sisters and I have done so many times, and Flame and I have planned this defeat for eons. The Devourer does not know Our plans, but it can recognize they are coming to fruition. It knows you are the final piece—which means it will stop at nothing to destroy you, and all who could take your place.

The Devourer, again. *How, of all beings, it could have been you....*

The final piece. Or, more precisely, the piece to bring the *final* two pieces into play. The mother.

My hand curled protectively over my abdomen.

Ben, oblivious to my stunning epiphany regarding our family's destiny, said in exasperation, "What Kor *couldn't* explain to me was this *third* Monarch."

"Oh, yeah," I said distractedly. "That's odd."

For some reason, that wasn't as much of a shocker to me as the revelation that I was the prophesied mother who would bear the children that could help bring about the end of the Devourer itself. Now their unconscious fluctuations of power in my womb didn't sound quite so premature...or excessive.

We can handle this, my son had said. *After all, it's what we've trained our whole lives to do.*

Their *whole* lives. Since day one. Because my children were going to need all the power they could get if they were going to survive. So, if I had to put up with a bit of discomfort for nine months to give them that chance...then so be it.

We sat for a time in silence, lost in our own thoughts about the future.

Finally, I sighed. "So, the conclusion is...this isn't over."

"No," Ben said grimly, holding me more tightly for a moment. "But at least we have as long as that time freeze holds over Earth, right?"

"Wait," I said with a start. "It's still *there?*"

Since our children said they were going to take it down as soon as I left, I guess I had assumed it was already gone. But then...wait, then this "final battle" would have already happened...and our children wouldn't have had time to grow up first....

Could I have held that time seal for *nineteen years?* I mean, it had *felt* like an eternity, but...how would I have gotten back to Ben, in the here and now?

My head hurt.

"Well, yeah," Ben said in surprise.

"How do you *know*?" I said urgently.

Ben shifted. "Well, er, because, first off, none of your family can see anything that's going on on Earth anymore. Every time they try to cast an image of Earth on ice, all they get is a blank. Second, you know...that moongate? The one that led...to your Tree? To...Earth?"

I stilled. "Yes."

"It's...inactive," Ben said quietly, giving me a squeeze. "I'm so sorry, Sarah. It's just...not working. Rachel tried—twice."

He hesitated. "She's rather broken up about your Tree. Seems to have this lingering guilt or something. Kept sobbing, 'I'm sorry' in front of the doors. Kor had to pull her away."

I sighed. "She...seemed to have come to care for the Tree, while she was tending to Her as the acting Royal while I've been with you. Then, at the end, the two of them had...words. Rachel said some things to Her that she probably regrets."

Ben echoed my sigh. "Haven't we all. I know I certainly have, to both Trees."

"Your Tree isn't dead," I said gently. Then I felt the staff in my hand.

Mirroring my thoughts, Ben craned his neck back to bonk his head against the staff's branchy, crystalline head. The glow from the crystals illuminated his soft smile. "Yours isn't completely, it seems. Hopefully that will give Rachel some comfort."

"Hopefully," I murmured.

Ben's smile faded. "Does it comfort you?"

I smiled wanly. "A bit. I still feel this tremendous...loss. Like a piece of me is missing. And, yes...like I failed Her. Even though She said this was the plan all along."

I turned the staff in my fingers, eyeing its head over Ben's own. "Whatever happens with this thing, I don't think things are ever going to quite be the same again. And that makes me sad."

"Er...what *are* we supposed to do with it?" Ben said, turning his head to eye it. He looked back at me and said, "Please tell me you're not going to have to carry it around for the rest of your life."

I laughed, surprised that this hadn't come up yet. Ben really had been so very patient with me.

"Oh, no. The Tree said to take it to your Tree."

As soon as I said the words, something felt off about them. While I pondered what I'd gotten wrong, Ben gave a deep sigh of relief.

"Oh, thank Flame. Because it really makes the thought of doing certain things with you a bit more...awkward. Especially considering it's a bit of a Tree."

I laughed and kissed him, certain a remnant of a Tree wouldn't mind that much.

Then it hit me: the part I'd gotten wrong. Again, the Tree's *exact* words came back to me.

"Her Sister," I exclaimed, breaking away from him.

"What?" Ben asked, nonplussed.

"The Tree—my Tree, the Tree of Ice—didn't say to take it to *your* Tree. She said to take it to *Her Sister*."

"Uh, Sarah. That's the only other Tree we know."

"Which was why I thought that's what She meant. But when I said, 'take it to *your* Tree,' I knew that was wrong. She's not the 'Sister' we're supposed to bring it to."

Ben stared at me. "Sarah...*how* are we going to find *another* Tree?"

A knock came on our door.

"Ah, torch it," Ben muttered, letting go of me. He shifted over to his side of the bed and stood up, grumbling on the way. "It's got to be in the middle of the night—*after* a battle. Whatever this is, it better be a life-or-death thing."

"Are you sure you want to make that kind of wish?" I teased shakily, iceheart pounding.

Ben opened the door. "What?" he snapped.

"Ah, good, you were already awake," I heard Kor say smoothly. "I thought you might be. And so is Sarah, right? Seeing as it's a bit after midnight?"

"Unfortunately," I called wearily. "Please tell me you're knocking on the door in the middle of the night with *good* news."

I said this with a pointed look at Ben.

"As a matter of fact," Kor said lightly, "I am. I just thought the two of you might want to know that Rachel says the moongate that formerly went to Earth is active again. As of, precisely, midnight. Our time."

"It...is?" Ben said faintly, then looked back at me, then back at Kor.

"Formerly?" I said, iceheart pounding again. I crawled off the bed and walked to the door—Branch in hand, of course. Fortunately, I was fully clothed in some loose, dramá-equivalent pajamas. Getting these on me while I refused to let go of a staff as tall as I was must have been a creative feat. I was a bit surprised I slept through that.

"Yes, formerly," Kor said, sapphire eyes glowing. "Because, of course, Rachel couldn't resist *opening* the doors."

I rolled my eyes. "Sounds a bit like someone *else* I know. You wouldn't have happened to, ahem, *encourage* such a thing, would you?"

Kor pouted. "What a hurtful accusation. Is that how you greet someone you care about after a near-death experience?"

Ben chuckled. "Tell me about it."

I elbowed him in the stomach. His dramatic hiss in response was just to make me feel good—I couldn't have possibly made a dent in those abs of his. If anything, it was my elbow that was stinging from the impact.

"You were saying?" I said to Kor, having never taken my eyes off him. "If the moongate doesn't go to Earth anymore, *where does it go?*"

Kor shrugged. "We don't know. Somewhere new, though. So, I suppose, technically, it could still go to Earth—but not to the Temple of Ice."

"Did Rachel go through?" I asked, pulse picking up again.

"No. Her *preliminary exploration* ended there. As soon as we determined that a new location lay beyond the ice, then I, as a diligent leftwing of the King of Flame, advised her, as a diligent Heir of Ice, to wait for the Queen of Ice to go through first."

I couldn't help a smile from tugging at my lips. "And so, of course, you ran right over here, hoping that if the parents were awake *anyway*, you wouldn't have to wait until Christmas morning to open your presents."

"Christmas?" Kor said in amusement.

I shook my head. "Never mind."

I looked up at Ben. "Well, what do you think? Do you feel like investigating a new gate now?"

Ben frowned. "There...*is* something odd about the timing." He looked at Kor. "You said precisely midnight *our* time?"

"Yes. Interesting, isn't it?"

Then, as my eyes fell on the Branch, it hit me. "That's...when I woke up."

When I could finally fulfill the last assignment my Tree gave me.

Ben looked at me, then followed my gaze.

"The third Tree," he said, eyes wide.

Kor frowned. "Third—"

Then his eyes lit up, glowing a brilliant sapphire. "Ooooh."

He looked at me again, with such a pleading expression that I wondered in amusement if he would have begged down on one knee if I'd told him to. "Come on, Sarah. If this is an invitation from another Tree.... Well, wouldn't it be downright rude to keep Her waiting?"

"Yes," I said softly, looking at the large crystal bud of my staff. "It would."

ABOUT TWO HOURS LATER, all the Linds, plus Ben and his wings, were once again assembled in front of the northernmost moongate of our small hold in the Seventh Realm—this time with the addition of Svyer, who, as a member of the Moontouched clan now, shouldn't be excluded.

Despite Kor's impatience, two hours was no time at all, considering how we'd had to wake everyone else up besides Rachel *and* convince them how important this was *and* for everyone to be conscious and presentable. I was surprised it hadn't taken us the rest of the night.

Trying not to think too hard about the last time we had done this—particularly since we had been just about as drained as we were now—I took a deep breath, slipped out of Ben's hand, and walked to those double doors.

I still couldn't help a couple of tears as I reached them and placed my free hand on the crack between. I bowed my head, resting my forehead for a moment against the cool stone and glowing white tree.

I wish I was coming to see You, I thought to the Branch in my other hand. Then I blinked away the tears, took another deep breath, and raised my chin.

Please open, I told the doors.

I'd figured out by now that they didn't need me to speak to them—just to give them some of my magic with intention. But speaking the words helped focus my intention, and besides, I never thought it hurt. If it helped me treat my Tree's gift of my magic and these gates with the respect they deserved...then I thought it did a lot of good.

It was the way I would teach my child to use their magic—whichever one took after me. Some moments I thought it would be the girl, some the boy, but I tried not to think too deeply about which would be which. I didn't want to pin them to a destiny any more than I had to, even in my mind. But I could think in general terms about how I could guide the one that followed in my footsteps.

I knew I should leave the teaching of the child of Flame to Ben. No matter how his philosophies might differ, I knew they would be good at heart, and our differences were what made us powerful together. I also knew he would be a good, patient teacher. He had been so to me.

The doors parted outward, giving me time to step back. Beyond, I soon saw a brilliantly lit room—so bright, at first I thought it was open to the sky, and that it was sunlight that spilled in through the cracks in the opening doors. But no—from what I could see through the ice, the ceiling in the next room was merely radiating a brilliant, almost blinding white, ever so slightly on the warm end of the spectrum.

Then my lights—the glowing spheres with an aura so vibrant we couldn't see their centers, who cared for our hold at night—began to hum with joy, as they had not hummed since my very first night in this place. All of them—all the *hundreds* of them—began drifting over, as if drawn to the open doors. My family, who hadn't ever seen them behave like anything more than polite, voiceless, bodiless servants, startled. Svyer stared, and Mom drew Abby and the twins closer to her nervously.

"It's alright, Mom," I said, looking back. "They're just happy. They did something a bit like this when I first came."

"Why would they be so happy now?" Dad asked curiously, tentatively reaching out to touch the one nearest to him.

He had his pick to choose from, since the lights were crowding around us in a thickening, brightening semicircle of light. They weren't even bothering with the grid pattern they'd used before, nor did they avoid touching anyone, even Ben and his wings, as Kor demonstrated when he, too, reached out to see if he could touch one, and it let him hold it in the palm of his hand. Perhaps because they were already bonded to me now.

"I don't know," I said to Dad. I was baffled. They hadn't reacted like this when we'd first gone to greet the Tree of Ice. If this was indeed another Tree, what made Her so special to these things?

Then my eye fell on one of the lights, in color so like the kind spilling from the open doors. My iceheart thumped as I had my first inkling.

Actually, perhaps my very *first* inkling came from when I was trapped in the darkness with the Devourer.

There was only one way to know if I was right. I turned and passed through the ice curtain...even though I wasn't sure whether I wanted it to be true.

We entered a room that was set up similarly to the entrance chamber of the Temple of Ice. Except where that one was dark, mysterious, and restful, this one was bright, open, and vibrant. All the white should have been blinding and sterile, but there was a softness to it that I couldn't quite put my finger on. It didn't come from the gold accents, which were in the trim on the white marble pillars or traced large diamonds in the white marble floor. The gold only added to the richness and awe-inspiring glory of the space.

As we walked across the floor, I saw that those diamonds formed what could have been the seeds or petals in a geometric flower, or perhaps the rays of a sun. The smallest started in a golden star in the center and grew to ever-greater sizes until they reached the ring of pillars, where they stopped. Those pillars supported a rotunda much like the one in the Temple of Ice's entrance chamber, but instead of a sky full of stars, this one was a smooth white dome. Light from an unseen source—perhaps even from above—rippled across its surface in a constant display of light and shadow. Then I realized what the pattern reminded me of: clouds moving across the sun.

Perhaps *that* was the source of the softness of the light. It wasn't stark sunlight. It was veiled, coming through shadow, and always in motion—and thus, to me, mesmerizingly beautiful.

My iceheart thumped all the quicker. The lights followed us in a bright cloud of their own—although their hums had stilled to reverent silence. Everyone else was just as quiet. Not even my rambunctious twin brothers said a word as they gazed around with mouths open wide.

There was something *special* about this place. It was in the very air we breathed: crisp but not cold, fresh but not biting, clear but not piercing.

It was the air of....

The word was just on the tip of my tongue when we reached the great double doors on the other side of the entrance chamber. Here was the greatest structural difference between the Temple of Ice and this one, since even this entrance chamber had wings to the east and west just as the one of Ice did: here, there was no dark hallway to walk down first. There, in plain view, was the entrance into the Heart Chamber. I didn't think a single one of us now doubted that a Tree rested inside.

Pulse pounding, I walked with slow steps to the doors. Unable to help myself, though, I took one look back, meeting the gaze of every member of my clan, asking them if they were ready for this. Their expressions ranged from inscrutability (Dad, Michael, Laura) to awe (Mom, David, Lizzy) to excitement (Svyer, Jonah, Noah, and Abby).

Tears were streaming down Rachel's face, and they didn't look like happy ones. But even she nodded when I looked at her.

I hesitated one more time...then looked at Ben. His gold eyes met mine, and he smiled softly at my glance. I knew, then, that he too had some inkling of what was coming. Still, I couldn't look away from him, hardly able to believe he truly was at peace with it.

Do whatever your heart tells you to, he said silently. *Whatever that is, whatever you choose, I know that heart will still be yours, and it will still be mine. And that's all I care about.*

Tears stung my eyes again. What had I done to deserve a man as good as Ben?

I nodded to him.

Then I walked back to Rachel. With both hands on the Branch of Ice, I offered it to her. She started, glancing at me.

"What? Why?" she whispered. "The Tree gave it to you."

"Because I was Her Queen at the time," I said with a tremulous smile. "But I think you are the one who should hold it now."

Rachel searched my eyes. "I...don't understand."

"Maybe not now, but...I think you will in a moment. Do you *want* to hold it?"

Rachel stared at it. Her eyes watered further as she looked into its main, glowing bud. She sniffled and nodded.

I held it out to her again. "Then I think that means you're the one who's meant to."

Hesitantly, gingerly, she reached out her hands and grasped both around the staff just above the spot where mine were doing the same. I gradually withdrew my hands...

...and felt a surprising lightness. Like a load had been taken off my shoulders. I knew what the difference was. With my decision made, the whole place seemed warmer, more welcoming. My pulse slowed, and my body relaxed. I felt a familiar love trickle back into my heart, and a deep sense of pride and approval that wasn't my own.

Rachel, far from looking burdened, seemed to feel the same release I did. She let out a breath, and her shoulders straightened. There was a light in her eyes again when she met mine. They were still sad, but they had a purpose. A meaning. A worth.

This was just...the way things had always been meant to be. I did not know why. It seemed like a long and difficult path to lead my sister and me to this point, but I had long ago learned not to question the wisdom of Trees. When I tried to think of any other way both of us could have grown into the roles we were meant to hold...I couldn't think of one.

"Thank you," Rachel whispered to me. "For giving me another chance."

"No," I said, smiling through my tears. "Thank you for taking it."

Feeling remarkably light for the heaviness of mourning that still rested in my iceheart, I turned and walked back to the doors...and put both hands on them.

Open, please, I said. Different magic, but I figured the same rules could apply. I was still the same person, after all. Just...more myself than I had ever been.

These doors, too, opened outward, and I stepped back to let them.

After the brightness of the entrance chamber, the room beyond seemed dark and shadowy. That only allowed the brilliance of the Tree inside to shine.

As we entered that darkness, and looked up at that light, I think every single jaw dropped, at least a little—even Kor's, even Dad's.

The mists obscured the confines of the room—if we were even in a room at all anymore. At the threshold, the floor turned abruptly from pristine marble to rich, dark soil that let out the pungent odor of life's potential with every step. The strongest scent in the room, though, was of that clear, beautiful, quiet odor of earth just after rain, the kind that made me just want to race through it with my arms wide open, lungs heaving in its wholesome purity. There was a third, subtler, cooler scent, though, and again that sense of familiarity I couldn't quite place nagged at me and kept me grounded as I tried to figure it out.

Thanks to the dark mists, the primary visible feature was the Tree—and oh, how glorious She was. She towered above us like a skyscraper, spreading Her limbs so wide they could have covered a football stadium. Unlike the Tree of Ice, She sat not on a rise but on level ground as far as we could see. Her roots didn't stretch long above the soil before they dove deep, so, unlike with the Tree of Flame, we could technically have approached Her from any direction—if we were willing to walk through the tiny forest of ferns with phosphorescent leaves that shimmered with all the colors of the rainbow and faintly glowing white mushrooms beneath. Which we did not. We stuck to the empty dirt path that led straight from the doors to the Tree.

As we got closer, I saw Her bark was smooth, and every bit of texture seemed to glisten, as if She had been sprinkled the entire way up and down with pixie dust. Her leaves were gassy vapors of warm white light, their shapes wavering with the slightest movement or bit of air.

They reminded me of nothing more than...my wings.

For the first time, I saw a Tree with fruit. At least, that's what I assumed they were at first: white spheres so bright I couldn't see their centers. They looked exactly like....

My lights, my dear helping lights, streamed in behind us and up toward the Tree's canopy. No longer could they remain silent. They vibrated with sheer, uncontainable joy in a song more exquisite than a chorus of nightingales.

The "fruits" flowed down to meet them, and the reunited kin spiraled around each other in a dance and song so mesmerizing that I couldn't take my eyes off them and stumbled along to our destination by instinct. If the path had been anything less than perfectly level and unencumbered, I would have tripped and fallen on my face.

That would certainly have been an undignified way to meet a new Tree. Yet all I could think of was my longing to join them.

Stay with us, now, Sarah, Ben teased me.

Fine, I huffed back to him, but I was glad of the reminder, especially when I saw we were almost to the Tree's base.

A large circle empty of ferns marked off the sacred space, with one opening that we passed through. In the center of the space between us and the Tree was a small circular fountain, about three feet in diameter and raised a few inches off the ground. Instead of being filled with water, white vapors flowed up from its center in a soft, continuous geyser only a foot high and flowed down from that peak to the black marble sides, dissipating just after it spilled over the rim. I could feel even from this distance that the vapors were cool.

As we had walked down that long path, every time I tore my eyes away from the dance and song above and looked ahead, I saw the circle was unoccupied. Yet by the time we entered the circle and I glanced across the fountain, Someone stood on the other side, and I nearly stumbled from shock and heartbreak.

There was a striking resemblance between this Tree's avatar and that of Her Sister of Ice's. She was dressed in the same kind of simple, sleeveless dress with a voluminous A-line skirt, albeit one made of white vapors like the kind pouring from the fountain. Her hair, too, was white vapor, but even as it flowed, it seemed to fall the same way and to the same floor-length as Ice's. Her skin, however, was black as night, and if She had not been standing with Her Tree's glowing trunk in the background, Her avatar's body might have blended with the mists.

The greatest resemblances, though, were in Her exquisitely perfect facial features and glowing white eyes; the near-exact similarity there brushed against the crack in my iceheart. Even the softness in those eyes gave me as much pain as comfort.

I felt a bit of a return of the heaviness of before as I walked slowly to stand on our side of the fountain, an equal distance from it as She was from it on the other side. Everyone else in my clan spread around the circle, while Ben and his wings waited just outside, just as they did before, when we all first met the Tree of Ice.

The Tree allowed us to settle ourselves without speaking or moving, only watching with a look of softness on Her face. After we became still, She gave us a few moments of silence before She spoke.

"*Welcome, Sarah, Queen of Ice—to you and to your clan.*"

I had to suppress a wince. Even Her voice was heart-rendingly similar: soft and peaceful. But there was an added measure of…energy. Aliveness. Potential.

I swallowed and bowed. "Thank you for Your welcome, my Lady. If I may ask, though…what may we call You?"

A smile grew on those ebony lips. "*I am the Tree of Light.*"

Even though I had felt this coming, I still had not dared put into words what my subconscious had told me all along. Hearing those words, especially coming from Her voice, sent a lightning bolt through my whole being, electrifying every cell.

She spread Her hands. "*Welcome, again, to My Realm—the Realm of Light. Though you know it better by another name: the Seventh Realm.*"

I heard audible gasps coming from behind me. I blinked.

"You mean...." I breathed.

"*You are indeed, in this moment, on the same world on which your clan has sheltered for these past moons,*" the Tree of Light said gently. "*The world I have carefully guarded for you, in secret, for a thousand years. And yes, have guarded and concealed for you from the Devourer from the first moment you arrived.*"

I blinked again. "Then...the lights...."

She raised Her hand, and a helping light that had been drifting downward settled into Her palm. It buzzed joyfully, and I got the impression it was preening. "*My little ones,*" the Tree said tenderly. "*Not My children, for the Creators have given Me none yet, but My own little creations I have made to keep Me company in the meantime, and to care for your hold and ease the difficulties of your beginnings there.*"

The light hummed in agreement and floated back over to me. I was too dazed to do anything as it rubbed my cheek affectionately.

The Tree smiled again as She watched. "*Though they do not have the full intelligence of a Tree's children, you have done well to care for them as living beings, for that is what they are. Continue to be kind to and thankful for them, and I will allow them to remain with you. Become slothful or ungrateful, or treat them as objects, and I will remove them from you...and more besides.*"

"Yes, my Lady," I said quietly. The light spun around me in its equivalent of a hug before flying off.

I took a deep breath, thinking of how to phrase my questions without sounding accusatory or heartbroken.

The Tree softened. "*I know what is in your heart, dear one, and so I will answer you. We never led you falsely. You truly* are *My Sister's child...as am I.*"

I inhaled sharply. "*What?*"

The Tree gestured behind me, and I turned to see She was looking at the staff in Rachel's hands. *"This is how all Trees begin, dear one. We all are merely Branches of our Mother Tree, going back to the Tree of Life Herself. I came from the Tree of Ice as a Branch just like this one and was planted here in this soil a thousand years ago in preparation for this moment. With that birthright, I could have grown to become another Tree of Ice like Her, but the Creators gave Me a different purpose, which I accepted."*

I stared at Her face, so achingly familiar. "That's why...."

"Yes," the Tree said, and this time, Her smile was sad—almost the exact same smile that my Tree gave me, at the end.

An ending...and a beginning.

I swallowed thickly. "If She was Your Mother, then why...."

"Even though I came from Her, Your Tree called Me 'Sister' because I am now Her equal, in the sense that I have reached maturity and am ready to be entrusted with children of My own."

I bowed my head, tears stinging my eyes. I would have had to have been an idiot to not see where this was going. I'd known it before I walked through the ice and into the Temple of Light. I'd had the first glimmer of it when I discovered the true source of my power. And yet....

Why?

"Speak your question, dear one," the Tree murmured. *"I will answer it."*

I looked up, my tears blurring my view of Her. "If I was always meant to be *Your* child, then why...."

"You have already felt this answer in your heart," the Tree said softly. *"Because you would never have fulfilled the measure of your creation if you were Mine from the beginning. You were born on My Sister's world, with Blood that mingled Her power and that of Flame. You had to fully explore your origins before you could fully choose what you wished to become. I only opened My door to you after you, in your heart, made that choice—though you did not realize that was what it was."*

The Tree sighed. *"That is the brighter reason. The darker is that the Devourer would have discovered you and sought your life much sooner had you been the*

Queen of Light—for that is the Queen it has sought to destroy ever since it learned that she will be the beginning of its end."

My eyes widened. *The mother,* I thought but did not say out loud.

The Tree nodded almost imperceptibly. *"Making you My Sister's Heir and then Queen confused the Devourer and thus gave you the time you required to discover, to grow...and to choose. And so you did, and on the journey, became all that We could have hoped for you."*

She smiled, Her white eyes tightening with such love and pride that I couldn't help but feel it stir within my soul again. Then She let that smile fade, becoming serious.

"Even now, you have a choice."

She looked behind me and spread Her hands. "All *of you of the Moontouched clan have a choice. You may remain children of Ice if that is what you wish. Indeed, We hope that some of you will choose to remain so, for We will have need of Ice in the days to come. Yet We will also need Light. If that is your desire, that is what I may give you."*

For the first time, someone else spoke. Dad took a step forward and asked with tightened eyes, "You are speaking as if you want us to receive a different power. How is that possible?"

He gestured to Svyer, who was also listening intently. "When this young woman joined our clan, she was told that she must retain her flameheart, that if our Tree tried to give her a heart of Ice, she would die."

"That was a different matter," the Tree of Light answered solemnly. *"The powers of Ice and Flame are too different to be changed from one to the other. Even temporarily combining them in one body is difficult and dangerous, as your Queen and King know well."*

Her eyes met mine for one moment, and my hand twitched, wishing to go to my abdomen. Hopefully everyone else thought She was referring to when Ben and I merged.

The Tree looked back at Dad. *"Even now, you are not so far from Light as you suppose, Jacob Lind. Even you have pondered why your two higher forms—what you call your lightform and your starform—are of Light, not Ice, have you not?"*

I blinked. Well, color me sheepish for not thinking of that myself. They just always felt so...natural to me. Then again...that was the whole point. I had unconsciously inclined myself toward Light from my very first day as Queen, when I discovered my higher forms. My forms...but perhaps not the only ones I could have chosen.

"Yes," Dad murmured. "Not in so many words, but...yes, I have."

"*I give you the answer now,*" the Tree said. "*In order to ease your way in this moment, in order to give you a chance to explore and grow into whichever power you desired the most, I gave to My Sister, the Tree of Ice, slivers of My Power, which She placed inside the icehearts She offered to you.*"

Dad frowned.

"*We were not deceiving you with Our gifts,*" the Tree said gently. "*As I came from Her, Light proceeds naturally from Ice—or, in other words, the power of stillness, of matter unorganized, of kindling not yet sparked, of the divine darkness. Ice is to Light what the night is to the dawn, what the winter is to the spring, and flows as naturally from the former to the latter as night and winter do.*"

Dawn. That was the feeling, the smell in the air! It felt like the very first moments of dawn. The *potential* of light was everywhere in this room, and the light itself was manifested in all its glory in the Tree.

Kor was having his own epiphany, which he couldn't help but burst out. "Is that why they can give us power?"

When everyone glanced at him, he had the grace to color a bit. "Your pardon, Lady," he said with a deep bow. "Forgive my interruption."

A crooked smile pulled at the Tree of Light's lips. "*I forgive you, Son of Flame. And yes, that is true. Yet it is the sliver of* Light *that feeds your power, because Flame comes from Light, as dawn gives way to day and spring to summer. Without that sliver, they could not have done so.*"

"Oh," I said numbly. If we had not been able to give power to the dramá....

That...would have been bad.

"*Indeed,*" the Tree said to me soberly. "*We knew you would have desperate need of Light, yet We could not risk openly giving it to you too soon, and it was the mystery of the combination that bewildered the Devourer for so long. For a time, it*" *believed We had somehow created something entirely new by combining the Blood of Ice and Flame."*

Her lips pulled at the corners again. *"And, for a time...We did."*

The smile faded, and She sighed. *"But the period of grace has come to its close. By the Creators' decree, you must now become wholly one or the other, so that you may be wholly governed by one or the other, as is the way of order."*

She paused for a moment to let that sink in, then continued. *"Even if your icehearts did not contain those slivers already, I still could have changed them into lighthearts without ending your life, because that would have been the natural progression of power itself. All those slivers did was to allow you to fully explore your choice, in ways subtle enough to protect you under the cloak of Ice. And those slivers can make the transformation less difficult and painful than it otherwise might have been. All that We did was out of mercy and love for you, to give you the power and knowledge that was necessary for your very survival, and for the survival of all the Realms."*

She looked at Dad. *"Do you see that now, Jacob?"*

His face was inscrutable, but he nodded slowly. "I...see."

She looked at me, inclining Her head, my Tree's softest smile on Her lips. *"I know your grief, dear one. I share it. I will miss My Mother—My Sister—with all My being. Yet I always knew this would be Her choice. If I, too, one day go down Her path, I know I will see Her again. As will you. Remember Her. But do not let Her death burden your heart with guilt any longer. You did not fail Her. Indeed, you did all that She asked of you, and She is prouder of you than you can know."*

My eyes swam with tears again.

"Do you understand now, dear one?"

I could only nod.

Then, the last of the heaviness in my iceheart left me...filling it with light. I had known for a while *what* I would choose, and even had an inkling of why. Now...I could choose it with joy. I could fully let go of what was never meant to be mine.

Not forever.

The Tree raised Her voice to declare to all, "*Now is the moment of your decision…. Heir of Ice, bring forth the Branch.*"

Rachel did so. None of the panic she had displayed on first approaching a Tree showed now. Tears were streaming down her face, but her eyes and expression were calm and dignified, full of surety and purpose. She even flicked a small smile at me as she came to my side. Then, when the Tree held out Her hands, Rachel tilted the staff to be horizontal, parallel with the ground, and then held it out in both palms over the fountain.

The moment the Tree of Light took the Branch of Ice, every crystal bud flashed with brilliant light before dimming to a bearable but still vibrant glow. As I blinked spots from my vision, I noted the healthy luminosity with relief, and one last, lingering bit of anxiety eased. It was as if my budding motherly instincts had known the Branch's significance all along.

Answering my thoughts, the Tree said with a smile, "*Thank you, both of you, for taking such diligent care of My new Sister until you could bring Her to Me. Rest assured, She will be safe and healthy in My care, until the day in which Earth is freed and I may give Her back to Her Monarch to plant Her on Earth.*"

She set the butt of the Branch on the ground and settled it in the grip of one hand as a staff. "*And now, by the authority lent to Me by the Branch of Ice, the time has come to determine who that Monarch will be.*"

She inclined Her head to me. "*Sarah Lind. Know that each of the choices before you is good; therefore, We leave the final decision to you.*

"*Know that if you retain your place as Queen of Ice—as is your right—you must recuse yourself from leadership of the Seventh Realm and the Moon-touched clan, for by the magic We have long since woven, they both belong with the dramá of the Six Realms. Know that the sliver of Light will be removed from your heart, and you will become wholly of Ice, Queen of Ice in exile, destined to one day independently rule Earth and care for humanity under the new Tree of Ice. You will retain your rights as consort of the King of Flame, but from this day forth, you will relinquish your right to rule in the Seven Realms, for your domain will belong solely to Earth.*"

Well, I thought. *I guess that's why the Trees kept being so vague about what They intended for my legal status.*

Even our heartbinding under the Third Covenant wasn't the end of the Trees' establishment of the new order...or of the space They had given us to choose.

Speaking of which, the Tree wasn't done explaining my choice. *"Know that if you choose to become My child, a child of Light, I will give you a new heart entirely of Light and make you My Queen, the Queen of Light. You will lose your powers of Ice and renounce any claim to Earth forever, but you will retain your rightful place at the head of the Moontouched clan and leader of the Seventh Realm, and you will rule over all the Seven Realms as not just the King of Flame's consort but as his equal—as the Monarch of Light will co-rule with the Monarch of Flame over the united Seven Realms forevermore, whether they be consorts or no."*

She paused, then said, *"Do you understand the choice before you?"*

I nodded. "Yes."

Without betraying a hint of partiality, the Tree of Light said, *"What is your decision?"*

Rachel inhaled sharply, stiffening. Not caring if this broke with the formality of the moment, I took her hand in mine and gave it a squeeze. I did not look back at Ben. He had already given me his answer, and I knew he would be hurt if I asked him if he was sure.

Besides, I was pretty sure all our desires were in alignment at this point.

The memory of Kor's voice again echoed in my mind. *How lucky we are that both of us can do precisely what we would have always wanted to do all along, and call it duty. Quite the coincidence, don't you think?*

Coincidence, where the Trees were concerned?

Never.

These things may not have been what we would have chosen for ourselves at the beginning. It had taken a long, painful, dangerous road, sometimes wandering down other paths for a time, before we finally realized where we truly belonged—and *wanted* to belong.

But after following the light of our Trees, after trusting in Their wisdom and love for long enough, we all eventually uncovered those parts of ourselves that had rested there all along, waiting for us to discover...

...and choose.

"I wish to join with You as Your child, my Lady," I said quietly.

The Tree of Light smiled ever so slightly, Her eyes tightening with joy. Somehow, I knew it wasn't just joy for Herself.

It was also for *me*.

For Her precious child, who had finally found her way home.

She held out Her hand, and a sphere of soft, white light appeared inside it. *"Then accept what I offer, and become."*

CONTINUE THE ADVENTURE IN...

DRAGON'S CHILD

Ready for the next one? Scan the code to find where you can get *Dragon's Child*.

ABOUT THE AUTHOR

Leah E. Welker graduated from Brigham Young University (Provo) in 2016 with a degree in English language and a minor in editing. She then edited for seven years and pivoted to writing in 2023. She is based in the DC area, where she lives with family and her rescue Australian shepherd, Wes.

You can connect with her at

https://www.leahewelker.com

Subscribe to her newsletter for updates, cover reveals, dog pics, and more.

https://www.leahewelker.com/follow

www.ingramcontent.com/pod-product-compliance
Lightning Source LLC
Chambersburg PA
CBHW031023030726
47497CB00004B/985